A FAR HORIZON

A Selection of Recent Titles by Brenda Rickman Vantrease

The Broken Kingdom Series

THE QUEEN'S PROMISE *
A FAR HORIZON *

Illuminator Series

THE ILLUMINATOR
THE MERCY SELLER

Novels

THE HERETIC'S WIFE

* *available from Severn House*

A FAR HORIZON

Broken Kingdom Volume II

Brenda Rickman Vantrease

This first world edition published 2018
in Great Britain and 2019 in the USA by
SEVERN HOUSE PUBLISHERS LTD of
Eardley House, 4 Uxbridge Street, London W8 7SY.
Trade paperback edition first published
in Great Britain and the USA 2019 by
SEVERN HOUSE PUBLISHERS LTD.

British Library Cataloguing in Publication Data
A CIP catalogue record for this title is available from the British Library.

ISBN-13: 978-0-7278-8840-2 (cased)
ISBN-13: 978-1-84751-966-5 (trade paper)
ISBN-13: 978-1-4483-0176-8 (e-book)

This is a work of fiction. Names, characters, places and incidents
are either the product of the author's imagination or are used fictitiously.
Except where actual historical events and characters are being described
for the storyline of this novel, all situations in this publication are
fictitious and any resemblance to actual persons, living or dead,
business establishments, events or locales is purely coincidental.

All Severn House titles are printed on acid-free paper.

Severn House Publishers support the Forest Stewardship Council™ [FSC™],
the leading international forest certification organisation.
All our titles that are printed on FSC certified paper carry the FSC logo.

Typeset by Palimpsest Book Production Ltd.,
Falkirk, Stirlingshire, Scotland.
Printed and bound in Great Britain by
TJ International, Padstow, Cornwall.

This is what the King who will reign over you will do: He will take your sons and make them serve with his chariots . . . to plow his ground and reap his harvests . . . to make weapons of war. He will take your daughters to be perfumers and cooks . . . He will take the best of your fields . . . and give them to his attendants. He will take a tenth of your grain and of your vintage and give it to his officials . . . Your menservants and maidservants and the best of your cattle and donkeys he will take for his own use . . . [Y] ourselves will become his slaves.

Excerpted from I Samuel 8:10–18.
The Prophet answers Israel's request for
a king to rule over them in place of judges.

INTERLUDE

Summer 1643

A
ll of England simmered. In the halls of Parliament, tempers flared. Quarrelsome voices echoed off the white-washed walls in the once hallowed St Stephen's Chapel as members of the Commons disputed. Some argued for making peace with the King by withdrawing their demands, while others – spurred by John Pym's fiery rhetoric – pumped their fists, shouting they had gone too far to turn back now. To acquiesce would surely return an emboldened tyrant to the throne along with his Catholic consort. It would mean a bloodbath for all who had dared oppose him, they argued.

In August, wearing white ribbons in their hair and armed with bricks to beat against committee-room doors, women marched on Westminster, demanding an end to the war. Some news books called them Southwark whores, bought by members of the emerging 'Peace Party.' One lone news book, from an independent printer on Fleet Street, suggested that perhaps they were simply the wives of laborers and merchants, their righteous indignation ignited by deprivation and the war's cruel reaping of their sons and husbands.

In the churches, Puritans, Separatists and emboldened Presbyterians pounded pulpits, demanding their God-given rights from the Church of England and their King. Wiping beads of sweat from their faces, their listeners roused themselves in resounding shouts of amen. In the Thames Valley, soldiers loitered in the shade of shriveled shrubs while their officers sought midday shelter in their tents to escape an unrelenting sun. Plotting, planning, spying, each side waited for the enemy camp to make a move. In the Midlands, the low hum of insects in dry pastures and hedgerows was interrupted only by occasional gunfire, brief skirmishes, unrecorded and unnoticed except for the occasional body rotting in a ditch. In the North, no breeze stirred as the regiments of Cromwell's Eastern Association trained until the general's dragoons fell like flies.

But at Oxford, the Queen's spirits remained buoyant. Since Henrietta Maria's joyous return from her year-long mission on the Continent, Charles was often away, but she was too busy trying to make a temporary court at Merton College to miss him overmuch. Inigo Jones helped her with the renovations, while William Davenant evaded the naval blockade to procure the needed furnishings and fine fabrics. On this late summer day, as she inspected with delight the silk hangings for the King's bed, she reminded herself of Charles's admonition against extravagance and his assurance that the Oxford quarters were temporary. But it *was* the King's bed and, for now, the royal bedchamber. With the infusion of resources she had brought back from the Continent, the treasury could surely afford a suitable bed for the King. And if Charles was right, and they were able to return to Whitehall soon, Inigo would find a place for this fine Italian silk.

In the meantime, when the King was away with his troops or closeted with his advisors, Henry Jermyn kept the Queen safe and provided merry company. If life was not perfect, it would be better soon. The King would secure his royal prerogative, Parliament would learn its proper place, and, in the meantime, Lucy Hay, Countess of Carlisle, in cooperation with Chancellor Hyde, had arranged a 'visit,' from Princess Elizabeth and little Prince Henry. The chancellor said it might not be a long visit because Parliament's consent was not given, which fact the Queen did not accept at all. She would die before she allowed her children to fall into Parliament's clutches a second time. Never again would Henrietta Maria leave her children to somebody else's protection. Not even their father's.

At Syon House, a few miles west of London, Lucy Hay was busy planning how best to arrange a way to carve out for herself an after-the-war strategy. Her lover and protector, Parliament leader John Pym, would not be pleased if he heard that she had arranged – without permission or Parliament's oversight – for the royal children to visit the Queen, but he was apparently too busy with the war to care about either them or Lucy. Elizabeth and Henry could be away a month or more before anybody ever thought to check on them, and would be back before anyone in

Parliament would know they had ever left. If she could pull it off, it would be enough to reclaim the Queen's grace and favor, whatever the outcome of this miserable war.

Within the city of London listless dogs with ribs showing nosed the gritty cobblestones, seeking moisture and a scrap of bone or gristle, but there was nothing to be found except the flung refuse of emptied chamber pots or filthy dishwater. Outside the city, the dry, dirty air from a summer of so little rain covered every surface, choking the throats of workers breaking hard ground to build the security earthworks. Even news of the fighting seemed to have slowed as England sweltered. In the surrounding countryside, the harvest was poor and the barns empty, boding ill for feeding hungry warriors during the coming winter. Grain dried in the field before it was harvested.

In Fleet Street, at the sign of the crossed swords, Lord Whittier and his one-armed apprentice printed only news of shortages and the women's protest and rumors of the Queen's return. There were also rumblings about Parliament's negotiations for an alliance with the Scots to take up arms against the King, but no hard news yet, only argument that the printer gleaned from loitering around the corridors of Westminster. James Whittier was growing more and more frustrated and more than the war was gnawing at him.

In the stifling heat of the Aldersgate schoolroom, John Milton was shorter tempered than usual as he brooded about the beautiful young wife who'd deserted him after only a few weeks of their miserable marriage. At Forest Hill, the home to which his wife had returned, a miasma hovered in the arid pasture. Mary Milton went about her dusty chores and tried to pretend her marriage had never happened. Her mind and body were occupied with helping her family maintain their manor holdings against an infestation of Royalist troops and diminishing resources, both human and material. Caroline Pendleton – her worst fear officially confirmed: that her husband William was indeed a casualty of the war – worried about what the future held in store, not only for herself but for her dearest friend, Milton's young runaway bride. Her own world turned upside down, Caroline was determined to devise a way to help the Powell family, who had once again offered her refuge.

It was as if all of England waited for the fall to bring relief, but when the first leaves of autumn fell, they were brown and brittle before they hit the ground. When the cooling weather finally came, it brought more devastation. Fighting resumed in earnest west of Oxford. In September, the King's forces reoccupied Reading and began the siege of Gloucester. Shortly after, the two armies collided at Newbury. The King's forces were defeated. Parliament was emboldened.

But the gods of war are fickle, favoring first one side then another, as though for sport. As the combatants and their families strive and bleed and die, Mars casts his cruel shadow over a kingdom about to break apart. Fortunes disappear. Lives are lost, and others are forever altered in unexpected ways by the never-ending conflict. The shattering of the kingdom has begun in earnest.

CORPSES EVERYWHERE

That night we kept the field where the bodies of the dead were stripped. In the morning these were a mortifying object to behold, when the naked bodies of thousands lay upon the ground and not altogether dead . . .

Words of Simeon Ash, parliamentarian chaplain,
after the Battle of Newbury

3 October 1643

I t was chilly in the laundry wagon and the ride was bumpy. As the shadows lengthened and the wind stiffened, Caroline was grateful for the warmth of William's greatcoat and cowhide hat. It was the one he'd worn on the farm in all seasons and it carried the smoky scents of hay and sheep's wool – and William. She was grateful now for the comfort it gave her, though she had never thought to put on a man's garment before Jane Whorwood suggested it.

'You will attract less attention if you are dressed as a man,' she'd said. 'I will give you a document to get you past the London sentries. If you should be questioned, just say you are the relief driver for the supply wagon. They will probably wave you through without even asking. They are used to our laundry deliveries and Jack is my regular driver for the Berkshire route. Jack will back you up.'

It had not been easy to reconcile the canniness and the courage of this savvy young woman with the innocent manner, blonde coiffure, and smiling blue eyes she also possessed. Mistress Jane Whorwood had from time to time stopped to purchase Ann's fine ale and, being an ardent Royalist and a youngish lady of jolly disposition, was a favorite of Justice Powell. Though they'd had no ale to sell and not much to drink, had none for weeks, the mistress of Holton Manor's neighborly visit to Forest Hill proved timely. It was the very day after Caroline, discovering how desperate things really were at Forest Hill, had naively offered a plan for temporary relief.

When Jane Whorwood had politely asked how they were faring under the occupation, Squire Powell's dire response had been more detailed than such a polite inquiry would usually elicit. Somewhat taken aback, the lady had stuttered out an expression of sympathy and asked if she could do anything to help. But before he could specify exactly how, she had hastened to say that sadly her funds were also depreciated by the war. It was a struggle to keep her business going, what with her contributions to the treasury and the bribes she had to pay to all the guards at all the checkpoints surrounding London – she had stopped here to draw a breath – but if she could help in any other way, anything, just ask. She would of course do whatever she could for so loyal a supporter of their dear King Charles, that most excellent of sovereigns. Caroline had noticed how her expression softened when she said the King's name, her eyes gleaming with the kind of religious devotion usually reserved for saints. Real saints – not the generic term with which the Puritans styled themselves.

Now, on her way to London and huddled in between Jane Whorwood's barrels of soap and her own personal possessions, Caroline pulled the greatcoat around her and withdrew into it, as though to find shelter from the chill of encroaching evening shadows. She inhaled, seeking comfort from the lingering essence of her late husband, but the scent had grown fainter, like her memory of William. She could no longer summon his face at will nor his voice, though it sometimes came to her at odd times, unexpected and heart-stopping, an ambush of crushing loss. She no longer waited, anticipating his sudden appearance or his call from another room, but sometimes still she saw a shadow that startled her. *William, is that you?* she had even called out once, thinking she had heard his familiar footfall. It was not the only time she had to remind herself that he was never coming home. A letter of condolence from the garrison certified that awful truth.

The wagon stopped, and the driver, appearing at the back of the wagon, nodded his head in the direction of a brush thicket a few yards away. 'Looks like a safe enough place to stop,' he said, his tone low and edged with embarrassment. 'Thou might want to stretch thy legs to make thyself comfortable. I'll keep an ear for trouble. Been a few outbreaks of heavy fighting around here lately, leftover skirmishes ever since Essex turned back the King's forces at Newbury. We won't stop again before Reading. Safer there than on the road since the Roundheads left and our side is occupying the town.'

Caroline did not want to stretch her legs. She wanted to hunch behind the piles of linen with her pistol in her hands, but she needed relief too. She waited until he was out of view and squatted on the ground with the wagon between her and the brush screen. No more privacy than an animal, she thought, as she gathered up the edge of the long coat with one hand, though God knew she should be used to such by now. Forest Hill had become so overrun with soldiers, peeking and poking into every corner, that a woman could scarcely avail herself of any modesty. But Jack was more considerate than the soldiers she'd left behind. He lingered longer than she thought he probably needed to and, climbing back into the driver's seat, he acknowledged with the briefest glance that she had returned from 'making herself comfortable.'

They had not gone very far when, through the open end of the wagon, they encountered, lying in the ditch, what was left of the first dead thing. Even the sharp odor of lye and ash from the barrels could not disguise the smell of decay. She buried her nose in the crook of her elbow. Just a bulky mess of blood and bone. No discernible head. An animal? The cart slowed to a halt as the driver pulled his neckerchief up over his nose and lit a coach lamp against the quickening twilight. A match flared. The wick smoked and spit a niggardly flame. Prompted by Jack's whip, the horses resumed their tired gait. Caroline stood up to risk a look but held onto the rails for support. The wind had stilled. A heavy silence hovered.

Her eyes adjusted slowly to the scene unfolding in the field. At first glance, denial stifled what reason would not acknowledge. But all too abruptly the images in the field ghosted to reality, revealing a tableau so nightmarish that it must be real because her imagination was incapable of conjuring such. Scattered like broken branches after a storm, the bodies of men sprawled across

the field, a score or more in various stages of undress, some
stripped to the waist, most with bare feet, some altogether naked.
At the near edge of the field, three of the bodies encircled the
ashen remains of a campfire. One corpse sat upright, nothing
where his head should be, a tin pot resting in his slack grip.

Thank God, she could not see the faces of the men – if they
still had faces.

A broad ribbon of darkness folded across the purple and
orange horizon, sailing like some great angel of death coming
to collect the souls of the dead. With one broad swirl the vision
spread its mighty wings, swooped downward and, breaking
into a host of chattering jackdaws and rooks, claimed the field.
At the whirring of the feasting birds, Caroline covered her eyes,
swallowed the gall rising in her throat, and slid back down to
the wagon floor. Her ankle scraped the iron band of a barrel,
but she felt nothing.

She sat in shock as the wagon bumped along the road. The
wagoner kept his steady pace, as if totally unaware of the scene
they had passed. The light dimmed to deep indigo and the road
receded. Caroline looked up at brilliant stars, flung like pinpoints
of light in the patch of sky above the environs of the cart's
wooden walls. These same stars would be illuminating naked
corpses and nesting carrion birds, shedding their light without
discrimination upon the living and the dead. Shivering violently,
she wrapped the greatcoat around her, but it did not decrease
the cold dread that gripped her. Like her, the dead men's wives
and daughters would never have a body to weep over. No grave
to visit. No place to lay a wreath of flowers. Some would wait
beside cold hearths for a homecoming that would never be.
Picked bones, gleaming in the starlight, belonged to no man. And
they belonged to every man.

The road narrowed. Hedgerows replaced the open fields.
Stars glittered overhead. Still the wagon groaned and bumped its
way southeast. Were Arthur's bones, like his father's, lying somewhere in a field beneath a starlit sky? She longed to see his easy
smile, to joy in the irascible spirit of the boy who had been
like a little brother to her. She had not heard from him since
before she lost William. Did he know his father was gone? If he
had heard, surely, he would have come to Forest Hill. Or was

he beyond caring about the living, buried in a mass grave some-where on a lonely fen? So many questions. So much unresolved.

What a fool she had been to think she could do anything in such a messed-up, ruined world. She couldn't stop Arthur from going and she couldn't stop William. What was she thinking? She should never have left Forest Hill, she thought, replaying it all in her mind.

'I will go to London,' she had said. 'William possessed a leasehold there. The woman who owns the property lived in the same house. As his widow, I will claim it, and if I am successful, I will send for you and you can come and stay with me until the war is over and you are fully restored.' She had offered this solution three days ago to the desperate squire when she'd found him in his study, head in his hands, sobbing.

'It's all gone, Caroline,' he had said. 'Except this. We can't buy food or fuel or anything with this worthless paper. My forests are plundered. There will be no harvest. The devil summer heat devoured what the soldiers did not. I simply do not know what we will do.' He flung a pile of the King's script. The useless notes scattered like dead leaves on the wooden floor.

'But, you have other resources. You have the dower rents from Ann's Wheaton properties to back you up.'

His face flushed with shame. He dropped his head. She had to lean in to hear.

'I borrowed against them years ago . . . Everything is gone, Caroline. You might as well know all. There is nothing left.' And then he lifted his head and added, 'I could have made it work, you know, I could have recovered everything. I could have. Except for this bloody war.'

Caroline had known things were bad. But she had thought they would be able to weather it. Were they truly so desperate? She'd had no idea he was such a bad manager, though she should have. It was all clear now. What else would have made the old Royalist barter his favorite daughter to a Puritan like John Milton?

The jolting of the wagon increased. Her ankle throbbed with pain. She touched the swollen bump lightly, rotated her ankle gingerly. Just a bruise, she thought, as she shifted her weight to test it. With one hand, she held onto a nearby barrel and stood up. Deciding the ankle would bear weight, she bent over a wooden chest secreted beneath a pile of clean linen and opened it with the key hanging from a leather thong around her neck. All there: the stash of leftover coins from the cellar, her token box with the pretty little gifts William had given her, buried beneath the few clothes and the linens she had brought with her. Of course, it was all there. Why would it not be? The chest had not left her sight since Jack loaded it for her. Why was she so frightened? She had to keep her senses about her. It was not like she was going to an unfamiliar city. She knew every crooked lane in London town. She had a plan. She just needed to stick to it.

After she had tied her ankle with a kerchief to stop the swelling, she folded a piece of sheeting from a pile of clean linen to use as a pillow and, leaning back against the hard planks of the railing, she closed her eyes and tried to sleep. They would not linger long in Reading and it was still a long way to London. She wrapped herself with William's coat like a blanket and pulled the wide brim of his hat over her face. The scent of decay was fainter, but it lingered in the chill night air. A hot tear slid down her cheek, praying that William, wherever he was, might rest in peace. As the wagon clinked and groaned on the rutted road, Caroline drifted off, thinking of all the mothers and wives and sisters who waited for their unburied dead. She was sleeping restlessly by the time they reached the Reading Garrison. Jack roused her with a warm drink and suggested she 'make herself comfortable' before they got back on the road. They would make London by midday.

John Milton felt the bright nip of autumn as he walked down Aldersgate to Cheapside. He was on his way to collect the quarterly revenues from his father's old business partner, who lived above the scrivener's shop in the house that had been John's boyhood home. Like the rest of London, the marketplace of London was much changed. Many vendors were still shuttered at midday. The Street of the Goldsmiths gleamed dully in the morning light, their empty shop windows offering no enticements. Most of the gold had been melted down to buy arms. Nobody thought of jewelry and plate, except the caches they had hidden, hoarding their diminished treasure as they did their foodstuffs.

As he turned down Bread Street, the once familiar aroma of

freshly baked goods was noticeably absent. Despite last night's frost, few chimneys smoked and those but scantily. Londoners were warned to be miserly with the dwindling stockpile of coal. With the royal forces owning Newcastle, the hearths of London would go begging this winter. Patience Trapford had likewise been instructed to conserve. He and the students didn't require a hot breakfast every day. Some days they could make do with bread and cheese and dried fruit, and a lump or two of coal would do for the schoolroom. On sunny days like this, Trapford could open wide the shutters to let the sunlight warm the front rooms. But hard times were coming. The fighting around Reading was too intense – its garrisons constantly under siege by one side or the other – and the fighting in the Midlands was escalating.

He looked down his father's old street for a welcome sign from a pie shop. There had always been pie shops in Bread Street. He'd told Trapford he'd bring home a meat pie. She was a good servant. He would hate to lose her now, especially when he was taking in more students. But the street did not look promising. The Mermaid Inn's sign was still swinging in the breeze. It had always been a local favorite known – among other, some less worthy things – for decent pies.

He was standing beside the bar, giving his order to be picked up about an hour hence, and it was not going well. 'No beef you say . . . what about lamb . . .? Not that either, and no chicken; well, it will have to be the fish pie, but please see that it is fresh' – when he heard a hearty voice behind him.

'John Milton. How good it is to see you. What brings you to the Mermaid? Not exactly the place I would expect to encounter an old friend of the Puritan bent,' he said with a half-smile. This was followed by an enthusiastic slap on John's shoulder.

John tried not to cringe beneath the familiarity. He liked Henry Lawes. Really liked him. And not just for his affable disposition, and certainly not for his loyalty to Charles Stuart. Lawes, despite his flaws in judgment, was an exceptional composer of very fine music. He had written the music for all the better-known poets and set many of the Psalms to beautiful polyphonic melodies. His use of counterpoint was totally original.

John smiled at him as he answered. 'If the Mermaid was good enough for Will Shakespeare and Ben Jonson, it will probably do my soul no harm. There might be some breath of inspiration still lingering in the air.' He inhaled deeply, as if to suck in the rarefied air he referenced. 'Though I am likewise surprised to see you here. I would have thought you would be in Oxford with the rest of the court. I haven't seen you since we worked together on *Comus*. I was truly grateful for that collaboration. Your music was . . . genius; perfectly accented each line of my verse.'

Lawes smiled at the compliment, acknowledging it with a slight shrug. 'I too enjoyed that collaboration. What are you working on now? That great epic you told me about?'

'Alas, for the time being, I have put poetry aside to offer my prose in the cause of liberty.'

'Ah. Yes. I have read some of your work. I am afraid I don't agree with the "root and branch" movement. I possess a total lack of understanding of the virulent diatribes against the King. And frankly, John, I am surprised that you too do not mourn the damage done to music, art and poetry by this radical Puritan faction.'

John pursed his lips in concentration, trying to decide how best to answer without offending his friend. 'I'll admit such suppression is a march too far for some of my colleagues. But I think it only temporary. The people will not long stomach such. If the people's true voice be heard.' He paused, sucking in a lungful of stale, smoke-laden air. 'But in the same vein I must insist that music, art, and poetry cannot abide for any length of time where true liberty does not, Henry. Charles Stuart, like his father before him, cannot comprehend the need for oversight from a freely elected Parliament. He is proving himself to be more tyrant than king.'

John Milton paused, consciously dropping the rising pitch of his voice to a more conversational tone. 'English Common Law should rule the people, not the royal prerogative of kings. Freedom of speech, freedom of religion, freedom of self-governance: liberty is the only nursery where the arts and artists can thrive, dear friend. The Star Chamber must not be allowed to decide what is art and what is not. Human liberty is God-given. The King's claim to divine right to rule is not.'

Mild consternation played on the composer's face. 'But, John, the arts *thrived* at the court of this same King you now rail against. Such music we made, such poetry – you and I, William Davenant and John Suckling were part of that. England has not seen the like since Queen Elizabeth's day.'

'There is one very important difference. This flowering you celebrate sprouted under the direction of a French, Catholic Queen. What the royal court did not commission or delight in was not performed. The song of a caged nightingale is very limited in its range – especially when that cage has a golden chain attached by the other end to Rome.'

'So that's the crux of it, then? The Queen and her religion. Should she also not be free to worship as she pleases?' Lawes gave a sardonic smile; some of the good humor had gone out of his friend and colleague. But Milton was in too deep to turn back now.

'Free, Henry? Yes, she should be free to murmur her prayers at whatever altar she chooses – if she is powerless to impose her corrupted belief on others and her golden crucifix is not paid for by the treasury. But she is not powerless. She is a Queen in thrall to a greater power, and I am not talking about our Lord. The religion of Rome is more about power than about God. Have you forgotten, Henry, the burnings under our last Catholic Queen Mary? She too promised tolerance in the beginning. Hundreds of burnings followed. Whole families tortured. Good church men, who dared speak against the yoke of Rome, were broken on the rack.' Milton could feel his temper rising. He inhaled again, this time seeking not inspiration but control. 'Come, friend. Let's not argue. Let's speak of other things. I am surprised you are still in London. How is your brother, William? Is he still composing?'

Henry looked relieved at the shift of subject. 'William has joined the fray. If he is composing songs, it's battle hymns for the royal army. He is more warrior than I.'

'And you? What sweet melodies does the muse whisper in your ear these days?'

'I am composing some music for the Psalms to be included in the liturgy.' He shrugged and gave a mournful shake of his head. 'At least I was. But with the archbishop in the Tower – and the court in virtual exile – I lack patronage. When the wolf shows up at the door, the muse retreats. Yet I remain hopeful and scratch out a melody now and then. And I still have the dear company

of a few fellows. Though not by their choice. Richard Loveless
has been confined to London for a couple of years, unable to
pass beyond the five-mile limit. His verse "To Althea from Prison"
is so beautiful in lyric and sentiment it would bring tears to your
eyes. Mildmay Fane is also confined.'

'I had heard that Fane was in the Tower. I hated to hear it.
For all his misguided loyalty, he is a good man.'

'He appealed to the House of Lords and they released him, thank
God, but, like Lovelace, they restricted him to stay within the Lines
of Communication. He pressed suit to join his family at one of his
country estates, but was denied and his estates sequestered.'

'Sequestered! What of his wife and children? How will they
survive?'

He shrugged. 'As a burden to relatives, I suppose. But what
of you, John? You married a year or so ago, I heard.' Then he
smiled – a little slyly, Milton thought – and asked as though he
was joking, 'You are not the J.M. of the *Divorce Tracts*, are you?'

Milton drew himself taller by half an inch, inhaling more stale
air. 'Indeed, sir. I am the same.'

The wide-eyed look on Henry's face showed genuine surprise.
'Oh. I am so sorry. I did not mean to pry. But I must ask how
your Puritan fellows have received your disavowal of the
sacrament of marriage?'

For friendship's sake, Milton ignored the disapproval shown
by this word choice, choosing not to reiterate his argument or
to point out that there were only two rituals in the liturgy
worthy of the term sacrament. 'My Puritan fellows have been
largely silent. I shall probably see their righteous disdain in
print before long.'

The innkeeper interrupted to present his bill for the pie. 'Excuse
me, sirs, but Mr Milton, I have given your order to the cook.
Could you please pay now? Times being what they are, we must
ask for payment ahead should some unfortunate circumstance
prevent your returning.'

'Of course,' Milton said, digging into his purse and frowning
as he counted out the coins. 'I will return in no more than two
hours. That should give sufficient time. It will be very inconvenient to have to wait.' And then he added another coin, 'Please
give my friend here a pint of your best.'

The innkeeper nodded in understanding and Milton turned back to his companion, saying, 'Henry, I am afraid I really must take my leave. I have a very important errand that should not be delayed, or I would stay to share a drink with you. But whatever the outcome of this war, let us remain friends. If I may presume upon our previous association, when that poem stirring in my soul is finally birthed, I have great hope it will be an epic achievement in every sense. Should I want to set any or all of it to music, well, there is none other than you who could do it justice.'

'I shall look forward to it. A grand epic, you say? Why, man, I will admit to envy of so elevated an expectation. May it come quickly before time and circumstance undo us all.'

As he walked the rest of the way down Bread Street, Milton congratulated himself. At least, unlike some of his peers, he was still his own man and required no court patronage. It was good for an artist to have a vocation to fall back on in hard times – much less capricious than fortune's patronage – and if he sometimes found his pupils burdensome, at least they gave him a base of income. And though he was without wife and progeny to offer the domestic bliss he had naively imagined, at least – unlike Mildmay Fane – he didn't have to worry about how to feed and house them. Mary Powell had relieved him of that responsibility by abandoning him.

Still at the Reading coaching inn, Caroline Pendleton had made herself comfortable after her long journey in the wagon from Forest Hill, as comfortable as she could with the ache in her swollen ankle. Her empty stomach ached too, but she couldn't afford to pay the puffed-up price the inn would be charging for a bowl of hot porridge, so she chewed on a hunk of stale bread and a withered apple scavenged from the bottom of her bag. She was grateful for the warmth of the fire. It was a hearty fire of good English oak instead of smoky coal. And it was free.

The public rooms outside the garrison were noisy with the cursing of Royalist soldiers, boasting of their recent encounter; how they had bested the Roundheads at Newbury and sent them scurrying back to London. Not all of them, she thought, remembering the carrion birds. She swallowed hard against the lump of bread lodged in her throat.

'Seems as I heard ye got as good as ye gave,' the publican said, slapping foaming tankards on the bar. 'Reading Garrison changes hands as often as a whore changes beds. But ye are welcome, just like the Parliament men whose heels ye tread, if ye have the price of a pint. That'll be sixpence each.'

They looked like an unruly lot. Though the publican had warned them his was a respectable coaching inn and he would brook no rowdiness or lewd talk, Caroline was grateful for the invisibility that William's broad-brimmed hat afforded. Jack, who was talking earnestly with the stable master, threw a concerned glance in her direction. Across the room a door opened. A gust stirred the heaping ash in the firebox. Caroline looked up to see a woman enter, carrying one child of about two years in her arms, a little girl – from her careful curls and little pink cloak. Another girl, wearing a pink cloak to match, an older sister, most like, held firmly to the woman's hand.

Caroline nodded and moved down the bench to make room for the woman and her children.

The older child stared at Caroline with a quizzical look. 'Why is that woman dressed in a man's big dirty cloak?'

The woman was fashionably dressed enough to be quality, but not so extravagantly as to call attention to herself. She scolded the girl, 'Don't be rude, child. Women's cloaks are sometimes not practical for travel. Just look at that smudge that your . . . little sister has on her jacket.' She glanced apologetically in Caroline's direction and said, 'It is a very practical choice.'

'My lady,' Jack's voice was low as he approached the bench. The young girl and her mother looked up expectantly, but her coachman was looking only at Caroline as he continued. 'Bad news. I have been warned that given the recent battle at Newbury and all, we might be turned back at the Lines of Communication – or worse. Security is very strict. I dare not risk thy safety or mine. I am turning back toward Oxford.'

'But Mistress Whorwood assured me that we could get through. She said it was your regular route. Surely—'

'A week ago, we could have. But thou saw the carnage in the field we passed.'

Caroline closed her eyes, trying to banish the vision of the ghost-like scene in the frozen field, the scavenger birds gleaning the remains of the battle. 'Don't worry. I will not abandon thee here. Accompany me back to Oxford. I will even take thee back to Forest Hill.'

Back to Forest Hill. Back through that dreadful landscape. And what would she find back at Forest Hill? More hopelessness. More desperation. Mistress Powell and Mary were depending on her to find refuge for them if they were forced to leave.

'That is very gracious of you, but I have nothing to return to. I will stay here until safe passage becomes available.'

'I will make inquiries and do what I can. But I doubt if any will try to make it through until things cool off a bit.' He shrugged as she shook her head. 'Very well then. I will bring in thy traveling chest.' He started to leave then turned back and asked, 'Be thou sure?'

'I am sure,' she said firmly.

At the other end of the bench, an officer of the King's army had approached and was speaking quietly with the other woman. She stood up and handed the youngest child to the man. The little girl started to cry and reach out to the woman in protest, 'Maman.'

'Stop crying like a little baby,' the older girl said in a long-suffering voice. 'You will see Maman soon.'

'Yes, my darlings. Soon, I promise. Now go with the nice soldier.' The child's wails became louder. 'He is a friend of your mother and he will give you a sweet, if you are good,' she cajoled. 'And you will see Maman soon. She will be so glad to see you.' She handed a packet tied with string to the officer. 'Give these letters into her hands only. That is very important.'

Maman – she will be glad. This woman was not their mother after all, Caroline thought. Manner and dress too fine for a governess. A young grandmother, perhaps, or godmother. But Caroline turned away, too preoccupied with her own dilemma to be too long distracted by this little domestic drama. She could sit here by this fire throughout the night. Maybe tomorrow things would look better, but if she had to stay too long, she would become conspicuous. There was nothing else for it. She had to dig into her hoard and come up with a night's lodging. Maybe if the current circumstances lasted, she could work in the kitchen for her keep. Her mind was preoccupied with her schemes for survival when she was startled by a light touch on her shoulder.

'I couldn't help but overhear what the coachman said.'

Caroline looked up to see the woman who had scooted down the bench, closing the short distance between them.

'My name is Lucy Hay, Countess of Carlisle,' she said. 'I will be returning to London in the morning. You can travel safely through the lines with me. You will be quite safe, I assure you. My coachman is skilled with the sidearm he carries, should we encounter any trouble, and I have a pass from Sir Edward Hyde to get us through the checkpoints.'

Caroline's first thought was relief. Her second followed closely. Why would this strange woman make such an offer? Truly out of compassion? Or had she some darker motive? Circumstances argued that she should presume the former.

'How very kind you are, Lady Carlisle,' she said. 'Please don't think me the disreputable vagabond I must look, though I do admit my situation is not optimal.'

The woman smiled at the understatement. 'I heard your driver addressing your plight and your speech is far above the common sort. There are many sad stories in these difficult times. I shall not pry into yours. But if all you want is to get to London, it would be no indisposition at all, I assure you.'

'In that case I would be pleased and very grateful for your assistance. Perhaps, I can help with the children to repay you.'

'They will not be returning with us. Payment enough is the pleasure of your company.' She stood up then and picked up the small valise she carried. 'I plan to leave at dawn.'

'I will be right here. And I am already in your debt. Thank you again, my lady, for not being put off by my unconventional attire. I am a widow. My husband, Sir William Pendleton, was killed fighting for the King. I am trying to return to my home in London. And his greatcoat seemed, as you so astutely observed, a practical choice.'

'I think your choice of traveling attire is very clever, Lady Pendleton. I will enjoy your company, I am sure.'

'My lady, you are an answer to prayer.'

Lady Carlisle threw back her head and gave a little musical

laugh. 'It has been a long time since anybody said that to me. It is quite a nice thing to hear. I will see you in the morning.'

Jack returned shortly and, placing the chest on the floor in front of her, said, 'I've had no luck in finding anybody going into London. Maybe things will settle down and we can get through the lines later. Mistress Whorwood has good connections.'

'Thank you, Jack. You have been very kind to me, and I do not blame you for not wanting to go on after what we have seen. Don't worry about me. Tell Mistress Whorwood that I can complete my journey by another means and that I am grateful for her compassion. I have found a friend. A lady from London who has a letter of passage from Sir Edward Hyde himself. She has invited me to accompany her.'

'Well. If that don't beat the devil,' he said, looking taken aback. Then he grinned and added, 'There's more to thee than meets the eye, I reckon.' He nodded at her and took his leave.

Something – the look of admiration, perhaps, or just the relief she felt – made Caroline laugh. For one moment that laugh broke the pall that was her constant companion. As she sat munching on her withered apple with a warm fire at her back, her knees propped on her smallish wooden chest, and a plan for the morrow, she almost forgot the throbbing in her ankle. She remembered too that this was the second time she had found a savior in an unlikely coaching inn, and was very grateful to whatever angel was watching over her.

TURNING POINTS

Remember, remember the fifth of November,
Gunpowder treason and plot;
I know of no reason why the gunpowder treason
Should ever be forgot.

Litany chanted by celebrants on Guy Fawkes Day

5 November 1643

The house was too quiet without Prince Henry's squeals of laughter and Princess Elizabeth's earnest scolding. Voices ghosted in Lady Carlisle's head. *Do not bounce balls in the salon, Henry. It is an outside ball.*

Lucy picked up the offending ball and stowed it away. In the three weeks since the children had been gone, the silent routines of Syon House had been broken only once with a brief visit from Edward Hyde reassuring her that the young Princess and her brother had been safely reunited with their mother. He had also delivered to Lucy a token of appreciation from Henrietta. It wasn't that she wasn't grateful for the small wooden box containing three exquisitely embroidered silk handkerchiefs – it was after all a gift from the Queen – but she would have preferred a personal note from the woman whom she had befriended and served since the Queen was scarcely more than a girl. Given the times and the circumstances surrounding their initial parting, the ivory inlay of a crucifix adorning the lid was at best an insensitive gift for a Presbyterian lady-in-waiting. At worst, it was a gouge.

'How fares Her Majesty?' Lucy had asked.

Edward Hyde had answered that the Queen was well and had established a somewhat festive court at Merton College. She looked a little pale, thinner than when she had left for the Continent a year ago, but she was putting on some weight now. At first, she had been unhappy because His Majesty and young James and Charles were away fighting in the West Country and had talked about joining them in the field. But that was before the younger children came. She appeared satisfied now and was already talking of celebrating Christmas with her ladies and the children. Then he had added with a flush as he looked away, 'She is *enceinte*,' he said, as if the Queen's condition sounded less earthy in the French tongue. 'Only a few months. The babe is expected in the spring.'

'Well,' Lucy had said, laughing. 'The war hasn't taken too much out of King Charles.'

Hyde had answered with an awkward little laugh and had taken his leave, promising to return when he had more news of the children. He did not know if or when they would be returning to Syon House, but he would keep her informed.

News of the Queen's pregnancy left Lucy feeling even more forlorn. Some women pushed out healthy babies – wanted and unwanted – like ewes, season after season, but after one disappointing attempt, her womb had shriveled. It was hard not to be resentful. Until she remembered the frightened young girl whom the Duke of Buckingham had coldly delivered to an indifferent bridegroom. Thanks to Lucy Hay, who by then had some experience in the art of love, the little French Princess had soon bound the young English King to her. Henrietta owed much to Lady Carlisle. Lucy hoped she did not forget the debt.

Some days she thought too about the young widow to whom she had bid farewell at a house in Gresham Street not far from the Guildhall. Caroline Pendleton had been surprisingly good company and in good spirits considering all she had seen. They had parted in front of a respectable townhouse in an area frequented by wealthy merchants. Lucy had offered to wait, but Caroline had seemed certain she could move right in, since her late husband held a lease there, and requested the driver to unload her chest. When the door opened, and Caroline went inside, Lucy ordered the driver to drive on with a feeling of unease and no small sympathy for the new widow. Caroline had lost so much to the King's cause, she deserved a little bit of happiness. Happiness did not come easily in these hard times, but Lucy hoped this new widow would find safety at least.

She thought too of going again to Westminster, an official visit, to tell John Pym of her independent decision to send the children to their mother. But no. Let the Parliament man, who had made himself scarce of late, come to her if he was concerned about their well-being – or hers. She even thought of writing him a formal letter, but determined that a communication of such a secret nature would not be secure. Spoken words could be denied. Words written in one's own hand could not. Besides, with the war, everything had become so much harder. Syon House lay outside the Committee of Safety's established Lines of Communication, making travel inconvenient and time consuming. There were always delays at the checkpoints. Surely, she would hear from John soon.

But when it came, it was not in the guise she could ever have expected. She and Carter were in the salon, returning the chairs to their proper places and the giant candelabra to its spot in the center of the table; who knew when or if the children would ever return, or if she would ever entertain again there for that matter, but seeing the room restored to its former use made it and her feel less empty.

Tom, the half-witted usher, shuffled in and stood leaning uncertainly against the door. Old Carter slid the covers from off the damask chairs and said, 'Well, say what it is you have to say, boy, speak up. Don't just slouch there like the cat's got your tongue.'

'A visitor is come. Wants to speak to milady.'

Lucy's breath caught in her throat. 'Who is it?'

The stupid boy just shook his head.

'Not someone you have seen here before?'

Again, a shake of his head, as though he were mute.

'Man or woman?' she asked, still hopeful.

'Woman, milady,' the would-be footman muttered, without looking at her.

'Go back and ask for her name,' Carter said with irritation in his voice. 'Oh, I'll go.'

'No, wait. I shall go myself,' she said. 'Any diversion is welcome.'

When she got to the foyer she was surprised to see a well-dressed young woman she did not recall at all. But this was no casual call, Lucy suddenly realized, as the sober-looking woman curtsied uneasily.

'Thank you for seeing me, Lady Carlisle. My name is Dorothy Drake, wife of Sir Francis Drake. We have not met before.'

Lucy's heart gave a little jerk of recognition at the name. 'You are John Pym's daughter. I have heard your father speak of you. He is very proud of his children. But pray, what brings you to Syon House? Though, of course, you are heartily welcome.'

'Thank you, my lady. My father speaks highly of you as well. He has sent me to summon you.'

The day was overcast but it was to Lucy as though a sunbeam had suddenly illumined the room.

'At his office in Westminster? Did he say when?'

'Not at Westminster. At Derby House in Canon Row.'

Derby House. That was not discreet.

The girl gazed at her with a knowing look but without resentment. 'My father asks that you attend him immediately. He requests that you return with me.'

Lucy looked down at her plain skirt and dust-streaked bodice. 'I am sure your father will not mind if I take the time to make myself more presentable. We have been house-cleaning. I will come in my own carriage and spare you the wait.'

Dorothy Drake inhaled deeply. 'My father insisted that I bring you back with me. I was instructed to wait.'

It took Lucy a minute to absorb what the girl had just said. Insisted? Why so demanding? His choice of messenger was puzzling. And to ask that she come to his house? She had never been invited to his residence. Through his spies he must have heard that she had allowed the children to go to Oxford. Why hadn't she had the good sense to tell him immediately? He must be very angry, might even consider her actions a betrayal.

'I will go with you now,' she said.

When they reached the checkpoints, the sentry waved the carriage bearing Parliament's seal through without so much as a look inside. Dorothy Drake was a woman of few words. The silence that lay between them was charged with an awkward kind of tension, as though something went unsaid – as indeed it did – precluding small talk.

Unable to endure the silence any longer, Lucy spoke. 'I must be frank with you, Lady Drake. The urgency in your father's summons as you delivered it, and the speed with which you insisted we depart, leads me to assume that this matter is of more than slight importance.'

She desperately hoped that John was not going to tell her that he felt she had betrayed his confidence by sending the King's children away without consulting him and therefore found their liaison too burdensome to continue. But that would mean that all along he had been using her to keep Parliamentary control over the royal children. That was not – could not be – true. She had won his heart, she was sure of it. A scolding perhaps – she probably deserved that – and would promise to make it up to him. Why hadn't the girl given her a chance to at least put on fresh clothes? His seeing her like this might put her at a disadvantage.

'Yes, Lady Carlisle. More than of slight importance.' She turned her direct gaze on Lucy and with a sober expression on her face said, 'Simply put, my father is very ill. He may be . . . dying.'

Lucy was momentarily stunned. 'Did you . . . did you say *dying*?' Her tongue could not shape the words. Her breath was shallow and quick. This was some cruel joke. Or he had an ague maybe, and the girl was just being melodramatic. He would recover. His will alone would not let him die. Not in the middle of a cause to which he was so committed.

The girl diverted her gaze to the clasped hands resting in her lap and said very softly, 'I do not know when you saw him last, my lady. But I must prepare you. He has not eaten in three days. He can only take water in drops. The doctor has bled him three times during this last fortnight and each time he gets weaker.' She paused to swallow and continued in the same low tone, 'His flesh has fallen away, and he is very pale. He cannot last long without a miracle. I hope that you can bring him some comfort. He says that you are a dear . . . friend.'

'Is he . . . is he in pain?'

'The apothecary has pounded some China seeds and mixed them with a few drops of wine. He cannot drink it, but a drop or two on his tongue helps him to sleep. Though he mostly refuses, complaining that it makes him drowsy and gives him strange dreams.'

Lucy rested her head on the hard frame of the carriage and closed her eyes, still struggling for breath, her mind as jumbled as her thoughts. Neither spoke until the carriage reached Derby House. She would have run into his chamber, but voices, men's voices, stopped them short. Dorothy laid a restraining hand on Lucy's shoulder.

'You should probably wait out here. I will go in and see if he is ready to see you.'

She came back shortly, whispering, 'He is with some members of the Committee of Safety. I always try to keep them away. I think Oliver Cromwell is with them this time. General Cromwell and Lord Essex are always at each other's throats. Manchester too. They are all strong willed and do not always agree on military matters.' Tears welled in the girl's eyes, her tone betraying frustration, as she said, 'They should not be bothering him now. He has given them all he can give. It would probably be best if you wait here.'

Before Lucy could protest that she was well acquainted with the Committee of Safety and they her, the determined young woman had hustled her into a tiny anteroom and was about to close the door. 'It will not be long now,' she said. 'I shall be quite firm with them. My father is past the kind of Parliament schemes that brought on the ill-humors sapping his life force.'

She was as good as her word. Lucy had no time to try to summon the innate optimism that had always seen her through before she heard the men leave, muttering to themselves about how Pym would never see the New Year and how they could think of none to take his place. Parliament was in the middle of a war for the soul of England, and England would soon be leaderless. Lucy cared not a pile of dog's dung about the soul of England. The soul of England was sucking the life out of the friend and lover on whom she had wagered all.

'You may go in now. I will see that you are undisturbed. Stay as long as he wants.'

The room was dimly lit, all but one of the curtains drawn.

John was propped up on the bed on pillows. This man bore little resemblance to the John with whom she had fallen in love. He was hollow-eyed and skeletal. His beard had not been trimmed and his hair hung in oily strands. The smell in the room was a sour mixture of incense and vinegar, underlaid with the smell of something rotten. Lucy painted a smile on her face as she approached but she could not sustain the smile or stop the welling tears that threatened to spill. He did not need to see her despair. She looked away, pretending preoccupation with smoothing the counterpane.

The only thing about the frail man lying in the bed that she recognized was the light in his eyes, a light still burning with some splinter of passion for living and doing. But the timbre of his voice was the same, albeit a little weaker. 'Lucy. Thank God you have come.' He took her hands in his. The skin felt dry and thin, like the desiccated wing of a dead butterfly.

'Of course I have come, John. I have longed to see you. Why did you not send for me sooner?' Dizziness threatened. She groped for the chair beside his bed and sat down. 'We have wasted so much precious time,' she said, 'so much precious time.'

'Please do not think my delay means that I did not long for you. There was so much to do and so little time to do it in. We are in danger of losing this war, and I know my time is short. I had to make a way.'

She said nothing, just struggled to choke back her tears.

'You understand that, Lucy, don't you?'

She just nodded, her head still down, unable to speak. He reached for her hand. It felt so fragile she was afraid even to squeeze it.

'Now we have finally secured all parliamentary signatures on a Covenant with Scotland for military support in exchange for a religious Protestant Union. It gives the Presbyterians a little too much control in church matters, but it will stop the Catholics and their political predation. You know, Lucy, for me it was never about their superstitious worship. It was about their greed and hunger for absolute power, and all that England has suffered under their power.'

His voice seemed to grow stronger through his will alone. She wanted to shush him, to tell him to conserve his strength, but she knew it would do no good.

'They must be stopped, or this King will take us right back to the days of Bloody Mary. England must be ruled by the people so that will never happen again. Charles will not even agree to equipoise, to any kind of balance in governing. Did you know, in the beginning, he tried to buy me off, offered me the exchequer's position. No better than a tax collector.'

She feared he was becoming agitated, patted him gently. 'I know, John. I know; all of England knows what an incorruptible man you are.' She stroked his forehead, pushing the greasy strings of hair away. 'Tell me, my love, what do the doctors say?'

'I have been poked and prodded by every money-grubbing charlatan in the College of Physicians. They agree on nothing but their fees. But I know what ails me. I have a mass in my stomach and it is growing, crowding out everything else. My father died this way. I knew it would devour me sooner or later. It appears it will be sooner.'

'But surely there is somebody that can help you. There has to be.'

'I am beyond their help, Lucy. There was one, a young astrologer and botanist. Nicholas Culpeper could have helped me if I'd found him sooner. Before the physicians leeched the life out of me with their purging and sweating and blood-letting. Culpeper runs an herbal apothecary – simples mostly, a few compounds – outside of London control. In Spitalfields.'

'Should we summon him?'

'No. He comes to examine me twice a week. Me – not just to sniff my urine and frown. He is a good young man; he was a Parliament surgeon on the battlefield until he was wounded and had to quit. I enjoy his company as much as his physicks. He left me some bishop's wort and suggested angelica tea, but nothing stops the pain except the devil seeds from China.'

He reached up and took her hand. She could feel it trembling. He was exhausted. 'Sit with me awhile, Lucy,' he said. 'I have some instructions for you, but I am going to close my eyes. Just for a bit.'

He did not stir for about half an hour, but she could see his chest move with his breathing. Once she tried to remove her hand, but he would not let go. The drapery on the window opposite his bed was open. The light outside was fading. She would have gotten up to close the drape and light a candle, but she did not want to disturb him.

She bowed her head and closed her eyes, wanting to pray, but she did not know what to pray for. A quick release from his suffering? A miracle? In this age when God's people were at war with each other? Who should He bless? Who punish? Why would He even listen? In the end she just prayed for peace. For John. For herself. For England and all its poor broken subjects. For all the children and the women who had been abandoned. Like the widow she met. Like the King's children. After a while she felt his gaze and looked up.

'Our Father who art in Heaven,' he began, as if he were reading her mind. 'Say it with me, Lucy.' As they repeated the Lord's Prayer, his eyes were open, looking at her, and his hand was still gripping hers. After his softly murmured *amen* he continued, his gaze still locked on hers. 'Yea though I walk through the valley of the shadow of death, I will fear no evil.' Then he sighed and closed his eyes again.

The bed on which he wasted away had strangely become to her as holy as any altar.

They sat again in silence, but this time he seemed more at peace, his breathing more even, until the sound of gunfire outside the window startled him. A yellow glow brightened the twilight. She went to the window and looked out.

'What is it, Lucy? Is there fighting in the streets? Have we been invaded?' She heard the anxiety returning.

'No. I see no soldiers. Just a crowd of people celebrating.'

The street below was filling up with revelers. Jeering and cheering, cursing and singing. Cacophony and chaos. Outside the window, a growing bonfire hissed and spit into the twilight sky as revelers once again burned their perennial Catholic conspirator in celebration.

'What are they celebrating? Have we won some great battle?'

'Today is the fifth of November, John. Once again Guy Fawkes will not live to blow up Parliament.'

He almost laughed, but the almost-laugh turned into a sigh, 'Ah, but Parliament may blow up itself, this time.'

Lucy watched the little scene play out in the street. She hated the annual celebration of the spoiling of the Gunpowder Plot.

Not because it had failed. But for what it had done to young Lucy Percy. That old conflict had stolen her youth and now it followed her into middle age, shadowing the last intimate moment she would share with her dying lover. What were all those boisterous revelers celebrating, anyway? It was not as if it was over. They were once again right in the middle of it. That old conflict had played itself out for ages, empires and peoples fighting over God.

Below, a shower of sparks lit the dark sky.

Where they once slaughtered animals in sacrifice, now they slaughtered themselves and others. But it was never about God. It was about power and ambition. More wanted to be God than serve God. And on whatever battlefield, in climes far and near, today and yesterday and tomorrow, where men butchered each other in holy war, the devil surely laughed and clicked his cloven hoofs in wicked delight.

'It grows late, Lucy. The streets will become unsafe with drunkards and ne'er-do-wells as the night progresses.' He reached for the bell at his bedside. 'Promise me one thing, before you go. Promise you will keep the King's children safe. Before you let Parliament get their hands on them, give them to their mother. Better they should be raised Catholic than become pawns in a game of "winner take all at whatever cost."'

Though he had shown compassion for the King's youngest children, Lucy was shocked to hear this admonition coming from John – shocked and relieved. She had feared that the man who wanted more than any other soul in England to see the King brought to his knees, the man who had sacrificed so much for that cause, had intended all along to use them as pawns to gain what he thought was a righteous and necessary outcome. But the awareness of a hovering death angel might well change a man's priorities.

'Oh, my love. I am so relieved to hear you say that. I must confess. They are already with the Queen. I delivered them to Hyde more than a fortnight ago. He has promised to bring them back if Oxford comes under siege. Please do not be cross.'

He didn't answer immediately, just looked at her, framed against the fiery window. She squeezed her eyes shut tight, praying that God would not let them part in anger. Not this time.

The ghost of a smile played around his lips. He swallowed hard and then said softly, 'Hyde is a good man, even if he is the King's lackey. It is just as well. I should never have burdened you with them. And if Parliament loses, you will have some protection. The Queen will be grateful.'

'It was no burden, John. No burden at all.'

His gaze studied her face, as if to memorize it. 'Come. Kiss me before you go, Lucy Hay.'

He didn't say, this one last time. But he didn't have to.

His lips tasted sour, but she would have held that kiss forever if she could. There was a knock at the door and he gently pulled away.'

'You may enter,' he said to the two strapping soldiers who came in. 'See Lady Carlisle safely to Syon House. Our business here is finished.'

STRANGE BEDFELLOWS

*We shall endeavour to bring the Churches of God in the
three Kingdoms to the nearest conjunction and uniformity
in religion, confession of faith, form of Church government . . . We shall endeavour the extirpation of Popery,
prelacy . . . superstition, heresy, schism, profaneness . . . We
shall . . . preserve the rights and privileges of the Parliaments
. . . We shall . . . assist and defend all those that enter into
this league . . . against all opposition . . .*

Excerpted from *Solemn League and Covenant*, agreed
to by Parliament and Scotland in September 1643

7 December 1643

'I 'll not sign it. It's not right. That is not what I was fighting
for. Instead of a Pope telling me how and when to pray, now
it's going to be a committee of Calvinists.' The printer's
assistant removed the last printed sheet for the day, the text of
The Solemn League and Covenant, the subject of his scowl. 'And
I know Patience will never sign it. She said she'd go to jail first.'

'So that is why you are in such a sour mood, Ben. You will
probably have lots of company. I don't intend to sign it either,'
James Whittier said. 'Don't worry. You and I are small fry. It
will be awhile before they get to our shop, if at all. Tell Patience
Trapford not to speak too loudly against it in her Independent
congregation, though it is probably unlikely the Committee of
Three Kingdoms will bother with a powerless young woman.
But they may go after some of those godly preachers she's so
fond of.'

That reassurance did little to lighten Ben's mood. Maybe it
was the approaching season that warned of a Christmas void of
all mirth and joy. Or maybe it was the pain. On winter days such

as these, his left arm hurt, and that was just crazy because the pain was in his empty sleeve, below the elbow joint where the barber surgeon had sawed off the splintered bone. The whisky they had poured into him had made him retch, choking on his own vomit, until there was only the searing agony followed by blessed nothingness. He tried to push it all from his mind. At least he had survived.

'None of the dissident preachers or their congregations will sign it,' he said. 'I can guarantee it. It will be a matter of honor for some, faith for others.' He paused in his pressing, resisting the urge to stroke the empty sleeve, then said quietly, 'You have been very kind to me, milord. I hope you know how grateful I am. But there's something I need to tell you. I haven't been exactly truthful with you.'

'About your service in the war? Who am I to fault—?'

'No. Not about that. I lost my arm right enough, though not in a grand battle as you might have imagined. I was a scout for Cromwell, not an infantryman. Got caught in the crossfire. A small roadside skirmish. Never knew if the musket ball came from our side or theirs, but, thank God, it was one of our own who hauled me back to camp.'

Whittier had paused in his typesetting and looked up with interest, curiosity in his arched eyebrow, 'What have you withheld that would be any of my business?'

'Well, start with my name. Benjamin is my second name. My first name, the one by which I have always been known, is Arthur. Arthur Pendleton. Not Pender.'

Whittier laughed. 'Well I'd say that's not exactly a lie. Maybe just an abbreviation. I'm guessing the godly Patience Trapford has raised your standards when it comes to truth-telling. But I am curious. Why did you change your name?'

'I just wanted to put the past behind me. Didn't want to think about it. Wanted to start anew.'

'The war, you mean?'

'Not just that. Family stuff. My father and his friends are fierce Royalists. You can see how that might lead to bad blood between us. He pretty much disowned me when I went over to the other side. But lately – well, it was something Patience said about having never really known her father and how she would give anything if she could just see him. She has no family at all. Put me to thinking what I had thrown away. I need your leave to go back to Oxfordshire and see if my father and I can come to some kind of reconciliation.'

The light outside was fading. Whittier got up to light the lanterns hanging high above the lines where the newly inked paper had been hung to dry before they were folded and cut.

'I have no right to stop you, Ben. You are not a bound apprentice. More an underpaid freeman. But there's a lot of heavy fighting in Oxfordshire. Must you go now?'

Ben picked up the rag and set his good arm to cleaning the platen. 'All the more reason I need to go. Before it's too late. I have a stepmother. More like an older sister than a mother. She is much younger than my father. If my father has been pressed into taking up arms for the King, she may need me. I know it is short notice, but I have finished this last lot and already packed a saddlebag.' He pointed to the said bag by the door. 'I'd like to leave tonight. It's a clear night. Full moon. Less likely to encounter soldiers on the road at night.'

'A man must do what a man must do. You do plan to come back, right? I have come to depend on you. And those newsboys you feed will really miss you.'

'I will be back, my lord, I promise. No more than a few days. You can count on it.'

Whittier blew out the burning end of the match he was using and flung it in the fire, started to scribble on a scrap of paper. 'Give this to the sentry at the checkpoint. It says that you are going to Reading to buy paper and ink for the shop. They will honor my signature.' Then, pulling Ben into a three-armed embrace he said, 'God go with you, Ben, and may you find all is well with your family. If you are going to be away more than a fortnight, try to get word to let me know you are safe.'

One hour later, Ben passed through the checkpoint, unimpeded except for a regiment of tartan-clad soldiers marching into London. They were accompanied by the groan and whine of a lone bagpiper. As the melancholy sound faded, he spurred his horse westward with a longing for home that was as deep as it was sudden.

*   *   *

When her landlady brought her the bad news, Caroline Pendleton was taking inventory of her rapidly depleting resources: the pistol, but she dared not part with Letty's silver plate, her last resort; two dozen sixpences, one gold sovereign, six guineas, one crown and two half-crowns – and one extra shilling a Roundhead lad had given her for sewing a rip in his sleeve and buttons on his breeches. Thinking of Arthur, she would have done it for free, but the youth had insisted and Caroline, feeling the pinch of poverty, had gratefully accepted payment. This she added to her little hoard in her token box and put the token box beneath her best dress in the chest, wondering what she was saving that dress for anyway.

Outside her small window, darkness was gathering. How she dreaded the long nights. She couldn't afford to waste even the cheap tallow dips on such a luxury as reading. Most evenings she just wrapped herself in William's greatcoat and huddled close to the chimney, warmed by the downstairs fire. From outside the only sounds were the comings and goings of the Trained Bands, some of whom were now quartered on the ground floor. For the citizens there was a curfew – though it was hardly necessary, Caroline thought. What honest soul would venture out in the cold, dark and stinking streets?

At least she had a roof over her head and had been able to find work in the kitchen of a nearby house sequestered for Parliament officers. It paid only sixpence a week, but she could eat what she prepared for the officers. Tonight, she had brought home two hunks of bread smeared with pear preserve, two rashers of bacon and some goat cheese – a feast. This she was planning to share with her landlady, as she usually did, when she heard the customary knock and the whispered 'Caroline.'

But she had only to look at her landlady's face to know this would not be their usual supper. 'Mistress Cramer, you look quite pale. Come, sit.' Caroline helped her to the lone chair beside the hearth.

'Oh Caroline, it is the worst news. They are taking the whole house.'

'They?' But she thought she knew.

'Parliament. A man from the Committee on the Three Kingdoms came today. He said they need the whole house to billet the Scots.'

'But what about the law? This house belongs to you. And William had a lease on a whole floor, which they have already invaded, pushing you and me into these attic closets like a couple of cupboard mice.'

The woman looked close to tears as she answered, 'They said all contracts are suspended. Private property can be sequestered for use in wartime though they promised that owners who have been loyal will be fully restored – and compensated – when the war is over. They gave me this as a receipt.'

She held out a familiar-looking piece of paper, except this one bore the seal of Parliament rather than the Royal seal.

'When the war is over. What are we to do until then?' And what if Parliament doesn't win, she thought, but she didn't want to make the woman even more anxious. She scanned it carefully. *The premises are to be vacated by the New Year of all civilian persons not authorized by Parliament.* Three weeks. The paper suddenly seemed too heavy to hold. She handed it back to her landlady. 'Put this in a safe place as your proof for restoration.'

The poor woman looked at it in bewilderment. 'Since when do Scotsmen have more rights than Englishmen?'

'Since John Pym negotiated a defense pact with them,' Caroline said. 'I overheard the officers talking about it.' But, as she explained, her mind was on this last catastrophe. Was God punishing her for her lack of gratitude? Suddenly the meager hearth and small chamber looked more than adequate. Then she looked at the woman sitting in front of her – a widow too. She would have been about Caroline's age now – when Caroline was just a girl delivering pies to William and his first wife in this very house. But she still had the same kind spirit.

'Have you any place to go, Mistress Cramer?'

'Yes, I have a niece in Hampstead. She is young with little ones. She's been asking me to come. She says the cottages around their village have not been bothered thus far. It is you I worry about. Will you try to go back to Oxfordshire?'

'There is nothing for me there. Don't worry about me. I'll think of something.'

She tried to sound convincing, but she'd tried the old neighborhood and didn't see one familiar face. Most were dead or

moved. There was one. Maybe. That man who had come to her
aid another time when she was desperate. He had said he was
from London and that if she was ever in London and needed
anything, to come to him. But he was practically a stranger,
though he had not taken advantage of her and had been the soul
of kindness. He might help her find a job and a new place to
live. His face was burned into her mind, but she could not
remember his name.

'Come, let's not despair,' she said. 'Let us enjoy our supper.
Something will come along. This war will end, and you will
get your house back. Merely think of this as a prolonged visit
to your sister while the ministers of Parliament are looking
after your property.'

Mistress Cramer nodded her head as if Caroline had said
something profound.

'Yes. That is right thinking. You are such a positive person you
make me feel much better.'

But as they munched on the bread and bacon, all Caroline
could think of was that they had a little more than a fortnight to
be out. Whatever was she going to do? If she could only remember
– they had called him Lord something. But Lord what?

On the eighth day of December, Lucy Carlisle did not follow
John Pym's funeral cortege as it wound from Derby House in
Canon Row to Westminster Palace. There was no place for her
in the processional of MPs and mounted cavalry – some of
whom, because of John's last political action, would be paying
tribute in Scots tartan to the late 'King Pym'. It had been a
name, coined by his enemies, now used by his friends in simple
recognition of his power.

As was ever her history, Lucy struggled to make a place for
herself. Even though her friendship with John was known, it
would be uncomfortable for his wife and daughters – and a cause
for gossip concerning the nature of that friendship – if she walked
with them in their mourning garb behind the coffin. Though she
did mourn, mightily. Loneliness enveloped her like an instrument
of torture: sometimes excruciating needle points of pain, sometimes pressing in, slowly squeezing the breath out of her
until she wondered if she would ever draw another. But it was

a familiar pain, and experience had taught her she would survive it. There might come a day when she would not. But, for all her sorrow, she did not think this was that day.

She never seriously considered placing herself in discreet disguise among the locals who reverently lined the street to catch a last glimpse of the celebrated Parliament man who had led them into revolution, raised their taxes to the precipice of starvation and sacrificed their youth in the hedgerows and fields and ditches, so she came early and sat alone in St Margaret's empty chapel, waiting for John to come to her, just as she had waited these many months. This time he would come.

They would be pausing in Westminster Hall now, she thought, as the sound of the pipes wheezed and groaned. The celebratory tones of 'A Mighty Fortress is Our God' penetrated her subtle grief. Martin Luther would have been proud – or would he? From Luther's saintly throne in heaven, did he celebrate what his simple rebel action had unleashed in Christendom during the last one hundred and thirty-seven years? Or did he mourn the years of blood and turmoil his theses had ignited?

'I come not to bring peace but a sword,' the Lord had warned with omnipotent foreknowledge. But whose side would Christ have been on in the continental wars? Whose side was He on now? Was John being rewarded with an early escape from an apocalyptic fury yet to come? Or was his premature removal punishment because he had incited revolt against an anointed king? Was John Pym a facilitator of God's plan – or was he a hindrance? She was not wise enough to figure it out. An archbishop wasting away in prison and about to be indicted, and the man who was foremost in putting him there had already wasted away: what did it signify?

From her seat at the back, Lucy watched as slowly the chapel began to fill with the select few who were allowed entry to the service, but she kept her eyes lowered. As the procession paused at the chapel door, she heard musket fire: the military salute, probably given by Oliver Cromwell's men. The new lieutenant general of the army in the North had been a friend and compatriot of John's since the beginning, though there had been some heated disagreement between the Independent General and the Presbyterian statesman about the Scots Covenant. Cromwell was no fan of bishops of any stripe but, in the end, John had persuaded him, asking point-blank if the new lieutenant general would prefer a presbyter or a Catholic pope, which they would probably have one day if Parliament did not accept the terms and troops the Scots offered.

The piping had stopped. Those assembled rose as six strong MPs carried the coffin down the aisle to its resting place in the altar. Feeling suddenly weak, Lucy clung to the back of the pew in front of her and stood slowly. *Carry him gently; you are carrying a piece of my heart.* Had she said that out loud? But no, thank the holy angels. Nobody was taking any notice of her.

To better control her emotions, she deliberately diverted her thoughts to the practicality of her surroundings. Of those who bore the coffin, she recognized four of the parliamentarians she had warned when she first betrayed her King to John Pym. The fifth, her cousin Lord Essex, like Manchester, was off somewhere licking his wounds since he had been relieved of his post as captain general in favor of Waller and Cromwell. A lifetime ago, it seemed. Now Pym was cold stone dead and the King she'd betrayed still lived.

The Reverend Stephen Marshall walked in his ungraceful gait to the pulpit, filling it with his thick-shouldered body, upon which his robes always hung wrong. There was so little that was attractive about him: a rugged plain visage, his ungainly manner. Yet he had a pulpit presence that was undeniable, a presence that demanded attention, as if some angel hovered over him declaring, 'This is a powerful man, hear ye him.' Edward Hyde had once reluctantly conceded to her that he thought Marshall more influential to Pym's cause than Archbishop Laud ever was to the King's. Marshall had served Parliament and John well, often preaching to the former in his capacity as chaplain to the House of Commons, and she had heard that, in John's last days, he was often by John's bedside in double office as facilitator and friend. Lucy had heard him many times – since he was Presbyterian and not Independent – and found his exhortations never boring. Sometimes they were filled with unexpected humor. Today, Parliament's prophet, the Very Reverend Marshall, looked out over those assembled and waited for them to be seated. Then he began.

First, he talked about John Pym's Spirit-inspired leadership, his courage in taking on mighty counselors who gave bad advice to a weak king. He was talking about Archbishop Laud, she thought, talking too about Thomas Wentworth. But her attention did not wander long under the dramatic rhetoric of Stephen Marshall. He celebrated John's faithfulness to his country and to the 'Lord of all lords' – as if they were one and the same – and praised the blueprint John had labored to leave for Parliament even on his deathbed. Finally, he built to a crescendo. As he placed John Pym indubitably in heaven, kneeling at the Mercy Seat among the martyrs and the angels, his voice boomed, echoing among the rafters, bouncing off the walls, every ear attuned, no one moving as he extolled that saintly fellowship.

Mercy Seat or not, somewhere John was surely smiling, she thought.

When the service ended, Lucy Hay, Countess of Carlisle, followed behind the procession, from an appropriate distance, to the North Ambulatory of Westminster Abbey, where they buried one of the two men for whom she betrayed her King. She lingered there until all had gone and she was finally alone with him.

After a time, she departed the empty chapel and went back to Syon House where, laying aside her grief, as she had done before, she began to plan for her survival.

On the day of the great man's funeral, Caroline and Mistress Cramer enjoyed a day of peace and quiet without the intrusion of the officers coming and going. All of London, it seemed, had deserted hearths and shops and lined the streets to watch the processional, so the women's domestic peace was broken only by the dolorous tolling of church bells throughout the city. But even that small peace was short-lived.

The next day, one of the men from the Committee of the Three Kingdoms returned.

It was early in the morning and Caroline had not yet left to begin her day's work. The first knock was brusque. Knowing that Mistress Cramer had gone to the shops to buy some pretty ribbons for her young niece (as if anything so frivolous could still be procured in this city of plain and godly folk), Caroline started down the third-floor stairs to answer the single barrier between the women and the military headquarters below. Her landlady had been in surprisingly good spirits for one who was about to be evicted. Caroline had no doubt she would return ribbons in hand.

The second knock was stronger, accompanied by a sharp command: 'Open in the name of Parliament.'

Caroline opened the door slowly and gazed eye-level at the MP from the Committee of the Three Kingdoms. She arranged her face into an expression of mild pique and asked curtly, 'Yes?'

'Where is Mistress Cramer?'

'Mistress Cramer has gone out. I am Lady Pendleton. My husband holds a lease with Mistress Cramer. State your business quickly. We are busy getting our affairs in order so that we can comply in the suggested time set for Parliament's request.'

It had hardly been a request and the time had been firm. But if Caroline had learned anything from her late husband, it was that one must never negotiate from a posture of perceived weakness.

The MP, looking somewhat taken aback, straightened his shoulders as if to make himself appear taller. He nodded his head briefly and murmured half apologetically, 'I am sorry, but I must inform you that we cannot give you the three weeks. You will need to be out within the week.'

'Within the week? The agreement was—'

'I am sorry for the inconvenience, my lady, but the city is full to bursting and it is part of the Covenant that the Scots soldiers will be billeted with shelter and provisions.'

Caroline said between clenched teeth, 'This is an unreasonable demand. As you said, the city is already full to bursting. If Parliament men cannot find rooms, how in heaven's name do you think two widows can find respectable accommodations?'

'I am only following orders. You will have to plead your case directly with the Commons. Maybe—'

'How many men are you planning to board here?' she asked, her mind whirling, building argument like a scaffold. 'This is not a large house. The rooms you are gaining from the two of us are very cramped and the bottom floors are shared space for the officers and sometimes rehabilitation for a poor wounded soul released from St Bart's. Surely, the Committee has been misinformed about any further usefulness to be found here.'

'The officers are to be relocated to Derby House now that it is – most unfortunately – no longer needed by Mr Pym.'

'But you said provisions? I am afraid your hapless Scots will find no provisions here. The kitchen is inadequate to feed a company of soldiers. I work in the large kitchen of a nearby house owned by the Worshipful Guild of Merchants. Even though the business of the usefulness of the guildhall is diminished, the Worshipful Master thought it should be kept open. As part of my pay, when the hall closes, I bring the leftover food from the kitchens to feed Mistress Cramer and myself. Sometimes, on a slow day, there is enough to share with the officers.'

The mustard seed she planted grew to biblical proportions. The MP visibly brightened, like a man visited by a brilliant idea. 'Then you might be able to likewise provide some provisions for the Scots boarders, might you not? If we speak to the Worshipful Master on your behalf?'

She gave him a long-suffering look. 'I can hardly do that if I am no longer working there. And I cannot work there if I have no place nearby to live, now can I?'

'Oh. I do see.' He considered for a minute. 'May I be permitted to see the rooms you and Mistress Cramer presently occupy?'

She stepped aside and, opening the door, indicated with her hand, 'Up those narrow stairs.'

He came back down almost immediately. 'I do see your point. Little would be gained,' he said. 'But would you be comfortable staying here? These are not officers using the house for workspace. This will be a company of soldiers, coming and going, sometimes sleeping here. I assure you they are well disciplined, but they *are* Northmen.'

She pretended to consider. 'I would be willing to give it a trial,' she said.

'You could bring any complaints straight to the local bailiff. I will instruct him about the situation, and he will check with you each evening. I will also speak to the steward of the guildhall. I am sure we can work something out with the Worshipful Master. We will offer him a food subsidy and – if the committee agrees – a small supplement for your pay.'

Caroline was flooded with relief. She had dealt with soldiers before. They couldn't be any worse than the Cavaliers at Forest

Hill; though Northmen, like Irishmen, were reputed to be an unruly lot. But at least such an arrangement would buy time. She would have some leverage as she was the keeper of the food. Did Scots even eat English victuals? She wasn't going to prepare something in a sheep's stomach. But at least she would have a roof over her head until something else came along.

'If I have your permission to take this proposal to my committee, I will get back to you on the morrow.'

'I shall look forward to seeing you,' Caroline said. She closed the door and leaned against it, tears of warm relief seeping beneath closed eyelids.

SOUL SICKNESS

*A Parliament is that to the Commonwealth which the soul
is to the body. It behooves us therefore to keep the facility
of that soul from distemper.*

From a speech by John Pym, delivered in
the House of Commons, 17 April 1640

John Milton did not like to have his morning lessons interrupted, so he looked up impatiently when his housekeeper
appeared at the door. 'Yes, what is it, Trapford?'

'A gentleman to see thee, Mr Milton.'

He started to tell her to send him away, but his curiosity got
the best of him. The fellow must have been persistent for Patience
to interrupt.

'Did he give his name?'

'No, but he said he has come a very long way; that he is an
old friend from Cambridge.'

'Very well, I will see him briefly.'

He turned to the pupils who, having heard this exchange, were
already sharing glances of scarcely suppressed relief. 'Mr Simms,
you are in charge. Be diligent in taking down the names of those
who do not give attention to their translations.'

Probably some would-be poet, trying to gain influence, he
thought, but when he entered the drawing room he could not
conceal his delight. 'Roger. Roger Williams. Old friend indeed.'
He rushed forward, grasping his fellow's hand, inviting him to
sit. 'How good to see you. What brings you back to London?
Have you returned for good?'

'For good? London was bad enough when I left.' He shook
his head. 'But now? By all the saints, it is a bleak and stifled
place: shops shuttered, soldiers everywhere and the town
surrounded by a great muddy ditch. New England looks a paradise

by this measure, even in winter.' He paused in his critique and smiled, slapping John on the back. 'But you, John Milton, you are a sight for sore eyes. Thought I should renew our friendship, maybe get a refresher from my tutor in Hebrew. How is your Dutch?'

'As rusty as your Hebrew, I am guessing, though I'll confess I got the better end of that bargain. You proved the better tutor. If you are not abandoning your Utopian dream for a newer, better England, what really brings you back?'

'Not abandoning it at all. Though I'll admit I have learned a thing or two about liberty. Hard to achieve and harder still to keep. I have made some enemies among the Massachusetts settlers. Serious enemies. The Boston Puritans didn't cross an ocean seeking freedom of religion – just freedom for their own religion. They brought the same old tyranny with them. No deviation allowed from their militant orthodoxy.'

'And I am guessing your free spirit rebels against that.'

'I have turned Baptist – an advocate for true freedom of conscience. My "free spirit," as you put it, has gotten me in some trouble. I was *invited* to leave Boston by the Puritan authorities in charge. The governor was preparing to deport me when I had to flee, in the middle of the night, leaving my family behind under the protection of a pastor friend.'

Intrigued enough to forget for a moment the occasional scuffle coming from behind the classroom doors, John gestured for his guest to sit. 'Where did you go? Mostly wilderness, isn't it, outside the colony?'

'All wilderness. And it was the dead of winter. I survived in a cave for weeks, praying I would not perish for my family's sake, until some friendly natives sheltered me. Come spring, I built a cabin and sent for my family,' he said, as matter-of-factly as if it were an everyday kind of feat.

Milton had always admired the man's brilliant, questioning mind, had admired his boldness, but this? This was a tale worthy of the playhouse. 'Is your new home comfortable? Is it safe?'

Williams nodded and gave a little half-laugh. 'Comfortable enough; tight against the winter winds. I was so proud of that house, cut every log and planed every board myself. We have lived there for a couple of years. I was cutting trees for a new barn when I discovered our new home was still in Plymouth jurisdiction.'

'Ah. That means your Boston enemies still hold authority over you.'

'Not for long. My Narragansett neighbors sold me a large strip of land. Large enough for a community of freedom-seeking people. I have returned to London to procure a charter from Parliament for "Providence Plantations" in the Narragansett Bay. God is good, John. We already have a few families and some single men. Lord willing, we will settle it as a free province, founded on the principle of religious liberty and with an elected president. No English governor controlled by Parliament or the Crown.'

'Have you considered that Parliament might prove as unfriendly to such a notion as your New World Puritan detractors? Have you made any progress?'

'I have indeed made progress. Just before he died, may God rest his soul, John Pym introduced me to the head of Commissions for Royal Plantations. The Earl of Warwick and I have already had one meeting. He said he would do what he could, and Sir Henry Vane I knew from when he was royal governor for Massachusetts. He has a powerful voice.'

'Bad timing about John Pym,' Milton said. 'He was a steady man, a reasonable man, though firm in his cause. He was the soul of that Parliament, the glue that kept the disparate factions centered. I already see signs of fracturing. They agree on nothing except being disagreeable. But Vane is a good man too, and he will assist the Earl of Warwick in getting your charter granted. Though I fear there are few such principled men left. Do you anticipate being here long?'

'Only as long as it takes.'

'If you should weary of your wilderness adventure and wish to bring your ministry home, you might find a Presbyterian bishopric less arbitrary than an Anglican one. London could use your voice.'

Williams shook his head. 'I cannot foresee such a circumstance. Speaking of the Anglican bishops, I hear Archbishop Laud is in the tower. Do you think he will be brought to trial?'

'Rumor says his trial is imminent. His enemies are more than ever determined. It will please the Scots Covenanters to see him tried and convicted. One could argue that it was Laud's imposition of his prayer book on the Scottish Kirk that started the war.'

'Do you think the Presbyterians will be any less tyrannical in their religious enforcement? I have heard about the Covenant. There will never be a place for Roger Williams to preach in a state-controlled religion. There must be a wall between God's garden and the wilderness outside; an impenetrable wall between Church and state that cannot be breached. Open one little gap in that wall and the wilderness rushes in. Soul freedom, John. It is a God-given right. In making Christianity the state religion of Rome, Constantine did more harm to Christianity than Nero ever did.' He sighed heavily and tossed his head, as though shaking off a burden, 'But now I've gone to preaching. Let's talk about you. You are teaching now, I hear, and married. May I be allowed to meet your wife? What about your writing?'

'My poetry is put aside for now. Most of my writing is political. As to my marriage . . .' He hesitated for the briefest moment, wondering if his old friend had heard about *The Doctrine and Discipline of Divorce*. 'When the fighting began in earnest, my wife was away visiting her parents in Oxford. It is not safe for her to travel now.' *All of it true, strictly speaking.* 'What about you? You mentioned your family. Do you have a wife?'

'When we left Cambridge and you went off to travel in Italy, I went to be the chaplain of a large house in Essex. I married a daughter of that house. We have been blessed with five, healthy, God-loving children and, by the time I return in the spring, I expect the sixth one. I miss them dearly, as do you Mistress Milton, I am sure. Do you have children?'

'No. No children. She is with her parents in Oxfordshire. We had not been married long when she was trapped outside the lines. She is very young.'

There was a pause in the conversation, as if Roger could feel his friend's discomfort. He was always an intuitive man. It was as if once again the subject of John's marriage had cast a pall on something he was enjoying.

'Well, John,' Roger said, standing up. 'I will not detain you longer, old friend. I know you are busy with your students. Perhaps we can meet again before I return home.'

'I would very much like that. Please come again. We can celebrate your progress concerning the Providence venture. If there is any way I can be of help, it would be my privilege. If you have the time, perhaps we might share a meal.'

'I shall look forward to it,' Roger said, then pausing added, 'Come to think on it, there is something you can do for me, if it is not an imposition. I need a recommendation for a publisher. I have two publications I would like to have printed and disseminated. The first is an alphabet of the Indian languages. I am often asked about the native populations of North America. People here are extremely curious, though they have some strange, misinformed ideas. I have found the indigenous peoples of the New World to be a wonderfully interesting and – from my experience – an honest, kind people, not the savages that some here seem to believe. Language provides understanding into cultures that anecdotes alone cannot. To that end I have developed an alphabet book which I think will provide some cultural insights. I need a publisher. Might you recommend one?'

Pleased to be asked, John considered for a moment. 'I have had several. Most recently I have used a young printer, name of Matthew Simmons. He is just down this street, next to the Golden Lion. Tell him I sent you. He will print your alphabet book cheaply and display it in the Stationers' network. As to your other, if it is political in nature or representative of the religious views you have just expressed, I would recommend a free printer, one who is not a member of the guild. Parliament has quite replaced the Star Chamber in its censorship, but uses the guild for much the same purpose.'

'The godly folk in London, then, have only embraced one tyranny for another.'

'That remains to be seen. Reasonable men will prevail, I believe, when the fighting is over. For now, there is a printer by the name of James Whittier who might be your safest choice. He prints news books and sometimes writings that will not pass the religious or political censors. He sells both on the street, distributes some with the booksellers in St Paul's Churchyard, some in coaching inns, and other places where people gather, but he will print for you privately to do with as you please. Tell him you are a friend of John Milton.'

'Good advice. I do not wish to join the archbishop in his current residence, nor do I wish to be expelled before I am ready to leave. Where will I find this James Whittier?'

'He has a small print shop in Fleet Street. Not too far from St Dunstan's, on the north side, just past Ye Olde Cock Tavern. There is a small printed sign in the window with the words "Print Shop" beneath two crossed swords. Not very fancy, but he does clean work.' Then John paused and added, 'When you are free we can meet at the tavern for lobster and beer and I will introduce you to him. When you are ready, of course.'

'I am ready now. I finished my language dictionary on the ship over. And I have brought with me also a manuscript entitled *Bloody Persecution for Cause of Conscience*, which I daresay Parliament will not appreciate. The dictionary I will give to Mr Simmons. The other, I will distribute here, but I also wish to take a hundred copies home with me. There are a couple of print shops in Boston, but since I am *persona non grata* there . . .'

'Tomorrow at three then?' There was the sound of a crash and then a scuffle from the schoolroom. 'That's my devil's summons,' John said.

Williams held out his hand and gave his easy smile, 'Ye Olde Cock in Fleet Street. Three of the clock. I shall look forward to it, John. And thank you.'

Mary Milton née Powell paid no attention to the sound of boots clopping on the hen-house planks until one of the girls tugged at her apron. Her youngest sister, Bess, wide-eyed and open-mouthed, was clinging to her so hard she almost lost her balance. It was only then she looked up, expecting to see her brother James. The Royalist soldiers never came into the outbuildings in the daytime – though two of their best egg-layers had gone missing in the last fortnight.

It took a moment for her to recognize the tall youth with the stitched-up sleeve. 'Arthur? Is that really you?' Her heart felt lighter just at the sight of her childhood playmate. He had been at Forest Hill so often, he was almost like another brother, but better, more fun than her real brothers.

He just stood there, grinning at her, as if he had only been gone a few days. But he was thinner and taller than she remembered and there was the empty sleeve where his left arm should have been. Underneath that shadow of a grin, his countenance wore a sadness that marked him as very different from the carefree lad she had known.

She handed a basket half-filled with eggs to the two little girls still clinging to her. 'Take these to the kitchen. Carry the basket between you. This is all there is.'

Still staring at Arthur, the older of the girls by only a year said, 'I remember you. You used to play hide-and-seek with us in the orchard. What happened to your arm?'

'Bess and Betsy. We had fun, didn't we?' Arthur said with forced cheer.

'Go on with you now and stop pestering Arthur with questions,' Mary scolded. 'Cook will be waiting for those eggs. If you don't break any she may give you a bun to share. Though you are not to ask. She may not have any buns today.'

'We know,' Betsy said, tossing her curls. 'Cook will be sad if we ask and she doesn't have any buns,' she mocked. 'You have told us that bunches of times.'

Mary ignored the impertinence and the two girls left, gripping the handle of the basket between them. 'They will probably trip and break the lot,' she said.

'They have grown in these last two years.'

'Yes, much has changed in the two years you've been gone,' she said. 'Sister Sarah has run off and married a Royalist soldier, and James is the only brother left at home now, and he's threatening to sign up with the Royalists. And,' she paused, looked away, not wanting to meet his gaze, 'I don't know if you have heard, Arthur, but I am married now.'

'Squire told me.' And then he added, his mouth twitching away a forced smile. 'He told me too that I am now an orphan. And it appears from the destruction I have seen at the farm, a penniless orphan.' He shook his head like someone trying to shake off a bad dream. 'As if that part really matters.'

'Oh, Arthur. I am so sorry.' She hugged him then, feeling the empty space where his arm should be. 'We didn't know how to reach you. We grieved – are still grieving – for your father. When he went missing, Caroline was so brave. She scoured the surrounding garrisons for weeks looking for him, hoping; finally, his loss was officially confirmed. He was ambushed on a mission to deliver supplies. We sent a letter to your last posting, but we never heard back. I wish Caroline was here to see you. She has gone to London. I think she just could not bear to be here without him.'

There was a silence of about half a minute while he stood there, chewing on his bottom lip. Finally, he asked, 'Did they find his body?'

'No. He was on a missing list while the garrison made inquiries. We all remained hopeful, especially Caroline, until they declared him dead.'

'So. No grave to visit. No real surprise there. I've seen what happens to the bodies of the fallen.' His feet shuffled on the straw-strewn floor, releasing the smell of dust and dried chicken shit into the space around them. When he looked up again, tears were welling in his eyes. 'So much left unfinished, Mary.'

And she knew he was not just talking about his father's grave, for she remembered what had passed between William and his son, how upset Caroline had been by the breach. Another silence. She waited until he stopped chewing on his lip, then asked softly, 'Can you stay with us awhile?'

'Squire offered me a job cutting wood – a one-armed woodcutter. Huh.' His mouth twitched again with that forced smile. 'He told me that Forest Hill is surviving on the sale of wood, said it is selling by the pound like cheese instead of by the cartload.'

'That's the one bright spot in our failing fortunes. Of course, even if we had anything besides the King's worthless script, there is nothing left to buy.' *Prattle on. Try to divert him from his pain.* 'But we do have room for an able-bodied man. You will be warm and fed. And loved . . . I mean you are part of us. You and Caroline, and your father too, will always be part of us.'

'Thank you for that. The "able-bodied," I mean. And the rest too.'

The girls had left the chicken coop door open and a stiff wind swirled. She shivered in her thin cloak.

'Let's go to the kitchen, give me time to persuade you to stay. We can get out of the cold. That's something to be thankful for. At least we have a warm hearth and enough wood to finish out the winter even after we sell most of it. Cook usually has a kettle simmering for the soldiers who come and go all during the day. It will not be hearty, but it will be warm.'

Still holding his hand, she led him inside the kitchen, which was thankfully deserted, sat him down at a table in front of the promised hearth and dished up the savory broth.

'We've sneaked many a sweet out of this kitchen,' he said, 'you and Caroline and I – before she married my father.'

She merely nodded, not trusting herself to speak.

He lifted the bowl with his one hand and drank its contents hungrily, while she cut a slice of cheese from a cheddar round and a hunk of bread from yesterday's loaf.

'Ann Powell still makes the best ale in Oxfordshire,' she said, putting a mug in front of him. 'The quality hasn't changed, just the quantity.'

He took a long drink. 'Something else hasn't changed. You are still the prettiest girl in the shire. Your husband is a lucky man, Mary Powell. Is he here? I would like to congratulate him.'

'No. He is in London.'

'You live in London then?' he asked.

'Not for a while. I came home when my father was sick and have been unable to go back.' She added, looking away, 'Because of the war.'

'I can escort you safely back to London. I have a pass.' When she hesitated, he offered. 'If you tell me where he lives, I'll take you right to his door.'

Pretending to rewrap the cheese, she turned her back to him. 'Thank you, but no. John does not miss me overmuch. He is very busy. And we've had to let most of the servants go so I am needed here.'

'What does your husband do there? Is he a member of Parliament?'

'No. He is a schoolmaster. And I think he writes some poetry and political stuff for Parliament.'

'You are not talking about John *Milton*? In Aldersgate Street?' He sucked in his breath. 'You are married to John Milton?'

'Do you know him?'

'I have only met him once. I am not exactly numbered as one of his close acquaintances. I know him mainly through his housekeeper, Patience Trapford.'

She could not suppress the sigh that escaped her rapidly constricting throat. 'Ah, the redoubtable Patience Trapford.'

He smiled knowingly. 'The same. Determined and very disciplined, and certain of what she believes; but there is a gentleness there when you get to know her.'

'I guess I wasn't there long enough to see that gentle side. How did you come to know her?'

He broke off a bit of bread and swallowed it. 'I wound up in hospital at Bart's. After they turned me loose I was fortunate to find employment with a printer. Patience brings copy to be printed from . . . your husband. Sometimes, I give her reading lessons.'

'What did you print for Mr Milton?' she asked, not really caring, just to ease the conversation away from her reluctance to return to London.

When he didn't answer right away, she turned around to face him.

He shrugged, paused as if he couldn't remember then looking down at his empty bowl as if to find the answer there, said, 'Political tracts, I think.' His face was red from being too close to the kitchen fire. 'I really didn't pay much attention to them.' And then to her relief he changed the subject abruptly. 'Your father said Caroline left a few months back. I feel guilty that I waited so long to write her. London is not really a good place now for a woman alone. Do you know if she is at the same house they kept in London?'

'Last we heard,' she nodded. 'She would be so relieved to see you. She worried to distraction when your letters stopped.'

'When I was wounded, more than my letters stopped. I felt broken away from myself, if that makes any since. I didn't want to be me anymore. I wanted to start over. Fresh. But you can't deny the truth forever. A man must acknowledge his responsibilities or he's not a man. And he must acknowledge too when he's done wrong. I am sorry that I abandoned everybody I ever loved. Sorriest of all that I . . .' his voice grew husky . . . 'can't tell my father that I am sorry.'

'Are you sorry you took up Parliament's cause?'

'No. But sorry for the way I did it. I left the people who loved me as if they would just be waiting for me on a shelf when I returned. I should have been more . . . deliberate about my choices and the consequences. I've seen things – unspeakable things done to innocent people . . .' He inhaled deeply, and a shadow crossed his face. She knew he was seeing some terrible image in his head, but she would not pry. 'And I have come to admit to myself that my rashness was born more from a call to adventure and my own stubborn certainty than sacrificing for any cause.'

'My husband is devoted to the Parliament cause. My parents think that same cause was birthed in hell. And I care not a whit for either side. When someone you love is killed or your property is confiscated, it makes little difference if the perpetrator carries a Royalist sword or a Roundhead pike. All I want is for it all to stop and things to return to the way they were. But even I am not so naïve as to think that can ever be.'

'There's something I don't understand, Mary. I am very surprised that Squire allowed you to marry a Puritan. It doesn't figure.'

'Not *allowed*, Arthur. Encouraged. Strongly encouraged.' She turned away from him so he could not read the bitterness in her face. 'But that's a long story best not gone into. Will you at least stay the night? Or a little longer? We still celebrate Christmas. Bess and Betsy would love it. I . . . I would love it too. For old times' sake?'

'Christmas.' He said it as if it was a forgotten thing. 'That would be really nice. Don't tempt me. There will be no "pagan" celebration of mistletoe and holly, no jolly wassailing in godly London, you can be sure. But I need to return. I have been gone almost a fortnight. My employer calls me his "good right arm." Thank you for the soup and bread and cheese. And the ale. I used to dream about Ann Powell's brew when we were in the field.'

He reached out as if to take her hand, but didn't, as if remembering they were not carefree children anymore and that she was a married woman now. But she couldn't help herself. She leaned forward and kissed him lightly on the cheek, tears welling in her eyes at the memory of the idyllic world they had lost.

'Don't worry about me, Mary,' he said. 'I will be fine. And I will find Caroline as soon as I get back.'

She lifted a small oiled-cloth package from the side cupboard. 'For the journey,' she said, handing him another slice of bread and cheese. 'God go with you, Arthur Pendleton, and tell Caroline that Forest Hill is not the same without her but that we are surviving, and she is not to worry if she cannot find a place for us. We are probably just as well off here. We have hunting rights in the surrounding forests and plenty of fuel.'

'May I take a message from you to Mr Milton?'

'You need not bother,' she said, feeling her face grow hot. 'He knows where I am.'

He only nodded, giving her a look that implied more understanding than had passed in their conversation. 'God be with you, too, Mary.'

She followed him out and watched him walk away with a heavy spirit, remembering all the good times they had had together. There was a time when she had even fantasized about . . . no use thinking of that now. But Arthur Pendleton and Patience Trapford? No two people could ever be more ill-suited. Not in the world she lived in. Sighing, she went in search of Cook to see if her little sisters had completed their errand, thinking what a crazy, mixed-up world they lived in now, a crazy, mixed-up, unhappy world.

Ben spurred his horse toward London with a heavy burden. He had lost the expectation of his future and the security of a world that he had taken for granted. When his mother died, he'd missed her, even cried after her as a child cries over a missing pet or a broken toy, but he'd been too young to realize the finality. But this time was different. He fully realized what he had lost and that it was never coming back to him. All that he had taken for granted: wholeness, family, a secure future, turned out to be as ephemeral as a soap bubble.

The carefree companion of his childhood was gone too. Should he have told her about what John Milton had written about marriage, his marriage to her? Was it cowardly not to do so? But such a thing was far too humiliating and painful to mention. How could any woman, especially a gently bred girl like Mary Powell, bear to hear that marriage to her was like being 'chained to a corpse' – and to read it in a pamphlet that all the world could see? If anyone was chained to a corpse, it was Mary. He'd only met the man once, but that was enough to know that the self-righteous, pompous and egotistical John Milton was no match for the beautiful belle of Oxfordshire.

As he surely must have anticipated, Milton's advocating for legal divorce on grounds of incompatibility had caused an uproar in Puritan London. Did he think that because his wife's name was never mentioned, and he only signed his argument J.M., that she would suffer no public shame? How many J.M.s in London could make such a relentlessly sound argument for something so universally unacceptable? Arthur hoped that Mary never had to learn of it. Few around Oxford read Puritan literature. Perhaps by the time she reconciled with her husband – if she reconciled – today's news would be yesterday's and who would even care? He was going to find Caroline. She would decide. She always knew what to do.

THE FICKLE TIDES OF WAR

*He [Charles I] was fearless in his person but not enter-
prising and had an excellent understanding but was not
confident of it; . . . And his not applying some severe cures
to approaching evils proceeded from the lenity of his nature
and the tenderness of his conscience . . . made him choose
the softer way . . . He was also an immoderate lover of the
Scottish nation . . . who he thought could never fail him.*

Edward Hyde in *History of the Rebellion* (1648)

Christmas was almost normal at Merton College. It was not Whitehall or Hampton Court, but the Queen did her best. There were feasts and merry revels, flowing French wine and singing and dancing to lute and harp. Forest greenery threaded the chandeliers and adorned the mantles and doorways. Inigo Jones transformed the dining hall into a fantasy of gossamer color, where statues of cavorting fairies shimmered in diffused light. Rupert and his brother Maurice joined them for twelve whole days and they all made merry as if the gods of war had gone on holiday. On Twelfth Night a troupe of jugglers and acrobats performed, much to the children's delight.

Henrietta's only real regret for the Christmas of 1643 was that she had not been able to join the hunting parties. But Lady Fielding and Genevieve attended her with great devotion, and in the evenings Jermyn and young Henry Percy were often there, jesting and playing the fool with her dwarf Jeffrey. Best of all, during the month of December, she enjoyed her husband and her children in a way that was wonderful and rare. Five months pregnant, she was a wren, albeit a wren resplendent in blue satin plumage, feathering her nest and glowing with health. She always felt better when she was pregnant. By her reckoning this child had been conceived in the military encampment at Edgehill, the day of her reunion with Charles. She loved the child growing inside her even more for what the timely circumstances of its conception augured.

While the hunting parties sported with their horns and dogs and peregrines, she was somewhat content as she watched her belly swell, exulting in each flutter and kick. '*Très bon, mon petit.* Learn to kick with vigor. Life is hard for a royal child,' she whispered.

The joyous season had begun auspiciously – only one day old – when she heard good news. She would not be likely to forget the day. The twenty-sixth of December, the feast day of St Stephen. That morning, Elizabeth had read Stephen's story to her, in good Latin, from the Gospel of Luke, and later Charles and their sons had come in from the forest, accompanied by their Stuart cousins, swaggering and boasting of success. Young Henry squealed with delight when his father picked him up and swung him in the air. The young duke had become very attached to the father he was just getting to know. 'Papa, one more time,' he said between giggles. And then again, holding up one chubby finger, 'one more time' and again 'one more time,' until Henrietta was getting dizzy just watching.

Charles nodded to Henrietta, 'We will feast on venison this night, *mon amour*,' then, laughing, he set his youngest son down, saying 'no more times.' He tickled the squirming child, who laughed so hard Henrietta was afraid he would lose his breath. 'That is quite enough, the both of you,' she said.

Smiling, Charles removed his hat and, bowing deeply in obsequious obeisance, said, 'Your wish is our command, my dearest lady in all the world. Please forgive our excess of good cheer.'

'You are forgiven. See it does not happen again,' she said, extending her hand to him, suppressing a giggle.

'I desire only your pleasure, madame,' he said as he rose and took the seat next to her. But the look he gave her made her wish they were alone.

'We bear good news. Do we not, Uncle? Splendid news that should put the Queen in an even better mood. Will you be the bearer, or shall I?'

Charles winced a little, and said, no merriment in his voice now,

'Rupert, think you not that it might be unseemly to gloat over the untimely death of one of England's able men and God's saints?'

'Able, aye. I'll grant that. Cunning too. But one of the saints – if he be truly a saint on earth, now he may be a saint in heaven right enough,' the brash youth sneered. 'But the King's enemy? If he is the King's enemy, he is England's enemy; if he is England's enemy, he is God's enemy. Think you there are saints in hell, Uncle? For that is surely where he resides, however he is called.' And then, not at all chastened by his royal uncle's rebuke, Rupert turned to the pages, who had accompanied them on the hunt and said, 'Fetch the steward of the cellar, lads. We must toast the King's health.'

Charles cleared his throat and said somberly, 'I would remind you, Nephew, that Christ admonished us to love our enemies. We should pray for his soul.'

Henrietta, who was preoccupied picking at a gnarled French knot in her embroidery, suddenly tuned her ear. Who were they talking about? The tension between Charles and the Prince of the Palatinate sparked in the distance between where Charles sat and Rupert stood. Not an uncommon occurrence lately, but all in all Charles was far too lenient with the nephew who presumed too much on his soldier's reputation. She watched in silence as the steward distributed cups and poured.

Rupert, ignoring his uncle's hard gaze, lifted his glass and bellowed, 'The King is dead. Long live the King.'

Members of the returned hunting party hesitated and then echoed the salute, even young Charles and James. To fail to toast the King's health was treasonous, despite the conundrum of the salute. The two younger children looked on with wide-eyed concern. The King was their father and the King was certainly not dead. Elizabeth looked at her mother in alarm. Henrietta shook her head, as if to say: pay them no mind. All is well. She reached for the girl's hand, as she waited for the scene to play out.

Then came the *coup de grâce*. She had to hand it to the boy; he had a flair for drama. Rupert held up his glass again, 'And to the swift and timely passage into heaven of "Saint" or, as they called him in London, "King" Pym.'

She put down her embroidery. Now they had her full

attention. 'John Pym, did you say? The Parliament leader? *Comment? Quand?*'

'In his bed. In agonizing pain. His innards eaten away. Hardly an honorable death. They entombed his body last week. With much weeping and gnashing of teeth in that saintly town, I am told.' Rupert smiled slyly. 'One would almost think it divine retribution – though all of the godly "saints" in London mourned him with a great funeral of state.'

'We will hardly wear mourning, here,' she said tersely. Charles's frowning silence warned her, and she hastily added: 'We will leave that to those who knew him.' Then, with a dismissive wave of her hand, 'Perchance even loved him.'

But in her heart, she was celebrating. The strongest voice in opposition to the divine right had been silenced by the grim reaper's skeletal hand, and blessed be that bony hand. And who was to say it wasn't the very hand of God that smote him down?

'Maman, I knew him. Should I wear mourning?' a small voice said.

Henrietta looked at her daughter with irritation. 'Don't be foolish, Elizabeth. You are mistaken. You did not know John Pym.'

The girl crimped her mouth in umbrage. 'I saw him twice. Mayhap thrice. At Lady Carlisle's house. He was kind to me. It was he who brought Henry and me to Syon House. To protect us,' she said.

'Protect you from what or whom, child?' her father asked, drawing her to him.

'From Lord and Lady Pembroke and others who were not kind and who would not let us celebrate the mass.'

'Did Lady Carlisle allow you to celebrate the mass?'

'Sometimes. In secret. We were also allowed the Latin Scriptures. And my tutor Mistress Makin came to me regularly.'

'Did John Pym know this?'

'Lady Carlisle said he arranged for the tutor. He was a kind man. Like you.'

Charles nodded slowly, directing his gaze at Rupert. 'I think that's enough talk about Mr Pym, may God rest his soul.' Then he took Elizabeth's hand between his two hands and said, 'We will pray for his soul,' and, looking directly into her eyes, added, 'But we will pray in English, which is your native tongue, Elizabeth. God hears in all languages.'

'Then why may I not pray in Latin like Mother?'

'Because you are a Princess of England, not of Rome. As to your mother, I suppose in some sense she is a Princess of Rome as well as France.' He did not look at Henrietta when he said that, but returned his gaze to his nephews. 'Now, the rest of you go and make yourselves useful after this morning's sport. Arrange with the gamekeeper about dressing out the deer from today's hunt. I shall abide here closeted with my family awhile.'

Henrietta's mood had in no way been diminished by Charles's little lecture on Christian charity. After all, it was an old argument between them. What mattered was that finally something was going their way. They spent the rest of that day and the next entertaining themselves in their little nest of family bliss. She finished embroidering the receiving blanket for the newest addition to their royal brood, watching while Charles played with Henry and Elizabeth or monitored James and Prince Charles in fencing contests with their royal cousins.

These halcyon days were only occasionally interrupted when the King went out to consult with Sir Edward Hyde and various other emissaries from the field. Once, the woman Jane Whorwood came with a gift of gold candlesticks and silver coins – from the King's supporters in London, she said. The King introduced her as one of his most loyal subjects and 'a great help to us.'

'We have met before, Your Majesty,' the woman said, falling into a deep curtsy.

'Yes, the gloves. I remember. We highly value your service, Mistress Whorwood,' she said, and meant it, wondering how she could have ever been jealous. The woman was obviously nothing more than a loyal subject. Henrietta had seen nothing pass between them that would indicate anything else, and Charles was too honest to hide his feelings. His expression showed only kind indifference when he thanked her.

They stayed thus for a fortnight as if the war did not exist, until bad news came: dire, unexpected news; news that broke that part of the King's heart where Scotland's thistle flowers bloomed. Despite all the concessions Charles had made to the Presbyterians in Scotland regarding Laud's prayer book and ecclesiastical rule, some of his Scottish subjects had betrayed him. They had made a devil's pact – a Covenant – with John Pym to join Parliament's rebellion. It was as if, with this last act before his death, the specter of King Pym now haunted them from his grave in Westminster.

She was in the presence room with Charles when Hyde delivered the harrowing news that a large army of Scots had taken up arms against their King in Covenant with Parliament. She tried to console him. Tried to advise him. 'Send Newcastle immediately to engage. They must not get to London,' she demanded. 'Grant them no quarter. They are rebelling against their sovereign. Take heart, husband. At least the Catholic highlanders are loyal. I met with them on my way to you. They gave their allegiance before God. They will not break their oath. Put your trust in them alone.'

'The Queen gives good counsel, Your Majesty,' Edward said. 'Put the rebels down swiftly, before their ranks swell. The Campbell clan is loyal: Lord Argyle will not betray you. And I can't believe Montrose will stay with the Covenanters. Even though he is Presbyterian, he is at heart the King's man.'

She sent the councilor whom she sometimes trusted, sometimes not, a look of gratitude. 'Also, you can look to Ireland, Charles,' she said quietly. 'You can raise a Catholic army that will quell these rebels both here and in Scotland.'

Hyde did not comment on that. She knew he was opposed but at least he kept his lips sealed in her presence. Charles just stared into the middle distance, not acquiescing to their arguments but also not disputing their merit.

That was just the beginning of troubles.

Mid-January brought news that Parliament had decided to put Archbishop Laud on trial, even though the evidence against him was as weak as it had ever been. She wondered if that had been part of Pym's agreement with the Covenanters – that with Parliament's help they could at long last be avenged on their old nemesis, who forced the Common Book of Prayer on the Scottish kirk. Finally, late in January, Charles came out of his closet to take some action. On St Vincent's Day he convened a new Parliament of loyalists at Oxford and, at his urging, they declared the Scots Covenanters foreign invaders and voted to raise an Irish army to defend the King of Three Countries. In February he dispatched the nephews to lead the fighting in Wales and the Welsh Marches. More than ever, the western territories must be held.

In March, the wind and rain exacerbated Henrietta's spiritual and physical heaviness. Occasionally they heard reports of cannon fire in Oxfordshire, and then came the devastating news that Newcastle's forces had been tricked and skirted by the large Scottish army, leaving them free to reach London largely unhindered. On Edward Hyde's advice, Charles met with his new Parliament members and asked them to broach negotiations with the London Parliament. Henrietta did not approve of this – it legitimized a rebel Parliament and showed weakness – but her energy diminishing with her growing belly, she held her peace.

At the first sign of spring, Charles said, she should retire to Bath for her confinement. She had taken to her bed with a headache. The waters would make her stronger, he said, and he could be called away at any time.

'What about the children?' she asked.

Sitting beside her on the bed, he kissed her on her forehead and said, 'James and Charles will go with me. Don't worry. Haven't they been well looked after in the field so far? Besides, since one or both will be King one day, they must be skilled in the art of war.'

She didn't like to think of them on the battlefield, even behind the lines, but she couldn't argue with the wisdom of it. 'I will take the young ones with me,' she said firmly.

He shook his head. 'No, they will be better protected here, away from Parliament's reach. And you will be freer to do what women must do.'

No. No. A thousand times no, she wanted to scream. Instead she said coldly, 'I will not abandon them a second time.' She did not say, *As you abandoned them at St James's Palace when you fled London*, but it was a struggle to hold those words back.

He paused for a minute as if deep in thought, pleating the fine fabric of her bed gown then, tracing her arm with his ringed forefinger, lifted her hand to his lips. 'Why not ask Lady Carlisle to come here while you are away? She seems to have done well enough by Elizabeth and Henry. When you return, you will enjoy her company. Only God knows how long I will be away defending against these rebels.' He stood up then, and began to pace beside her bed, the hand that had held hers smoothing his chin in contemplation. 'This time we can prepare properly for the children. They will be here with the court, with Lady Fielding and Chancellor Hyde and Lady Carlisle, if you decide to send for her when you return with the babe.'

'But no, I—'

Before she could finish her protest, he sat down beside her again, cradled her belly with his hands. 'It is not like the last time, dear heart, when you were away, and I had to leave them at St James's Palace.'

'I . . . shall think about it,' she said, closing her eyes to hold back untimely tears. 'We will talk about it later.' Then as he walked to the door, she said, 'Please close the drapery, *mon amour.* The light, it is too harsh.'

Upon his return, Ben did not go that first week to seek out his stepmother at the Gresham Street address as he had promised Mary Powell. Mary Milton now. That was a bitter pill to swallow. He told himself that he did not seek out Caroline because he had too much work. The boys had nearly flogged him when he'd returned, demanding to know why he had abandoned them to the unsatisfactory victuals that milord provided, and there was a small backlog of printing, which Whittier ignored, absenting himself, possibly making up for lost time at the Southwark taverns. Two nights he had come in just before dawn, smelling of incense and whisky. It was not pique because of his own absence from the shop. His employer had seemed congenial enough upon his return, not complaining at all, and expressing genuine sympathy when Ben told him about the death of his father.

But after that first night, when he had gone out, saying with a grin that now it was the 'printer's devil's' turn to provide dinner for the newsboys, he had seemed distracted and oddly troubled. Ben thought it necessary to stick close to the shop those first few days. At least that was the lie he told himself and, oddly enough, deep down, he knew it was a lie – a convenient excuse. As much as he longed to see Caroline, and did not doubt that it would be a great relief for her as well, it would be a painful reunion, a reminder of all that had been lost.

'Didn't you tell me that your stepmother was here in London? Have you seen her yet?' Lord Whittier asked on the Saturday after Ben's return. 'And Patience Trapford, does she know you are back? She came here looking for you, worried that you might be ill when you did not appear for Sabbath services for two weeks running. I think she even went to the big ditch looking for you there. I told her you had gone to take care of family business and wasn't sure when you would return. Though she tried to hide it, I could tell she found that news distressing.'

He should have told Patience he was leaving. She was a good friend. Maybe more than a good friend. But that was a dead end. What woman would want to be wife to a one-armed orphan with no prospects?

Wife? Where had that come from?

What would Patience say if she knew the companion of his youth was Milton's wife? Might she share some insight into why he thought her an unfit wife? It was Milton who was unfit. Old enough almost to be her father. But Ben would say nothing to Patience, beyond a casual mention that he had known Mistress Milton growing up. Any suggestion of criticism of the godly man Patience adored would only serve to complicate their relationship.

He also delayed going in search of Caroline because deep down it was good to be just Ben again, roughhousing with the boys, pulling on the press until his muscle quivered with fatigue, pretending that the war was happening far, far away, even though the newsprint he was pressing talked about a skirmish not ten miles upriver and a bunch of Parliament troops drowned.

The next Sabbath came and went. This week, he told himself, I will go to Gresham Street to find Caroline. This coming Sabbath I will go to church and tell Patience about my father and casually comment that now they had a mutual connection. But on a Tuesday morning, his excuse for yet more delay walked in the door with the promise of another contract.

Ben was cleaning the press when Roger Williams came into the shop looking for a publisher for his pamphlet on the 'Bloody Persecution for Cause of Conscience.' He looked up briefly as

Lord Whittier greeted the visitors. And there was John Milton. Within an arm's distance. Wearing his pompous demeanor as stiffly as his starched lace collar, brown velvet suit, and carefully curled hair. A sudden vision of the sadness and resignation with which Mary had said, 'I am married now,' engulfed him.

He brought the press down with enough vigor that it groaned in protest and, wiping his stained hand against his apron hard enough to flay the skin right off, regarded the man whose mannered speech and arrogant opinions had merely been amusing when Patience spoke of him. But that was before.

'Ben, have you met Mr Milton? We printed some pamphlets for him.'

Ben stepped forward reluctantly, nodded at Milton without looking him in the eye, then straightened his spine to tower over the man despite Milton's high-heeled shoes. 'Yes. We met here once before.'

The other man held out his hand. 'Roger Williams,' he said. 'Very pleased to meet you, Ben. I understand that you not only work the presses but help set type.'

Ben merely nodded and tried to smile. But the man's easy manner was calming. He was jovial, with a warm smile and sincere eyes.

'Reverend Williams is a preacher from across the ocean. He has returned to London to get a land grant for a plantation in the colonies. Along with a little publishing that might fall outside the confines established by the Stationers' Guild. Do you think he's come to the right place, Ben?' Whittier smiled, the kind of smile Ben had not seen lately.

'I do indeed, milord.' Still thinking of the last unorthodox pamphlet they had printed, and regretting his part in that.

'I am sure my words will be in capable hands. I was fortunate that my old friend John Milton steered me toward you,' he said. 'Here is my manuscript. I'll check back with you in a week. Will you have something to show me then?'

'Enough that you can approve the type. Shall we say early next week – Monday or Tuesday?'

'Let us say Tuesday. I have a meeting with Henry Vane on Monday about the Plantation.'

Whittier took the manuscript and the men shook hands, then James followed them into the street where they talked for another few minutes. When he returned he seemed thoughtful, remarking how much he had liked Williams and almost envied him. 'It must be something to build a country so far removed from government meddling. No king. No governor except one chosen by the people – and no religious squabbling; every man free to worship as he chooses or not to worship at all.'

'Sounds radical. What does Mr Milton say about it?' Even he heard the sneer in his tone, but Whittier seemed not to notice.

'He agrees with you. Said it was a radical and a foolhardy attempt, but for the sake of their friendship he would do what he could to help him get the grant. Radical it may be, but it seems to be working for him so far. He can't wait to return.' He shuffled through the written pages. 'Parliament censors will not be happy with this. They like to think only the Catholics and the Church of England persecute. We need to get on this right away.'

'Why the hurry?'

'Williams wants to get passage home as soon as his grant is finalized. You know, Ben, we may eventually be frozen out by the guild. A little outside business is good. It will keep the press running and put a little money in our pockets too. There's a thriving market for underground pamphlets and we are going halves on this one.'

'I am ready, milord. Whenever you are,' was all Ben said, as if he had no other obligations at all.

LONGINGS

God bless you, my sweet child and wife, and grant that ye may ever be a comfort to your dear father and husband.

In a letter to George Villiers, Duke of Buckingham,
from James I (1623)

I desire only to live in the world for your sake . . . I will live and die a lover of you.

George Villiers, Duke of Buckingham, to James I

'Is it my fault, or yours?' Lucy asked James Whittier as he lay beside her, breathing heavily like a man who had just dropped out of a race he knew he could not finish.

Her voice was soft with passion – or unshed tears. Since John's death, the spring that produced those tears had flooded at the smallest cloud.

He did not answer immediately.

Suddenly self-conscious, she pulled the coverlet up and her shift down to the ribbon garters securing her silk stockings, lest he find her breasts too flaccid, her belly too flabby – though verily that was not all that was limp between the sheets. She charitably shared the coverlet, covering them both, then lay back, each staring at the bed canopy as if its tapestry held some newly discovered secret. What he was thinking she could not fathom. But as for her, the passion that had prompted her overtures had receded and she had quite exhausted her bag of tricks.

It had all started so innocently, just the sharing of a simple repast. She had not exactly seduced him. At least not deliberately. It was just that since John's death all joy, even the expectation of joy, had gone out of her life. When Whittier showed up at Syon House to deliver his belated sympathy, and pump her for information, she had greeted him with delight and flirted shamelessly, even inviting him to her boudoir to share an intimate meal. But truly, male companionship was all she was seeking.

Botticelli's *Venus*, woven into the canopy above them, mocked her. *Ah but admit it, Lucy. Truly, you did seduce him. That was not what he came for. You made the overture this time. You are always most needy when you mourn. Remember how quickly Pym replaced Thomas Wentworth in your bed.* No. Really it signified nothing, she reasoned. She had only insisted Whittier join her because she hated to eat alone.

Carter had served them slices of duck dressed in wild berry sauce, along with small root vegetables roasted with savory herbs, all cleverly salvaged from the remains of yesterday's dinner. The butler, always the soul of discretion, if not approval, had closed the door behind him as he left. Pouring her visitor a glass of wine, she coaxed, 'My brother Algernon's best. This horrid war has not taken everything from us. We might as well drink it before his cellar is looted by the Royalists. You heard, I suppose, how close they came. I have a hole in my garden wall from a cannon ball. Though now I think on it, the hole might have been made by Parliament's side.'

'I heard. I printed an account in my daily broadsheet.'

As his gaze settled on her, he took the glass, his eyes glinting with pleasure. She had so missed that look of appreciation in a man's eyes. 'Now.' She sat across from him. 'We are quite alone, my lord. We will not be disturbed. We may talk about anything you desire. But first, you have come a long way during a busy workday. Let us enjoy this feast together, shall we? Though I will admit it is disheartening how one's standards have changed. At least Cook has tried to dress it up for us.'

He laughed. A wonderful, deep-throated laugh. 'Feast enough for any man, no matter how discerning his taste,' he'd said, his gaze not wavering. He was such a practiced flirt. Beneath his bold gaze, her skin tingled with warmth. How she had missed this: the flattery, the flirting glances, the hidden meanings in each jest, the coy answers.

Reaching across the table, she took away the chunk of fowl

he was raising on the tip of his knife and put it on her plate, sliced it into smaller pieces, saying, 'What is the hurry, my lord?'

Curiosity raised an eyebrow. A half-smile played with his mouth as he watched in silence. She leaned across the table and, lifting a morsel to his lips said, 'Good things should be savored slowly.'

He parted his lips and waited, enjoying the game. As she placed the sliver inside his mouth, some of the red sauce dripped onto his chin. She made a little clucking noise of mock dismay then, wiping it away with the tip of her finger, sucked at the stain with a pouting mouth.

He chewed slowly, not taking his eyes off her. He swallowed the meat and, sighing with satisfaction, said with a smile, 'I see what you mean, my lady.'

Leaning across the table, he kissed her, a prolonged kiss, slow and filled with passion. His lips were firm, and the taste of berry lingered on his tongue. She had reciprocated in kind, more in kind than a lady should have done, but it had been so long, and suddenly they were making the beast with two backs and what started out slowly elevated to a frenzy before coming to an abrupt halt.

He sat up, his back to her and pulled on his breeches.

'I assure you, loveliest of ladies, 'twas not your fault. You are a beautiful woman. Any man would . . .'

Was he just being charitable to a woman almost old enough to be his mother? 'Would what, my lord?'

'Find your beauty an . . . inspiration. It was churlish of me to take advantage of your grief. Realizing that is what unmanned me in so . . . untimely a manner.'

She opened her mouth to protest, but he shook his head. 'Your bond with Mr Pym was no secret. But lest you need more assurance . . .' With his back to her and his head bowed, she struggled to hear as his voice trailed off. 'It was not the first time lately,' he said, running his fingers through his dark hair in a gesture of frustration.

She sat up and turned her back to his as she reattached her bodice. 'If you will be so kind as to hand me the skirt that you so skillfully removed.' She could feel her cheeks burning, scarcely knowing if it was for his embarrassment or hers, yet wanting him desperately to stay just for the comfort of his company. 'We did not finish our food, or our wine . . . or our conversation. Pity to let good food and good company go to waste.' She turned to face him then, both now fully, if not carefully, clothed. 'Will you tarry awhile?'

'I would like that very much,' he said, then added sheepishly, 'but if it is all the same: this time I'll feed myself, lest I be tempted to repeat my sorry performance.'

It was a rare man who could laugh at himself, especially in matters of intimacy, she thought, as he seated himself at the table and began attacking the food as if he had earned it. She watched him eat in silence. The meat had congealed in the berry sauce, though he seemed not to mind. She sipped her wine. But not seductively. She knew when she was beaten. A quiver of insecurity lingered. Maybe he was one of those men who was all talk and no action. But if that were true, his reputation was certainly a lie. Maybe it was something – or someone – else.

'Have you ever been in love, Lord Whittier?' she asked, not challenging him with her eyes, but looking down at the glass she toyed with.

When she glanced up, he had put down his fork and was looking at her. He picked up his wine glass. Took a sip, hesitating, as though he was trying to frame his words.

'Once,' he sighed. 'When I was very young. I fell in love with a beautiful girl.'

'And did she love you back? Silly question. Of course she did. How could she not?'

'I thought she loved me.'

'And she proved false?'

'She married my brother. He was the heir.'

'I am sorry,' she said. His was a common story. Grace and good looks usually weighed lightly against title and wealth. Handing him a cloth, she said, 'You have a little bit of berry sauce on your mouth.'

Taking the bit of linen, but careful not to touch her hand, he acknowledged both the gesture and its underlying truce with a shrug and a half-smile.

'What did your brother have to offer? Besides the title, which I suppose is no small thing. Are they happy?'

'They are both dead. She died giving birth to a stillborn child.'
He grimaced. An old scar, she thought, that he did not wish to
probe. Still she waited, wanting to hear the rest of the story. He
took a swallow of wine then continued in the same flat tone.
'Five years later, my brother squandered the family fortune on
ill-timed ventures and then he died of drink.'

'Leaving you to inherit the title. And not much else.'

'And not much else.' He drained the last of the wine. She refilled
both glasses. 'What about you, my lady. Have you ever been in love?'

She laughed. 'Several times. But that breathtaking, full-of-giddy-
dreams fever – only once. I was very young too. And already
married to James Hay.'

'You did not marry for love, then?'

'No. I married to get out of Tower Prison where my old father
insisted I share his incarceration. James Hay was a means to an
end. I never loved him. Though I liked him. I am in no way
complaining. James Hay was much older than me, the old King's
ambassador to the Continent, and he was gone a lot, leaving me
to my own *entertainments*. He gave me freedom, a life at court,
and a title. When he died, I mourned. It was like losing a kind
patron. I have survived on the courtly graces and necessary
cunning that he taught me.'

'Survived very well, I would say. This young lover, did he break
your heart?'

'Into tiny little pieces,' she laughed. 'And he wasn't even my
lover, though we flirted: a lot of dancing and groping in closets,
a little kissing; all very exciting and causing a lot of court gossip.
But I'll have to say, Lord Whittier, looking back he was not as
good a kisser as you.'

She wasn't sure, but she thought she saw him flush with embarrassment. And well he might, given his performance.

'He broke a lot of women's hearts. It was rumored even the
Queen of France succumbed to his charms when he went over
to arrange for the marriage between Henrietta and Charles.
Though I think it was probably no more than a flirtation, because
in his heart he preferred the King. And when old King James
died, then he preferred the son.'

'You have aroused my curiosity. Was your young lover the
notorious George Villiers, Duke of Buckingham?'

'You knew him? You were scarcely more than a boy when he was assassinated. I would never have mentioned him, if I thought you knew him.'

'I only knew of him. It has long been rumored that he was the old King's catamite. Rumored too that he poisoned the King because he preferred the Prince. Do you think the rumors true? I mean, you obviously knew him well.'

'True that he was a catamite?' She shrugged. 'A little old for a catamite. He was twenty-one when he first caught the eye of a King. And I was not the only woman who found him irresistible that first year he came to Whitehall. He was an Adonis. But it was no secret at court that James Stuart adored him.'

'Do you think the rumor true, that Buckingham poisoned his King because his eye wandered to the son?'

She shook her head. 'Never. Buckingham's enemies and Charles's enemies fostered that lie.' She was surprised at the vehemence with which she defended him after all these years. 'George was mad with worry when the King became ill. He truly thought the royal physician vile and incompetent. That was why he shut him out and dosed the King himself.'

'What about Charles? Was he also seduced by his father's lover?'

'That is also a vicious lie. George Villiers was a kind of mentor to the young Prince. More like an older brother. Though not altogether in a good way. They did get up to some mischief in Spain before Charles married Henrietta. But no. I am sure of it. Charles Stuart adored Henrietta. To this day he is devoted to her. They have enough children to prove it.'

Suddenly feeling uncomfortable with this line of conversation, she gave him a hard look. 'Why are you so interested in old court gossip? You are *not* going to put this in one of your news books.'

'I was only interested to see what kind of man could break the heart of a woman who could have any man she wants.'

'Well not all,' she said archly, taking another sip of wine. 'You know, it has been my observation that sometimes . . . when a man is besotted with a particular woman . . . he is sometimes slow to respond to another.'

She could see from the expression on his face that her words pinched.

He was suddenly very serious. 'Besotted? In your experience, do you think it possible for a man to become *besotted* or enamored of a woman whose name he does not know and with whom he has had only the briefest encounter?'

'Maybe,' she said, thinking that she had cut close to the bone and relieved to have found a probable cause other than her own fading charms.

'Do you believe that the face of said person, even the sound of her voice, could haunt a man's dreams? If I believed in witches, I would say I have been bewitched.'

'And I would say, you are in love, James.'

'How can a man be in love with a fantasy? I only had two brief encounters with the woman, the first of which I am ashamed. I cannot even remember her name. Though God knows I have tried.'

'This fantasy, as you describe it, obviously has a hold on you. There is only one way to find out. You must seek her out. If she is only a romantic dream, then you will find it out soon enough. But if she be real, you do yourself no good service by trying to bury her beside the dead love of your youth. Go back to the place you met her. Ask if anybody knows your mystery woman.'

A late afternoon sunbeam sent a shaft of light through the window, picking out the now empty wine glasses.

'Thanks for the advice. I will think on it. I will. But I have been thinking of going away. There is nothing left for me here.'

'But your printing business is thriving, is it not?'

'Not for long. Parliament is forcing out free printers. Just like the Covenanters are forcing out free thinkers. We are merely exchanging one tyranny for another. Catholic, Anglican or Presbyterian, pick your poison – doesn't matter what name you give it. It's still tyranny that deprives a man of the right to his own soul.'

'Where will you go?'

'I haven't decided. Far away from kings and parliaments. Maybe to the colonies.'

She couldn't help but laugh. 'You in a Puritan colony? They would have you in the stocks before you even got off the boat. And if they didn't, you would drown yourself in the Atlantic out of boredom.'

He gave her a look of mock astonishment. 'You don't think they have taverns? And pretty ladies?' Then his tone turned serious. 'I met a man who is starting a free plantation. Freedom of speech. Freedom of conscience. A man can believe or say what he wants to believe or say. A radical experiment, to be sure. But it would be an adventure. There is not much to hold me here.'

'Except your mystery woman.'

A lift of his shoulders and a nod. 'Except my mystery woman.'

'Is that why you came here today? To bid me goodbye?'

'That. And to pay you my sincerest condolence for your loss. But I also came to return something that belongs to you. Now that your uh . . . circumstances have changed. And with the war . . . well, who knows how that will turn out? Depending on who wins – though I will admit you have played the middle better than most.'

Smiling, he reached into the pocket in his jerkin and pulled out Wentworth's diamonds, the same diamonds she had donated to the Royalist cause two years ago. He held them up to catch the sunbeam, as she had held them up to catch the candlelight in her long-ago salon. Seeing them again took her breath away.

'You didn't really mean to give these to Charles Stuart, did you? After the way he betrayed Thomas Wentworth?'

'What? How did you . . .? You were there that night. I remember. You were there. And you left right after Councilor Hyde . . .' A sudden shock of realization and she laughed, 'And Councilor Hyde was robbed.'

'Did the King know he was robbed?'

'Oh yes, Hyde is nothing if not astute. He told the King. He wanted Charles Stuart to know how hard he was trying to raise funds. He even wrote me a note explaining about the robbery and assuring me that he had told His Majesty, who was "very moved" by my gracious understanding and loyalty.'

'Good enough then. You got credit and now you have your jewels back. They are much too beautiful to be used to fund a war. They were given in love and should not be stained with blood.'

'But why give them back to me? Especially now? You could have used them to buy your passage to Utopia.'

'I have other resources. Anyway, I never intended to keep them. I got enough from the melted plate, which I stole at the same time, to buy the press I wanted. I decided to give them back to you because we, who are forced to live by our wits, deserve not to be robbed by each other.'

'But James, you know I dare not wear them again.'

'Not here, not now. But you will have them like an ace hiding in your sleeve. You can always sell them if necessary. Your brother's fortunes are tied to Parliament. Your cousin Essex's too. The House of Percy could lose all. If the King wins.'

Then he stood up brusquely, like a man who had accomplished what he came for. She followed him out and, as he took his leave, she reached up as if to kiss him on the cheek and whispered in his ear. 'You know, Lord Whittier, highway robbery is a hanging offense.'

He put his forefinger to his lips and whispered, 'But you will never tell.'

'Not even if they rack me,' she said. And she meant it. 'One more thing,' she said, putting her hand on his sleeve as he opened the door, 'find that woman you told me about. Does it not say somewhere in the Bible, "Man was not made to be alone?" Go find your Eve, James. Maybe you can take her with you into the wilderness.'

A pan of potatoes in one hand and a skillet of bread in the other, Caroline used the crook of her elbow to push her straggling hair back from her forehead. It had been a difficult day in the guildhall kitchen. The March drizzle and wind whipped down the flue of the makeshift stove, scattering smoke and ash. The Scots soldiers had complained about the half-roasted potatoes, though they didn't blame her. They were boisterous and noisy, and she sometimes had trouble understanding their thick brogue, but all in all they were kinder to her than the English officers had been, thanking her, calling her 'bonnie lass.' She was grateful for even the difficult days because she had a roof over her head and she shared the same food the soldiers ate. Provisions in the market were exorbitantly priced. The Committee for Three Kingdoms made regular delivery of foodstuffs that were mostly unavailable for the rest of London.

She stirred the recalcitrant coals once again and was bending over to place the last pan of potatoes in the oven when out of the corner of her eye she saw the one-armed soldier approaching. Probably one of the several disabled from the war who had learned that they could share the leftovers from the soldiers' mess.

'I am sure to have something for you today,' she said without looking around, 'though you will need to wait a bit. I can give you some bread and broth if you cannot wait.'

'I didn't come for the food,' the voice behind her said. At first, she didn't recognize it. Then he said her name. 'Caroline?' It was low with a little break in it.

She almost dropped the pan, managing just to shove it in the oven, yet afraid to turn around, for fear it was an illusion – like other tricks of her imagination, the hearing of a voice she longed for or a shadow out of the corner of her eye.

'It's me, Caroline.'

She turned around then, heart pounding. 'Arthur? Is it really you?' Her breath caught in her chest when she noticed the empty sleeve. She grabbed hold of him, crushing him in an embrace. Only one arm hugged her back, but it was not a boy's arm. It was a strong arm that pulled her tightly to a man's muscled chest.

When she pulled back, she ran her fingers along the line of his face, as if to reassure herself that he was not a mirage. He touched her face, too, smiling as he wiped at the track her tears had left.

'I went home looking for you. When I didn't find anybody, I went to Forest Hill. They told me . . .' He choked and could not finish.

'I am so very sorry you had to find out about your father's death that way.'

'It was my own fault. I should never have stayed away so long. I should have been there for him. For you. They said you tried to find him . . .' His voice trailed off.

She waited for him to gather his emotions.

'The farm is not the place I remember. It is a very desolate place. And Forest Hill is not much better.'

'I know. But I have been assured we will all be made whole when the King wins the war.' *As if you, who have lost a father and more, and I, who have lost a husband, could ever be made whole.* But she did not say that to him. The young needed hope.

'When? If he wins the war,' he said.

'You are still on Parliament's side, then?'

'Nay, I've seen too much cruelty and suffering on both sides. I'm on nobody's side except mine and yours and maybe . . .' But he let his voice trail off again and then said, 'I went by the townhouse. Looks like it's been overrun with Scotsmen. They told me you would be here.'

He put his one strong arm around her shoulders and pulled her closer to him.

'I want you to know, Arthur, how hard I tried to find your father.'

'I know,' he said. He hesitated, shuffling his feet, unable to look at her. 'I should have been there to help you. They told me how brave you were and how you worried when I didn't write. That's just one of the many things I regret. Like the way I left. The harsh words between Father and me. I can never take those words back.'

'It is all right, Arthur,' she said, touching his face, lifting his chin so his gaze would meet hers. 'William grieved your leaving, but that's only because he loved you so much. He wouldn't have wanted to let you go, no matter whose side you were on. He knew his son loved him.'

That wasn't exactly true, and she knew it. But she knew too, if William could see his son now, he would forgive both the lie and the boy.

'I reckon his death happened about the same time I lost my arm. Father and son broken by the same war at about the same time but on opposite sides.'

He picked up the corner of her apron to wipe her tears away and, seeing that it was almost as smoke-stained as her face, he laughed, an awkward, choking laugh, releasing some of the grief made new by the sharing. 'Hey, what do you say if I unstop that flue for you?'

'Please,' she said, grateful to be diverted. It was such a relief to see him, and yet it took her to a place she had tried so hard to shield her mind from. If she ran fast enough, drove herself into the ground with worrying about all the daily chores of just surviving, her mind was too exhausted to remember all that she had lost.

'Let me retrieve the potatoes first. I'll peel them and drop them in the broth pot to boil,' she said, nodding in the direction of the iron pot hanging over the hearth. 'They will have time to cook before the stragglers come in,' she said. 'The afternoon patrol shift comes in just before dark.'

'Guess it would be best to wait until the coals die down, so we don't smoke up the place more. The Worshipful Company of Mercers won't be happy if we blacken their pretty paneling and gilded girders. All right if I sit here?' He pointed to a stool in the corner.

As the potatoes cooked, she listened with a mixture of horror and grief at all he'd been through. He told her about how the war had wounded more than his body, about how a young mother, her wits totally gone, haunted his dreams as she cradled a doll in her arms. How in his dreams he could still hear her singing in her gentle voice, *lulay, lulay my little child* to her dead infant. He told her too how he had seen men blown apart, about how he wound up at Bart's without really knowing how he got there. But he'd never had to kill anybody, he said. That was a blessing.

When he grew quiet, she knew he had gone to that place where men who were not meant to be warriors, unlike others who thrived on the thrill of the fight, always went. So, trying to pull him back, she prompted, 'You went to Forest Hill, you said. Were Squire and Ann and the children doing well enough? How is Mary?'

'Pretty as ever. Though changed. All grown up, I guess. She said to tell you not to worry. That they have enough to eat and a roof over their heads. And they are all still hearty. She said you should just look out for yourself. You will always have a home as long as they do, if you need to return.'

'I left because I thought I might be able to help them. But it is all I can do just to keep a patch of roof over my own head. I'll not go back. I don't want to burden them with one more mouth to feed. Squire and Ann have been so good to me, taking an orphan in at thirteen, treating me like their own.'

'Don't feel burdened by any debt to the Powell's, Caroline. Squire was good to you. But they got the better end of that bargain. Mary was so much happier after you came. She never enjoyed her siblings like she enjoyed you, though we tolerated the young ones. When you made us. What fun times we had,' he sighed. 'As to your being a financial burden: you know Father paid Justice Powell for your upkeep? Right up until he married you and you came to live with us.'

'No. I didn't know.' That was a little unsettling but not altogether surprising. 'But, Arthur, he did not pay them to love me. They were the only family I had after my aunt died. I will always love them and be grateful to them.'

'Still, Richard Powell got the best of that exchange. He always had an eye out for a shrewd deal. Even Father said that.'

She remembered the sad, tired man she'd encountered shortly before she left, despairing over the state of his finances, and she could feel no resentment for him, except for his betrayal of Mary: that was some shrewd deal too.

'Did Mary tell you she was married?'

'She told me plainly,' he said, 'just blurted it right out. But, Caroline, Mary is not happy. And no wonder. Her husband may be brilliant, but I find him pompous as a peacock. Very demanding and full of himself. Not a pleasant man at all. Squire should never have pushed her into a marriage like that.'

'No. I agree. It was a shrewd deal gone sadly awry for everybody concerned. You talk about John Milton as though you know him.'

'I have only made his acquaintance on two occasions. That was enough. I know him mostly by his writing, which I find offensive. I work for a printer who published some of his work.'

He paused, as if about to go on, then looking troubled said, 'Caroline, have you read any of John Milton's work?'

'Only some of his poetry, which was actually quite good. What did you publish for him?' she asked, not really caring, thinking how wonderful that he had found employment and wondering where he was living. Please God, do not let it be on the street like so many of the others, yet knowing that he was hardly likely to have found a place to rent in a city full to the brim. 'Where are you living?'

'I sleep at the print shop, like a glorified apprentice. The printer has a couple of young boys who sell papers for him. I sort of look after them, cook for them, keep them busy so they stay out of mischief. In between print jobs. You'd be surprised what this one arm can do. I pull the press. I am even learning to set type.'

'Your father would be very proud of you. The way you are making a life for yourself in this troubled time. I am very proud of you.'

He smiled, a faint smile, but real. 'I even have a new girlfriend. Well, sort of. I have just lately begun to think of her that way, though we have been good friends for a few months.'

'Tell me about her.'

'Her name is Patience, though she's sometimes not very patient. I think you would like her. She is very strong like you, though at times a little . . . stern. Disciplined too, when she sets her hand to a task; but what else could be expected of a godly Puritan girl? She drags me to church at least once a week when we are not working on the big ditch together. Sometimes the preacher even lets her speak. She preaches better than some of the men.'

The coals heaved a dying sigh and fell in bright embers into the ash pan. He closed the iron damper to cut off the flow of oxygen to any embers, then grabbed a poker and looked around for something to thicken it into a ramming tool.

'There,' she said, pointing to a threadbare pillow sack filled with rags. 'Dip some of those rags in that bucket of dish water so we won't start a fire.'

He wrapped the wet rags around the poker and poured the rest on the embers. 'Do you have any old broadsheets around we can spread to catch the mess?'

'There is a stack under the cupboard. The officers bring them in. I rarely have time to read them. The soldiers use them to wipe their bums. Did you print any of Milton's poetry?'

He looked at the stack of papers he was riffling through and frowned. 'Nah. No poetry. Just his opinions. Not worth the price of the ink.'

He opened the damper and jammed the poker up the flue with more vigor than was necessary. His effort was answered with clumps of black soot and creosote.

'That's what you get for burning good English oak instead of coal,' he said. 'That should hold it now that we have coal again.'

Together they cleaned up the mess. 'A man with a good right arm is hard to find,' she said. 'The potato soup should be ready.

It is seasoned with a bit of bacon. Would you like a bowl and some bread?'

'Tempting as that sounds,' he grinned. 'I'd better get back. The boys will be wanting their supper.'

'Will I see you again soon?'

'Of course you will. Now that I know where you are. Caroline, we are family. If you need anything . . . They told me at the house that you and the old mistress who owns it are still living there. But do you have enough money to get by? I have saved a little.'

A great wash of relief flowed over her. Here was William's son in the flesh. Really here and offering his help: what she had prayed for, the boy found at last, safe and sound. And claiming her as family.

'I am doing fine, better now than I have been in weeks, just knowing you are safe.' She took his hand, pressing it firmly between hers, and brought it to her lips, not wanting to let him go. 'You and I will be fine, Arthur. If we have each other, we have not really lost William. He binds us together. He will always be with us in our shared memory. You must make a life for yourself. Your father would want you to be happy. Maybe when the war is over, and Mary returns to London, we can all be friends again. Even the impossible Mr Milton.'

'Not Mr Milton. I can't see us ever being friends. Though Patience would like that.'

'Does Patience know Mr Milton?'

'Patience adores Mr Milton. He is her employer.'

Patience. That name sounded familiar. Patience . . . Patience Trapford. Milton's housekeeper. Mary had spoken of her and how her husband thought the girl could do no wrong while his wife never did anything to suit him. Patience Trapford and Arthur. What a strange world.

'She thinks he is brilliant and any flaws he might have should be overlooked.'

'Because he is such a good poet?' Caroline asked.

'No. She's not much for poetry. For reading of any kind – except the Bible. She thinks he's a most marvelous theologian and a very godly man. She gets really cross with me if I criticize him.'

'So, you don't criticize him.'

He grinned in resignation. 'So, I don't criticize him.'

'Does Patience know that you and John Milton's wife are friends, practically family?'

He looked down then, scooped up a last bit of ash and dropped it in the trash bin. 'I haven't talked much about my life before. It was too painful.' Then his face colored a little with embarrassment. 'At the print shop they know me as Ben.'

'Ben.' And then she repeated it, trying to wrap her mind around it, 'Ben. Ben for Benjamin.' She thought she understood. He was looking for a place to hide, too.

'I can't explain it.'

'You don't have to. After all, Benjamin is your middle name. Your mother named you after her father. I shall call you Ben also,' she said, 'if you would like me to.'

'I was hoping you would understand.'

'Will I see you again soon?'

'We are working pretty hard on a new project, but I'll be back first chance I get. In the meantime, Caroline, if you should need me for anything, just come to the print shop. It's on Fleet Street. There's no name on the door, but you can recognize it by a printed sign in the window: two crossed swords. Just ask anybody for James Whittier's print shop. They'll tell you.'

'Whittier,' she said. 'Whittier. I think I can remember that.'

ABANDONED

But what, Sweet Excellence, what dost thou here?

Sir William Davenant, Cavalier, poet in exile, and
supply runner between Paris and Oxford,
addressing Henrietta

'Think you, Husband, that I should have returned to Paris with William Davenant,' Henrietta asked, 'risking both your child's life and mine?' She was pacing now, hands gripped across her belly as if to protect it. 'Would you have me give birth to a prince or princess of England in a supply boat?'

'I want only what is best for you and the child,' he said without looking up from his writing desk. 'Your presence here puts a target on the court and, most importantly, on you. Chancellor Hyde says—'

'Edward Hyde cannot wait to have me gone so he can talk you into signing away your royal prerogative.' She wanted to scream in outrage but, having learned what scant purchase that gained with her stubborn husband, she stilled her frantic pacing and stood beside his desk. Since Christmas he had sat at that desk, or hovered in conference, preoccupied with endless schemes that always came to naught. The only fruit he had produced in months was heavy in her womb.

He put down his pen and reached up to take her hand. 'Henrietta, you need not fear that I shall sign away the King's prerogative. It is a groundless fear. I would never. Not ever. In any case, Parliament has refused to negotiate with the Oxford Parliament by countering with their original proposal. Against Chancellor Hyde's recommendation, I have terminated any further hope for rapprochement.'

'*Vous êtes arrivé en retard au jeu!*' she wanted to retort, but squeezed her lips shut.

'There is nothing now to be done and there will be nothing more to be done until either I or Parliament rules the field. General Essex knows you are here and will blame you for the failed negotiations – though, of course, as always, it was my decision. But I know the way Robert Devereux thinks. When he learns that I have rejected Parliament's proposal again, he will put Oxford under siege. I cannot stay here to protect you, Henrietta. It is not honorable that the King should tarry here in his wife's arms, eating and drinking by a protected hearth, whilst his loyal soldiers take the field. I am King. I must lead.'

She wanted to scream at him, *Verily? When have you ever led?* But she did not. There was logic in what he said. She sank into the chair beside his desk, suddenly too weary to stand. 'If it were not for the babe, I could go to the field with you. It would not be the first time.' She said this softly, more to herself than to him.

'For mercy's sake, Henrietta, distress me no more than I already am! Extreme remedies are requisite for extreme evils, and of two evils we must choose the one to do least harm.'

Startled by his intemperate tone, she found enough energy to match it with her own. 'And where would you have me go? Back to Den Haag to beg for more money for you?'

'That was your idea, remember, madam. Not mine.' He looked down at his hands, flexed his ringed fingers, examined his nails, inhaled deeply. 'I think you should go home. To Paris. To be with your family.'

'Home? Where you are, that is my home, Charles. Buckingham took me from my *home* when I was just a girl,' she said in disbelief. 'And family? I have no family in France. Who will be my royal protector in Paris? A six-year-old nephew whom I have never seen? Or Cardinal Mazarin, the protégé of Richelieu, who hounded my mother into exile?'

He just looked at her with that long-suffering expression she had observed in his negotiations with Parliament. It was an expression that presaged a turn of mind beyond influencing: eyes closed, implacable, just waiting for the appeal or argument to run its course, his mind already made up. Then he said, 'You are not your mother. Marie de Medici was a schemer and a reckless spendthrift. Cardinal Mazarin is a friend of the Queen

Regent. He will see you as an asset. As I do. He will receive you graciously.'

'If I am an asset, then why are you sending me away like some discarded mistress?' Her tone changed from outrage to pleading. 'My brother, the King, is dead. My mother is dead. I have no family but you. I. Am. Your. Wife.' The last word broke on a sob.

Opening his eyes, he stood up then and drew her to him. Wiped at her tears. 'Dear heart,' he said softly. 'Do you have any idea what a sacrifice it is for me to send you away? But I know that it will not be forever. And when we are reunited, it will be as sweet as last time. Remember Edgehill,' he said, speaking softly, patting her belly.

'I am not likely to forget,' she said, trying to calm herself. For the baby's sake. For his sake.

'Your sister-in-law has sent you a gift for the baby and an invitation for you to come to Le Louvre, to wait out the war at the French court, *dans le sein de votre famille* – in the bosom of your family: her words, not mine.'

Le Louvre. That dreary pile that her mother had scorned. If Anne of Austria, her brother's widow, was to be her only family, she was destitute indeed. Though she supposed she should be grateful. It was better than wandering friendless among the Hapsburgs or going back to Den Haag.

'And what about Elizabeth and Henry?' she asked.

'I would like them to stay in England a little while longer. Susan Fielding will look after them until I can get them permanently and safely settled.'

Her heart raced. What was he saying? 'Permanently? *S'il vous plaît, mon cheri . . .*' Was she truly being sent into exile then? 'I beg you, Charles—'

'No. Do not work yourself into an emotional state. It is not good for the child. I only mean away from Oxford. I will see that the children are protected until it is safe for you to return. If that doesn't happen soon, I will send them to you in France. I promise. It will only be a little while, dearest. In Paris, surrounded by your beloved Capuchins, you will be a prayer warrior for me. For England. Every day I will know that you are praying for our cause. We can be nothing if not victorious. God is on the side of a dutiful and divinely anointed king – even one who makes mistakes. Remember King David? He made a mistake or two.'

'You will not make that mistake, will you, Charles? Remember how his children paid.'

His soft laughter fell like gentle rain on her wilted spirit. 'You are Bathsheba enough for me.' He embraced her before adding firmly, 'You do not have to go immediately, but soon.' He pulled her closer. Kissed the top of her head. 'You will be able to move slowly, stopping often to rest,' he said. 'It is best, I think, for you to go southwest. Our hold on the West is solid and, if you cannot return here, Falmouth would be a safer port from which to depart. They will be watching the eastern ports. Davenant said he barely kept the supply boat from being boarded at Harwich.'

'I will go to Bath for my lying-in,' she said, some of the old self-assurance returning to her voice, 'I will not birth this child on the Continent. This child will be an English subject, as are all my children,' she said, trying to sound brave, but thinking how exhausted she felt, wishing she was already in Bath, lying in the spa, her mind floating, soothing waters washing over the white mound of her belly.

'The Royal physician is with Rupert's company in the North. But I will send for Sir Thomas Cademan. I know you prefer him.'

'It is not only because he is Catholic. Remember how skillfully he tended Lady Carlisle when she had the pox. He has helped me with the headaches. I need to rest now, Charles,' she said. 'Just thinking about birthing this child alone has given me a wretched ache in my bones.'

'Of course, my dearest heart,' he said. But his attention had already returned to his writing. He did not glance up again.

That was how she left him, as weary as she had ever been, but she did not go to her room to rest. She went instead to her altar to pray: for the child in her womb, for all her children, for her husband. for his kingdom; so many Ave Marias that her voice grew hoarse. Spirit restored, she left the chapel, determined. She would go to Bath for her confinement as Charles wanted. But she would return to Oxford. She was the Queen of England. She would not run.

*   *   *

Several days later, Edward Hyde looked up in surprise when the Queen stormed into the chancellor's office. He stood up and delivered a perfunctory bow. 'Your Majesty, how may I be of service?'

'I wrote a letter to General Essex demanding safe conduct to Bath.' She slapped a paper down on his desk, her hand like her mouth, trembling in rage. 'This was his reply.'

Hyde picked up the paper calmly and, scanning its context, sighed heavily. He recognized the beginnings of a royal tantrum. 'Please, Your Majesty. Calm yourself. It is not good for the child. Come, sit.' When she had seated herself, he handed her a pillow to put behind her back and said as gently as he could, 'How did you expect him to reply? I wish Your Majesty had sought my advice before you saw fit to write to him. Did His Majesty give consent?'

'I did not ask for consent. His Majesty agreed that I should go to Bath for my lying-in. For this traitor general – to whom Charles once offered the highest office in the land – not only to refuse his Queen's request but to threaten to provide safe conduct instead to London is beyond outrage. He said I should answer to that devil's Parliament for my part in *fostering the conflict*. This insult to the Crown simply must not go unanswered.' Her voice was rising.

He rang the bell and a page appeared. 'Bring Her Majesty a glass of honeyed cider.' As her pregnancy had progressed, so had the storms. Some passed as quickly as they came. His fervent hope was that this one would pass as quickly. He chose to overlook the implied insult that he had not been the King's first choice for chancellor. The offer to Essex had been a bribe to get him to switch sides. Charles knew Essex was war-weary. That's why he was always pursuing negotiation. Had the King succeeded in turning Essex, it would have been a lethal blow to Parliament. The Queen and Robert Devereux had never been on good terms. Henrietta had spoken against his preferment, so little wonder he was not anxious to accommodate her, especially now that prospects for peace were over.

'Your Majesty,' Hyde said, 'it is unfortunate that you provided your plans to the enemy, but I think Lord Essex may have done you a great service here.'

'*Mon Dieu! Il n'est pas possible* that you should defend—'

He handed her the honeyed drink, then lowered his voice, hoping she would mirror his calm. 'Essex's response, aside from its obvious disdain for royal regard, is a warning to you. To us. We must take every precaution. You must travel in disguise. In an unmarked carriage. Did you give him the date for which you were requesting the safe conduct?'

'I told him I was leaving in two weeks.'

'From when?'

'I wrote the letter last week.'

'Then you must leave immediately. And plan to tarry in Bath no longer than you have to.' He tried to keep his tone calm, even matter-of-fact. 'Your enemies know that is your destination. You will need to make your way to France as soon as you can travel. The general and his siege machines are probably already on their way to Oxford. The King will accompany you south as far as he can. The captain of the Queen's Guard will accompany you all the way to France and the royal physician will meet you in Bath and travel with you also.'

'And Genevieve?'

'Genevieve will be there when you arrive.'

She started to cry softly then. Sometimes his enemy, rarely his friend, the slight woman and her silent tears moved him. If it were permissible, he would have hugged her to him.

'*Pardonnez-moi, s'il vous plaît,*' she said. 'I . . . I made a grave mistake.'

Nodding, he smiled weakly. 'Nothing that cannot be remedied,' he said with more surety than he felt. 'But it is good you came to me so soon. With swift action we may even turn it to our advantage.'

She sniffed hard and stood up, straightened her frail shoulders. He walked with her to the door. 'Your Majesty,' he said, 'I have always admired your courage. It will not fail you now. When you are safe in France, His Majesty will be greatly relieved. Do you think you can leave tonight? Hours count.'

'I will be ready when the King comes for me.'

'You will be a great asset to His Majesty, as you were the last time you went abroad.'

For the first time since she entered the room she gave him a faint smile. 'That is all I ever desired.'

When she had gone, Edward Hyde turned back to his desk. He had one other distressing chore to complete before he went to help prepare for the Queen's flight. Archbishop Laud had been indicted by Parliament for treason and had written asking for advice as he prepared his defense, a singular event from the proud old archbishop. His time in the Tower must have dulled the edge of his pride. A letter would have to do. Hyde stared into space, dipped his pen, stared again, but the words would not come. Finally, he wiped his dripping quill and went to help his King prepare for the perilous departure of his pregnant wife.

UNEASY ALLIES

What shall our nation be in bondage thus
Unto a nation that truckles under us?
Ring the bells backward! I am all on fire.
Not all the buckets in a country quire
Shall quench my fire.

From 'The Rebel Scot' by Cavalier Poet,
John Cleveland, in response to the
presence of Scots Covenanters

James Whittier had set aside this day for a quick turn of profit,
but the day was not proving good for either profit or sport.
Instead of the usual midday adventurers and ne'er-do-wells,
or the occasional bored Cavalier confined within the city, the
tavern was crowded with Scottish soldiers. Their enthusiasm –
fueled by the cartloads of barley corn they'd brought with them
and bootlegged to every publican in London who sought to avoid
the newly levied English tax on Scotch whisky – made any tavern
seem full to bursting.

'How aboot one more wee dram, lads, to celebrate the
going-to-trial of Archbishop William Laud?'

They passed around the jug to shouts of 'to Archbishop Laud
and may the devil take his own,' then rolled the dice and whooped
and moaned when they lost.

'To the Englishman who is skinning us,' one of them shouted,
winking good-naturedly at James.

Skinning? Hardly, James thought.

'To all of London's godly souls and a pox on the Cavalier.'

Round and around the table went the jug, from which
James only pretended to sip, though he tasted enough to
know it was the good stuff. Even in their cups, they were a
good-natured lot, which should have augured well for James,

except their drunken exuberance tempered their frugality not one whit. Two more rolls of the dice. He won again, but the pot was meager.

'To the covenant.' Each man cheered until the timbers shook. Another jug was produced. 'To John Pym, may he rest in peace.'

It was well enough they should drink to John Pym and the agreement he had pushed through Parliament, James thought, as he pulled in his tiny pile of earnings. Usually he let the mark win a roll or two, but this lot didn't seem to really care. They just wanted to celebrate. With just cause. They had threatened to invade England because of Laud's forced liturgy. But in a twist of fate that even they could not foresee, instead they had been invited in and were being paid for their *invasion*. And it just got better. Upon their arrival they had learned their arch-enemy William Laud was going to trial for treason.

So soon it would be the Presbytery instead of the Church of England who meddled in Englishmen's prayers. Parliament was already pressuring every English male above eighteen years to sign onto the Covenant or face 'severe consequences.' They had already posted a notice on his door, which he promptly burned. It was enough to make a devout Christian say to hell with the whole hypocritical lot of them. But James was only marginally Christian by Church of England standards, and not at all devout by godly standards. Somehow, he could not see the humble Galilean carpenter they all pretended to follow beckoning from the end of their bloody paths to power.

'That'll be enough for me today, lads,' James said, gathering in the paltry few coins he'd won, but they were still drinking and back-slapping and scarcely noticed his leaving.

It would only be the same story if he went to another of his favorite haunts. The Scottish exuberance was everywhere. Anyway, his heart was not in it. Maybe his luck was running out, or he was just tired. They had been working hard at the print shop and there was still more work to do on the Williams project, but he didn't need to go home. Ben had said he wanted to design the cover, so James had left it to him. His presence would only interfere with the boy's concentration. He'd told Ben he would be out for most of the day. God knew he needed some diversion to take him out of the malaise he was in, so he headed across

London Bridge to Southwark. Moll knew how to soothe a man's frustration.

But not this time as it had turned out.

As he pulled on his breeches and piled a few silver coins on her bedside table, she said, 'James, there is no need for that. I failed. Unless you want me to try again. I have other ways,' she teased.

'No, Moll, girl. You were not the one who failed.' He gave a rueful little laugh. 'I think I just need a change.'

'I have a new girl,' she said, her hands gently stroking his chest as she helped him button his shirt. 'Bella. From the Continent. All blonde loveliness. Lips like cherries. Nipples too. All natural. Very clean and very enthusiastic in her work.'

His lips briefly brushed her fingers, as he removed her hand from his chest. 'Tempting, but no,' he said. 'Not that kind of change. Something . . . else.'

When he kissed her goodbye, he tried to make it a passionate kiss. Nothing. He looked at her full-figured body in frustration. A body a man could lose himself in. Most men, anyway. What was wrong with him? Maybe he was ill. Maybe he was dying. Maybe he should see the apothecary. Maybe a potion against witchcraft.

'Goodbye, Lord Whittier. I hope you find whatever – or whoever – it is you are looking for,' she said with a little half-smile.

He made his way back across the river, ignoring the vendors and the beggars, the raucous children who roamed the streets and alleyways, screaming, playing battle, using sticks for swords as they chased wild dogs and parried and thrust and cursed each other with shouts of 'Roundhead swine' and 'Cavalier fool.' In his frustration he would have kicked whatever cur crossed his path.

'Whoever it is,' she had said. Moll was the second woman in as many weeks to suggest a 'whoever.' There was a 'whoever.' Of late, her image came to his mind at odd times and often. But he had racked his brain, trying to think of the woman's name. He'd heard it in the guardhouse at Reading. He could see her, clutching her old-fashioned pilgrim's bag, dark brown hair spilling around a plain cap, desperation in her wide eyes as she pleaded with the commander to give her back her pistol. The same fine pistol that belonged to the husband he knew was dead. He had heard her first name too. Before that meeting. Her husband had called her name – that name just out of reach – when he had ordered her back in the wagon at that first encounter. He could still hear the righteous outrage in her voice. God's blood, if he could remember everything about her, from the feel of her arms around his waist on the back of a speeding horse, to the way her neck arched, curved and graceful as a swan's when she bowed her head, why in the name of all the saints could he not remember her name? Or at least the address he gave to the coachman. Somewhere around Reading or Oxford? Hampshire, maybe?

Useless to dwell on it. He was thinking too hard. Her name would slip into his consciousness like a thief on some day when he no longer cared or was not trying to remember. The mind worked that way. It was not the servant. It was the master.

His boot slid in a pile of filth lying right in the middle of the street, causing him to almost lose his balance. Holy crap how he hated this stinking city. He wasn't lying when he said he needed a change, he thought, as he scraped the mess from his boot with the side of a flat rock. And it would only get worse, no matter who won. Maybe it was time for him to go. But where to? The Continent was no different, with its endless religious wars. He'd been thinking about the colonies since listening to Roger Williams talk about his Narragansett Bay plantation. But that was a real long shot and such a radical idea: that a group of freemen – that's what they called themselves – could decide their own governance. He couldn't quite wrap his mind around it. But it seemed to be working for Williams and his family.

Family. That was something else. Sometimes he longed for a different kind of intimacy – not the ephemeral kind that was bought with silver coins or achieved through a sudden fire in the loins and as suddenly extinguished. He had watched Ben and Patience, both as innocent as lambs he was sure. The girl was a Puritan, and the Puritans held some strange tight-arse ideas about relations between the sexes. That kind of thinking was probably what blasted John Milton's marriage to hell. But the way Ben and Patience laughed together, argued with each other, sometimes touching hands lightly, almost shyly – something about that he envied. Maybe it was companionship he was missing. He needed to find himself a good woman and settle down. Maybe. But a good woman was hard to find.

The sun was sinking just as he approached the door of the print shop. What a wasted, unproductive, godawful day. As he entered he noticed through the doorway of the print room that Ben was not alone. Probably with Patience Trapford. He hung his coat and hat on the hook by the door and settled onto a bench with a rag and wiped the filth from his boot heel so that he wouldn't track it into the press room.

'Master James?' Ben said, coming toward the entry.

James did not look up. 'What?'

'Remember I told you my stepmother was in London?'

Whittier grunted, his mind still on his humiliation with Moll.

'Well, she's here and I would like you to meet her, if you have time. I don't remember if I told you her name. It's Caroline. Caroline Pendleton. I told her you wouldn't mind if she visited me here on her days off.'

'Of course not,' he said, looking around for a place to fling the dirty rag he was using before he got the dog shit on his hands. 'You must have told me,' he said, inspecting his boot heel. 'I remember that name. I think. Not Caroline, but . . . did you say *Pendleton?* I thought your name was Pender.'

Ben sounded a little sheepish. 'Milord, I told you my real name weeks ago. I know I did because I was worried about it. I remember the conversation well.'

James let the rag drop to the floor.

'I remember the important part. We had a good talk, and I told you I understood and that some days I'd like to be somebody else too.' Like today, he thought. He stood up. 'Of course,' he said, trying to sound more enthusiasm than he felt, 'just let me wash my hands and then I would very much like to meet your stepmother.'

Minutes later, when he entered the print room, the woman was sitting on the tall stool beside the press. He froze in recognition. She looked up at him and smiled.

A voice in his head warned, *Look away, man . . . she is an enchantress, a siren, a witch . . . a dangerous woman. But you don't believe in witches, James. No. I don't believe in witches.*

As he looked down into a pair of dark eyes, something inside him shifted, trapping his breath inside his chest. Maybe he was hallucinating. Maybe he'd caught the French pox and his brain was being eaten away – that would explain a lot. But no, this woman who faced him now with a startled look on her face was real. Same face. Same slender neck. Same wide eyes as the enraged woman he'd first encountered outside Rickmansworth. Only that time they had been flashing anger at the rogue who held a pistol on her husband. *Get back in the coach, Caroline.*

She was here. In his print shop. In the flesh.

'My lady, I . . . I am very glad to see you again,' he stammered. 'A pleasant surprise.'

She returned the smile. 'And I you, my lord. A fortunate encounter. To think that fate has thrown us together twice.'

Three times. But, thank God, she only remembered the man who had rescued her from a town under siege. Why had he not recognized her then? Or had he, deep down in his guilty soul?

'Life does work in strange ways,' she said. 'I am embarrassed that I have not looked you up before to tell you how grateful I am for your past kindness to me; I am ashamed to confess it, but in the desperate circumstances surrounding our encounter, I quite forgot your name.'

'No need for embarrassment. It happens to all of us. I am glad that you are in London and that Ben has found you. You look well.'

Turning to her stepson, she said, 'Ar . . . Ben, this is one of the kind strangers I told you about. I am sorry. I still do not remember—'

'James Whittier, Lady Pendleton. And may I say I am so very glad you have been reunited with Ben and he with you. I think you need each other. And may I also say that you look . . . much better than when last we met.'

She blushed and laughed. 'I should hope so. You must have thought me a beggar.'

'I thought you very courageous and really quite . . . lovely.'

'*Lady* Pendleton?' Ben asked. 'When did that happen? And just when and where did the two of you meet?'

'It is a long story, Ben,' she said, still looking at James with something like disbelief. 'We'll have time for getting better acquainted later, I hope, Lord Whittier. Right now, I see through the window that darkness is falling, and I need to return home. I came today to ask Ben if he could help me fetch some things from the farm at Forest Hill. Things I could not bring with me. With your permission.'

Forest Hill Manor. Of course. James could suddenly see the address written on the paper that he had given the coachman. He remembered thinking what a pleasant place that name evokcd.

He pretended to consider her request. 'Ben is really busy right now, working on a very important document. Against a deadline.' And then, summoning an expression as though the thought had just occurred, 'But I could take you. I have business near Oxford,' he said as he tried to make his tone casual. 'You could show me what you need to retrieve, and we could bring it back, or ship it by river if there is too much. There are a lot of Cavalier soldiers twixt here and Oxford, and I am known at all the checkpoints.'

She looked somewhat taken aback. It crossed his mind that he was being too forward. 'That is very kind, Lord Whittier. But there is no hurry. Really. I have made do this long, and I do not need to impose on your generosity further.' Then, turning to Ben, she said, 'You are blessed that you have found employment with such a kind man.' She glanced out the window at the fading light. 'Now. I really must go.'

Still giddy with having found her, he was not giving up this easily.

'My lady, I insist you do not leave without one of us escorting you. We have a couple of newsboys we feed. Ben is a much better cook than I am. The boys will riot if they must eat what I cook for them again. It would be my pleasure to accompany you.'

'I appreciate the gesture, Lord Whittier, but it truly is not necessary. It is only a short walk, scarcely more than a mile. I know every shortcut and close in London. As a girl I grew up navigating these streets. I will not get lost.'

'Aye lass, but then thou dinna have to deal with drunken Scotsmen.'

Her answering laugh was delightful, 'You are a very good mimic. You could be on the stage. If London still had a stage. Very well. I accept your offer.' She looked thoughtful and then added, her tone growing a little sharper as he helped her into her coat. 'As we walk, perhaps you can make me understand why a respectable and compassionate man such as yourself published Mr John Milton's scandalous document on divorce. Did Ben tell you that the wife he so despises is a friend of ours?'

'He did,' he said, opening the door. Twilight had descended in the interval since he'd returned, he noticed. Thinking on how his prospects had changed in such a short time, and not wanting to fall from her good graces, he scrambled for an explanation that she would accept. 'But as I told Ben. We only print it. We do not endorse it. And I share Ben's dislike of Mr Milton, as a man. As a writer,' he was struggling to keep his tone more apologetic than defensive, 'as a writer I must confess to a grudging admiration for him. I may not agree with his argument, but he states it well. It is merely an argument for the legal right to divorce for causes other than abandonment or adultery. I am sure he has already received a barrage of puritanical criticism in print. But he has a right to say it – and he did not call his wife's name, or even put a personal frame around his argument.'

'For shame.' In the gloaming he could not see her face well but there was no mistaking the disapproval in her tone, a tone he'd heard before. Her pace quickened with indignation. 'Do you not think how humiliated his wife would feel if she should be aware of it? Did you even read it? I mean *really* read it?'

There are three of us and only one of him. The melody in her voice carried that remembered beat of indignation. He wanted to stop right there in the middle of the street and kiss her. But not bloody likely – he was blundering this badly.

'Of course I read it. I am not that irresponsible. Maybe not every word, but enough to get the gist. He repeats himself a lot.'

'Indeed. Well to me his argument sounded very personal.'

He did stop then, right in the middle of the street. 'You read it then?'

'Don't sound so surprised. Do you not think I can read?'

Good God. He had only just found her, and they were already arguing.

'No. It is not that at all. It is just that I would not think that sort of polemical writing would be the kind of thing that young women read. Please, I am very sorry if I have offended you. I would not . . .'

In the growing dusk it was hard to read her expression, but as they turned into Gresham Street she bent her head, avoiding his gaze, 'No. You are not at fault. I apologize for my tone. As you said, you didn't write it. You only printed it. If not you, then someone else. I should not have let my personal disappointment spill over onto one who has proven his generosity and compassion to me and my family. We shall not speak of it again.'

The bells signaling evensong pealed out from block to block. They walked the rest of the way to her house without talking, stopping in front of what looked like a respectable townhouse, but there was no welcoming light in any window.

'This is it. Thank you, Lord Whittier, for seeing me safely home – once again.'

Before he could think of something charming to say, she turned and fled up the steps and quickly closed the door behind her without so much as a backward glance. But at least he knew her name, knew where she lived, and had a connection with her through Ben. He would see her again, and soon.

The unfortunate events of the day were receding. He had found her. Now all he had to do was win her.

Henrietta supposed Charles – or most likely Edward Hyde – chose Abingdon Abbey as the place to say goodbye. It was a truly godforsaken place because it had been abandoned and looted by the Church of England more than a century gone. At sunset it was particularly foreboding. The locals never came except to steal stones for their hovels and fences. Its once proud structure was subsumed by negligence and decay. Now, in mid-April, new green tendrils grabbed at dead vines and crept over the skeletal remains. Ancient apple trees, bent and broken, bordered an overgrown vineyard that no longer bore fruit, mocking the holy rites that had long ago been celebrated in this once holy place. More than just the cold wind chilled her as they pulled into the ragged yard. She found its desolation soul-searing.

Charles had not ridden in the carriage with her, preferring, he said, to 'ride beside, the better to defend you.' Only when they pulled into the shadow of the abbey had he climbed in beside her. Henry Jermyn, now Baron Jermyn, Captain of the Queen's Guard and her always-friend, stuck his head in the door and offered them refreshment presented in Jermyn style on a golden plate. She took the plate to please him, but only nibbled at the pretty confection. It was her favorite. How thoughtful he was.

He well deserved the title that she had insisted on, even though
Charles had been reluctant. She did not drink at all from the
silver cup. Who knew how long it would be before she could
relieve herself. There was certainly no place here.

'*Merci beaucoup*, Baron Jermyn,' she said, handing back the
cup and plate. 'Your service, like your presence, is always a
comfort. I am so glad you are accompanying me.'

Charles frowned then, closing the door against the newly made
baron, said, 'Don't look so sad, my dearest. This will all be over
soon. You will once again sit beside me at Whitehall. Our court
will be restored with the music and light and laughter you and
I created together. Our kingdom will be whole again.'

'I will pray for that, Charles, with every waking breath.
Even as I sleep, my soul will petition the saints to protect you
and our children.'

He took her hand, saying nothing.

'Remember your youngest children, Charles. Do not get so
caught up in the fighting that you neglect them. Do not leave
their well-being to servants and convenient courtiers as you did
when you fled London. That was a mistake.'

'I know. I had no choice. It broke my heart. But it turned out
well enough. Chancellor Hyde thinks we should return Elizabeth
and Henry to Syon House for the time being. What think you?'

She hated to admit it. But for once she agreed with Hyde. She
did not like him. Did not think him capable. But he was not the
kind of man to put children in danger, and he had proven himself
loyal. 'Elizabeth speaks very fondly of Lady Carlisle,' she said.
'Even asked if she could come to court at Oxford.'

'Our spies say that Essex has received orders to begin the
siege against Oxford. That will occupy him for a while. When
he prevails, he must find the royal nest empty.'

Henrietta replied, 'I remind you that Lucy is Essex's cousin.'

'Yes, but he has been her cousin all along and still she kept
them safe. Just until you can get safely to France. Hyde will
arrange for them to come to you. I promise.'

'I have no choice but to trust her. She might even be persuaded
to escort them to France herself. I would like that. In Lucy I
could have a friend at Le Louvre. We could be strangers together.
In Paris there would be no false religion to come between us.'

'It will be over soon. I promise,' he said again. 'The Irish troops from the North will turn the tide for us.'

She bit back the reminder that this would all be over if he had taken her advice when she first wanted to raise a Catholic army to put down the rebels. Now it might be too little too late. But she did not want a bitter parting between them.

Then, with no more fanfare than a merchant bidding good day to his wife, he kissed her goodbye and exited the coach. She watched him out of sight. Framed by the coach window, silhouetted against the brilliant afterglow of the dying sun, without his broad Cavalier's hat or royal robes, and mounted on an unremarkable steed, she was surprised how ordinary he looked.

When the horizon was empty, she leaned out the window and motioned to the captain of her guard. 'Henry, please ride in the carriage with me for a while. I need your company.'

The kitchens at the guildhall had become emptier every day since the weather had warmed enough to make war a constant pastime. Caroline was glad she no longer had to work until she was too exhausted to stand, but she remembered the endless stream of young men who came through her kitchen and wondered how many she would never see again. Because of attrition, the soldiers of London's Trained Bands were away for longer and longer spells. The Scots who were not joining the march on Oxford were encamped around London's environs. On most days Caroline only prepared a porridge breakfast and sent them off on patrol with a plowman's lunch.

But today was Sunday, and she did not have to work at all. She rolled over in the small bed, wedged under the eaves, for another hour of blissful sleep. Then she had another thought, the kind of urgent, wide-awake insight that springs full-blown into the waking mind and will not be denied. She needed to get her name on the church roll if she was ever questioned about her attendance. If Parliament was positioning itself as head of the church, seeing as how they no longer recognized the King's right to that duty, they probably had a committee to enforce church attendance. They had a committee for everything else.

Only last week a bailiff had approached her at the guildhall kitchen, asking about her church affiliation. Thinking quickly, she had mentioned the one closest to her, the Church of St Lawrence in the old Jewry. He had asked her name and written it down, then smirking had said, 'Wouldn't have taken you for a Church of England type,' before he passed on. Why had he written down her name? So today, even though she wanted to sleep, she heaved herself out of bed, put on her best bodice and skirt and headed down the three flights of stairs and out the door to the Church of St Lawrence. A good thing, too. As she entered the narthex, a churchwarden with a quill and paper had asked her to sign her name. She had never been asked to sign her name at St Nicholas in Oxfordshire.

The crowd was small. The Anglican priest noticed too. He preached about following false prophets, plainly warning the few congregants he had left, admonishing against the siren's song of new and strange doctrines. Clearly, he was talking about the new independent congregations that were siphoning off his parishioners. Like the one Patience and Ben attended. She wondered if they had asked for Lord Whittier's name? She didn't see him as an especially pious man. If a churchwarden asked for his name, would he give it? Or would he just raise an eyebrow and laugh?

But all in all it was a pleasant enough experience. She sat there in the quiet, surrounded by the stained-glass windows casting rainbows of soothing color across the nave, and was comforted by the familiar liturgy. As usual the service ended a little after midday. As she emerged she thought that today was as good a day as any to run the hateful errand she had decided was necessary.

Ever since she had visited the print shop, she had been thinking about her conversation with Whittier, and the looming threat to Mary Powell's future should Milton try to divorce her on grounds of abandonment. Caroline had decided that she needed to take some preemptive action of her own. What could it hurt? She would introduce herself to Mr Milton as a friend of Mary's, come to pay her respects at Mary's request, explaining that Mary had never meant to tarry so long, but circumstances and the war had intervened. It would be a little bit of a lie. But not really. Mary had upon one occasion made mention of wondering how her husband fared and she'd not ever said that she *never* intended to return. One thing was sure. If Caroline approached Mr Milton, he would know that his wife had a witness who would defend her against any charge that she had willfully and knowingly abandoned her husband. Thus, he would have no grounds for divorce under existing law. It would at the very least keep Mary's options open until she was fully aware of her choices: go back to her husband and try to build a life, or live forever with the shame of divorcement.

Caroline hailed the churchwarden just as he was leaving with his book of names tucked under his arm and asked if he knew where John Milton the poet lived. He gave her directions, but then added, 'He's a Puritan. I'd steer clear of him, if I was you.'

On this first day of May, she emerged from the interior of the church to see that the bright Mayday promised by a clear dawn had turned to London gray, as if to remind the godly that the Lord frowned on all pagan revels. In anticipation of the coming holiday, Parliament had passed a law against all maypole festivities, pronouncing them filled with superstition and idolatry and leading to licentious behavior. Since it fell on Sunday this year, any Mayday celebration or assembly was sure to be met with more than righteous indignation. But at least the rain held off. No excuse for her not to carry out her dreaded errand.

As she walked the half-mile down Gresham toward Aldersgate Street, she saw no signs of celebration. Only church-goers, clutching their New Testaments tightly, scurried down the higgledy-piggledy lanes to their homes like rabbits to their warrens.

When she turned into the street where Milton lived, she saw a small crowd had gathered at the end of the street, just in front of the arch. Beside a bright ribbon-festooned pole – some brave souls must have erected it under the cover of night – a Puritan preacher's voice harangued his listeners. At Mr Milton's townhouse, about halfway down the street, she paused to listen but could only make out a few words: 'profaning the Sabbath,' and 'abomination' and 'shameful pagan rituals.' As a girl, how she had loved Mayday with its music and dancing, girls with flowers in their hair, couples weaving in and out, braiding rainbow ribbons around the pole. No merrymakers in the crowd today. It was one thing to erect a forbidden maypole under cover of darkness in an act of defiance, another altogether to celebrate in the open daylight. Or maybe it was simply that there was nobody left in London who felt like dancing.

She ascended Mr Milton's steps and knocked on the door. Nobody answered. She knocked again louder, wondering if the housekeeper had the day off and perhaps Mr Milton had not yet returned from church. She was thinking of walking to the end of the street to see if there would – after all – be a confrontation, when the door opened. 'Yes, what is it?'

'Mistress Trapford,' Caroline said, 'may I please be admitted? I am a friend of Mistress Milton.'

The girl stared at her from bold, bright eyes. Instead of an apron she wore a gleaming white cap with just a hint of lace on it and a wide lawn collar. Tucking an escaping curl into her cap, she blinked and cocked her head to one side. Her eyes narrowed with suspicion. 'How dost thou know my name?'

'Your friend Ben told me about you.'

'Ben the printer's devil? How dost thou know Ben?'

'I am his stepmother. He speaks very highly of you.'

'Funny, he never mentioned thee to me.' Then her face reddened as if she realized that sounded cheeky. 'I am sorry, Mistress—'

'Caroline.'

'Mistress Caroline, Mistress Milton be not here.'

'I know she is not. That is why I am here. To give Mr Milton news from his wife.'

The girl looked a little startled at this and strangely flustered, as if she was trying to decide whether to admit her. Finally, she said, 'Mistress Caroline, I was leaving when I heard thy knock. 'Tis the Sabbath. This is my day off. Mr Milton has just returned from church. I will announce thee, but if . . .' She paused and sucked in her breath, as if sucking in courage, 'If he asks thee if thou would like some refreshment, I would take it as a favor if thou wouldst decline. I have an . . . appointment.'

Caroline could not help smiling. 'It is my day off as well. I understand,' she said, wanting to ask if she was going to meet Ben, but she knew it was not the right time or place.

'Come with me then,' she said, and led Caroline down a narrow hallway that opened into an alcove. 'This is . . . this is Mistress Caroline Pendleton to see thee, a friend of Mistress Milton. If it pleases thee, I will be leaving now.'

He was sitting in a straight-back chair, gazing out the window. 'Mistress Pendleton? Ah yes, I remember. You are from Forest

Hill. I met you and your husband at . . .' But his voice just trailed off here, as if he could not bring himself to invoke his wedding day. 'An unexpected pleasure,' his voice said. But his tight expression denied it. Then, calling out to Patience, 'Tarry just a moment, Trapford. My guest might enjoy some refreshment.'

Patience looked pleadingly at Caroline.

'Do not trouble your servant on my account, Mr Milton. I imagine since this is the Sabbath, this is her day off.'

He looked slightly annoyed then and said, 'Quite right, of course. I can find something, I am sure. There is some syllabub in the kitchen, isn't there, Trapford?' Then to Caroline, 'She always prepares a syllabub for me on holidays. Though this is no real holiday.'

'Syllabub. Yes, sir,' the girl said, visibly wilting.

'No. Really, Mr Milton. I would like nothing except a few minutes of your time,' Caroline said, thinking longingly of the cool creamy goodness. Syllabub had been one of William's favorite desserts. Though in such a godly household it would probably be whipped without brandy. 'Please. Do not tarry, Mistress Trapford. I wish you blessed company on this Sabbath afternoon.'

'Thank you,' the girl said, with a smile that betrayed her gratitude, a surprisingly pretty smile that went all the way to her eyes.

Milton moved another straight chair from a table scattered with books and papers close to his by the window. 'Trapford seems in a fine mood, I must say. I wonder where she goes on Sunday afternoons.' He said this as though it had never occurred to him to question it before. 'I do hope she is comporting herself as she should.'

'She seems a very devout young woman. I would not worry overmuch.'

'Quite so.' He drummed his fingers on the side of the chair. She longed to slap them still. 'How is your husband, is he well? What brings you to London?'

'I am a widow now. My husband was killed in the war.'

'I am sorry,' he said. 'Many brave men have been lost.'

She looked down, not wanting him to read in her expression that she did not accept his sympathy. She just needed to accomplish her mission and leave as quickly as possible. 'I will not keep you, Mr Milton. I will discharge my errand quickly. I know that it is the Sabbath and you are resting from your scholarly labors. I came to see you so that I may report to your dear wife concerning your welfare.'

He tilted his chin up and frowned. 'Indeed.'

She ignored the skepticism in his tone. 'Just before I left for London, your wife beseeched me to carry a message to you that she is indeed sorry that the war has prevented her from coming to you.' Smiling with what she hoped he would perceive as sincerity, she added, 'Mary will be so relieved to hear that you are well. I think the separation has increased her fondness for you.'

It was as though, from a narrow distance, she was watching herself watching him, and was surprised and even alarmed that the lie came so easily – so convincing, she could almost believe it herself. She was less certain that he did.

'Will she be relieved?' he asked, lifting his eyebrows to almost touch the carefully coiffed fringe on his forehead.

'Oh, most certainly.' She allowed herself a sympathetic sigh. 'I am sure you must be lonely here without her. But life at Forest Hill has not been easy. It has been difficult for Mary there. They are overrun with churlish soldiers foisted on them, all those extra mouths to feed and no help. The manor to be maintained. Her brothers have gone off to war and the younger children are no help. Endless days of drudgery. And the boorish soldiers.'

'Boorish soldiers?'

'Oh, do not worry. Mistress Milton is quite firm with them. There was just one really who required setting straight. A captain. Quite smitten with her. But she did not hesitate to tell him that she was a married woman and her husband was a famous writer in London who had written for the Queen and he would not tolerate any disrespectful behavior.'

'Did she really say that?'

She tried to feign disbelief that he would question it. 'Yes, she told me herself.'

Or some version of that. When had she become such an accomplished liar? Distressing really. And on a Sabbath. But the ox was truly in the ditch.

'I can't help but observe that the war did not stop you from coming to London.'

'Oh, my dear sir, you would not have wanted your wife to

travel the way I did. I traveled most of the way hidden in the back of a wooden cart. A torturous and frightful journey. I had nothing left to stay there for,' she said. 'I would only have been a burden to my friends. No home. No livelihood. My husband had a leasehold in London. I thought to go there, only to find it had been claimed by the Committee of Three Kingdoms for their officers. Though I am allowed a small apartment, so don't think that I have sought you out asking for help. I am fine and have found employment.' She clapped her hands together in a gesture of satisfaction. 'And seeing you looking so well I am quite relieved that I can assure Mary that her husband is well and waiting for her to return.'

He didn't say anything for a long moment, neither denying the truth of her last remark nor affirming it. He just looked at her with an inscrutable expression. Had she overplayed it? 'You may report that I am well,' he said finally, not smiling.

'Mary says you are a famous poet. Are you writing?'

'No. No poetry. I have been busy with . . . other things.'

'Well, I can quite understand if this horrible war has chased inspiration away. It provides no fit environment for a great poet.'

He smiled at that.

'Now,' she said, 'having accomplished my mission, I must say good Sabbath to you, sir. I shall write to Mary and tell her that her husband is well. She will be greatly relieved, as am I. Thank you for seeing me,' she said, standing up.

He stood up too, bowing slightly. 'Feel free to come again. Sunday afternoons are sometimes . . .' for a moment she thought he was going to say lonely, but he finished with, '. . . very quiet.'

She departed Mr Milton's threshold with a troubled conscience but a sense of accomplishment. A light mist was gathering. It would turn into a drizzle before nightfall. She looked down the street at where the maypole stood deserted, the color of its ribbons melting in the damp. There would be no dancing this Sabbath afternoon, nor bonfires tonight, even if Parliament had not prohibited them. The London of her girlhood was gone, and she realized that it was probably never coming back.

UNEXPECTED VISITORS

*They are indeed our pillar fires. Seen as we goe. They are
that citie's shining spires.*

Stephen Marshall's sermon at John Pym's funeral

Mid-May 1644

On the day that the Very Reverend Mr Stephen Marshall
came to pay a pastoral call, Lucy Hay was gazing out
the tall windows in the salon but not seeing the sun-
dappled lawn or the first flush of color from the roses around
the garden fountain. Shrouded in the mists of her own misery,
she paid no notice of the rugged, plain cleric with the thick
shoulders and commanding presence striding up to her door.
Lucy saw nothing except the long string of empty days she
imagined lay before her.

The salon had been restored to its former state shortly after the
children left for Oxford, but it had not and would not – for
the foreseeable future, if ever – return to its former usefulness.
No courtiers in proud plumage, no music, no tinkling laughter. No
sound of Elizabeth's officious scolding or Henry's bouncing balls
and raucous squeals either. It had been five months since John's
funeral. If she had to be honest, she would admit it was not so
much his presence she missed, for that had long been scarce, but
the fact of him, the expectation of his coming. With no husband,
no lover, no child to ease her into old age, and all her friends
either dead or exiled, Lucy had never felt so alone in her life.

Carter coughed discreetly, arousing her from her torpor.

'It is a lovely day; perhaps my lady would like to take a turn
around the grounds,' he suggested, as he cleared the remains of
her half-eaten breakfast. 'But first there is a gentleman to see
you, a Reverend Marshall. Shall I send him away?'

'Stephen Marshall? No, he preached Mr Pym's funeral. I will see him.'

Lucy smoothed her hair with her hands, wishing she had a cap under which to hide her unkempt curls, bit her lips and pinched her cheeks, then looked down at her simple skirt. She should have at least put on an overskirt, but she had so few visitors now. For propriety's sake, she laced her bodice to the top – after all, this visitor was the most acclaimed Puritan preacher in England. Carter ushered him in. The Very Reverend Mr Marshall not so much entered the room as inhabited it. 'How kind of you to call,' she said, extending her hand. 'Your presence honors Syon House.'

'The honor is mine, Lady Carlisle,' he said, brushing her proffered hand with the briefest touch of his lips. 'I came to see how you are doing since the loss of your dear friend, and dare to harbor a hope that I may offer some small comfort to you.'

'Carter, bring us something cool from the cellar. Cider?' she asked, looking at her guest.

'Thank you, no. I cannot tarry. I just came to beg your forgiveness for not extending sympathy sooner. Because of the press of ceremony at the funeral, we had no opportunity to speak privately. I have been away with the troops, but I am called back to speak at Westminster this afternoon. I return to the field on the morrow.'

'A much-needed respite, I am sure,' she said, indicating that he should sit beside her. 'It must be hard duty, comforting the dying on the battlefield.'

How incongruous he looked among the graceful chairs, almost comical with his great hulking manliness. But there had been nothing comical about the way he had looked in the pulpit at Westminster. With his expressive face and booming voice, he had commanded the attention of every creature he addressed. It would be no wonder if the spiders in their shadowy corners ceased their spinning to listen.

'I assure you, sir, your words at John's funeral gave me solace. I remember especially the part where you talked about great men as our "pillar fires." It reminded me of how the Israelites followed a pillar of fire at night.'

A wide grin spread across his face. 'As it was intended to do. I do appreciate congregants who bring a knowledge of Scripture with them. It not only makes the sermon easier on the ears, but shorter. I don't have to explain every allusion if the hearers are grounded in the Word.' He added, rolling his large eyes: 'Some of those Puritan preachers do drone on and on. The mind can only absorb what the posterior can endure.'

She laughed aloud at this very un-reverend-like observation.

He smiled and said, 'Laughter is good medicine.'

'It does feel good,' she admitted. Then, taking a deep breath, she said, 'I was glad when I heard you were going to preach John's funeral sermon. I think John would have been very pleased and honored by your tribute. I heard you preach once at Cole's Abbey in Aldersgate. John was there too. I encountered him at a gathering sometime later and we talked about how you drew your listeners in with your personality and humor,' she said.

It was not really a lie. They had indeed had that conversation, though it had been at a very private gathering.

In gentle acknowledgement of her compliment he only nodded, then said, 'Is there anything I can do for you? Some service – spiritual or practical – that I may render?'

'You are very kind. I am not lacking for any creature comforts, though I will admit my friend's passing has left a hole in my heart. I think in some way John was also a casualty of this awful, endless war. He worked ceaselessly, dragging his body down, scarcely sleeping or eating, almost obsessed with the need to control the King's usurpation of Parliament's power. But I suppose there are few on either side whose fortunes and fate have not been altered by the war.'

'Some worse than others. We must all pray for peace and be open to peace, but not at any cost. A peace not honestly gained is no peace at all.'

'What must we pray for then? Victory? Do you not think both sides are praying for that? If Holy God is father to all, then how does He decide between his children?'

'Justice, perhaps. The child that is least wrong and will do the least harm to His creation. God takes a long view.' He shrugged his giant shoulders and added, 'His children not so much. But the Scriptures teach us that we must pray for forgiveness of our transgressions and that we must pray for our enemies.'

'Do you have enemies, Reverend Marshall?'

'We all have those who we think, rightly or wrongly, wish us ill and would act on those wishes. We call them enemies.'

'Do you think the King is your enemy?'

'If he prohibits or restricts me from preaching God's word as I perceive it, yes. But I wish Charles Stuart the man no harm. I bear him no hatred.'

'What about Archbishop Laud? Is he your enemy?'

'Ah the prayer book, the forced liturgy.' He paused, seeming to choose his words carefully. 'I think William Laud is an enemy of God's true church, a tool used by Satan, and that is a very tragic outcome for any human being, but I have no authority heavenly or otherwise to condemn him. Yes, I do pray for him. I will work to have him removed from his position of authority over the Ecclesia, but I have great compassion for him. I believe he has chosen wrongly and will ultimately bear the consequences. We must always pray that God's will be done in our lives, whatever happens to England. Christ's Kingdom is not of this world.'

'Reverend Marshall, do you think God has a "will," a divine plan for each of us?'

'I do. A path clearly marked, if we choose to follow it.'

She hesitated, thinking about the choices she had made. But what choices had she really had? What choices would she have going forward? She wanted to ask him more, but he stood up, a signal the visit was ending. She stood too. He reached out and covered both her hands with his large ones. 'May I pray for you before I go, Lady Carlisle?'

She nodded, and as he prayed she was comforted by the gentle cadence of his supplication more than his words. And when he had gone she felt better somehow, not less lonely, but it was almost as if his faith had softened her loneliness, like the scent of flowers in a closed room.

'Almost there,' Edward Hyde said to the two children who sat across from him as the plain, unmarked coach turned into Syon Lane. The young Duke of Gloucester clapped his hands and exclaimed, 'Won game, Henry won game,' whereupon he snatched off his beribboned bonnet and threw it at his sister. This time his sister, who was looking out the coach window with wide eyes, did not scold. 'I see it. I see it,' she said with rare excitement, 'I see the house.'

Edward Hyde saw it too. For the first time since approaching the guarded ramparts surrounding London, he released his nervous grip on the pistol beneath his plain cloak. His eyes, ever watchful of 'his two young granddaughters,' turned to gaze upon the house looming in the distance. The first time he had ridden down this lane, he had been relieved of the King's treasure the courtiers had 'donated' at the urging of London's most celebrated hostess. He remembered the elegant salon, the music, the laughter; so incongruous he had thought even then, poised as they were on the cusp of war.

Much had changed here now. The canopy bordering Syon Lane shut out the sun with its untended overgrowth. Of course, there would be no gardeners to tend them now. The house looked almost deserted. No coming and going now since the house lay outside the greater London battlements. Even the river traffic was sparse. He looked anxiously at the King's children. What if Lady Carlisle no longer lived here, or what if she said she could not accept them? Once he heard Parliament forces were preparing to lay siege to the Oxford court, there had been no time to request her consent. His only thought had been to get the children out.

So far all had gone as planned. Suspicious eyes had not been aroused by the single coachman holding the reins, one of the King's soldiers in simple disguise but with a long rifle hidden beneath his bench. The two children had been remarkably compliant, taking the perilous journey as a game they had played before. The princess had kept her little brother engaged, even when he protested at the girl's clothing he was forced to wear for 'the game.' As they had approached a patrol of soldiers, Elizabeth had whispered to him, 'Remember the mouse game, Henry. If we win we will get to stay with Lady Carlisle while Maman and Papa are away. You can play with your toys in the room with the tall windows and we can picnic in the attic.' Then she had said loudly enough for the lone guard at the checkpoint to hear, 'Grandfather, why have we stopped?' A cursory glance inside the coach and the guard waved them through. 'Well done,' Hyde had whispered, and smiled as he watched the children exchange satisfied glances.

As the coach pulled to a stop in front of the entrance to Syon House, a woman's figure, holding a spade in her hand and shaded by a wide sun hat, bent over a rose bush. When she turned to look at them, he recognized her, even with one hand shading her eyes. 'Thank the Lord and all the saints,' he breathed, climbing out of the coach. He turned his back to her and instructed the children. 'Stay here until you are called. We don't want to spoil the surprise.'

Elizabeth nodded her eagerness to conspire. She took Henry's hand in hers and, when he started to call out, his sister shushed him with a warning finger to her lips.

As Hyde exited the coach a familiar voice called out. 'Are you lost? I do not recognize your carriage.'

He drew closer, removed the tall-crowned Puritan hat as he said, 'Edward Hyde, my lady.'

'Counselor! Have you also deserted His Majesty for parliamentary causes?'

He was Chancellor now, but he did not correct her. Slapping the hat against his thigh, he said, 'This ridiculous thing? This is my disguise.'

She laughed good-naturedly. 'It suits you. What occasion brings you to Syon House? News from the Queen? Are we about to be invaded by Royalist troops?' She was only half-joking, he could see. She let the spade fall to the ground, wiped her hands on her apron. 'I am afraid you find me ill-prepared to receive visitors. Though you are the second one I have had today, and much welcome.'

'I have two others with me who are very anxious to see you, Lady Carlisle. They have come a long way.'

He turned and motioned for the children, who tumbled out of the coach toward them, Elizabeth holding tightly to Henry's hand. But if they had forgotten in their excitement the royal decorum, Lucy had not. She offered a deep curtsy as Henry broke free and ran toward her. Elizabeth, suddenly shy, held back until Lucy closed the gap between them, pulling them both into her embrace.

It was only then that Edward Hyde breathed freely. This was not the behavior of a woman who would refuse to take the children. Officially, they were under Parliament's control, assigned to the House of Northumberland. Of all the options available, this was the best possible outcome. Parliament would leave them alone here, and they would be loved and safe. For the time being.

'Let us get out of the sun and go in,' she said, picking up Henry, and exclaiming in mock surprise, 'Oh I beg your pardon, mademoiselle. What is your name?' she said, putting him down again and pretending to look puzzled.

'I am Henry,' he said, indignation pursing his lips into a pout. 'Pretend game.' He stuck out his chin instead and pointed to his sister. 'She made me.'

'And you did a really good job with your disguise, Your Grace. I'll bet you fooled all those pesky guards.'

'They were very brave,' Hyde said, tousling the boy's hair. Away from the court it was easy to see them as just ordinary children. But they were not; they were children of the King. He removed his hand from the royal pate. Whoever's care they were under had a fearsome responsibility. He would be glad to be rid of it.

'Come,' Lucy said. 'Let's find Carter and tell him to bring some refreshments for us and our guest. You can tell me what fun and adventures you had at Oxford.'

As the children ran ahead calling Carter's name, Hyde motioned for the coachman to unload two large trunks. Lucy Hay looked at him and raised one eyebrow, reminding him briefly of the shrewd, much younger woman who was once Henrietta's favorite.

'Has the Queen tired of them so soon that she would send them back to Parliament's clutches?'

'The Queen had no choice. She is heavy with child and is in Bath for her lying-in. Parliament has ordered a siege of Oxford. The King and his sons have gone to the battlefield. The Queen says to tell you that in all England the person whose love and loyalty she most relies on is that of Lucy Hay, Countess of Carlisle, and she trusts you to keep her treasures safe.'

For what seemed like an eternity the countess said nothing, just stared at him as though the very thought was shocking to her. The chancellor had a momentary fear that she might refuse; might say that she had not the resources, or that she could not accept this extra burden. But when the children came running back out and took her hands to drag her into the house, she laughed and followed them in. He sent another prayer of thanks heavenward.

'In the salon, my lady?' Carter asked, trying to avoid dropping the serving tray as Henry ran to the door.

'Yes, please, Carter,' she said, as Henry stopped abruptly in the doorway and looked around puzzled.

'Henry's toys?' He looked troubled.

'I put them away while you were gone. We will get them out soon, I promise. Just like before.'

Odd, he thought, as he watched her interacting with them, maternal for the courtier he had known and, who it was said, was incapable of bearing children.

'What about my tutor? When is Mistress Makin coming?'

Lucy hesitated before answering, throwing a beseeching look in his direction, then said, 'She quit coming while you were away. I am not sure . . .'

The girl looked at him too and exclaimed in the commanding voice that royal children must be given as birthright. 'You must get her back. I need her for my Hebrew and Italian. Nobody in Oxford could teach me.'

The child looked almost panicked. He had ceased being amazed that such a brilliant mind and strong spirit lived in the girl's frail body. 'I will see, Princess, if she can attend you again, but it has become very difficult to travel now. You remember the checkpoints we had to pass through to get here.'

'Why can't she live here with us?'

He looked at Lady Carlisle with a questioning lift of his brow.

'It is fine, Mr Hyde. Bathsua Makin may be a scholar, but she is surprisingly good company when she is not buried in her books. I would be glad if you can arrange it. I don't think Algernon will trouble himself to make it happen. He is away with the navy anyway. It was Mr Pym who arranged for her to come before. I think she will be open to the idea if you ask her. She thought Elizabeth an excellent student.'

He glanced at the children at the other end of the table. They seemed to be occupied with their sweet cider and biscuits. His voice low, he said, 'I will do what I can. I cannot approach her myself, I must not be taken prisoner.'

'But surely you have diplomatic license.'

'Not since the London Parliament declared the Oxford Parliament void and its members treasonous. Lord Essex has even put a price on the Queen's head. When he learns that she is not in Oxford . . .'

Lucy Hay went white. She looked away from him at the children who had finished eating and were growing restless. Elizabeth took Henry's hand and led him to the window. 'Remember, Henry? You can see the river from here. We will ask Carter to put the chairs back against the wall and bring down your balls and soldiers and it will be just like it was before.'

As the children stared out the tall windows, remarking on the familiar, Lucy turned back to him. 'We must talk,' she said, her voice low. 'Certain arrangements must—' She broke off her whispering and turning away said, 'Carter, please take the children up to the attic and find their toys.'

Henry turned from the window and, holding up his hands to be carried, ran to the servant.

'Oh, Your Grace, you are quite a young man now,' Carter said. 'Do you think you could walk up those stairs holding my hand?'

There was something about the way the child slipped his hand inside the footman's that wrung at Hyde's heart.

When the children had gone, she said, 'I must talk candidly. I cannot accept this responsibility with the skeleton staff now serving Syon House. I do not even have a lady's maid. One old man, though Carter serves me loyally and willingly, and when the children were here – well, you can see that he is very good with them – but one aged servant and his bumbling grandson are not adequate. I have a cook and a laundress but they each will need another pair of hands in the scullery and the laundry. I will also need another housemaid and a nurse for the children.'

His mind was spinning as fast as she was talking, wondering how he could satisfy what seemed reasonable demands. He had not anticipated her reduced circumstances.

She broke off her recitation of requirements to ask, 'Has Henry been breeched or is he still wearing a dress?'

That at least he could answer from experience. 'Yes, but he has the occasional accident. Lady Carlisle, I don't think I can—'

'I suggest you start at St James's Palace. That was the royal children's household before Parliament took custody of Henry and Elizabeth. Henry had a nurse there. John brought her to me, but I let her go back when the children left for Oxford. Her name was Colette. And I will need a maid for the laundry. I do understand your security concerns, Mr Hyde, I do. But the servants at

St James's Palace were loyal to the children. At least John said they were. They will not betray you.

'As for the other three servants, I shall request them from the Percy Household since they are officially designated custodians by Parliament and commissioned by Parliament to send me a quarterly allowance for provisions. A payment is due . . .' she paused as if doing a quick calculation in her head, '. . . midsummer, and I doubt John told the commissioners that I let the children go to their mother. He had too much on his mind. Besides, he was as anxious as I that they not fall into Lord Pembroke's hands. I think the payment will come on time. Algernon's new wife will complain about the needed servants, but she will comply. She will not want the children at Northumberland House. Find that nurse and see while you are at St James's Palace if you can find a suitable groom for Henry. Go to Chelsea. Try to convince Bathsua Makin to come. Without her I will never be able to keep Elizabeth's mind occupied.'

'I will try my best,' he said. 'If Mistress Makin cannot come, I will send the tutor from Oxford – though Princess Elizabeth is not much impressed with him. Yet he will be better than none.' He reached for his Puritan hat. 'Best wear this if I am going into the lion's den. I had hoped to avoid Westminster, but perhaps I can fulfill my errand and slip through the Lines of Communication with all the other tradesmen who are leaving. I have found the busiest times are the easiest.'

'You have sneaked in before?'

'Only once. At the request of Archbishop Laud. Poor man is facing trial. He wanted me to advise on his defense. He is hopeful, but I fear a bad outcome.'

'I am no lover of William Laud, but surely . . . treason? They'll never prove it. John said that was why they had not already brought him to trial.'

'You of all people know they do not have to prove it. The Covenanters will push for a bill of attainder.'

As she walked him out, he turned and asked, 'If you don't mind my asking, you said I was your second visitor. Who was your first? Anybody I know? I get so little news of my few friends still in London.'

'I doubt you know him. The Very Reverend Stephen Marshall. It was a pastoral call. He preached John's funeral.'

'I know of him. Even heard him preach once before the war broke out. A formidable presence in the pulpit. There could be no better advocate for the Presbyterian cause,' he said, remembering that Lucy Hay was a Presbyterian. He'd always supposed that her refusal to attend mass in the royal chapel was the reason for her abrupt departure from the court. 'I think, in Stephen Marshall, Parliament found an advocate every bit as powerful as the Archbishop Laud was for the Anglican cause,' he said. 'One is credentialed by the law of the land, the other by the sheer force of his gift of rhetoric. Two of God's prophets on opposing sides. It will be interesting to see which one he favors. Though it's looking more and more like Marshall.'

'Some think the outcome of the war will tell us that,' she said archly. 'Or perhaps not. It may be that, disapproving, God will turn his back on all who make war in His name. Who can know?'

He wanted to ask which side she favored, but he thought he knew. She favored whichever side was victorious.

'God go with you, Counselor,' she said. 'I trust that you will remember and remind them of my loyalty in this very important thing.'

'I shall remember and remind, but I think they already know,' he said, climbing into the coach. 'When you see the nurse, you will know I have succeeded, and I shall send you word regarding the tutor.'

By the time the coach had turned east off Syon Lane and headed toward Westminster, Lucy was already in the nursery, replacing the children's beds with clean linen. Her heart felt lighter than it had in months. Syon House had been lonely without them but, more importantly, the fact that the King and Queen trusted her enough to send them back showed they did not suspect she was the one who'd informed the Parliament five of the King's planned action against them. Since John had died, and with the children gone, she had felt herself more vulnerable. Now, whichever side Almighty God chose, because of the children, her future looked less precarious.

PROOF OF LOVE

I hope yet to serve you. I am giving you the strongest proof of love that I can give; I am hazarding my life, that I may not incommode your affairs. Adieu my Dear Heart. If I die, believe that you will lose a person who has never been other than entirely yours.

From Henrietta's letter to Charles, July 1644

Mid-June 1644

'Why must we leave Bath tonight?' the Queen asked Henry Jermyn. 'Truly, I have not found much comfort here, but I would much prefer to wait until tomorrow. *Je suis fatiguée.* I was preparing for bed.'

The pleading in her voice almost persuaded him. He wanted to take her in his arms and comfort her, kiss the shadows beneath her eyes, place his hand upon her belly to feel the life growing inside her. But he could not. Such an act would of course be treasonous. He could only keep her safe. He didn't exactly remember when he became aware that he loved her. It seemed that he had always loved her. And being alone with her was torment.

'As your most loyal subject, I wish only to serve your desires, Your Majesty, but as your captain, I am charged with your safety. I am truly sorry, but it is imperative that we leave within the hour. The King's messenger says that not only has Essex put a price on your head, but he has disobeyed Parliament's command to lay siege to Oxford and is instead diverting his troops westward. He knows, or at least suspects, your presence here. That is why he is abandoning the Oxford siege. His men will have the roads cordoned off by dawn, if they have not already. If we head south now we can make Glastonbury Abbey before that happens.'

'I cannot go without the doctor.'

'He has already left. He will meet us in Glastonbury. He can check you there and see if he thinks it is safe to travel the sixty miles from there to Exeter. You will be safe at Bedford House. Lord and Lady Russell are very loyal and are prepared to welcome you and provide you with every comfort. It will be a much safer place to deliver the King's child. Genevieve has gone on ahead to prepare for your arrival.'

'But I thought Parliament held the garrison at Exeter.'

'Prince Maurice routed them last fall. It is solidly a Royalist garrison now.'

'I would have known that fact if his brother had taken it. Rupert always makes sure everybody knows his triumphs. Maurice just does what he needs to do, an admirable trait. I shall be ready within the hour, but, Henry, you know I cannot ride in my condition.'

'You will not have to,' he assured her. 'Put on the plainest, loosest garment you have and wear this,' he said, handing her the plain cloak and bonnet. 'As soon as you are dressed, meet me at the kitchen garden gate – do you know where it is?'

She nodded.

'I will be standing beside a carriage, wearing a roundhead haircut and Puritan doublet,' he said.

This at least got a smile out of her. 'You are going to cut your beautiful hair.'

'A small enough sacrifice to keep my Queen safe,' he said. 'Now we must hurry.'

One half-hour later, as he helped her into the small coach, she looked up at him, worry lines crimping her forehead, and said through the faintest smile, 'Not too bumpy, please, unless you want to deliver the King's child on the side of the road.'

He thought her the bravest woman he had ever known, and more devoted to her husband than Charles deserved. 'Not too bumpy,' he confirmed with a smile. 'Midwifery is not an occupation to which I aspire.'

He climbed onto the coachman's bench and, with a flick of the reins, the pair moved forward. The urge to spur them on was strong, but mindful of his precious cargo, he kept a sedate pace. They were only about three miles out of Bath when a party of riders approached, almost running him off the road.

Fast horses. Buff jerkins. Sidearms flashing in the moonlight. Roundheads this far west meant only one thing: Essex's men. And they would know what they were looking for. So great was his relief when they thundered past with scarcely a glance in his direction, he almost dropped the reins. But that relief was short-lived. Intuition told him that at least one or more might circle back. In their place, he would have done.

The light of a bashful moon high in the sky picked out a small copse of trees behind a shepherd's hut. Pulling on the reins, he leaped down, tethered the horses to a bush and signaled for Henrietta to get on the floor. 'Company,' he whispered, 'probably nothing. But stay down, low as you can. Cover your whole body with the coach blanket.'

He walked several paces away, stopping in plain sight, in front of, but not shadowed by, the trees, so the riders could plainly see him doing his business. It wasn't long before he heard the horses returning, followed by the sound of men's voices. He patted the inside of his jerkin to make sure the pistol was there. From the corner of his eye he could see that there were five of them. Not good odds.

'Who goes there?'

He noted the thick East London accent. Not King's men. He turned around, pretending to fumble at the button closure of his pants. 'Ye gave me a start,' he said. 'Until I saw thy buff coats. 'Twere a relief to see good Parliament men. Thought sure ye might be robbers or worse. Maybe Royalists.' He scrunched up his nose, as though some foul smell had just offended. 'These parts be ripe with the stinking lot of them.' Inspired, he thought, as he heard his own voice imitating the colloquial dialect. Many of the Puritans, especially in outlying dockside areas, still used the English of the old King James. 'Cyrus Pitcock,' he said and, wiping his hand on his britches leg, offered it to the lead rider who ignored it.

'Why are you on this lonely road at night, Mr Pitcock?'

None of the soldiers made any movement to dismount. The lead rider leaned forward, loosely holding the reins, his posture casual, but a flintlock lay in his lap.

'No reason that I asked for. On me way home and anxious to get out of this Royalist-infested country.'

'Where is home and what is your business here?'

Henry thought quickly. They would likely be on their way to scout Taunton for Essex, who would like to take their Royalist garrison back. If he should run into them again, they would not be likely to stop him a second time. 'Parliament town,' he said, praying that the Queen did not raise her head to look out the window. He spoke loudly, hoping his voice would carry. 'Just tryin' to make it to Taunton to pick up me wife. Her mother lives there. She's sick with the palsy. Traveling by night to avoid the King's soldiers.'

'I don't follow.'

'I hear they are more like than not holed up after sunset, whoring and drinking.'

The soldiers laughed at that. The leader said, 'Speaking of whoring, Mr Pitcock, I don't suppose you happen to have heard any news of the King's French whore hereabouts?'

Henry scratched his head, praying Henrietta had not heard their vile insult. The coach was tethered on the other side of the hut, and the soldiers had their back to her. He dropped his voice to a conspiratorial whisper. 'Ye mean the King's Catholic consort? Papers in London said she was in the Netherlands.'

The lead rider guffawed at that. 'Nay, man. Surely you heard. She came back months ago, bringing Catholic soldiers with her and pope's gold to pay for her papist invasion.' He leered as he added, 'She brought something else back with her as well. The bitch is about to drop another mongrel pup into the King's lap, so this time she'll be movin' slow.'

Henry's fingers itched to grab the gun and shoot the blackguard's face to bloody hell. But there was only time to get off one shot. And then he would be food for crows and she would be theirs.

Another of the soldiers chimed in. 'My sister-in-law's cousin worked at the kitchen in Whitehall. She says all the King's children are bastards.'

Jermyn would go for him next. It would be a pleasure to see his blood spurt. He was trembling with rage as he tried to gain control of his twitching hands, but when he answered, he was surprised to hear his voice low and calm. 'In her letters the wife hasn't said anything about the Queen being in these parts. I am sure she would have heard. Isn't it a large undertaking when a Queen makes a progress?'

'Oh, this will be no royal progress. She's a sly fox this vixen,' the second soldier said.

Then the lead soldier glanced toward the coach. Studied it for a long moment. 'Mind if I look in your coach, Mr Pitcock?' Not waiting for an answer, he dismounted and strode toward the coach, jerked open the door, stuck his head inside. Henry took panicked inventory. Beside the pistol he had a small sidearm at his waist under his shirt and a dagger in his boot. One of the five was scarcely more than a boy. He would shoot the one opening the coach first. The others were still mounted, giving him the advantage, he was thinking, when the first soldier stepped back away from the open door of the coach. He was holding a blanket. Even with the thin crescent moon sliding behind a cloud, Henry could see the coach was empty.

He thought that he would melt with relief. She must be hiding in the hut. Please Holy Virgin, let them not look there.

The virgin must have heard.

Holding up the blanket and shaking it out as if he expected to find . . . what?

'I be cold natured,' Henry said. 'Sometimes it gets a mite nippy up on the driver's bench.'

The soldier folded the blanket and put it back on the carriage seat. 'No stone unturned,' he said half apologetically, and shut the door. Mounting his horse and giving the signal forward, he said, 'God's speed, Mr Pitcock. Maybe we will see you down the road.'

As they rode away, Henry took his time, pretending to untie the reins, slowly mounting the driver's bench, making a show of wrapping himself in the blanket. He waited until they were out of sight before leaping down and rushing into the darkened hut.

Enough light spilled in through the open door to see the room was empty. Had she run out onto the moor while their backs were turned to the coach? There were predators there too. But his back had not been turned. He would have seen her. He whispered, 'It's me. They have gone. You are safe.' Nothing. 'Your Majesty?'

Silence. A deadly, looming silence. Not even the scuffle of a rat. Then a shadow separated itself from the wall, and thank

Christ and all the saints in heaven, she was there, standing before him, her face so pale and sad in the moonlight, for one heart-stopping moment he thought she might be a ghost. A ghost with a very round belly.

'You heard them?' he said.

'I heard,' she said, her voice frail and tremulous. 'Every malicious, vile lie,' and then, her voice grew stronger, 'Charles will make them all pay.'

Wanting nothing more in the whole world at that moment than to take her in his arms and comfort her, he only said, 'Pay it no mind. They are just an ignorant lot who believe what they are told to believe. They don't know you or anything about you.'

'Why do they hate me so? What have I ever done to them?'

Now was not the time to explain that it was not her they feared. She was just a stand-in for their nightmare memories of another Queen Mary, who had racked their grandfathers for their Protestant beliefs and burned their clerics. Instead, with his hand, he gently wiped away the tears tracking her cheeks and wished with all his heart that Charles Stuart was half the man she wanted him to be. She removed his hand from her face brusquely, as if to let it linger there would somehow make her weak.

'Do you feel well enough to continue?' he asked. 'I think they will not bother us again.'

She nodded and led the way back to the coach, climbed back in with his assistance. When they left Bath, he had given her a bell and told her to hold it out the window and ring it if she needed him. He listened closely, but the only sound that punctuated the night silence was the clip-clopping of the horses and the occasional hooting of an owl.

Just before daybreak they reached Glastonbury.

The second Sunday in June, Caroline waited outside the Church of St Lawrence. Arthur had said he would meet her there and they would have a nice Sunday afternoon stroll and a chance to visit if the day was fine. The day was indeed fine: a rare blue sky, with little clouds like white lace handkerchiefs – mares' tails, her dear auntie used to call them. A soft breeze teased at her hair and the sun shed a delicious warmth on her face.

She had only seen Arthur once – she must remember to think of him as Ben now – since their meeting at the print shop. He had come by the guildhall last week to check on her, apologizing that he had been busy with a new project, telling her that she should feel free to come and see him there if she got lonely. 'Milord said to tell you that you are welcome anytime.'

James Whittier was the reason Caroline had not tried to visit Arthur again. Despite his former kindness to her, or maybe because of it, she couldn't quite decide, the printer made her ill at ease. She couldn't tell Arthur that, so she merely said she did not want to be a pest, and it was enough just to know he was near. He assured her that they were almost finished with the big project and he would be able to see her more often, adding that since he and Patience Trapford had been attending church together, he might bring her with him the next time. He was anxious for them to get to know each other.

'I have already met her.'

'Where? How?'

'I went to see John Milton to reassure him that his wife had not abandoned him. I did not want him to have recourse for claiming desertion.'

'How did he take that?'

'Skeptical and tight-lipped, very noncommittal, but at least he knows Mary has a witness. Patience met me at the door. She was very nice to me . . . after I told her I was your stepmother.'

He laughed. 'She can be a little brusque for a servant girl, until you get to know her. She is loyal. Clever too. And very kind. I hope you will like each other.' He said this with a sincerity that spoke more than words about his feelings for the girl.

'I am sure I will like her,' she said.

'Next Sunday?'

'I shall look forward to it. I will go right home after church. The soldiers will be gone so we can talk in the parlor.'

Now, in anticipation of that visit, along with the few congregants of St Lawrence Church, Caroline filed out past the heavy wooden doors, one or two generous souls even giving her a nod of recognition. She noticed a lone carriage making its way down the street and paused to let it pass before crossing. But it did not pass. It pulled to a stop in front of her, and the driver dismounted with easy grace.

Was that? It was.

'Lord Whittier. If you have come for Sunday services, I am afraid you have arrived too late.'

'I have not come for service. I have come for you, Lady Pendleton.'

'For me? I am sorry, my lord, but I have an appointment with—'

He smiled and gave what might pass for a courtly bow. 'Ben told me you would be here. I . . . we . . .' He pointed to the carriage from which Ben waved sheepishly and called out, 'It promises to be such a fine day, Patience and I thought you might enjoy a picnic in St James's Park.'

'St James's Park! That's a goodly distance.'

'That is why I suggested the coach.'

'But that must have been a terrible expense. I hope you hired it for another, worthier, purpose.'

'What could be worthier than a Sunday afternoon in the park with a lovely lady? But lest you think me profligate, the stable gives me a discount. I mention them in my broadsheets from time to time.' He gave a little shrug as if to say it was nothing. 'Ben and his friend want a Sunday picnic. And propriety requires a chaperone.'

Did a wink accompany that remark, or was it just a tic? Definitely. A wink.

Her heart skipped a little, as she was trying to decide whether she should be pleased or dismayed. There was a familiarity in that wink that was almost insulting. But then she remembered, embarrassed, how tightly she had wrapped her arms around him and how solid and reassuring his body had felt as they fled a city under siege. Familiarity there too. He had shown nothing but kindness to her; still, there was something in him – his impulse to take charge of whatever situation he was in; the easy way he manipulated those around him – that meant just being in his presence incited a feeling of heightened excitement in her that she had never felt before.

He did not wait for her to give consent but, bowing from the waist, opened the door of the carriage to reveal the prim young Mistress Trapford, clutching her picnic basket in her lap with a white-knuckled grip. The girl was dressed in the plain clothes of the godly, but her simple bonnet and collar were gleaming white and braided in the plain bun beneath that proper bonnet was a string of yellow ribbon. Something about that bit of ribbon was endearing, that and the trusting way she looked at Arthur. At Caroline, she only nodded and smiled, then lowered her thick lashes to cover the bold eyes Caroline remembered.

Arthur reached out for Caroline's hand to help her inside the carriage. 'I hope that you don't think me presumptuous. I thought you deserved an afternoon lark. We all deserve it. And the day is so fine . . .'

'It is a very generous gesture. From all of you.' Caroline forced a smile, trying to include the girl.

'Good day to you, Mistress Caroline. I am glad to see you again,' Patience said, a very becoming blush blooming on her cheeks.

'It is good to see you too,' Caroline said, thinking that she wasn't the only one nervous here.

'How about letting the printer's devil drive?' Arthur said.

'Only if you take an extra pair of hands with you,' Whittier said, with a sideways nod at Patience.

'Always,' the boy laughed. Jumping from the coach, he reached up with his strong arm to assist the girl, who looked as though she needed no assistance whatsoever, so eager was she to escape.

Suddenly alone with him and wondering if she was being manipulated by Arthur or by James Whittier, or both, her backbone so straight against the seatback that she might be giving more support to it than it to her, she resolved to be on her guard.

'Tell me about Arthur's father,' Whittier said as the carriage began to move. 'William Pendleton must have been a remarkable man.'

With that one casual remark from him her resolve loosened – a little.

'He was, my lord, but how would you know that?'

'Because of the remarkable courage that his son – and his wife – have shown in adversity.'

'Remarkable courage?' That was hardly the first attribute that came to mind when she thought of William. Good, compassionate, wise, careful, but courageous? She pondered this for a minute, remembering how his hands shook when he opened the King's summons, but remembering too that he answered it anyway.

'He did have remarkable courage,' she said. Disarmed by the question, she blinked hard and looked down at her hands clasped primly in her lap. 'Not fearless as are some, loving the fight for the sake of the fight, rushing out in eagerness to meet the enemy. But if by courage you mean right action taken in the face of trepidation, then, yes, he was very courageous. I miss his quiet strength most of all.'

'That is exactly what I mean. Ben has that kind of courage. The way he refuses to allow the loss of his arm to stop him; the way he doesn't wallow in pity, or become bitter. And since you are not his natural mother, I can only assume he inherited that courage from his father.'

Diverted from her surge of grief by his comment about Ben, she looked up. Whittier was watching her with a calculating eye, almost like a hunter stalking a deer. An inappropriate comparison, she thought, when he had been nothing but kind to them, yet there was something about him that incited a kind of restless longing that she could not quite define. It was a disconcerting feeling. She turned her gaze to the open window, but not really seeing, not noticing that they had left behind the winding lanes of the crowded city for the wider green expanses of greater London.

'I am very grateful to you, Lord Whittier, for your kindness to Ben. And for your kindness to me. You very well may have saved my life and most certainly much distress.'

'Please. Call me James. I am lord of nothing except my own decisions. I expect we are kindred spirits in that regard. I shall call you Caroline and you will call me James. As for gratitude, you don't know me very well. I don't usually go out of my way to play hero. Self-interest is more in my nature. From the beginning I saw something in Ben that I knew would serve both of us. He is turning out to be a remarkable printer.'

'And the two newsboys you shelter?'

He shrugged, 'They hustle my ink. It is a trade that serves us all.'

'And rescuing a lonely, frightened woman on a fruitless search, how was that in your best interest, my lo . . . James?'

'I don't know. The impulse of a man following a beautiful

woman into the night?' He grinned. 'That is not so hard to understand. And then when I heard your story at the garrison, I became intrigued because I knew then, or thought I knew . . .' he paused, glancing away briefly, as if considering some inward impulse before continuing, '. . . that the man you were seeking was probably already dead.'

Had she heard right?

'You knew William was already dead? How is that possible unless . . .' But she couldn't say it.

'Unless I killed him? No. I have many sins blotting my account, but murder is not one. I never saw his body or knew who killed him or even for sure that he had been killed. But the same night I encountered you inside the city wall at the Reading Garrison guardhouse, I had been playing at cards with a man who carried the same pistol that was in your possession – or one just like it. You told Lord Aston it was one of a pair. When I had admired its mate earlier in the evening, the man said he took it off a dead man.'

'Why did you not tell me then?' She looked straight into his eyes, her gaze demanding an answer.

'Would you have believed me? A stranger? And I had no way of knowing for sure. But I did know that you were in danger and in no condition to continue the search, and that if you had a home and some place where people loved you, you needed to be with them when you learned that you were a widow. If I was wrong in that assumption, I apologize.'

She could not speak for the great lump in her throat, remembering that night, the fear, the futile hope. When the horses pulled to a stop, she was facing the window, looking out over the wide green meadow that led down to a lake in the distance, but not really seeing it.

'It appears that we have arrived at our destination,' he said, breaking the silence. 'I'll just help secure the horses.'

His self-assurance seemed a little threadbare, she thought as he stepped out. Ben, wreathed in smiles, was at the door offering to help her down. Of course, Ben did not know what she had just learned, how fate had conspired to bring the three of them together . . . the four of them, she corrected herself, as she looked up to see John Milton's housekeeper standing behind him. The wind had pulled tendrils from beneath the girl's bonnet, framing her face, and even her eyes were smiling as she reached in and, with strong arms, pulled the picnic basket out.

It just seemed to happen that they walked in pairs down to the lake.

'Sorry,' James said, spreading a blanket. 'It has a bit of ink on it. You don't have to worry. It won't wipe off. It won't even wash out with lye and hot water. I've tried.'

'I am not afraid of a little ink,' Caroline said, just for something to say as she helped him spread the corners.

He laughed, 'I think that is a very good thing, since everything in my life seems to have ink stains.'

She ignored the subtle invitation there. Or was that just her suspicious nature? Maybe it wasn't meant to be flirtatious at all.

'This looks quite a feast,' Caroline said, as Patience and Ben unpacked the basket: cheese and pickles and fresh bread and slices of roast fowl. 'Wherever did you find the greens?' Caroline asked, thinking of the scarcity of all produce in the markets.

'They are fresh-picked this morning,' Patience said. 'I keep a little patch behind Mr Milton's back door.'

Ah. Mr Milton. The uninvited fifth guest, Caroline thought, remembering Mary and the hateful divorce papers. The publication that their host facilitated. And her stepson too, if she was honest. How could Arthur stomach Patience's association with the man? But, she thought bitterly, what real choice did either of them have?

'And my contribution – French red,' James said, producing a large bottle and four glasses. 'Now don't worry about the expense, Caroline. I mention the vintner—'

'From time to time in my broadsheets,' Caroline chimed in, laughing despite herself.

She took a sip eagerly, savoring it. 'I haven't had French wine since . . . well, in a very long time.'

It was indeed a fine picnic, especially in these hard times. The food was fresh and good, the fowl roasted to perfection. Ben and Patience joked and teased each other like children. It was all so carefree, an interlude out of time in grim London, she thought, her mood warmed by the day, the company, the wine. The only reminder of the war was how few people were enjoying the park: no children playing *pallemaille* on the green, no lovers strolling together – if one didn't count Ben and Patience, who were walking down to the lake with the leftover crumbs to feed the few skinny ducks.

'Well,' James laughed. 'It seems our companions have abandoned us,' he said. 'What shall we talk about?'

Emboldened by the wine, or the sunshine, or just her realization that she needed to take control of the conversation before he did, she answered quickly, 'Let us talk about you, James. Tell me how you came to be a printer, and I am especially interested in how you decide what is worthy to print.'

'Ah,' he said with a smile. '*The Doctrine and Discipline of Divorce*. I wondered when we'd visit that subject again.' He lifted the bottle, but when she declined, he emptied it into his own cup. 'First things first. You are entitled to know a little of my history.'

Why would she be 'entitled to know'?

'When I woke up one morning to find myself suddenly a penniless lord, my older brother having squandered what remained of our father's fortune before his own untimely death, I realized that I needed a livelihood. Being truly not suited for the Anglican Church, for which I was Cambridge trained, or the military, for which I had absolutely no inclination, I was faced with a conundrum. One day, not long after I had been glancing at a broadsheet and thinking there was so very little in it that was, as you say, "worthy" of print, I remembered hearing that my great-great – one of the greats – grandmother on my mother's side once owned a print shop in Paternoster Row. I spent a few days considering whether ink might run in my blood too. I decided that would be as worthwhile and lucrative a venture as any.'

'But if you were penniless, how did you get the funds for the press and the ink and the paper?'

'Well, I . . .' he paused, appearing distracted by a bird pecking at discarded crumb he tossed its way, '. . . that's a story for another time. We shall just say that I had a string of good luck.'

He didn't have to say. She thought she knew. As upset as she had been that first day she had encountered him in the coaching inn, she remembered there had been a table of card players. It was all a blur, more dream than memory. She couldn't remember seeing him there but, in her imagination, she could see him there.

'Cards or dice?'

'Both, but I prefer cards. More skill, less luck,' he answered, looking a little taken aback.

'Do you always have good luck?'

'Not lately,' he said, frowning. 'But I am expecting that to change. You play the law of averages and limit your losses. But, most importantly, you must be able to read people. I am pretty good at that. But it is not the way I want to make my living.'

'And what of the second part of my question?'

'Second part?' He sipped his wine and paused, as if considering his answer. 'Yes, Mr Milton and his worthiness. I have lately come to the opinion – no, it is more than an opinion . . . I have come to the belief that if a man is denied his voice, then he is denied his freedom, and if he is denied his freedom, he is denied his God-given right to his own soul. And that is a true sacrilege.'

What a mind-bending notion, that even fools and insidious ideas should be allowed an audience. And he delivered it with such sincerity, not pausing long enough for her to offer this observation.

'Who am I to decide whether Mr Milton's diatribe was worthy? He came to me because his voice was being suppressed. His argument was cogent, even sound, and his rhetorical worthiness well established. His contention slandered no person. Forgive me if I did not then have the personal perspective on it that I have since gained. But I did not endorse his argument. I merely allowed him a channel in which to offer his views in the marketplace of ideas by printing it when others would not.'

Marketplace of ideas. A strange expression. As if ideas could be traded, bought and sold like goods. If he was so intent on voices, she would let him hear hers. 'So, you think then a man's voice should be heard even when it slanders?'

'Slander? That has no basis outside your private knowledge of Mistress Milton and exists only in that personal scheme. As we have already discussed, John Milton did not call his wife's name or even say that his argument was predicated on personal experience. He merely made a broad argument for opportunity of divorcement on grounds of incompatibility by showing rather pointedly, I thought, the suffering that can ensue from a bad match.'

She opened her mouth to protest but he held up his hand in a halting gesture.

'Mistress Milton also has a voice. If she should wish to use it, then I will of course provide her a channel in which to do so.'

'If the authorities don't shut you down for illegal printing first,' she said.

'That,' he said, 'is a risk we are prepared to take. For the time being . . . I believe that while it is unfortunately true that people sometimes get hurt when we wage war with words, there is much less blood-letting than when men wage war with guns and knives. I say "we" because Ben has worked very hard with me on a new project dealing with issues of persecution and freedom, which also will not be well received by Parliament. You should be very proud of him, Caroline.'

'I am. I always have been. Even when he defied his father and joined Parliament's cause, though I did not agree with him, I understood. I listened and even agreed on some points. And I was proud of him for standing up for what he believed. Though when I see what he has lost,' she said, bitterness in her tone, 'I wish we had locked him up until the war was over.'

'Then he would have been locked up for a very long time. But I don't think you really mean that,' he said. 'A boy cannot become a man if his most sincere decisions are obstructed. And even the voices of the young deserve to be heard. They are not always wrong. And speaking of the young,' he said, glancing sideways toward the lake, 'they will be back soon.'

He reached out and took her hand. 'We are wasting this interlude.' She should have withdrawn her hand, would later wonder that she had not. 'I find talking with you very stimulating, Caroline. I think you and I are a lot alike in that we are both survivors. Whenever I engage with a strong, intelligent woman, I cannot help but be in sympathy with Milton's argument. Even if a wife is beautiful, obedient, and dutiful, a man needs something more.'

She still did not withdraw her hand. The moment had become

suddenly so abruptly intimate, so personal, she was frozen in it, like a startled rabbit.

He leaned forward and kissed her.

She broke away, but not quickly enough not to taste the wine on his lips, not quickly enough to fail to realize she had never been kissed like that before.

The look on his face was bewilderment. He was not a man used to rejection, she supposed. He just looked at her as if he was due an explanation.

'You must not get the wrong idea,' she said, her cheeks burning with embarrassment. 'I . . . I still feel like a married woman. I will always be indebted to you, but not . . . not enough to dishonor my husband's memory.'

'I don't want a woman who is *indebted* to me,' he said with some pique. 'I can't believe you think me such a churl that I would exploit your situation or whatever kindness you think I have done for you. I can only plead that I was simply overcome by the moment. I understand. William has only been gone a few months. I should have been sensitive of that. Though I do dare hope, Caroline, that at some point we might be more than friends. I would be less than honest with you, if I did not tell you that.'

She heard Ben's distant laughter, glanced at the two of them, strolling back, captured in a pastoral scene, a portrait torn from the fraying fabric of another time. Another place.

'But for the time being, please be assured that I will settle for the pure pleasure of your company, whenever and wherever you should deign to give it.'

Not really knowing how to answer such a declaration, Caroline said, 'We should gather up the picnic things.'

He got up to help her gather the plates and napkins.

'Friends then?' he asked. Then grinned, as if what had passed between them was trivial, but weighting even that with intimacy by adding, 'But good friends, yes?'

She nodded and murmured, 'Yes, of course, Lord Whittier, friends,' she said casually, busying herself with folding the blanket as carefully as if it were an altar cloth. He reached to take it from her, just brushing her hand with his. It was almost like an electric shock between them.

She would try to avoid being alone with him again. 'Would you mind driving us home, James?' she said. 'Arthur said he wanted me to get to know Patience better. I think she will be more comfortable if Arthur is riding in the carriage too.'

He cocked his head to one side and looked at her knowingly. 'Whatever my very good friend desires,' he said.

ARRIVALS AND DEPARTURES

Cromwell's own division had a hard pull of it; for they were charged by Rupert's bravest men both in front and flank; they stood at the sword's point a pretty while, hacking one another; but at last (it so pleased God) he (Cromwell) brake through them, scattering them before him like dust.

Scoutmaster-General Watson to Henry Overton,
after the Battle of Marston Moor, 2 July 1644

16 June 1644

'The babe is crowning, Your Majesty. Once more. Push. Now,' the midwife insisted.

'*Je ne peux pas! Aides-moi. Je sui trop faible. S'il vous plaît, s'il vous plaît,*' each plea accented with a breath.

It was Anne Villiers, Lady Dalkeith, and not the midwife, who had been standing behind the birthing chair for the last eight hours, crooning to her, gently wiping Henrietta's brow.

'Yes you can,' she said. 'You must, for the sake of your child.'

'For the sake of the King's child,' Henrietta said, tasting the blood on her lips where she'd bitten into them. Drawing a deep breath, as if she could breathe in strength, she asked, 'Did you remember to light the candles for St Margaret?'

'I have checked them every hour. They are burning brightly.'

Another wave of pain crouched, waiting to pounce and maul. Henrietta tightened her grip on Lady Dalkeith's hand, feeling the soft flesh give beneath her nails, but she could not let go. Anne flinched, but neither woman lessened her grip as Henrietta pushed and screamed.

Henrietta had not been all that pleased to see the grandniece of the late Lord Buckingham when she had arrived at Bedford House; had even thought of refusing her when she offered to stay in the birthing room. But Genevieve had said they needed her, pointing out that the chatelaine of Bedford House was too fussy and there were no other ladies-in-waiting to assist. Feeling foolish and a little petty, Henrietta had conceded. Now it was Anne Villiers whose hand she gripped as another wave of wrenching pain swept through her body, taking with it her last vestige of strength and determination.

'*Appelez le docteur!* Cademan must cut the babe out of me. The King's child must not die!'

The midwife dragged a bloody sleeve across her face, wiping the sweat that dripped down her nose. 'For God's sake, someone open a window. And tell Sir Thomas that we are past women's work here. The Queen requires his scalpel.'

Genevieve flung open a window and rushed from the room to search for the doctor. When she returned to the chamber, doctor in tow, the Queen, pale and still as death, was slumped in the birthing chair. The midwife was already at work kneeling over the child. 'The King's child lives. She appears healthy and none the worse for the extended labor. Give your attention to the Queen,' she said to Thomas Cademan.

Anne and Genevieve half carried, half dragged her, supporting her on their shoulders. They positioned her gently on the bed, bending her legs at the knee, covered her with clean linen. Clean linen between her legs too. She heard Sir Thomas giving instructions and Anne answering him, their words broken as if they floated through bubbles. *I want to see the baby*, but her lips would not move. She was only half conscious of hands working on her body.

A tall shadow moved from the end of the bed and hovered. The hand that pressed at her throat smelled of vinegar and herbs.

'She has a pulse . . . weak . . . bleeding heavily,' he said. Then, his voice louder, he asked, 'You gave her blue cohosh? Where did you get it?'

'From a local apothecary. He said it came from Nicholas Culpeper in London. I thought it would strengthen the contractions. Her labor was long. And she was already weak when it started.'

'That explains the excessive bleeding,' he said. 'Your decision was justified. It probably saved the child's life, but she is very weak. The Queen is a woman whose will is stronger than her constitution, and she is no longer young.'

The words formed in her mind, but she could not voice them. *I am here. Don't talk about me as if I am dead.*

'I have packed the cavity with a cotton compress. The flow seems less vigorous than it did. I will check on her throughout the night. I think she will sleep, but if she stirs put two drops of this beneath her tongue. Be precise. More could kill her. It is Culpeper's tincture of poppy and very pure. You have had a long day, but you have not finished. I suggest you take turns here. We do not know how long the Queen will need a constant watch.'

Henrietta struggled to speak. The words were close. So close.

'The baby. Does the child live?' Could they hear? Did she say the words out loud?

'Your Grace.' She felt the pressure of the doctor's hand forcing her shoulders back into the pillow as she struggled to lift herself up. 'You have given the King another beautiful Princess,' he said.

'I wish to hold her,' she whispered.

Thomas Cademan nodded. 'Just for a minute. You need to rest. We will take care of the babe.' He gently lifted her head and shoulders up onto the pillows.

'*Merci*, Sir Thomas. *Merci d'avoir sauvé mon enfant.*'

'I did not save your child. God saved your child. And you did the hard work. Her entry into the world was easier for her than for you. She is breathing well, and all her parts are perfect.'

The midwife had finished cleaning and swaddling the infant. When Henrietta looked down at the tiny little girl in her arms, tears streamed down her face, so many tears, she could not stop them. The baby screwed up her rosebud mouth and started to whimper.

'What is wrong with her?' Henrietta asked, her heart racing.

'She is a very healthy infant, Your Majesty. She feels her mother's heart beating. She is trying to suckle.'

'Minette. *Ma petite* Minette,' Henrietta said. 'I have nothing for you.'

'Shhh. Do not worry, Your Grace. You must rest. The nurse-maid is standing by.' He looked at the midwife with a question in his eyes.

'Lady Dalkeith has secured a good woman from the village, capable of both nursing and taking care of the princess,' the midwife said, 'but today another nurse arrived. She said she was sent by Anne of Austria, Queen of France, from the royal nursery. Madame Peronne.' She reached down and took the child, who was crying loudly now. 'Which would you prefer to have primary care of the infant?'

'The French one,' Henrietta said, her arms falling back upon the bed like dry sticks as she released her daughter.' *So that she will learn to sing in her mother's tongue.* She did not say that aloud, did she?

'Both women are waiting in the nursery. Lady Dalkeith will take the child to her and we will use the village nurse for feeding and swaddling.' He motioned toward the midwife and handed her the squalling infant. 'Let me put this tincture under your tongue, Your Majesty. It will help you to sleep and regain your strength, so you can care for your child.' The drops tasted bitter. 'It will make you feel better.'

The doctor picked up each of the little bottles the midwife had laid out. 'Use the herbal salve when the bleeding stops.'

To Henrietta the room looked as though it was melting around her. Sir Thomas's voice faded away, the words coming and going.

'All . . . is good . . . little of the elderberry syrup . . . clove . . . complain of cold . . . a lot of blood . . . red wine laced with honey and cinnamon. No blessed thistle . . . increases mother's milk . . . too weak . . .'

Henrietta's mind faded into oblivion then and she dreamed strange dreams with vivid colors, bloody reds and bright yellows and deep greens, swirling in and out and around, drawing her into their black center. Sometimes she heard people talking and sometimes thought she felt wet swabs on her tongue.

On the third day, she awoke to a strange woman by her bedside spooning tiny bits of calf's-foot jelly into her mouth. It tasted of salt and broth. The woman called Henrietta's name and explained in blessed French that Her Royal Majesty, Anne of Austria and Queen of France, sent greetings to her beloved sister-in-the-law and her best wishes for a soon-to-be reunion. She proved herself a worthy and determined nurse, insisting that Henrietta get up every day and walk in the garden. She prepared her food herself and limited the time the Queen spent with the baby, so that she did not get too tired, all the while keeping a watchful eye on the nursemaid. When Henrietta protested – even though it was truly wonderful to be pampered – that she wished madame would care for the child, the nurse retorted that the child was thriving under the care of Madame Villiers and the nursemaid. '*J'ai été envoyé pour prendre soin de vous,*' she said. And take care of her she did. Henrietta was grateful.

As Henrietta's strength returned, so did some of her optimism. She had heard from Charles, who had sent her a letter celebrating the birth of the little Princess, filled with sweet endearments. It was accompanied by an exquisite pair of embroidered boots, fit enough even for the French court, he said. He said also that he hoped to see her again before she left for the Continent and could not wait to hold her and the babe in his arms. She had to call for Henry Jermyn to interpret the code for the rest of it. Her head ached just trying to decipher it. Charles was always changing the code.

Henry glanced at the letter briefly and reported the gist of what it said. Since Newcastle and Prince Rupert were securing the North and trying to open a path for Lord Montrose's Highlander Catholic troops to counter the Covenanters, the King was leading a regiment of horse into the West Country to protect their garrisons from Essex. He hoped she would not have to leave for Falmouth Harbor before he arrived.

Henry had looked up then and said a little reluctantly, 'And His Majesty also says that he wishes to have the child baptized into the Church of England as soon as you can arrange it.'

'But the King is not here, is he?' she said.

'He also says that you should not wait for his coming, and to see that it is done "with all speed."'

She should not have been surprised. Charles had always insisted on the Anglican baptism with every child, and she had complied – after the child had secretly been baptized by a priest. She had done that with the first child – and thank the Blessed Virgin she had, because that first little Princess had died, and her soul would exist forever in Limbo if she had not. What did it really matter if all her children's births were listed in Church of England records? That church had no authority in holy matters and their baptism was hardly more than a bath and an English legality. Though admittedly the surreptitious Catholic baptism had been much easier in her chapel at Somerset House with her own priest.

'There is no hurry. The King is not here.'

The look in Henry Jermyn's eyes betrayed his understanding. 'I doubt that Lady Dalkeith is acquainted with any Catholic priests. She is devoutly Church of England.'

'Henry, you have always gone out of your way to befriend me, even at times of great danger to yourself. You know how important this is to me,' she whispered as though the walls had ears.

'Yes, Your Majesty, I do,' he said with a sigh. 'I can try to find a recusant priest somewhere in the village. I shall make discreet inquiries.' Then suddenly his aspect brightened. 'I believe I should start with the good doctor. What do you think?'

She nodded and smiled her agreement.

That very evening, whilst Henrietta was enjoying her time alone with her little Minette, a tall man of some years dressed in everyday britches and shirt was ushered in by Henry Jermyn. He was carrying a small satchel. He looked startled when he saw the Queen, but he did not question or comment except to say, 'I am Father Andrew, Your Highness. I understand you require a private christening.'

Henrietta smiled her gratitude to him. 'It is necessary, Father Andrew.' Turning to Jermyn she said, 'Lord Jermyn, will you please summon Madame Peronne? She will witness the baptism.'

While he was gone, the priest withdrew from the bag his vestments and little silver vials of oil and blessed water. 'Is this the prepared space?' he asked, motioning to the altar with candles and crucifix that Henrietta had set up in a small corner of her chamber.

'It was the best I could do,' she said, doing a mental inventory in her mind: a small silver bowl to hold the holy water for pouring, a larger bowl beneath to catch the water, a basin of clean water for the priest to bathe his hands in, bits of bread to remove the anointing oil from his fingertips, and even an embroidered white linen handkerchief to cover the infant's head.

'It will do,' he said, donning his purple stole. 'She feels warm,' he said, taking the child in his arms.

'I was perhaps holding her too closely. She has been healthy.'

Madame Peronne entered the room, quietly, closing the door behind her, saying only, 'Lord Jermyn will not be present. He was called away by a messenger.'

'You will be witness then?' he asked the nurse.

'*Oui.*'

'Then let us begin.'

The child was quiet in the beginning as though asleep. '*Exi ab ea, immunde . . .*' Even as the priest made the sign of the cross with his thumb on her forehead and breast, she did not stir. But when he poured the holy water over her head, she opened her eyes and howled. Father Andrew continued chanting the liturgy as if this was not an altogether unusual occurrence. At first Henrietta was not disturbed by it either. Prince Charles had howled, and James had released a noxious amount of gas, but by the time the priest finished the last *Pax Tecum* this child was shivering and wailing, that intense, breathless crying that signals trouble.

Even the priest looked concerned as he handed the child to Madame Peronne. 'She may be feverish.'

'According to the nursemaid she was colicky earlier. How was she with you?' she asked Henrietta.

'Slept in my arms like an angel.'

'I will bathe her limbs in cool water, while keeping her body covered. A few drops of elderflower or yarrow tea on her lips might help bring her fever down if she has one. It can do no harm. *Ne vous inquiétez pas, Votre Majesté.*'

But it was hard not to worry. She remembered another baby girl who had failed to thrive all those years ago, even as she tried not to think that this baptism might have happened just in time.

After the nurse had carried the child away, Father Andrew stood by the door, sans vestments, sans official demeanor, just an ordinary workman in plain working clothes.

Not sure of the protocol but suddenly remembering that this was no house priest, she said, 'Father, I have no money to offer, but please know that this day you have rendered a great service

to the Queen of England, who will always be a loyal daughter
of the Holy Roman Catholic Church.'

'It was my honor, Your Grace. Lord Jermyn made a generous
contribution to my ministry.'

God bless Henry Jermyn, she thought.

When the blessed one returned she was removing the basin,
the silver bowls, the white lace cloth that covered her dear child's
head, lest the accoutrements be noticed and commented on by
the servants. 'No need to apologize for your absence, my lord,
I know in these difficult times your involvement in a clandestine
Catholic rite could be dangerous.'

She looked up from her chore to tell him how much she
appreciated his service. But his aspect stopped her. His face was
as white as a snow hare. He just stood there, looking at her.

'What is it, Henry? Why so pale? The priest. He was discovered.'

'No. The priest was not discovered, Your Grace. But I have
just received a message from the Northern Front, and I am afraid
the news is . . . devastating.'

Her heart squeezed. 'Not Charles. Not my sons.'

'No. Not as bad as that. Calm yourself. But the North has
been lost. When daylight broke this morning, four thousand of
the Prince's finest soldiers lay dead on a muddy field in York, at
a place called Marston Moor. It was the worst battle of the war
so far. Witnesses said the fighting was hell and that General
Cromwell, aided by a few of Lord Leven's Covenanter Scots,
ruled that hell.'

Her first thought was to thank God that Charles was headed
west with his battalion. But Henrietta knew the strategic importance of such a loss. With Montrose's loss, loyal Scots Catholics
would never find their way to joining the fight. Ports closed.
Resources denied.

'The King's nephew and the Earl of Newcastle?' she asked.

'Newcastle has fled the country in shame. Rupert escaped
through a cornfield. But you know that little white poodle he
carried with him like a talisman. He was a casualty.'

'*Mon dieu. C'est triste.* Prince Rupert loved that dog like a
child, carried him into battle for years on the Continent. He
thought as long as Boye was with him, he could not lose.'

'That's what the Protestants thought too. Some of the print

rags called him a devil's familiar. The superstitious fools will be as emboldened by the dog's loss as much as by the Royalist dead.'

'Rupert's sorrow will be boundless, and his grief will distract him. What of Essex?' she asked, hoping for some good news at least. 'Please say he lies dead somewhere in that muddy field.'

'Further bad news, Your Majesty. Essex was not there. He is on his way to lay siege to every Royalist stronghold between Devon and Land's End. Soon. I think we are still ahead of him, but only just. You must get to Pendennis Castle in Falmouth. It is well fortified and will be one of the last to fall. With the loss of the North, the northeastern ports will be closed. Falmouth Harbor will be our only escape route to the Continent.'

'But Charles is on his way. He will stop him.'

'With Rupert's losses, it will be hard to stop him. The King will be outnumbered. How soon can you be ready to depart?'

'Depart? Before Charles gets here? It is not yet safe to take the baby. I think she might even have a fever. And I am still not strong.'

'Then you will have to leave her here.'

'Leave her! I will not. How can you even suggest—?'

'It is for her own safety as well as yours. If Essex's men come here and find you gone, they will not search for the child. If they capture her with you, what will that mean for you and her? Here she is safe, and Lady Dalkeith has already proven her loyalty, as has your doctor. He will stay here as he is needed to tend to the child's physical needs. Madame Peronne will go with you to tend to yours. When the war is over, and you return, your daughter will be here waiting for you.'

'But what if . . .?' She could not allow herself to even think it, let alone say it. She did not have to.

'Then, Lady Dalkeith will bring her to you in France.'

'You have it all figured out, don't you?' She couldn't help the bitterness in her voice, even though she knew it was misdirected. What could he know, what could any man know of how hard it would be to abandon the flesh of your flesh, the heart of your heart.

'It is my job to figure it out. I have thought of nothing else since I received this message an hour ago.'

'I know,' she said, not looking at him. 'I will give you my answer in the morning. I cannot even think on it now. I must rest.'

'In the morning then. No later. I beg you.'

'Tell Anne Villiers I wish to see her. And tell her to bring her Protestant Bible.'

The next morning, having procured Lady Dalkeith's oath of loyalty to the young Princess and to the Queen, as well as her promise to act as godmother at the formal christening, Henrietta left Bedford House for Pendennis Castle. For all the latter's formidable fortifications, she did not tarry. The sooner she made it to Paris, the sooner she could persuade her brother that he must send money and troops to Charles's aid.

On 14 July 1644, a wool merchant with his 'wife and two of her sisters' sailed out of Falmouth Harbor on an unremarkable Dutch merchant vessel loaded with wool sacks. The four were the only passengers. The crossing was uneventful.

When they disembarked in Calais, Henrietta squealed with delight. '*Regarde*, Henry. *La crête de Bourbon. C'est le chariot royal.*'

'And look who is driving, Your Majesty.' Henrietta clapped her hands and laughed as Jeffrey Hudson, on the coachman's seat, blew his horn.

Young Henry Percy, in full footman's livery, leaped down and with a sweeping bow, said, 'Welcome to your home away from home, Your Majesty.'

'As we are all to be in exile together,' she said, 'let us make the most of it, *mes amis*. We shall find it more hospitable than Den Haag, I am certain.'

But though her words were hopeful, she remembered all she had left behind and wondered how she could bear it.

BLOODY PERSECUTION

*God requireth not an uniformity of Religion to be enacted
and enforced in any civill state; which enforced uniformly
(sooner or later) is the greatest occasion of civill warre,
ravishing of conscience, persecution of Christ Jesus in his
servants and of the hypocrise and destruction of millions
of souls.*

Roger Williams in *The Bloudy Tenent of Persecution
for Cause Of Conscience*

'Y ou are late today. I was just about to close the line and
clean up,' Caroline said to two Scottish soldiers who
lined up with their bowls at the guildhall kitchen. 'The
stew is thin. With so many of your ranks away in the fields, I
never know how much to cook. I wish you had come sooner,'
she said, fishing with her ladle for the last bits of meat and
vegetables. 'Why are you so late? Are you just back from the
battle in the North?'

'We have been assigned to latrine duty on the London perimeter
until His Lordship tells us different.'

That accounted for the smell. 'McDuff too? Is he coming?'

Of all the Scots who came through the food line, the cocky
young McDuff with his infectious good humor was her favorite.
She handed his usual companions steaming bowls of stew.
Their shared glances showed some discomfort, as though it was
a hard question. Finally, one of them said, 'McDuff be not here,
mistress.'

'Well I can see that,' she said, handing each a chunk of bread.
It was plain that they didn't know how to answer her. 'He wasn't
killed in the battle?'

'No. Not killed in the battle,' the younger one said, shooting
a glance at his companion.

'Thou best ask Lord Leven where young McDuff is,' the older one interjected roughly. Taking their bowls and bread, they went past the few stragglers who lingered and sat alone at the back of the hall.

'There is pudding,' she called.

They did not even look up. Just in case, she set out two plates of flat honey cake. McDuff was probably being disciplined for some prank or other. Maybe they were too, since they had been given such hard duty. She hoped he was not ill, she thought, as she dipped her ladle into the dregs one more time. Less than a cupful left, but with bread for dipping, that would do for her supper. She was almost too tired to eat anyway. Ever since the first returns from Marston Moor, a sadness had hovered over the usually boisterous lot, infecting her spirits as well. Though there had been casualties, at least they had won the battle. She would have thought they would be strutting and celebrating.

By the time she had eaten and cleaned the last pot, the sun was almost setting. Not dark yet. Still time to make the short walk to the print shop. Since the picnic she had seen Ben only once, and that briefly. Ben. Surprising, she thought, how quickly she had adapted to his new name, but not surprising really, when she considered how the war had changed everything. Her life with William, even her life in the London of her youth, seemed like a fading dream. She no longer looked up expecting to see William. Not here. Not in this place. But Ben was in this world. Outwardly the boy she remembered had changed, wounded inside and outside, but she could tell his heart was still the same. She could be at the print shop by deep dusk if she left now. Maybe Ben would walk her home. Time was when she would not have been afraid to walk home alone. But in this London, nobody waved and called out her name, just hurried by, grim faces turned toward home, as if the shadows hid demons.

She arrived to find the door to the print shop open. She watched him from the street, intent on his work, the muscle in his one arm bulging as he pulled the lever forward then back, before lifting the frame and removing the printed sheet, surveying it carefully through squinted eyes. Then, sighing with satisfaction, he hung it on a line to dry. From the sheets hanging around the room it looked as though he had been at it for a while. When her shadow crossed the threshold, he looked up to see her and smiled broadly.

'Caroline. Just in time. The last copy of the last page of our big print.' He pointed at the neat stacks of folio pages, four images to a sheet, each sheet waiting in its stack to be folded and assembled.

'How many pamphlets will this make?'

'Four hundred,' he said proudly, and then laughed. 'Now all we need do is fold and assemble each one, sew them into folios and send them out to the vendors.'

'That's all? Did you do all this by yourself?'

'Milord helped when he was not hanging around outside the Commons listening for news. And Patience too, when she could get away from Mr Milton. Though she has not had much time lately either, working later and later. Milton is taking on more boarding students. He has leased a bigger house in the Barbican. Patience had to pack up the kitchen and help him pack up his study. Every slate, book and pencil just so.' He picked up a rag and began to clean the type.

'Here, let me at least do that,' she said.

'No, I'm used to it. You might get ink on your clothes. But you can help me fold. No, on second thought,' he said, looking out the window at the afterglow, 'we'd best call it a day's work. It'll be dark soon. Little John and Ralphie will be wanting something to eat. I think I've got some dried beef, if they haven't eaten it all,' he said, as if to himself.

'Dried beef?'

'Yes. Not too bad. You just cut any kind of meat into strips, trim the fat, salt it and dry it over slow coals. It will last for weeks without spoiling. The boys like it, especially when I rub it with crushed herbs and spices before I put it in the embers. Stay and eat with us. You might like it.'

'How did you know how to make it?' she asked in wonderment.

'Roger taught us.'

'Roger?'

'Roger Williams. The man from the colonies who wrote that pamphlet about the Indians.'

Caroline had seen it in the stack of pamphlets accumulating

at the guildhall. She'd not had time to read it, but she had scanned it, thinking she could not imagine living among savages.

'The Narragansett natives taught him the recipe. He brought some with him on his voyage over.' Ben made one last hard rub on the type plate and then threw the ink rag onto a pile. 'Our big project is his newest pamphlet,' he said, pointing to the papers lining the room.

'Did you print the Indian book?'

'No. But we're printing this one. It's sure to raise Parliament's ire. He wanted an unlicensed printer.'

'Isn't that dangerous?'

'Not for him. He's already got his charter for a free province signed and he's headed home. Took ship in April. Probably already there by now, or close to it.'

'Leaving you and Lord Whittier to take the blame.'

'Don't look so alarmed. We haven't put our imprint on it. No crossed swords. And we are not the only unlicensed printers. Just the best. Milord is careful. He doesn't want his press and type confiscated.'

Ben went over to one of the stacks of already dried sheets, and pulling one off the top, handed it to her. 'This will be the cover and first three pages.'

Caroline laid it on the table and sat down to read it. 'Good job with the cover page. I remember James said that you designed it. *The Bloody Tenent of Persecution for Cause of Conscience, Discussed, in a Conference Between Peace and Truth.*'

'Go ahead. Read the introduction.'

She scanned it quickly. It briefly outlined the contents in twelve coherent points.

'I don't think either the Presbyterians or the Anglicans will approve of this,' she said. 'No wonder he couldn't find a licensed printer. This is radical even for these times.' She read aloud, her alarm growing, 'All civil states with their officers of justice in their respective constitutions and administrations are proved essentially civil, and therefore not judges, governors or *defenders* of the spiritual or Christian stand and worship . . . Ben, what if the magistrate showed up right now to inspect your business? You'd be arrested and sent to the Tower.'

'That is a concern, I will admit. That is why we need to get them folded and tied and out to our network of distributors as soon as possible. It's been a slog. If you've some time Sunday afternoon, we could use help with the sewing. Patience is coming to help. The boys can do the folding.'

'And what of James?'

'He'll be crating them up and delivering them to his distributors. Roger only asked for fifty. He said if we bore the expense, we could print as many as we wanted and distribute the rest all over England, saying that was the audience he wanted to reach anyway. He did ask that we keep the profit margin as low as we could, so it would be more widely read. I know what you are thinking. But don't worry, Caroline. If I should be caught, the printer who owns the press is the only one liable. I am just a poor apprentice. They would have no legal grounds to hold me.'

'He's right about that, Caroline,' a voice behind her said. She looked up to see James Whittier standing in the open door. He closed it behind him. 'Don't worry. I will see that Ben and the boys are protected. If I am caught I will confess that the fault is mine and mine alone. But we are not really taking that much risk. By the time Parliament raises an objection and tries to ferret out the printers of unlicensed works – of which we are just one of many – there will be no evidence whatsoever. If they come here, all they will find is a bundle of broadsheets and type being set for another.'

He went over to the drying line. 'Is this the last page?'

'You are looking at the last sheet of the last page.'

Caroline noticed the pride in his voice.

'Good work, Ben,' Whittier said with a broad grin of approval. 'Sorry I wasn't here to help, but I was eavesdropping on the Committee of Three Kingdoms. Got the complete reports of the Battle of Marston Moor for this week's news book.'

'Preliminary reports give it to Parliament forces,' Ben said. 'What will our headline be?'

'Haven't decided yet.' He reached in his tunic pocket and pulled out a sheaf of papers, pitched them to Ben. 'You decide.'

Ben scanned the hastily written scrawl, his eyes widening. 'Royalists lost four thousand men and Parliament only three hundred? Did you leave out a zero?'

'That is the correct number.' His face looked grim. 'Muddy field just outside York. A couple of hours in the early morning rain. Forty-three hundred souls slashing and screaming and praying in the mud and blood and guts amid the sound of big guns and the choking smoke, until many ceased to hear anything at all. Mostly young men, some old. The Earl of Newcastle fled to the Continent in disgrace. Rupert of the Rhine escaped through a cornfield.'

A familiar dread gripped Caroline. If William was ambushed, at least he was spared that kind of carnage.

'The headline will be: Royalists Lose Control of the North. Turning Tide?' Ben said.

'Sounds about right,' James said soberly, then tried to regain his usual demeanor. 'Our boy here has a real knack for cutting to the pulsing heart of the matter.'

She appreciated his praise for Ben, but the assumed familiarity, the possessive 'our' linking them all together was irritating, and yet, if she really admitted it, in an odd way comforting too.

'I have drawn a line under Lord Manchester's Eastern Association,' Whittier said. 'But it was truly not Manchester so much. Lieutenant General Oliver Cromwell and his Ironsides Brigade saved the battle. Cromwell himself was wounded but he led his troops back in. Some credit will accrue to Lord Leven. He was the lead commander since his Covenanter Brigade of Horse, about a thousand strong, was the largest. Some of them broke and ran when the fighting got hot. But he was able to rally the remnants and, with Lord Maitland's regiment, to assist Cromwell.'

'I am not surprised at the Ironsides Brigade,' Ben said. 'I served under Cromwell and I can testify that his men are well-trained. They would never retreat unless ordered to do so, and that order would be slow in coming. General Cromwell is always right there in the thick of it, giving blow for blow.'

'From what I have heard,' Whittier said, 'he is probably the only man as committed to the cause of defeating the King's forces as John Pym was. Now that he is the hero of Marston Moor, his voice in Parliament will be enhanced. Henry Vane, the heir apparent, is no John Pym. He will be looking for a strong voice to fill that void.'

Ben scrunched up his face, that same face Caroline remembered seeing when he was in deep study, often just before arguing with his father. 'That seems like a lot of power for one man to have, political and military; for a man as disciplined as passionate as Cromwell,' he said.

'It is. That is why we will only print the facts of the battle and not let Cromwell's role obscure that of the Scots. All of London doesn't need to be hailing him a hero. Not yet, anyway.' Then he stood up and, wiping his hands together as if dismissing the subject said, 'But we are boring Caroline.'

'I assure you, Lord Whittier, I am not in the least bored. I frequently have contact with the Covenanters whenever they are in the city. Young lads mostly. Some of them conscripted by clan leaders. I had heard a little something about the big battle. They have been straggling in all week. Fewer than before. Were many of them killed?'

'Hard to say how many were killed in the fighting. Leven's troops were decimated at his own command.'

'Decimated?' Caroline said.

'An old military punishment. From the time of the Romans. Whenever a battle was lost, one out of every ten soldiers was killed by the legion commander.'

'You don't mean . . . but the battle wasn't lost.'

'When the fighting heated up, some of the Covenanters fled.'

'And Lord Leven—'

James nodded, 'Just lined them up and counted them off. No trial. No defense.'

'Not killed in the battle' had been the answer to her question about young McDuff. She thought for a moment she was going to be sick. The cheery, always joking boy, scarcely old enough to wield a pike. *Decimated.* A fancy word for murdered. All that youth and energy – he was about Ben's age; all that exuberance, that happy smile, just snuffed out, and to what purpose? Did he have a wife at home? A mother? Maybe even a child of his own who would never know a father?'

'What of the other nine?' she asked, barely able to force out the words.

'Flogged. Shamed. Given hard duty, jobs that nobody else wanted to do.'

'Like latrine duty.' She wasn't even sure she had said it out loud. But from his expression she knew she had. 'Print that in your broadsheet, Lord Whittier, what Lord Leven did. See what the wives and mothers who read your paper will think of such military justice.'

'I understand, Caroline, I do. I agree there should have been a court martial before pronouncing execution. But there is no mercy in war and only crude justice.'

From outside came the sound of querulous voices.

'That will be our boys,' Whittier said, looking relieved to change the subject. 'I picked up a fish pie from a vendor outside Parliament House. Figured Ben would be too busy to think about supper. Got it cheap. She was just closing up shop.'

The door opened and Ralphie and Little John came in still quarreling. 'He didn't even try to sell all his papers.'

'Did too.'

'You should have never taught him his alphabet, Ben. He just leans against the wall trying to pick out the letters and looking for his name.'

'I counted seven in the first paragraph. I saw my name twice,' the youngest boy said.

'I had to sell his papers and mine too.' Ralphie scowled. 'He's a sluggard.'

'Well then. I guess if you have to do all the work, maybe tomorrow, he'll just stay behind with me,' Ben said. 'Help me with the chores and stuff.'

Ralphie's eyes widened in surprise. 'I did not say he shouldn't go. He's my partner. I can't sell the papers by meself.'

'Then in that case, I guess you'll just have to either teach your partner how to sell better – or settle for selling alone.'

Ralphie looked down at his feet, scuffled them back and forth then said grudgingly, 'He does bring in some customers. The women like him. I do all the work and then he collects the money.'

Little John grinned and turned his pockets inside out. A shower of coins fell to the floor.

Ralphie shook his head in disgust. 'Sometimes they even give him an extra ha'penny. But I suppose he deserves something for all them hugs and cheek-pinching.' Ralphie shuddered.

Caroline marveled at how cleverly Ben managed the boys, turning prosecutor into defender.

'Stop your quarreling and mind your manners. We have a visitor,' James said. 'Say hello to Mistress Caroline, Ben's stepmother. I expect you'll be seeing more of her.'

'Stepmom! She's too young to be his . . .' But he broke off at a raised eyebrow from James.

'Are you sleeping at home again tonight, Ralphie?' James asked. Then he turned to Caroline to explain, 'Sometimes Ralphie's father has too much to drink and gets a little unfriendly. But lately, it seems he's found the Lord and the Lord is helping him stay sober.'

Caroline was surprised to hear that godly language as if it was Whittier's everyday parlance, but she supposed he was quoting the boy for the sake of the boy.

Ralphie's eyes grew wide as he explained, 'The preacher says the Lord has wrought a mighty miracle. Seven nights in a row. Me dad's even found work helping build the new meeting house. Me mum is singing again.'

'That is wonderful, Ralphie,' Caroline said, wanting to hug him, but he'd already made plain what he thought of hugs and cheek-pinching.

Ben cut a slice of the pie for Ralphie. 'You need to head out before it gets too dark. Your mum will be worried. Eat this on your way. We'll be expecting you bright and early tomorrow to help with the folding.'

'Looks better than the devil's dried beef,' Ralphie said, and bit into it with a grin.

'I should be going too,' Caroline said. 'I just stopped by to reassure myself that Ben is doing well. Sometimes I can hardly believe he is real,' she said, thinking of McDuff.

'He is very real, Caroline. And doing well, you can rest assured. Please don't leave yet. Ben will be worried if you go back alone after dark. Stay. Share our pie. Ralphie seemed to like it.'

'If she doesn't, there's always dried beef, eh, Johnnie?' Ben said with a wink.

Suddenly reluctant to leave, she said, 'I will stay on one condition. That you allow me to come back on Sunday afternoon and help expedite your new project – Ben has said speed is important – and, since I have already had my supper, Johnnie can have my portion.'

The boy grinned from ear to ear, his thoughts written all over his face. This was so much better than hugs and a cheek-pinching.

It had been a good two weeks for James Whittier. Caroline was as good as her word. She not only came back the following Sunday, but the next Sunday after that. With the four of them, Patience and Ben folding (they always worked as a team), Caroline sewing and James binding the bundles for shipping, *The Bloody Tenent of Persecution* was now for sale in St Paul's Yard and far beyond; as far away as the Netherlands and of course the New England colonies. He agreed with the substance of it and hoped it would be endlessly copied, until it washed up on every shore like the old Tyndale Bibles his grandmother had told him about when he was a boy. He wished he could be there to see the satisfaction on Roger's face when he uncrated it.

There was a lot about the preacher and author he admired. James had never met anyone as confident in his beliefs – or as persistent in defending them. Maybe that was why he left England. To make a place where he would not be required to defend them, at least at the end of a gun. With his banishment from Massachusetts, things had not turned out exactly as he had hoped. But the man was nothing if not persistent – and optimistic. He had invited James to go back with him. 'When you no longer feel free here to live by your conscience,' he'd said. James was already feeling it, though now he had more to keep him here than ever.

He had been scratching about in his mind for days to find an excuse to keep seeing Caroline now that their big project was finished. He couldn't confess that he was totally, completely besotted with her. That would scare her away. She was not like the women he had known; women whose affections were given on a whim or traded for favors. He was sure, after his clumsy blunder in the park, she would have avoided him forever, had it not been for wanting to keep her connection with Ben. Later, when Ben mentioned that her hours had been cut back at the guildhall kitchen because so many of the soldiers had gone to besiege Newcastle, the importance of that bit of war information to his pursuit of Caroline did not really hit him. He was reading his competitor's Thursdays weekly *Intelligencer*, the London edition of *Mercurius Civicus* – since the Licensing Act it had become Parliament's propaganda tool and a most unlikely source of inspiration – when he got the germ of a strategy.

The header promised: *Truth Impartially Related from Hence to the Whole Kingdom to Prevent Misinformation.* The irony of that made him laugh out loud. But reading the article about the siege of Newcastle, he remembered how Caroline talked about the young Scottish soldiers and how few came to the guildhall now. He should have thought then of the opportunity that circumstance presented, but he had been preoccupied with thinking about the implications of the paper's capitulation to parliamentary pressure.

The pandering slant of the article disgusted him. It severely criticized the Scots for being slow in capturing the northern town, mentioning too how some Covenanters had deserted at the battle at Marston Moor. Omitting the part played by the Scots in the victory at Marston Moor, their coming to Cromwell's aid, with no mention of the missing Essex or Manchester in the crucial siege, was not 'Truth Impartially Related.' It was clear to James that Parliament was using its mouthpiece oracle to turn sentiment against the Scots in justification of their neglect in paying them under the terms of the covenant. But fear-mongering or not, if Lord Leven's extraordinary discipline could not inspire his soldiers to take the impregnable fortress, it would indeed be a brutal winter. James had been to Newcastle. Its medieval walls were ten feet thick and surrounded by a ditch bigger than the one around London. No way to penetrate it with limited artillery. Lord Leven was charged with mining the walls. James pitied the poor souls who had to set those mines so that the walls would crumble, and a black river of coal could flow south.

And then it hit him. Of course. While the Scots were engaged with Newcastle, and most of London's Trained Bands were guarding the ever-widening circle around London, troops boarded and fed in relatively secure London would be few. That meant Caroline's income would suffer. Being patient, when he wanted something as he wanted her, was not his long suit, but he was determined to practice it. Everything about her appealed to him. Not just her body or her eyes or the shape of her mouth – though he took pleasure in just watching the way she tilted her head when she laughed, or walked across the room, or swept her hair away from her face – but he thought that if he were blind and deaf, he would know when she entered the room. Of all the women he had known, she was the one who he imagined might sustain his interest for a lifetime.

His plan was simple. He would offer her work in the print shop to supplement her lost wages. Or, better yet, get Ben to offer it to her on his behalf. And when she accepted the offer, as surely she would, if only to be nearer Ben, James would be patient. He would bind her to him gradually, make her feel safe, earn her respect and friendship. But there were a couple of obstacles to the happy outcome he envisioned: one was her fierce loyalty to her dead husband, and the other was the small matter of their initial meeting of which, thank God, she seemed to have no memory. The former he was confident would fade with time, provided there was time. And the other? He would consider later how best to overcome that one. But one thing was sure. He would have to tell her. There should be no secrets between them.

THE POWER OF WORDS

Give me the liberty to know, to utter, and to argue freely according to conscience, above all liberties.

From *Areopagitica*: A Speech of Mr John Milton, for the Liberty of Unlicensed Printing to the Parliament of England, 1644

The back door of the shop was open to the light and to draw the breeze through, but so intent was she on her task that Caroline did not hear the clattering of horses and cartwheels against the cobblestone street outside, nor did she hear the printer's footfalls when Lord Whittier returned. She looked up to see him peering over her shoulder.

'You are really very fast at this. Only three weeks and you are already setting type.' He looked approvingly at the neat rows. 'Faster than Ben. He was right to suggest hiring you.'

'Ben is a good teacher,' she said, thinking that after all she had two hands, so she should be twice as fast. 'I wanted to show you that I can do something besides file the letter blocks and sweep. Does this mean I am a printer's devil now?'

'Oh no. You are much too . . .' he paused as if searching for the word, 'kind to be anybody's devil. I was going to say beautiful, but I thought you might take offense and think me too forward. Come to think of it,' he said with a grin, 'I've known some beautiful women who surely were apprenticed to the devil.'

I'll wager you have, she thought. Returning to her task, she said, 'How can any woman be offended at such a compliment? I don't think anyone has ever called me beautiful before.'

That was true, though she'd never really thought about it. Mary Powell set the standard for beauty at Forest Hill.

'Then blindness must be endemic where you come from.'

Endemic – not a word the tutor at Forest Hill had ever

included on their lists to be memorized, but from the context it must mean common, she thought. Feeling her face redden, she finished the last word of type in the last row. 'There,' she said. 'Tomorrow's broadsheet. Please proof it before you ink it. Is *proof* the right word?'

He smiled. 'Exactly the right word.'

Feeling suddenly very aware that she was alone with him for the first time since coming to work at the shop, she said, 'Ben has gone to take Ralphie and Johnnie the afternoon edition' – another new word she had added to her list – 'and I am going to the market before it closes. The boys said they were tired of dried meat strips. I am hoping for something fresh.'

Taking her bonnet down from the hook by the door and replacing it with her apron, she said, 'I shan't be long.'

'Wait,' he said. 'Let me get you some money.'

'I have money. Ben paid me last Friday. And I shall eat the food as well.'

'I believe our terms were that the print shop would replace your lost earnings.'

'Which you have done.'

'Did not the guildhall provide the food you cooked?'

'Well, yes but—'

'And did you not also eat from what they provided?'

She nodded.

'Well, then.' He reached inside his tunic and withdrew a sovereign.

'But this is too much.'

'If you have some left, hold it for next time. If it is not enough, tell Ben, and he will make up the difference. We have a little puddle for everyday expenses like food.'

'You are more than generous, my lord.'

He frowned, 'Thank you, my lady.'

She corrected herself, 'You are more than generous, James.'

'Thank you, Caroline. And you are more than beautiful. Now off with you. I am going to proof this, and Ben can print it when he returns.'

She went out into the late August sunshine feeling more light-hearted than she had in longer than she could remember. She had lain awake at night trying to figure out how to replace her lost income. Two days at the guildhall kitchen was not enough. Her little hoard would be gone in no time. It seemed that once again James Whittier had come to her rescue. And though she hated to be beholden to anyone as she was to him, this was a new day and, as the Psalmist said, she would be 'glad in it.'

In the green market, Caroline found parsnips, spinach and a cabbage to add to Ben's pottage pot and cucumbers, onions, some lightly wilted sorrel leaves with a bottle of apple vinegar to brighten them. She decided to pass on a white-fleshed melon in favor of a jar of honeycomb, remembering how the children at Forest Hill had loved sucking the sweet nectar and chewing the wax. With a loaf of fresh rye, she could crumble the stale wheat loaf-heel into Ben's pottage pot and add some fresh sage and precious pepper for seasoning.

Despite her careful shopping, she was a little shocked at how much she spent – only three crowns left, and she had not even bought a small bird for the pot. She went to three vendors before she finally complained that what used to cost pennies now cost shillings.

'Aye, mistress, 'tis the war. Most of what we sell comes from outside the Lines of Communication. Most kitchen gardens don't have enough to sell after Parliament takes its bite to feed the soldiers. Trust me. The overage is not going into my pocket. I can't sell what I can't get.'

So that was how the guildhall kitchen was supplied, she thought.

When she returned to the shop Ben, inventorying her basket, grinned from ear to ear. 'I cannot believe you found vegetables. I didn't even know we could get honey.'

She noticed with a conflicting mixture of relief and disappointment that James had left. That thought might have confounded her if she'd had time to consider it.

'You just didn't know where to look,' she said. 'We have all this and more in the guildhall kitchen, but it wasn't cheap,' she said as she handed him the change. 'This is all that's left for the "puddle," as milord calls it.'

Ben's insinuating smile was a little irritating, 'If you bought all this, and had two crowns left, then he's more generous with you than with me. Wonder why that is?'

'Maybe it is because he is tired of dried meat,' she said. 'I will boil the bird and the parsnips before adding them to your pot, so it will be ready when the boys return. Unless you need me to help with the printing,' she added, remembering that the boy of yesterday who she once bossed was today a man and her superior.

'Apples! Caroline, you found apples. No. You go right ahead with your preparations. The sooner the better. I am tired of tough beef too.'

The skinny little chicken was already boiling, and she was peeling the parsnips when the bell on the front door tinkled. 'I will see to it, Ben,' she called, wiping the sweat from her face with the corner of her apron.

She recognized John Milton immediately. It took him a minute, even though she had visited him at his home.

'Mistress Pendleton, I believe.' He was staring at her apron. 'I . . . I did not expect to see you here.'

'The printer's helper is my stepson. I help out too on occasion.'

'Is Lord Whittier about?'

'No. Is there something I may do for you?'

'I stopped in to see if I could purchase the new pamphlet by Roger Williams.'

'We don't usually sell anything here, Mr Milton. But they are widely available at the vendors in St Paul's Churchyard.'

'But surely you have a copy,' he said, smiling a little sheepishly. 'I dined at the tavern down the street with friends. This is much more convenient than walking to St Paul's.'

'I will see if I can find one in the back. If you would care to wait here.' She indicated the bench in the entrance.

Ben looked up from the press with a frown.

It was plain he had recognized the voice. 'We have a man who wants to purchase a copy of the *Bloody Tenent of Persecution*. Do we have any?'

He pointed with the ink mop toward a chest on the other side of the room. 'In there,' he said, 'hidden under yesterday's broadsheet. About a dozen.' Then he added, mumbling, 'Make him pay, Caroline. He's a pinchpenny.'

She nodded, wondering how he knew that, or if he just automatically assumed the worst about him, and closed the door to the print room as she went back out. 'That will be three pence,' she said, handing him the pamphlet.

He looked a little surprised. 'I am sure that Lord Whittier would discount the price for me.'

She did not want him to get the best of her. Ben had said to make him pay for it. How was she to know if James would give him a discount? But neither did she want to prejudice him against her. For Mary's sake.

'Unfortunately, Mr Milton, Lord Whittier isn't here, and I have no notion when he will return. I shall be glad to hold it for you. I will take care of it personally.'

Milton did not look pleased. She was thinking maybe she would pay the three pence herself and not tell Ben, when a tall shadow paused in the door open to the street.

'John Milton,' James Whittier said. 'How good to see you. Give the pamphlet to him, Caroline. Compliments of the print shop. Without his referral, there would be no pamphlet.'

Caroline handed it to him, trying to hold her irritation against Milton's smug look as James said, 'Come on into the print room, Mr Milton. I have just returned from Parliament House, and I have news which, distressing as it is, you will want to hear.'

'I can guess what you are about to tell me. I have already heard from friends in Parliament.'

Caroline removed herself to the kitchen in the side alcove to be less conspicuous, but she could still hear.

Milton continued, 'Parliament has condemned my treatise on *The Doctrine and Discipline of Divorce*. I understand they are planning a book-burning.' That had her complete attention. 'It is not that it is my book. The ideas in the book – my words – are already out there. Parliament will sweep up the local copies, but people will be reading my arguments for a hundred years. Maybe more. Despite their best efforts, my work will endure.' Then came the clap of angry hands. 'But it is the thought that they dare burn any book. Better to burn the man than to burn his words, his ideas. To kill a good man is to kill a reasonable creature; to burn a good book is to kill reason itself.'

James nodded in agreement. 'That is why this shop publishes unlicensed voices and will continue to do so or it will close – or be closed by the censors. I have seen what the licensed printers are printing. Parliamentary propaganda, exaggerated tales designed to seed discord and feed the flames of war. How can an Englishman learn the truth about the war, about anything, if he cannot trust the source?'

Milton's small mouth pursed in anger. 'I am going to wait until after they have their big bonfire. And they will have a public bonfire. Political spectacle always engages the ignorant. But I will not be silent. I am going to write an open letter to Parliament, decrying this tyranny. Will you print it for me?'

'If I am still in business when you finish it. Which is no sure thing.'

'We are agreed then. Let us firm up terms for publication. I want enough copies to place in St Paul's Churchyard, of course, but also to post in every coach house and every tavern in England and surrounding. They will not be able to find and burn them all.'

'How many copies are we talking about?'

'About two hundred. I will try to keep it spare but, as you know, Lord Whittier, I am not a man of few words.'

'Try to keep it to forty pages. Even that will be expensive: two hundred copies, ten sheets per each printed in quarto – that's two thousand printed pages.'

'I know it will be expensive. That is why I am willing to forgo any profit. Print it as cheaply as you can. Cheapest paper. Some of them will be burned anyway.'

'Can you underwrite my expense?'

'Some. But I was hoping, Lord Whittier, that since we are like-minded, you might take on some of the cost.'

'I cannot afford to underwrite it. Not with so much risk. I could be shut down if I am discovered, deprived of my livelihood and my investment. Being a very good writer, perhaps a great one, you are at less risk. But I will price it so that perhaps I can recoup my costs along with – I am not promising, you understand – something for you. Banned books always increase demand.'

His boldness almost took Caroline's breath away. He would wind up in Tower Prison, or worse.

'All that depends on how quickly you finish it. If they trace Williams's *Bloody Persecution* back to me, I won't be able to print it for you.'

'I will get the manuscript to you as soon as possible.'

'Do you want your full name on it?'

'Not J.M. this time. John Milton. My name will carry some weight, I think. Are we agreed, then?'

'We are agreed then. I will be in touch.'

Milton stood up and started toward the door and then, approaching her said, 'I bid you good day, Mistress Caroline. Have you any news from Forest Hill?'

'Not since we last spoke, Mr Milton.'

'I would appreciate any news you might have in the future.'

James had not followed him over to Caroline, but stood staring out the window as if in a deep study. She was considering the best way to answer, when James interrupted.

'Mr Milton, I have given another thought to our arrangement.'

The poet's back stiffened, so that Caroline could swear he grew taller by half an inch.

'How would you feel about a barter? My labor for yours. And you will have to pay nothing toward the expense of publication.'

'My labor for yours? Do go on. I am intrigued.'

'I have a young boy who works for me, an orphan named John – we call him Little John. He possesses an extremely alert mind for a boy of six years. I think there is a potential there to be realized, if the boy but had a chance. He displays a remarkable eagerness to learn but has nobody to teach him. You are a teacher. I am curious to see what a gifted teacher could make of him. Patience and Ben have taught him his letters, but he needs more.'

'Patience? Patience Trapford?'

'Patience and Ben are good friends. She comes here on her days off.'

'She told me she was going to church,' he said indignantly.

'She does go to church. An independent congregation, Baptist I think, in Norton Folgate. Ben goes there too. Mostly because she goes there. They met when she brought your first manuscript to me. She started helping him with his work in exchange for his teaching her to read.'

'Teaching her to read! She couldn't read? Are you sure? I often gave her lists for the market and other things. She never said. If she needed to learn to read why didn't she ask me?'

James laughed. 'Ben asked her that same thing once and she

told him in an outraged tone that it would be like asking a master violin-maker to carve a reed whistle. She just wanted to be able to read the Bible. Not translate Latin and Greek.'

'And your young John? What does he want to learn?'

'I don't know. I just have a feeling about him. My labor for yours?'

Milton paused in consideration then said, 'Maybe two days a week, but I will have to evaluate him myself. I have one other child his age who is just beginning. Send him to me Monday next and I will see. Better yet, I shall send Patience to fetch him, since he is familiar with her. I should know if he has the mind of a scholar by the time I have finished *Areopagitica*.'

James raised his eyebrow. 'Is that your title?'

'Named from the *Areopagus*, the ancient Greek tribunal that met on Mars Hill. I am addressing our *Areopagus*.'

Even Caroline knew that was a bad title. The man was too clever, always soaring to heights that ordinary people could never reach or simply did not want to. No wonder Patience hadn't told him she couldn't read. While Caroline was thinking it was kind of James to want to help the boy, she wasn't sure this was the way – or that John Milton was the best person – to do it.

After he had gone, James came into the kitchen. 'We have a new project,' he said.

'I heard.'

'Your tone suggests disapproval.'

'It is not my place to approve or disapprove.'

'I value your opinion.' But he did not wait for her to give it. 'You met with success in the market place. I can smell it.'

'I gave Ben what was left. I spent—'

Before she could give him a reckoning, he held up his hand to halt her. 'No need. I trust you. We will eat and drink well – I brought a bottle of wine – until our business dries up or Parliament shuts us down.'

We. He had said, we. 'And what then, James?' she asked.

He shrugged. 'We will think of something else. You, me, Patience and Ben. And we will take care of the boys too. We are a team.'

'Is that what that was about just now with Little John?'

'It is an avenue to explore. If Milton becomes attached to the boy's quick mind, he might be persuaded to take him in. His own little scholar to mold. That might appeal to him. After all, he is expanding to run a boarding school. If something should happen here, I mean. You and Ben could survive. Ralphie too. He's almost old enough to be apprenticed to a printer. I know a licensed printer who would be more than willing to take him in for room and board.

'Don't look so worried, Caroline. I am just preparing against whatever might come. But, for now, we are going to print up some more copies of Roger's pamphlet – St Paul's has already sold out – then we're going to eat our food and drink our wine and celebrate that fate has brought us all together. Let tomorrow bring what it will, it will anyway.'

As she finished slicing cucumbers and peeling an onion, a merry little tune ran through her head. Before long it had found its way to her throat. Ben called out to her, smiling for the first time since Milton had gone, 'You used to hum that at Forest Hill. Sounds good, Caroline. Really good.'

The workload was heavier for the next few weeks. James had been right about the popularity of banned books. Ben, Caroline and James worked feverishly, Patience too when she came on Sunday afternoons. They were ever mindful of the urgency and the need for secrecy as they printed out a second edition of Roger Williams's censored pamphlet and increased the price a ha'penny. On Sundays they had to keep all doors and windows shuttered even in the golden light of early autumn, because it was unlawful to work on the Sabbath.

In the meantime, the broadsheets still went out under the mark of the crossed swords. James had become an associate member of the Worshipful Company of Stationers and had registered his mark when the Licensing Act passed. That relationship gave them a measure of cover to print the other pamphlets that bore no imprimatur. Lord Whittier even showed up at some of the guild meetings on Ludgate Hill, paid his licensing fees, was companionable to the masters in the hall. They were careful. Yet it was only a matter of time, Caroline thought, before they were caught – but that would be on some hopefully distant tomorrow, and this was today. She worked as hard as she could. And as the Sundays passed, she grew more comfortable with Patience. The girl was a hard worker, and the way she worked with Ben at the press was comforting to watch. Except for the high esteem she held for John Milton, she also had a keen eye for reading people.

'Thou needest not worry, Mistress Caroline. Little John is doing well. I have never seen Mr Milton dote on a lad so. I think some of the others are a little jealous.'

The child appeared happy when Patience showed up each Monday to escort him. When it was official, and he was to be allowed to go on Tuesdays as well, Mr Milton suggested that he stay Monday nights to 'spare Trapford a trip,' he said, though Caroline knew Patience looked forward to those trips.

'Has Mr Milton settled into his new house in the Barbican yet?' Caroline asked this Tuesday when the girl looked less energetic than usual.

'Aye. At last,' she said. 'Every pencil in its angel-ordained place.' Then she immediately apologized for her cross tone, saying it was just that Mr Milton had taken on two new students already. More mouths to feed. More chamber pots to empty. More slates to wipe clean.

'You are too conscientious,' Caroline wanted to say. 'Some men will use you up and never even know they are doing it.' But she did not. Though she decided that, come next Sunday, she would see that Ben and Patience had some time to be together without having to work so hard. She would speak to James about it tomorrow.

TIES THAT BIND

Had it any been but she,
And that very face,
There had been at least ere this
A dozen dozen in her place.

From 'The Constant Lover' by John Suckling
(published posthumously in *The Last Remains*
of Sir John Suckling, 1659)

October 1644

With Caroline close to him, it was hard for James to concentrate enough to keep the hackney out of the ditch. When he first asked if she would like to join him on his trip to Reading to order supplies, she had declined. But when he suggested they go on to Forest Hill, so she could have a short visit with her friends and retrieve some of the belongings she had left behind, she appeared open to the offer.

'Is Ben going?'

'No. He said he was too busy.'

When she seemed to at least be considering the invitation, he said, 'Consider the expense of your private lodging in Reading a gift from me for all your hard work these last weeks.'

'Can you not buy paper in London?'

'The Reading broker is cheaper. Fewer taxes. Anyway, if the London stationers' guild pokes around and sees how much paper we use, they might get suspicious. I plan to leave early in the morning. You are heartily invited to accompany me.'

She had said that she would think about it but had not mentioned it again.

When the ostler delivered the coach and pair to his door a little after dawn, James loitered, casting a hopeful eye down the empty street. He probably should take the coach back to the stable and swap it for a horse. It would be faster. He could get the contraband pamphlets meant for Reading and Oxford in his saddlebags. The paper and ink supplies were to be shipped via the river anyway. But just as he was about to head out, no more reason to linger – she wasn't coming – he clicked the reins, cast one last glance down the lane.

Was it? Yes, not quite running, closing the distance between them.

'I would have picked you up,' and then before she could answer, he had added, 'I hope you brought your pistol. Just in case. Mine is already under the driver's seat.' Alarm bloomed in her face. 'I expect no trouble, of course, but two would be better than one.'

She pointed to the familiar scrip he remembered seeing spread out on the table in the garrison guardhouse when Arthur Aston had questioned her.

'Do you want to sit in the back or on the bench with me?'

'It promises to be a beautiful day. I will enjoy the autumn sunshine and the scenery better if I sit outside. At least until we stop.' But when they paused at a roadside alehouse for refreshment and relief, she had climbed back up and had ridden with him the whole day.

Above the steady clopping of hooves, they spoke of many things: of the scarred countryside and the beauty of the autumn light; how she missed the country even though she'd grown up in London's crowded streets, delivering pies for her aunt's bakeshop; how, when her aunt died, she'd gone to live with the Powells at Forest Hill Manor before marrying William. Most of her story he had already gleaned bit by bit from Ben, but when she paused he asked questions, just to hear her voice so close. In answer to her tentative questioning, he told her about his childhood, how he came to be alone without family. It was easy talk, sharing opinions: political and religious, of which she had plenty. They talked print-shop talk, about how grateful she was that Ben had found work he loved. But when he mentioned that if Ben could get journeyman status, he would probably ask Patience to marry him, she grew silent.

The hedgerow shadows lengthened and crawled across the

road. He hoped to make Reading without having to light the coach lamp. Maybe he shouldn't have put her at risk, remembering how easily a robber could stop a small coach; remembering too that he was smuggling unlicensed pamphlets out of London. He shifted in his seat, making sure the pistol had not been jolted out of reach.

'Your arms must be tired,' she said. 'Would you like me to take the reins? I know how. I sometimes drove the wagon and team for William. I also had a little mare and trap of my own.' He thought he detected a catch in her voice when she added, 'My mare's name was Lilybud.'

'I am fine. Won't be long now. You said "had." What happened to Lilybud?'

'She was stolen by marauders.'

'Royalists or Roundheads?'

'I don't know. I never saw them. Just the bloody mess they left. But it really doesn't matter who, does it?'

The huskiness in her voice made him want to put his arm around her to comfort her, but he resisted the impulse, saying only, 'No, I don't suppose it does.'

'I came home from Forest Hill and she was gone. Our dogs, William's Splendid Pair, he called them, were slaughtered, along with his prize Merino sheep.' He felt her sigh in his own throat. 'I left that next morning, desperate to find him.'

These last words were so softly spoken he scarcely heard them. The wind had picked up. With one arm, he pulled the coach blanket up to her lap.

'Thank you,' she said and fell silent again.

Seeing a hedgerow up ahead, he pulled sharply to the middle of the road. The horses' response was a little slow. 'There is an alehouse at the next crossroads, as I remember. We will stop there and rest the horses.'

By the time they drove through the stone archway of the coaching inn at Reading, the evening star had risen. In the courtyard he handed the reins off to the stable boy, tucked the pistol into his belt and jumped down. 'Give them each an extra nosebag,' he said, handing the boy two silver coins. 'One for the extra nosebag and one for you. I will call for them in the morning. Early.'

Every nerve in his body tingled as he reached up and lifted her down. Other parts of his body responded too. Quickly releasing her so she would not notice, he reached for her bag and escorted her in, motioning for the innkeeper, who signaled in recognition. 'Lord Whittier, may I be of assistance?'

'I would like a clean, well-furnished room for Lady Pendleton. With fresh linen, soap, towels and a sturdy lock on the inside.'

'A single room, my lord?'

Whittier shot him a warning look, 'For the lady. She is a dear friend. I will take a bunk in the merchants' dormitory. Lady Pendleton and I will share a meal in an hour. In the merchants' dining area. A snug, if one is available. What is the inn specialty today?'

'In the merchants' room, my lord, it is stuffed breast of partridge in a savory sauce with a salad of braised greens and an apple custard. Would you like wine or beer?'

Judging from the great number of wagons in the courtyard, the many sieges Reading suffered had not diminished the popularity of the inn. The food would be fresh and the cellar adequate. 'Wine. Whatever you are serving the merchants.'

She was silent as he walked her to her chamber and stood in the doorway. He did not trust himself to go in to test the lock – never had he wanted a woman so much in his life as he wanted her – so he ran his fingers over the rusted metal, imagining the softness of her skin, remembering the taste of her lips. 'Seems sturdy enough, and the bed looks fresh,' not mentioning how he longed to lie down beside her. 'A maid will bring you fresh water and towels,' he said brusquely, putting her satchel on the bed. 'I want to get to the stationer's before closing. We will leave for Forest Hill before he opens in the morning. I will be back in about an hour and we can go down to dine.'

She did not answer but only nodded. Come to think of it, he had not heard her utter a word since they approached the gate to the coach house. Of course. She would be remembering her previous experience with this inn. The memory would have come crashing in on her as they entered the courtyard and crossed the common room. He cursed his choice. There were other inns.

'Are you well, Caroline?'

She rewarded him with a weak smile. 'A little tired. That is all.'

But the haunted look in her eyes told him it was more than fatigue as she said, 'You go on. I will be ready when you come back. And thank you for this nice room. I am sure you will not save enough on your paper purchase to pay for it. Let me help.'

'The pleasure of your company is more than payment enough. You rest. Take this hour to refresh yourself.'

A maid knocked on the door with fresh bed linens.

'When she leaves, lock the door and don't answer it to anybody else. I won't be long.'

James was as good as his word. One hour later he knocked on Caroline's door and softly called her name. She had attempted to refresh her appearance and her spirits. For all his courtesy and expense, he deserved, at the very least, a cheerful companion.

'Shall we go down, milady?' he asked extending the curve of his arm, which she took as though they were descending the stairs to a ballroom.

'We shall, milord.'

As they passed through the main room, she averted her gaze from the bench beside the hearth where she had huddled, frightened and alone. Some days it seemed a lifetime ago, but seeing it now, it seemed only yesterday. The room into which he ushered her was nothing like the common room. Much more elegant. It was lined with booth-like alcoves where several merchants with neatly trimmed beards and quality doublets talked softly, some pushing papers between them as they drank and ate and perused their contracts. She could almost see William among them.

The 'snugs' were hung with velvet drapery. 'Shall we keep the curtains opened or closed?' he asked, settling across from her.

'Closed, I think, James. Since there are no other women here, I would not want to call attention.'

When he pulled the curtain, the space grew more intimate. He sat opposite her across the table. They were close enough to touch hands. She kept hers in her lap, wondering if she had made a mistake, but she would insult him now if she asked for the curtain to be pulled back. Their food appeared through the parted panels and she suddenly realized she was famished. Not wanting to deal with the repercussions of too much food and drink, she had eaten almost nothing and drunk less at their two breaks.

The food tasted wonderful. James must have thought so too because they were halfway finished before either of them started a conversation.

'Did Ben mention his intentions toward Patience specifically, or are you guessing?' she asked between forkfuls.

'He asked me about how he could achieve journeyman status, and when I inquired what was the hurry, he told me what was rolling around in his head. I had recently upped his pay and he said he was saving the extra to afford a place where they could live so Patience could leave Mr Milton's employment and work with him in the print shop. I pointed out to him that he was earning journeyman pay already.'

'But if you are paying him enough already, then why does he need journeyman status?'

'It is a step to his being a master printer. Before he takes a wife, he needs the security of the Worshipful Master of Stationers' Guild stamp. Then he can hire himself out to any of the guild masters and not have to worry about the fortunes of any one. He would be his own man.'

'But surely he would not leave you when you have done so much for him.'

'More, I think that he thinks I might leave him. He said he thought that I was getting restless because of the Licensing Act and might want to close the shop. Or be forced to do so. He and his new wife would need to be able to survive without me.'

'Are you?' she said, the suffocating closeness of the heavy curtains suddenly too near. He was the hinge that held them all together in some semblance of security. 'Are you getting restless?'

He shrugged. 'Not so much restless as hemmed in. I know that we can't go on forever printing unlawful material. When Parliament finds that we can print faster than they can collect and burn, they will shut all the unlicensed printers down one by one, even if it means heavy fines or imprisonment. They will go after the most subversive first.' The cocky grin emerged as he added, 'And I am proud to say that we probably head that list. But I will abandon the venture before that happens.'

Venture? Was that all it was to him? Just another scheme to be easily replaced?

'Then Ben is wise to seek the official stamp of approval.'

'Yes. I have already applied to the council for a license for him. But we are going to have to print a few more materials bearing the crossed sword and Stationers' Guild imprimatur to make us look legitimate. I've signed up a couple of projects; a cookbook and a guide to women's health, but when the *Areopagitica* arrives in the bookstalls—'

Caroline interrupted him. 'But maybe Milton's pamphlet will persuade Parliament to be more lenient. His argument is powerful. For freedom to speak, I mean – not divorce.'

She looked at the expensive meal only half-eaten on her plate, her appetite suddenly gone. What he was saying was very troubling. Not the news about Patience and Ben's plans. More how all their lives, their choices, should be so determined by circumstances outside their control.

'That is wishful thinking, Caroline. Not going to happen. No matter who wins the war. We are all right for now, simply because Parliament is too busy to ferret out all the unlicensed printers. But we need to be realistic.'

'What about Mr Milton? He wrote it. Will they not go after him instead of you?'

He shrugged. 'Not like they will come after his printer. Milton is well known and respected by many in Parliament. His writings concerning the failures of the Church of England – and especially the Laudians – have been very helpful to the Puritan cause. They will go after the independent presses, so they can control the flow of his pen. That is why we need to have a plan.'

A plan? How did one plan for the unknown? They were all pawns in the war. A gust of wind shook the window of their snug. Outside, a sprinkle of leaves buffeted the glazing before settling in a sodden heap. For all their yellow and crimson glory, tomorrow they would just be a pile of dying brown matter. She looked down at her half-finished plate. 'This portion was too generous. I am quite full.'

He poked his fork into her plate and transferred the slice of partridge to his own.

'It will not go to waste,' he said. And when the apple tart

appeared, he ate that too, between forkfuls saying, 'Don't worry, Caroline. Whatever happens I won't abandon you. I will try my best to keep you and Ben and Patience – if she is indeed his choice – safe. Have you ever considered how our little orphan quartet functions like a family?'

'I guess I never thought of it that way. We are all orphans – alike in that we are alone. Even Patience. Ben said all she had was a grandfather who died last year. And though Ben has me and I have him, we are not bound by blood.'

'Not by blood maybe, but we are all bound together by friendship and by work. More than that, we share a stubbornness, a will to act, a kind of inner resourcefulness, a determination to survive, and a sense of loyalty to that bond.' He scraped the last bit of tart from her plate. 'That is more than you can say for some blood families.'

She smiled then, trying to look reassured, telling herself how fortunate she was to have a friend in him. But she and William and Ben had been a real family and the war had shattered that. 'An all too unfortunate truth,' she said, fatigue ambushing her. The hours on the road, the memories attached to the inn with the shadow of her loss looming ever larger here, and now this disquieting conversation had suddenly sapped her strength.

'Thank you again, James, for dinner and for inviting me, but I think I would like to go up now. You said we needed to leave early in the morning, and it has been a long day. A lovely day, but long.'

Scraping back his chair, he stood up and offered her his arm. 'Allow me to see you safely up the stairs to the gallery.'

She looked neither right nor left as they walked through the common room and up the stairs. When they reached her door, she thanked him again and bade him goodnight, wondering if he would spend the evening at the gaming table in the main room. After she had slid the bolt on her bedroom door and heard his receding footfalls, she resisted the urge to call him back.

Caroline found Mary Milton in the brewhouse with her mother. It was mid-afternoon. The hut was hot and close with the smell of mash and yeast. Sweat rolled down Mary's face as she helped Ann pour the steaming wort to cool in the fermenting tub.

Caroline stood, unnoticed in the open doorway, watching them, drinking in each word, each movement, even the pungent smell. Ann Powell bent over the last of the three vats. 'This one is ready. I will bottle it while you grind the coriander seeds for the next barrel.'

Coriander seeds. That was Ann's secret to the hazy, golden ale that Forest Hill was known for. Coriander and wheat added to the barley. Ann Powell had never used hops in her ale. She said she didn't like the bitter taste of beer. Mary dragged the mortar and pestle from its shelf and began to grind the seeds, stopping only to massage her slender neck.

Her glance fell on the open door. 'Caroline?'

Anne Powell looked up. 'Caroline. Girl, are you a sight for bleary old eyes.'

Mary dropped the pestle and ran to the doorway, threw her arms around Caroline then withdrew, laughing. 'Sorry. Hope you haven't forgotten the way a country girl smells.'

'I have forgotten nothing. Even the smell of sour mash is something I miss. Do you need some help?'

'Of course, we need help,' Ann said. 'We always need help. You are sorely missed, my girl.'

'Where is sister Sarah?'

'Married – at least she says she is. Gone off with that Captain Potter. Followed after him like some slutty camp follower when he was posted out of here.'

'War makes unexpected alliances,' Caroline said, reaching for her old apron still hanging on a peg by the door.

Ann gave her hand a playful slap. 'Do not go reaching for that dirty old thing. We are going to the kitchen and will have something cool to drink, and talk like the civilized folk we used to be. I will come back here later and finish. How long can you stay? A long time, I'm hoping. Christ and all the saints, how Mary has missed you. We all have.'

'I have missed you too,' Caroline said. 'Sorely. And I will be grateful for a cool drink. We left Reading early this morning and it's been a pretty good clip.'

'We?' Mary asked.

'I'll tell you about it. All about London and what I've been doing these days. I've time enough for a good long chat. I can stay the night. If that's all right?'

'All right? We wish she would stay forever, don't we, Mother?'

'We want you to stay with us as long as you can. As always,' Ann said, tearing a little. 'The girls will be so glad to see you. Squire is away. He will be sorry he missed you.'

'My brothers have deserted us. They found more glory in fighting for the King,' Mary said. 'The last we heard from them they had survived the battle on Marston Moor, thank God.'

In the stillness of the afternoon kitchen, they drank cool buttermilk from the spring house. 'I can tell you have the same cook,' Caroline said between bites of gingerbread. 'What about the other servants?'

'Just the women. We can't pay them much, but they are loyal. And we share our food and fuel with them – we have plenty of wood. You have probably noticed how most of the oaks are gone. If the squire doesn't stop cutting soon we will have to rename the manor No-Forest Hill.' She shrugged. 'But it's the only income we have, except the King's worthless script. Even the rents have all dried up.' She drummed her fingers nervously on the table. 'That's enough about us. How did you get here? Did you have any trouble?'

'No trouble. A friend brought me. He has business in Reading and Oxford.' The words were hardly out of her mouth before she shook her head, forestalling the frown on Ann's face. 'Don't get all worked up and think I have abandoned virtue. He is my employer. James Whittier. I work for him sometimes in his print shop. Arthur – he calls himself Ben these days – works for him.'

'Is he a good man? Is he kind to you and Arthur? Is he a Puritan like . . . John?'

'He has shown us both every kindness, though we do work hard on his behalf.' She gave a little half-laugh. 'But hardly a Puritan. He sometimes ducks the churchwardens by closing shop and disappearing to some of the taverns that play Sunday round-robin secretly for their regulars. His little protest, he calls it, against forced piety. He shows up once in a while at St Bride's. It is close by.'

'Is he a King's man then?'

'He says he is neutral – if one can ever really be neutral on something so important.'

Ann excused herself then to fetch Betsy and little Anne, who were supposed to be in the orchard gathering pears. They would want to see Caroline, too, she said. Mary and Caroline went up to the room they had once shared.

Mary took off the kerchief and hung up the smock. It shed a faint smell of peat smoke and coriander in the pretty bedroom painted with green vines and unicorns.

'Are you living in William's London leasehold?'

Caroline picked up a brush from Mary's dressing table, 'Sit down in front of the mirror. Let me brush your hair like old times.' Then, running the brush through Mary's long hair, while the girl sighed with contentment, she explained how she now lived. 'Like here, the military has taken over the townhouse. Mistress Cramer has gone to stay with her niece. Since the war began, London has become a cold and lonely city, no music, no festivals, no familiar friends. At least we have coal again – thank God for that – but now it is a very dirty city.'

'I am so glad Arthur found you. At least you have him. Do you ever run into John?'

'We don't exactly travel in the same lanes. But he comes into the print shop sometimes. Most times he just sends his servant. She and Arthur have become friends. She is a very good worker.'

Mary's blue eyes looked at Caroline from the mirror, a tiny smile working the corners of her mouth as she said, 'Patience Trapford? And Arthur. Well. I would have never put them together.'

'They are not exactly together. Not yet anyway. Did you know that your husband has moved to a bigger house on the Barbican?'

'How could I know? I have not heard from him in months,' she said bitterly.

Caroline put down the brush. 'There. Shining and beautiful as ever.'

'Thank you. That felt good. I miss you so much. It feels almost like old times, having you here like this. Though I know it is not.'

'There is something I need to tell you, Mary.'

Mary swiveled around and faced her, the contented expression on her face fading. 'Spare yourself, old friend. I know about John's latest masterpiece. Father told me. He found a copy of it at the coaching inn in Oxford. It was signed J.M. but I know it was his. Same wordy style.'

'You read it then?'

'Enough to get the gist of what it said. How awful it is to be bound to a wife who is too much of a dullard to be a suitable companion for a man of his great intellect. I didn't finish it. For a man who prides himself on his great intellectual capacity, he doesn't seem to understand the concept of the beauty of brevity.'

Caroline laughed with relief. Mary didn't seem that hurt, just angry. The war – or her unfortunate marriage – had changed her from a girl into a woman.

'He is stupid, selfish, vain, and blinded by arrogance.'

'At least he didn't name you or sign his own name even.'

'Small comfort that. If a country bumpkin like me can pick out his overwrought style, I am sure his peers will have no trouble.'

'I have a confession to make, Mary. I hope you will not be angry with me. But I read it too, and I was so angry and so afraid that he would try to divorce you on the grounds of abandonment, that I told him a bit of a lie. I told him that you asked me to inquire about his welfare and to assure him that once it was safe to travel you would return to him.'

Mary's laugh startled her. 'Did he believe you?'

'I think he did.'

'How did he take it?'

'Somewhat soberly, I think. Trust me, Mary. I only wanted to give you a choice by stripping him of the right to a legal divorce, should he choose to charge abandonment. I am not saying you should go back to him. Just that it need not be his choice alone.'

'When have you not looked out for me, Caroline? Now you have sinned by lying for me.'

Caroline smiled. 'Each day I grow fonder of Martin Luther's "grace."'

'You have less need of forgiveness than anybody I know. And you may have done me a great service. If the King loses this war, I may have to go back. Just to have a roof over my head. If that roof is still available to me, I will have you to thank. But for now, it is indeed unsafe to travel. Tell Mr Milton, when next you see him, that you have spoken with his wife and she bids him be patient a little while longer.' She paused long enough to take a breath. 'You said he has bought a bigger house – well, he very well may need it if he has to succor his in-laws too.'

Caroline laughed out loud. 'Squire Richard Powell, beholden to a Puritan for his bed and board, and the Puritan Milton beholden by his own elevated estimation of himself and his strict code of honor to shelter his Royalist in-laws – the gods of irony are working overtime.' Then she said soberly, 'But it is not fair to you, Mary. Not fair that you should suffer all the burden of it when you had no choice.'

'There is enough burden in this situation to go around, believe me. And who gets fairness these days, Caroline? Anyway, I might as well be slave there as slave here,' she said, wiping at her stained skirt. 'But I am not going back yet. If the tide should turn and Parliament loses, then who knows? It may be the highly esteemed Mr John Milton who comes to the Powells' looking for shelter?'

'Would you take him in?'

'I would have no choice. I gave my oath. He is my husband, and I will not seek to divorce him because he is short, pompous, and not a merry companion.'

That night, as she lay beside Mary in the old bedroom they once shared, where the painted unicorns were showing wear and the twining vines specked with peeling, Mary whispered, 'Do you still miss William terribly, Caroline?'

'Terribly,' she said. 'Sometimes, not as often now, I think I see his shadow or hear a footfall and think *William is coming*, and then I realize he is not. William is not there. Will never be there. That piercing thought, the final truth of it, follows me everywhere, a silent ambush: a word, a slant of light, an object; something familiar or unfamiliar. When it strikes, seemingly out of nowhere, it almost stops my heart. Being alone is a hard thing, Mary.'

In the darkness, Mary reached for her hand and squeezed it. Grateful, Caroline squeezed hers back.

A DECLARATION OF INTENT

[E]very man should say to every man, 'I authorize and give my right of governing myself to this man, or to this assembly of men, on this condition that thou give up thy right to him, and authorize all his actions in like manner.'

Thomas Hobbes, Chapter XVII in *Leviathan, or the Matter, Form, and Power of a Commonwealth, Ecclesiastical and Civil* (1651)

By late November the traffic on the Thames was already confined to a narrow middle channel and threatened by a growing scrim of ice clinging to the banks. Icicles hung like daggers from sagging roofs, and the few street vendors who ventured out huddled over braziers. But they had coal aplenty. London choked on soot. At the sign of the crossed swords in Fleet Street, the press creaked out sheets of Milton's *Areopagitica* as well as legitimate broadsheets and the recipe book that Ben was to present to the Stationers' Guild. He sheepishly mentioned to Caroline his plans to ask Patience to marry him as soon as his license came, saying, since she was his only living relative, he hoped she would approve.

Caroline had brought back some of the furnishings from Forest Hill, telling him he could have whatever he wanted. Fighting back tears, she said she would like only to keep William's desk and some of the linen. James offered to store the two cupboards, a table, two chairs, and the two beds upstairs.

'Set up your bed down here, Ben,' he said. 'We can fit it into the corner. It'll be better than the cot you are sleeping on now.'

'You take Father's bed, Caroline,' Ben said. 'You can put it in the townhouse.'

'I don't have room for it,' she answered, 'certainly not now and maybe never. If you and Patience can't use it, you can sell it later.'

The short days and waning light were an obstacle to productivity. Caroline enjoyed being at the print shop, but it was exhausting too and the return to her cold attic room was every day's dread.

'You could stay here. But then you'd have to marry me,' James said, grinning. It was not the first time he'd hinted at that possibility. She just scowled and ignored him, choosing to pretend he was joking.

He had first broached the subject several weeks after their trip to salvage what she could from the farmhouse. As soon as they had entered the lane leading to the farm, she regretted her decision to come. Where the lovely old copse of oak trees had bordered the sheep pasture, now there were only stumps – part of the squire's new woodcutting enterprise. The house was still standing, but little else. The fields and pastures had been burned to stubble. The barn door sagged on one rusted hinge, and the roof was gone. Its skeletal structure brought tears to her eyes.

The door to the house creaked open at the slightest push. The front room was empty and smelled of dead ashes and neglect and decay. A charred log remained in the fireplace and an abandoned fry-pan spilled gristle and grease globules onto a cold hearth. Acanthus leaves carved in the chestnut mantle bore burn marks.

'Some vagabond or soldier trying to stay warm, I suppose,' James had said.

'This was once such a beautiful room. For the first time in my life I felt like I had something that belonged to me. William was generous that way. He said what was his, was mine too.'

When she started to cry, he had taken her in his arms and held her like one would hold a child, whispering, 'It will be all right, Caroline. You can restore it. Ben and I will help you.'

Striving for self-control, she pulled away from him. 'I will never return to this place. William only leased it from Richard Powell. But the furnishings – there might be something here of value still,' she said. 'It looks like the lock to the back rooms has not been broken. I think . . .' She went to the hearth and removed a brick from the inglenook. Held up a key.

The bedroom had not been violated. Squire had shoved some of the best pieces from the parlor into this room. She had gone straight to her closet and emptied it, pausing to press her cheek against a hooded cloak of soft wool. 'I need this. You are tired of seeing William's old greatcoat, I am sure,' she said, attempting a laugh to chase away the desolation. She dug through some of the larger chests. 'I will never wear some of these things again, much too fine for a servant, but maybe I can use some of the fabric for something more practical . . . These I can definitely use,' she said, pulling out a pair of soft leather boots.

'A pair of fine shoes can always be counted on to lift the spirits of a woman. This place doesn't really look that bad. You should see the ancient pile I abandoned. But I do know something of what you feel. At least you and Ben have this . . .' he said, pointing to the furniture they had tagged for saving. 'My brother mortgaged everything. He would have sold the title if he could have found a buyer.'

'I am sorry. Forgive me for whining.'

'You are not whining. I did not mean that. I was only pointing out how much we have in common.'

And he had continued pointing it out at every opportunity since they returned.

'Ben is still working on his cookbook, so I will walk you back tonight,' he said, pulling on his coat.

'You do not—'

'Don't even say it,' he said. His hand lingered a little long on her shoulder as he helped her with her cloak. He lowered his voice to an almost whisper, 'I would wade blood chin-deep for you, Caroline. What is a little bit of cold and damp against the pleasure of the company of a woman I adore?'

'How can I resist such a gallant offer?' She reached for the soft wool cloak she had brought back from Forest Hill, fastened its fur-trimmed hood under her chin and said, as lightly as she could, 'I shall try to avoid any blood puddles, lest your sincerity be put to the test.'

In Paris the approaching winter was also entering with uncharacteristic bluster. But in the Palace at Le Louvre, Anne of Austria and the French courtiers took care to see that Henrietta had every comfort. In the company of Jeffrey Hudson and Henry Jermyn, young Henry Percy and the other Paris exiles, Henrietta did well enough in the daytime. But the long winter nights she spent either huddling over her letters to Charles, or praying for her children in the dim glow of the palace chapel.

A trusted messenger who spoke good English made the channel crossing regularly. Her letters to her husband were frequent. His dispatches to her less so. But he was busy with the war in the West. His letters were filled with news of the skirmishes between his forces and Lord Essex's. In his first dispatch he had praised his 'dear heart,' for giving him another beautiful daughter, whom he had seen christened Henrietta Anne after her mother and her godmother. After that he had not mentioned the child once, except to reassure Henrietta in her persistent inquiries: all reports were that the babe was safe and thriving under the careful stewardship of Anne Villiers.

He also wrote – with bitter complaint – about his nephew Charles Louis, the oldest of his sister's remaining sons who, after his older brother's death, had inherited the title Elektor of the Palatinate. Unlike his brothers, Rupert and Maurice, he did not come to his Stuart uncle's aid, but was even now in London cozying up to Parliament. Of course he was, Henrietta thought angrily. Of all Elizabeth Stuart's sons, he had always shown himself to be the most cunning. Perhaps his sympathy with Parliament was born of pique that his uncle had refused to support the Protestant wars in Europe, but more probably it was out of ambition. Parliament might just see Charles Stuart's Protestant nephew as the perfect candidate to lead a war of succession against an unpopular monarch.

As usual, Henrietta did her best to advise her husband. It was frustrating being so far away, having to rely on Charles's assessments, which – truth to tell – were not always as keen-eyed as they should be. He was becoming increasingly vague when she asked him for details of the war. Better intelligence was to be gleaned from her friends in London and Oxford.

She corresponded frequently with Lucy Hay. In between anecdotes about the children, Lucy wrote that Archbishop Laud was being tried for treason. He was mounting his own defense 'with spirit,' as was reported in the news books. Henrietta had never really liked the pompous little man, but at least he was not a Puritan or a Presbyterian rebel. He had been loyal to Charles in his role as Defender of the Faith. But she had always known Laud was a man torn between two masters. The Archbishop rejected the Holy Father, but with his devotional love of liturgy he tiptoed around the Holy Mass. It was hard to pity him, though she had to admit he and she had somewhat in common. He had sighed with near longing when he first saw her beautiful chapel. She determined to pray for his soul when Parliament took his head, as they surely would. It was almost certain King Pym had promised it to the Presbyterians before he went to his own well-deserved hell.

While the musicians played softly on their lutes and Jeffrey made rude jokes, she spent the short gray days with her ladies, hovered over their needlework in the candlelit hall: a soft blanket to be sent to baby Minette in Bedford, a fur-trimmed hood and embroidered mantle for Princess Elizabeth, a stuffed bear with onyx eyes and a sassy red tongue, sporting a belted toy sword to match Henry's own. She was almost finished. Her gifts should reach Syon House by Boxing Day. Finishing a blue French knot, she lifted her sewing needle to her lips and bit the thread with her teeth. 'Jeffrey, I have not seen Jermyn in three days. He is not ill, I hope.'

The dwarf did a little half-twirl, came to a full stop and stood on one leg like a confused sea bird. 'Lord Jermyn?' Supporting his chin with the heel of his hand, he peered into the middle distance, as though she had asked a deep and philosophical question. He snapped his fingers and exclaimed, 'Methinks I saw him yesterday, delivering a turd wrapped in scarlet ribbon to Lord Flatrock.'

Henrietta stopped her smile with a twitch of her lips. Poor Jermyn. His piles were often the butt of the court's jokes. She must not encourage this disrespectful jest. But the fool needed no encouragement. Mouth pursed into a thoughtful pout, he pondered aloud, 'Or was Lord Jermyn splashing a pipe of liquid gold on a faerie hill in the rose garden? The latter, I think. The faerie queen was not amused. She evoked in him a mighty wind.'

Her ladies looked to her and stifled their own laughter. She managed a scowl. 'I think, Lord Minimus, that the French court is a bad influence on you. Your wit grows coarser every day.'

He splayed his hands, palms out, and pulled a disappointed face. 'But, I was trying to answer with discretion and panache.'

'You did not answer at all. Have you seen him?'

'His lordship said for me to tell you that he will attend you on the morrow.'

'Scoundrel! And you waited to be asked. Watch yourself, fool, or I will send you to the front to try your humorless jokes with the big strong soldiers there.'

Whereupon the dwarf began to rend his clothes and plead with such exaggerated tomfoolery that the ladies' laughter spilled out as they pleaded indulgence for him. Finally, giving in, she laughed too.

Le Louvre, the palace that her mother had hated, was not home. But, surrounded by her friends and a court already in preparation for the season of Advent, it was not a bad place to spend the winter.

If she couldn't be with Charles and the children.

And Jermyn was coming on the morrow.

'It is freezing in here and there is no light in the house or on the stairs. Even the chimney is stone cold. What happened to the officers who worked downstairs?' James asked when he entered her room.

The whole house was in darkness. In the main parlor, lit only by the moonlight, James had retrieved a tallow dip from the mantle and sparked it by poking a few near dead embers in the fireplace to light their way up the narrow stairs.

'The officers have stopped coming every day,' she said, retrieving the key hanging around her neck. With a practiced hand she opened the door, took the taper from his hand and groped for the lantern hanging on the chimney wall. 'I usually leave an oil lamp burning on the table inside the door. But I have fumbled my way through this room so many times I can find my way in the dark.'

The flame leaped up, painting a ghostly circle on the open roof beams of the attic, releasing the smell of burning wick and oil. 'When the officers don't come, the fire downstairs doesn't get lit. The heat from this chimney wall has been enough, but when there is no fire downstairs . . .' She shrugged away the rest of her answer. 'But I have blankets.'

With a rap of his knuckles James broke the icy skin in the water basin on the makeshift dressing table. 'Caroline, you simply cannot stay here alone under these conditions. It is not safe. I insist you come and stay at the print shop.'

When she started to protest, he said she could have his upstairs room all to herself and he would bunk downstairs with Ben. There was plenty of room since Little John was now boarding with Mr Milton and Ralphie was sleeping at home. 'This is simply not a situation that Ben nor I can tolerate.'

'Maybe I can persuade the Committee of the Three Kingdoms to let me have our old quarters back now that they are no longer being used. There is a fireplace and large windows to let in the light. Even a cook stove with a flue. It was quite comfortable and lovely . . .' Her voice trailed off, as she remembered the first time she had seen it. William had told Letty to bring the girl with the pies inside, so she could warm herself by the fire. That had been wintertime too. She had warmed her girlish self by the great fire and thought it was the prettiest room she had ever seen and Mr and Mrs Pendleton the nicest people in the whole world.

James's voice broke in. The memory faded as quickly as a spider's web at the end of a broom. 'If you can find somebody to authorize it,' he said. 'But that is not helping now, is it? In the meantime, pack your things and come stay with us.' He lowered his voice, reached out to touch her but let his hand drop. 'Caroline, I don't think William would have wanted you to stay here like this. Not if he was the good man you say he was.'

When he said he was going to stay with her until she relented, she gave up and went back to the print shop. Two weeks later she was still sleeping there, and she had to admit it was much more comfortable. She slept wonderfully well, never awakening in the night with her heart pounding and her legs numb with cold. But she didn't like to be beholden to him when he had already done so much for her. On the days she went to the guild kitchen, she checked the house in the hope she would find one of the officers there and ask if she could move back to the old apartment. She thought about returning to it without permission, but good sense prevailed – and something else. She wasn't lonely anymore. At the shop, they laughed and worked and supped together and, after a long day when the printing jobs were heavy and Caroline was clearing away the remains of a hastily thrown-together meal, James would say – with a grin that said he understood her concern for propriety: 'Ben, go upstairs and see that your stepmother's room is warm enough. Don't forget the warming pan hanging by the hearth.' Sometimes he would add, 'Carry up a fresh pitcher of water as you go.'

'Aye, Cap'n,' Ben would answer, scooting back his chair with a smile.

Between them they made Caroline feel secure and cared for. And needed. She felt as though she earned her keep, and that was good, but still something nagged at her peace. It didn't seem right that she should sleep under another man's roof, and worse that she should take pleasure in his company with her husband so lately gone to an unmarked grave.

Then came the night when the usual evening ritual did not happen. Ben excused himself, saying that he was going to see Patience at Mr Milton's house. They needed to tell Mr Milton of their marriage plans. It was Patience's idea. She thought that as his servant of so many years, she needed to at least solicit his approval.

Caroline was pondering how their marriage would affect her living arrangements; she really should make a greater effort to find something acceptable, so she would not be a hindrance to their plans. She was scouring the last skillet with sand when James asked if she would linger downstairs awhile.

'We have some things to talk about. Private things. Just between you and me.'

'As you wish,' she said, hanging up the pan on its hook above the hearth. She settled at the table across from him.

For a long moment he just looked at her. She could feel herself blushing under his scrutiny. Finally, he began. 'You must surely know by now how I feel about you, Caroline. If you are in any doubt, let me explain it to you. I am not flirting with you or playing at some careless courtship when I compliment you or make excuses to be with you. I am totally and hopelessly in love with you.'

She shook her head in protest, not wanting him to continue. Just because – especially because – she was under his roof, he should not talk this way.

'No. Hear me out. Don't interrupt. I have been rehearsing what I wish to tell you for weeks in my mind.' He paused to clear his throat.

She prayed for some timely interruption, some knock at the door, anything to forestall what she was not ready to hear.

'I have been with several women in my life – fascinated by some, infatuated with others – but it never lasted. Nor did I want it to last. These dalliances grew out of mutual boredom, loneliness, lustful curiosity, or sometimes just opportunity – and the attraction faded as quickly as it flared. Always. Except once. And I was very young and vulnerable, my pride hurt more than my heart. It was the certainty of the temporary nature of all those alliances that made them possible for me. The way I feel about you is singular, unique, at least to me.'

She took a deep breath. Looked down at her hands, unable to meet his gaze and said quietly, 'How do you know this time is different, James? Could it be merely that you want something that you cannot have? How do you know that you will not tire of me as you have tired of others?' She couldn't help but think of how quickly John Milton had tired of his wife.

'Because I want a different kind of intimacy with you. I don't want just two bodies grinding together, although after only one stolen kiss by a duck pond in St James's Park, I knew we would fit together as surely as Adam and Eve. I want a true intimacy: body, mind, and soul. I want to stand before an altar and make a lasting vow to you before God. I want you to be the mother of my children and the nurse for my old age – or I yours, whichever fate decrees. But most of all I want you to want that too.'

He ran nervous fingers through his hair, forcing it back with both hands and continued, 'God knows as a husband I have little to offer you. But I would strain every sinew in my body to provide for your sustenance and protection. And for any children that we might have.'

He stood up then and began to pace, looking at the floor and not her, his voice tight with frustration. 'You have made it clear that you need time. But I cannot go on like this, lying down here night after endless night, sleepless, trying to stop myself from thinking about you, picturing you in my bed alone. Or picturing you in my bed and not alone.'

Caroline, heart racing, unable to think how to respond, concentrated on dribbles of rain reflecting the firelight in little prisms on the window glaze behind him. A chaos of color. Separating. Combining. Separating again. Light without illumination. She became aware of the silence hanging between them. She looked up and met his gaze.

'I understand all that you are saying, James. I am honored. What women would not be? I am sure you have left a string of broken hearts in your wake, each of whom would give everything to hear you say what you have said to me. But I do not wish to be one of those broken hearts. I see now that it was a mistake for me to move in here. It was wrong of me to think that such an arrangement would not send false signals. I am sorry. I will move back to Gresham Street tomorrow. You do not need to worry about me. I am no fragile flower that can't stand a little frost.'

She heard those words coming out of her mouth, and yet that was not what she wanted to say. But how could she give the answer she wanted without explaining it to William? No grave to visit. Not even the spot where he died. Sometimes she fantasized that he was still alive. Was it the prospect of betraying him or accepting the reality of his death that was holding her back? The heart of any sane woman would leap with joy at such a proposal. If they could just roll back the last week, go back to the way they were, she could have more time.

'No,' he said, his mouth firm and unsmiling. 'I will move out if it comes to that. I am leaving for the Continent tomorrow. I will be away for a fortnight at least. You might as well know all. I have sold the press to one of the guild masters. They will be picking it up this week.'

'Sold the press! James, why?'

He had stopped his pacing and resumed his seat across from her.

'Do you know what the big November bonfire was, Caroline? The one outside Parliament House?'

'Just the same old celebrations, I suppose,' she said, wondering at the relevance.

'It was a book-burning. We didn't report it. I didn't want to publicize it. All the copies Parliament could get their hands on of Roger William's *Bloody Tenent of Persecution*. Milton's *Areopagitica* will be next. And then they will begin to seek out the contraband printers in earnest. By then, if they should look my way – and trust me they will, every man has enemies – the press will be long gone. I will merely say that I suffered from lack of large projects and was forced to sell the press. I have destroyed the proofs of the Milton pamphlets. They won't go after any of us. But they will still have won.'

'Oh James, I am so sorry. You are so good at what you do. Think of all the readers you have reached.' And then she had another thought. 'James, what about Ben?'

'Ben's journeyman status has been approved. He can work anywhere he wants. The masters all have their own presses. He will keep the type and blocks and trays. He and Patience can live here. They can have the whole downstairs and you can keep the upper chamber. I will not be here. The lease is prepaid for two more years. Parliament will not interfere with it, I think, since Ben fought with Cromwell's army.'

Outside the window the light had dimmed. The color was gone, and only gray streaks of water marked the pane. 'You will not be here? Where—'

'This city is choking me. I don't belong here. No matter who wins. Maybe if John Pym had lived . . . but, without strong leadership, Parliament is splintering into factions. If the King loses – and I think he will eventually – there will be a period of bloody chaos and retribution, jackals converging on the spoils. Then the military will take over. The strongest man standing will rule. I have fallen in love with the idea of freedom almost as much as I have fallen in love with you. Freedom, but not chaos. The idea of self-governance has rekindled a hope in me that I thought had died. I want to help build the kind of society that Roger Williams is working toward on his plantation in Narragansett Bay. It is a venture that, if it succeeds, might just make a new world.'

His voice grew soft, his tone almost regretful. 'Roger invited me to leave with him when he went. Said he and his sons would help me build a house, clear a patch of land, plant a crop. Said there was already a growing fishing industry and fur trade. Even jokingly said they would soon need a printer. There was already one in Boston, but it was a Puritan press. In six months I would earn the status of freeman and I could vote. Imagine that, Caroline. A man could have a voice on the kind of government he wanted to live under. No king, no royal fees or Parliament taxation without the consent of the governed. A people governed by their own settled law, and not by whimsy; each man given his right to due process. It was so tempting. I told him I wanted to stay to see his project through, but I could have found a printer in Amsterdam for him. I would have taken ship, right then, had it not been for—'

Leaning across the table, she put her fingers to his lips, to stop his saying it. She could not bear the thought of his leaving. But he had drunk a magic elixir and she knew there was no stopping him now, and she would not stop him if she could. Then, hardly knowing what she was doing, on some unfamiliar impulse that suddenly seized her, she pressed her lips to his. The kiss was long and filled with pent-up passion, a kiss unlike any she had ever shared with her late husband.

She could almost feel William's presence. She pulled away, her face burning, shivering inside.

He sat still as a statue, smiling, a hint of self-satisfaction in his eyes.

'William will not always be there between us, Caroline. He will fade. The dead always do. But I want you to remember that kiss while I am gone. That is real. That is now. Whatever you owed to William is in the past.'

She was not likely to forget it. She would take the guilty pleasure of it to her grave. But even if reason taught her to ignore her sense of betrayal, how could she leave everything she'd ever known? If what he said was true, she just might be able to hold him here. But to what purpose? He would learn to resent it. To resent her.

'I am going to Amsterdam tomorrow. I think the Dutch merchant ships are better built and their sailors more knowledgeable of trade winds than the lighter English ships. Their crossings are more frequent and faster than the Massachusetts Bay Company.'

He had been thinking about this for a while, she realized. It was no impulsive scheme.

'Caroline, while I am gone I want you to think about what I have said to you. Think about our building a future together. Think about new falling snow on evergreens and virgin hardwood forests. Think about fertile fields with soil that is not blood-soaked, and skies so clear you can see the glory of the firmament against a night sky. Think about what it will be like to breathe free air and build something together, unhindered by the whims of a tyrannical government. Ask yourself, Caroline, what have we to lose, balanced against all that we could gain?'

What indeed? But how could she leave Ben?

'Ships make frequent crossings. If you are not happy there, we can always come back and start over here, once the war is over. Or maybe Ben and Patience will join us there. Start their own newspaper. Print what they want without guild or government interference. Build a cabin next to ours so our children can play with their children.'

No mention of sickness and hardship. Even thinking of the long crossing made her queasy. Nothing but water around them for weeks. No mention of pirate ships? No mention of stormy seas? But what a landscape he painted to tempt her. It was as though he read her mind. No wonder he was so good at cards.

'They probably don't allow card-playing there, James. They are pretty godly folk, I hear.' She tried to resume the easy bantering tone they often enjoyed.

He laughed then. 'Unenforced piety, my darling. That's the beauty of it. Every man to his own conscience, to worship when and how and if he pleases. Consider it. We could be married here before we leave. Just think about it, Caroline. And in the hope that you make the right choice, I am going to book a cabin instead of a single berth.'

She felt something akin to panic.

'James, you are too optimistic. The picture you paint is not realistic at all, and I am not sure . . . But I will think about it while you are in Amsterdam. I promise. I will give you my answer when you return, God willing.'

'That is good enough,' he said. 'But since I believe that there is a certain hope that your answer will be affirmative, and since I want there to be no secrets between us, I have something I wish to show you. With your permission, I shall retrieve it from upstairs.'

She heard him climbing the stairs, his steady footfalls crossing the floor, then hurrying back down. Resuming his seat, he rested his closed fist on the table.

'I fell in love with you I think the first time I saw you. And it was not in the coaching inn or at the guardhouse in Reading.'

'It wasn't? But when? Where? I would have remembered.'

He opened his fist and a pearl ring fell onto the table.

Was that? She picked it up. It was. Her ring. The pearl ring William had given her. The pearl ring that was stolen by a highwayman brandishing a pistol just outside of Reading.

'You . . . I don't understand. How did you know it was mine?'

'Because it was I who took it from you.'

The thief's face had been covered. All she had seen was his eyes. And one strand of dark hair – hair as dark as his – pulled tight behind his low-brimmed hat. For a moment she almost lost her breath.

'You? It was you? A common thief? You pointed a gun at William, threatened to shoot him?'

His voice was quiet. He did not look at her as he tried to explain. 'It was a spur-of-the-moment act. A lark. I had never stolen anything before. But that night I had been to a royal gathering and they had taken up a collection for the King. All the courtly sycophants were there, the ones who had not run to the Continent with the Queen. I just kept thinking how useless it all was. Charles Stuart didn't need their sovereigns and crowns, their gems and gold chains. At worst it would only go to buy guns and bullets. At best some Flemish painting or gilded saint for the Queen's Royal Chapel.'

The drizzle had turned to sleet. Caroline was conscious of it pinging the window. Every little piece like the prick of a needle somewhere inside her.

'I could put a haul like that to better use than the King. A haul like that would buy a new press I had my eye on. I followed Edward Hyde out when he left and relieved him of it and more besides – a bundle of silver candlesticks and gold plate he had collected earlier. It was so easy.'

He looked up at her then. His eyes, dark and troubled, squinting, like a man startled by the light. 'I was on my way to sell it when I saw your coach.'

'Was that a lark too, my lord? A lark to rob a poor merchant and fright a helpless women half to death?'

'Helpless? You, Caroline, are the least helpless woman I know. But I repented it before you were out of sight. I don't know why I took your ring. I knew the King's haul was more than enough. Maybe it was the thrill. You must believe me. I would never have hurt you or the coachman or William or anyone else. You know me by now. You know I would never shoot a stranger.'

'I thought I knew you. But now I see that you are not the man I thought you were.' She hardened her gaze, feeling betrayed, wanting to hurt him, and said, 'Highway robbery is a hanging offense. You, my lord, are nothing more than a common criminal.'

He visibly flinched under the lash of her words. Words she hated even as she said them. She did know him, or at least some part of him. 'Is that why you went out of the way to help me? Because you suddenly found a conscience? Or was highway robbery just another adventure?'

'I didn't recognize you then. Not for months. I dreamed about you. I could hear your voice in my dreams – strident, strong, taunting an armed criminal; the voice you are using now – but I could not recall your face or even remember your name. It was maddening. But I didn't try to find you. I knew that you were married. I had never seduced a married woman knowingly. You must believe me, Caroline, when I saw you in that coach house, just another woman, frightened and alone, all I wanted was to help you. I was drawn to you without any ulterior motive other than to protect you. That should have been the first time we met.'

The silence lay between them, the weight of it choking her. Finally, she found her voice. 'I have much to be grateful to you for, James. I thought you were a good man. Exemplary in compassion and resourcefulness. I suppose in some ways you are. I could overlook the gambling by telling myself that it was a game, a sport that men played with each other. But now I am questioning your good sense, your character, your judgment.'

A ghost of a grin returned. 'That's why you would be such a good wife for me, don't you see?'

But if he meant it to be disarming it was not.

'No man is all good, Caroline. I don't pretend to be better than

I am, but with you I can be better. It was important to me that you knew the worst. Doesn't that count for something?'

'William was so humiliated to think he could not protect his wife. He could hardly look at me.'

'I will confess, I regretted it as soon as I saw the lightness of his purse. I had reasoned that he was probably some incognito nobleman. Anybody out on that lonely road with a crested coach would be a fool. I misjudged the target.'

'Target. That says it all, doesn't it? He was just a target. Not a person. A target.'

The ring lay on the table between them. He picked it up, fondled it almost lovingly.

'The ring was a good piece. Your husband had good taste. But I couldn't sell it. I wanted to keep it for some reason that I didn't even know. I think it was because that was the day I fell in love with you.'

The bell on the door jangled in the silence between them. Ben came in with a gust of wind, shaking off the rain. 'Surprised to see the two of you still up . . .'

'We were waiting for you,' James said. 'Did Mr Milton give his blessing?' His voice sounded flat and tired, lacking in the passion with which he had just made his declaration.

'Sort of. His biggest concern was for himself. No surprise there. He wanted to know if Patience could stay long enough to train a new girl. I told him he'd better get two to replace her,' he said, going over to warm his hands by the fire. 'Feels more like January out there than November.'

'I am happy for you, Ben,' Caroline said, standing up, giving him a little kiss on the cheek, 'really happy. It is late, and I am suddenly very tired. I think I am going on up.'

As she stood up, James slid the ring across the table. 'Don't forget this, Caroline. It would be a shame to lose it twice,' he murmured.

DEATH COMES FOR
THE ARCHBISHOP

*I most willingly leave this world being very weary at my
very heart of the vanities of it, and my own sins many and
great, and of the grievous destruction of the Church of
Christ almost in all parts of Christendom, and particularly
in this kingdom.*

William Laud, Archbishop of Canterbury, upon
the imposition of his death sentence by
Parliament's bill of attainder

January 1645

W inter in Paris was not easy for Henrietta. Cold seeped
into the walls of the palace and into her bones,
bringing boredom and fatigue. At a dimly lit stone
altar each dawn (how she missed her glorious chapel, with its
Rubens paintings and glittering candelabra), like some ancient
cloistered nun, she prayed the Hours of the Virgin: *Ave Maria,
gratia plena, Dominus tecum.* The prayers for Prime were
followed by Matins and Lauds and throughout the day, ending
with Vespers and Compline. Her prayer book, her treasured illu-
minated *Horae*, had belonged to her mother, a gift from Cardinal
Richelieu when they were on better terms. Being little used by
Maria de' Medici, its jeweled binding was scarcely worn at all.

After each *Ave* and in between the proscribed prayers, Henrietta
beseeched the Holy Mother to imbue her husband with the
wisdom she feared he lacked and, in tearful petition, to protect
her youngest children, left behind in England without father or
mother to protect them.

She prayed also for Lucy Hay. Henry and Elizabeth's welfare, and mayhap their very lives, depended on her former friend's loyalty and resourcefulness. She prayed too for Anne Villiers, Lady Dalkeith, who still was caring for little Minette. Sometimes Henrietta's arms ached from wanting to hold that child to her breast. She had been the hardest one of all to birth, and somehow that made her more precious. *Ave Maria, gratia plena, Dominus tecum.* The Virgin knew that ache.

Edward Hyde had written assuring her that the children were well and still being cared for by their guardians, whose names he wisely did not write. 'Lord willing,' he'd said, 'and Parliament's consent, it should not be long before Lady Dalkeith can bring the child to France to join her mother and her brothers.' Henrietta suspected he'd thrown in the bit about Parliament, implying permission would be sought, in case the letter fell into the wrong hands. She had to concede that she might have been wrong about Edward Hyde. He was now her only link with her children, and she was beginning to trust him. What choice did she have?

In her misery, the Queen shunned the company of her favorites, weary of Lord Jermyn's huddled conversations with Henry Percy, their secretive whispers and sober faces, too quick to put on false smiles and feigned cheer whenever she appeared, as if they were all enjoying a jolly holiday away from the fray, as if across the channel her husband's kingdom was not tearing itself apart. Jeffrey's foolishness became so offensive to her in his silly disregard for the war in England that more than once she had shrieked at the dwarf, banishing him from sight.

Only good news from England could lift the pall that had settled over her spirit. But there had been no real news of late, good or otherwise. Not since Newbury. Charles's letters had become infrequent and shorter, just a few lines assuring his 'dearest heart' that he sorely missed her but that, despite having sustained losses at Newbury because of the treachery of the Covenanters, he was confident that the loyal Scots in the North would rally in support of their King. As to the defeat, he blamed the 'cowardly' Earl of Newcastle more than he credited parliamentary forces. The tone of the letter did not bode well – it was as if saying everything would turn out as he wished it would make it so. This was a characteristic fault in her husband that she had long dealt with, but this time she was no longer there to manage it.

Henry Percy had said he'd heard that the Earl of Newcastle 'fled the field.' Henrietta had no love for the general, but he was not a coward and had proven himself to be an able commander. With some coaxing he could be brought back. She had written Charles, advising thusly, but he did not answer. Since that time there had been one brief message at Christmastide, containing no real news, saying only that because he was in the field it was harder to write. A veiled warning to her that he was shutting her out? That he no longer required her advice? That did not bode well for the House of Stuart.

'Lord Jermyn, has there been no message again this week from the chancellor? This is the fourth week. They have all gone strangely silent. I feel our correspondence is being intercepted – or worse . . .' But she could not voice the worst, could not even allow herself to think it.

'Nothing, I am afraid. But don't worry, Your Majesty. Bad news rides a swift horse. I am sure everything is going well, or we would have heard even without the chancellor's reports. Many in France would cheer bad news from England, and I have heard nothing in the taverns. Will you dine with us tonight? We miss your company.'

When she did not answer, he tried to tempt her out of her mood. 'We can bring in your favorite court musician. He is beginning to need the practice. The King would not want you to worry yourself into ill-health.' Then he added softly, 'Nor do I.'

But even his entreaties did not move her. 'The King should write and tell me that himself,' she said. 'I will sup in my room tonight. If any messenger should come, seek me in the chapel or my chamber, no matter the hour.'

Lucy Hay had never witnessed an execution and, having grown into womanhood with the threat of the dreaded executioner's axe within her family, had no wish to. That she had not attended Thomas Wentworth's was a cowardly act of which she was ashamed. In her darkest moments she had wondered if he had searched in vain for her face in the crowd that horrible day. That thought haunted her. The last words she had spoken to him had been the hollow reassurance when she had visited his Tower cell, that everything was going to be all right. The same last words

Charles had given. But Lucy would have moved heaven and earth to make those last words true, while Charles Stuart would not even use his royal prerogative.

On the day that the frail old archbishop met his maker, Lucy took Princess Elizabeth to visit her tutor in the Strand, where Bathsua Makin was recovering from an ague at her home. The girl had badgered her for two weeks, begging Lucy to take her to see the most learned lady in England, saying she was falling behind in her Greek and Hebrew, until finally Lucy gave in, thinking: What could it hurt? If the woman was too ill to see her precocious royal pupil, they would just leave. At least it would stop the girl's nagging. And there was one errand Lucy had been planning in London.

The tutor looked frail but seemed pleased to see her royal pupil and dismissed Lucy summarily, telling her to come back in three hours. Three hours. In London. In January. With dirty snow lining the gutters, and none but the most desperate souls hazarding the slick streets. Little past nine bells. Whatever was she to do for the other two? This was no longer the London of thriving shops and pretty store windows.

'Where to, my lady?' the coachman asked, his words muffled by his thick wool scarf.

She fingered the clasp on the tiny embroidered purse. 'Goldsmith's Row, Cheapside.'

The creaking of the carriage wheels echoed forlornly. No other soul was in sight in one of the most celebrated shopping districts in all of Europe. Cheapside market had been a source of pride for Charles Stuart. More than a decade gone, he had ruthlessly banished all who hawked cheap jewelry and recruited the most skilled artisans and saw that the guild regulated them to the highest standards. But the war had exacted its due here and the few shops still in business were curtained.

She leaned her head out the window and shouted, 'There. Stop there.'

The driver pulled over. No glittery merchandise brightened the window, but the curtain was partially drawn, and the sign of the jeweler's little golden hammer was clearly visible. Thomas Simpson's sign. She knew him. He had once made a counterfeit piece for her that even she thought must surely be real.

She exited the coach carefully since there was no footman. She could not really blame the coachman for not stirring his blanketed legs. 'Wait here,' she shouted over her shoulder. She tried the door, but it was locked. Peeping through the half-drawn curtain into the darkened interior, she saw no movement. A stiff wind stirred the fur trim of her hood as she pounded on the door and called out. At last she heard the latch lift and Simpson himself appeared in the doorway.

'We are not open today,' he said, and started to close the door in her face.

'Please, Master Simpson, just a short consultation. We have done business before. I have come a long way.'

He opened the door just wide enough for her to squeeze through. Shutting the door behind her, she threw back her hood and gave him her brightest smile.

'I shan't take up much of your time, though I will confess that I am surprised to find you not open for business.'

'Not a good day for doing business. Only drunkards and riff-raff abroad on such a day.'

How was this day different than any other? she was wondering, when he said, 'I remember you, Lady Carlisle. It has been awhile. I am afraid my merchandise is much depleted. Not much market for fine gems these days – even counterfeit.'

'I am not here to purchase. The war has beggared both my need for fine jewelry and my capacity to afford it – a reordering of priorities, as I am sure you can understand. If you would be so kind as to indulge me, I simply wish a moment of your time for an expert opinion.' When he didn't immediately answer, she flashed him a smile. 'Please. It will only take a moment, I promise.'

He frowned and for a moment she thought he was going to refuse, then he said with a frown, 'A moment only. Now, how may I be of service?'

She pulled the little embroidered purse from without the pocket of her mantle and fished for the contents. The jewels lent their light to the dim interior of the shop. 'I wish to know if these are genuine or if they are imitation,' she said, handing him the earrings Thomas Wentworth had given her before he died.

He took them over to his desk and looked at them for a long moment through a small round glass. 'They are genuine. The diamonds are from India and, frankly, my lady, I have not seen any that might surpass them in clarity.' He handed them back. 'I cannot give you an estimate of their value in such uncertain times. In England they would not bring what they should. In Paris or the Netherlands perhaps. The Dutch still have a thriving trade.'

'What if you broke the diamonds up into their singular stones? Would they be easier to sell? I would like to keep the two emeralds for myself. Perhaps in a plain gold ring.'

He looked thoughtful. 'The smaller stones perhaps would find a ready buyer – the two pendant cuts would be harder because of their value. But, Lady Carlisle, I would strongly advise you not to do that. They are much more valuable as they are. The workmanship of the setting is exquisite.'

'I cannot wear the diamonds in these uncertain times and, frankly, good sir, it would give me peace of mind to have their value in ready coin – except for the two small emeralds,' she repeated. They were the color of Wentworth's eyes.

The jeweler examined the earrings again then looked back at her, pausing as though weighing something in his mind. 'I have many clients who share your reservations about the value and safety of their belongings. They have made certain arrangements with me for their safe-keeping.'

'What sort of arrangements?'

'May I have your word that you will keep our conversation private?'

'Certainly. I am the keeper of many secrets.'

He smiled. 'I can well imagine,' he said. 'It is a simple arrangement. Some clients deposit valuables with me for safe-keeping: gold bars, guineas, ducats, precious objects, jewels. Many of the owners are out of the country for various reasons. A few are off on the battlefield, some in exile, and some just feel that their more valuable and portable goods are safer on deposit. It gives them a certain peace of mind against marauders, thieves, looters, confiscation.'

'Deposits? Is such business legal?'

'It is sanctioned by the Worshipful Company of Goldsmiths, though the practice is not commonly known. Again, I am trusting your discretion.'

'Be certain of it, sir, if you will grant me the same. It would do me no good service if my possession of the diamonds should be noised about. But still, it gives me pause to leave them with you without some surety.'

'You will have surety. I give you a certificate of deposit with my signature as a guild master and a description, approximate value, and quality of the items deposited. You may draw against that amount at any time, should you desire. There is no redemption fee. You simply present your certificate.'

'Please don't take offense at my skepticism. I am a simple woman. What if you should die, what claim would I have?'

'Or abscond with your diamonds? In the first unfortunate event, you need only present your document to the Goldsmiths' Company to claim your jewels. In the second, you will be compensated by the guild, and I will be hunted down and hanged.'

It sounded a little like a scheme to her, but she could see the appeal. 'If I may have some time to think about it.'

'I understand.' He smiled at her knowingly. 'You are a "simple woman."' He handed her back the diamonds. 'Perhaps if you saw the place where your diamonds would be kept? I have a safe vault in my cellar. Would you like to see it and what others have given into my safe-keeping?'

He went to the back of the small showroom and motioned for her to follow, seemingly having forgotten that he had no time for her. 'My work room is down here.' He opened a door and she could see down into a daylit basement. Beneath the leaded window that fronted on the alley was a workbench littered with bits of metal and a tiny pick and hammer. On one side lay a half-strand of pearls with a clasp of lapis. On the opposite was a wall of shelving containing jars of shiny bits of metal and small colorful stones – most of them semi-precious. He turned his back to her and, as if by magic, the wall of shelving shifted to reveal a sturdy oak door with iron hinges. Taking a key from around his neck he unlocked it. A creaking of hinges and she was staring into a small windowless stone chamber that smelled of stale air.

Drawers, with numbers scrawled on the face of each, lined one whole wall. On a table immediately to the left was a table covered with a threadbare damask cloth. He held his lantern high and drew back the cloth to reveal gleaming gold and silver utensils: candelabras, candlesticks, goblets set with rubies and pearls, bowls of inlaid rock crystal, heavy gold chains, each item tagged with a number that she assumed corresponded to the heavy ledger bound in leather and chained to the wall.

'What a fantastic hoard. But I don't understand. There is tremendous responsibility here. A lot of work just keeping up with it all. Where is your profit from such an endeavor?'

He smiled. 'Well, you should ask. I like to see beautiful things preserved, but I am a businessman too. Those large drawers hold caches of gold coin, given to me on deposit for safe-keeping, which I can loan out for interest within the time of the contract.' He went over to one of the small numbered drawers and pulled out an object wrapped in soft wool. 'This item belonged to one who is awaiting trial. Upon his death, if the certificate is not presented by one of his heirs before its redemption date, then by terms of the contract, this will become my property.' He unwrapped an exquisite little snuffbox inlaid with emerald and rubies. 'This and other of his effects he put into my safe-keeping before he went to Tower Prison. He will not need it much longer.'

'How can you be so sure?'

He looked surprised. 'You mean you have not heard? All of London is preparing for a celebration at his execution. Archbishop Laud is much despised in this town. There will be plenty of drunken Scots celebrating with their raucous pipes. There may even be looting. Have you not noticed the street is shut down and all the windows empty?'

'Today? He is being executed today? I did not even know the trial was over. Are you sure?'

'I am sure. Why else would I close my shop?'

What if Princess Elizabeth should witness the execution? Or be threatened by ruffians? Why had Bathsua Makin not warned her?

'I had no love for the Archbishop, Master Simpson, but I have no wish to see his bloody head. I am sorry, I must go. I will get back to you about the diamonds and maybe some other things. Thank you for your advice, and be assured I shall keep your confidence. But, right now, I must see to it that a child in my care does not witness such a spectacle. We must get out of town before the crowd turns violent.'

'The execution is scheduled for noon today. The crowds will already be gathering on Tower Hill. Which way are you headed?'

'Chelsea, to gather my charge. And then west toward Richmond.'

'If you go now you will likely escape the greatest press of people.'

When she arrived at the tutor's house, Mistress Makin met her at the door, her face ashen. 'Thank God. I felt sure you would come as soon as you became aware. I am sorry, Lady Carlisle. I have not been out, and I did not know until one of my servants asked for the afternoon off. You should have no trouble going back to Syon House. Everybody will be in a hurry to get good viewing positions for the spectacle. I have already explained to the princess that you will be coming back to get her sooner than expected, but that she may come again. Is your coachman trustworthy?'

'Yes, I have used him often.'

'*Dominus vobiscum*,' Bathsua shouted as Lucy guided the princess into the carriage.

'*Pax tecum*,' Elizabeth called back.

If anything was different about the London streets, Elizabeth seemed not to notice, only once asking why the horses were in such a hurry. She chattered constantly about how Bathsua had praised her, stopping only to ask when they could return.

'When she is feeling stronger,' Lucy answered, relieved, as the coach turned into Syon Lane, that both had been spared the bloody spectacle. Her heart squeezed a little thinking of the frail old man and the manner of his death. The magnificent little snuffbox, smaller than a human heart and encrusted with gems, was symbolic of a prideful life marked by power and ambition. *All is vanity, sayeth the prophet.*

As they hurried across the lawn, the garden dial pointed straight at 12.00. A shiver that had nothing to do with the cold crawled up her spine. She said a little prayer for William Laud then, importuning mercy for the soul of the old churchman. Surely, he would get some consideration before a throne of judgment for his lifelong devotion to the Church of England. And then she remembered the cruelty he had imposed on those who disagreed with his interpretation of the sacred, and the prideful imposition of his arbitrary liturgy that had ignited the war. But weighed in the scales of Divine Justice, how could any soul survive? Christ, have mercy on him.

Christ, have mercy on us all.

How empty the print shop feels without its chief workhorse, Caroline thought as she swept gray spider wool from the spot where the great press had crouched. She already missed the wooden giant they would no longer need to feed. It was mid-afternoon now, and Ben had gone with the buyer from the guild to help set it up in its new home, leaving her alone with her thoughts.

James had been gone only a week. It seemed an age. When she was not terrified that he would not return at all, she dreaded his return because he would demand an answer. And whatever answer she gave would surely change her life forever in ways she could not possibly foresee. How could she know what hazards, what hardships, waited beyond the waters? He was a man too driven by reckless impulse. How could she trust him? Right now, he was bewitched by a dream. She wished Roger Williams had never come into the print shop, spreading his contagious freedom talk. Freedom for what? Freedom to starve? Freedom to be killed by savages? Freedom to wrestle bare sustenance from raw, unyielding land and fickle seas?

She opened the door to sweep the broom's gleanings into the dirty, stinking street, and tried to imagine what visions James Whittier conjured in his head: pristine snow on green trees, clear blue skies unsoiled by smoke from ten thousand coal fires. Birdsong instead of cannon fire. And every man master of his own land and household.

But she could not see what he saw. No clean air filled her lungs, just grit that made her cough. All she felt was the dagger-edged wind whistling down Fleet Street, empty now, the crowds, satiated with revenge, having gone home to sleep it off. All she smelled was the stench of the river. Shivering, she shut the door. Very probably, despite his earnest protestation of love, she was no more to James Whittier than a prop in his imaginary utopia. And when his golden dream turned out to be thinly gilded, would his love prove likewise of baser substance? She bent to retrieve a piece of straw that had broken away from the broom, threw it on the fire. It flared and was consumed. Like love too easily won, promises too easily made.

Yet, what could be worse than here, she wondered, remembering the morning's horror. To remain in England without James meant meeting each new day's struggle alone. Did not Scripture promise a new heaven and a new earth? Could there really be a new England? What sane person would not wish to abandon the old kingdom after having witnessed what she had seen this noon?

She had been coming home from the Smithfield market, exhausted from searching out a bit of stringy stew meat, when she turned toward Fleet Street. Just after eleven bells she noticed a growing crowd of people, striding purposefully toward Tower Hill. It was a hostile crowd. Something or someone had stirred a hornets' nest. And then it occurred to her.

Today was the tenth day of January. Preoccupied with her own emotional turmoil, she had remembered too late the screaming headlines of last week's news books. How could she have forgotten something so horrible to contemplate?

She paused only long enough to take two deep breaths and shift her bundle safely under her arm. If she hurried she could get safely home before the streets became too clogged. Peering anxiously as the pace of the mob quickened, she darted down an alley, thinking to avoid the main thoroughfare, only to discover the alley too was filling up, cutting off her exit. Angry voices assaulted her ears as, jostled by the growing mob, all headed in the same direction, she struggled against a surging tide. Too late. Her heart was seized with a cold dread. Trapped in a foul knot of humanity pressing in upon itself, she was carried along like a swimmer fighting a swirling current,

At the western edge of Tower Hill, the mob slowed to a standstill. Wedged between an ill-smelling tanner and a pair of stable boys, Caroline tried to get her breath. Neither they nor she could move for the press of people all around.

In the distance, Caroline caught only a glimpse of the small, bent stick of a man, slowly climbing the last steps he would ever climb. *Oh God. Please. No.*

Shouts erupted all around her as she shut her eyes, but she could not shut out the cries. 'Laud. Laud. Laud. Give us his head. Give us his head.' Raised fists pumped the air, around, behind, in front, as a chant rose up. 'Cut off his papist head. His head. His head. Give us his head.'

The great mass of flesh inched forward. She could not breathe. But her companions had no trouble. Their chants and curses paused only when the Puritan chaplain, who towered over the condemned priest, lifted his powerful arms and thundered, 'Silence. Let the condemned man speak.'

When the Archbishop stood to speak, she could not hear his fainter words from her great distance. Unfortunately, the platform was high enough that no man or object blocked her vision. As the old man lowered his head on the block, she lowered her head too, so that all she saw was brown earth being scarred and beaten beneath shuffling, stamping feet. But no matter how hard she pressed her hands against her ears, she could not stop the jeers and cheers of the crowd when the axe fell. A great moaning of bagpipes joined the chants and shouts as the bloody head was lifted high. For one flashing moment she thought this must be what Hell was like. Her throat closed against the burning that erupted from her stomach. Dizzy with horror, she fought to keep her balance as the crowd surged forward and around her. But, arms flailing, she held her footing, working her way backwards until she was on the outer fringe. From somewhere she found the strength to run. Somewhere along the way she had dropped the hard-won meat she was carrying; all that was left was a smear of blood that had leaked onto her sleeve.

She had not heard Ben come in. Nor did she have any memory of how long she had been sitting in the chair, rocking back and forth, thinking of nothing, watching the embers in the fireplace sputter and fall away, the only other sound the numbing rhythm of the rocker, back and forth, back and forth, solace in its repetition. Slowly she became aware of his voice, close to her ear, leaning over her.

'Caroline, thank God, you are here. I have been looking everywhere for you. I came home too late to remind you against going out.' Then, his voice catching on his breath, 'Is that blood on your sleeve?' He tilted her face toward him. 'Talk to me, Caroline. You have a bruise on your cheek. Are you hurt?'

She touched her cheek. It felt warm and knobby. She flinched, finding her voice slowly. 'Did you see, Ben? Did you see them cut off the Archbishop's head?'

'No. I was too busy looking for you. The last thing milord said when he left was for me to look after you.' His voice broke then, 'My father would have been so angry with me for not keeping you safe.'

She looked down at the rusty stains on her sleeve. 'I was coming from the market. I lost the meat that was to be your supper.'

'Never mind about that. You need to rest. Drink this. It will calm you.' She took a swallow from the cup he was holding before her, scarcely feeling the burn in her throat. 'Let me help you upstairs. It is over now. You are safe. Try not to think about it. I will bring you something to eat after you've rested.'

But she did not sleep. Each time fatigue claimed her, dreams and visions of the day jolted her from her dozing, and she felt the fear rising. She longed for William. The warmth of his body, his sturdy presence, was the kind of assurance she needed now. But when Caroline envisioned the man she missed, try as hard as she might, it was not William's dear face she saw.

When the printers came to haul away the press, she was still awake. She waited until they were gone, and Ben with them, to go downstairs. Fatigue clouded her mind and slowed her steps. She picked up the broom and began to sweep. When Ben came back, she would need to help him set up his father's bed. Soon to be his marriage bed. The banns for his wedding to Patience Trapford had already been read. They were planning to wed when James returned. When James returned, he would want an answer from her. For the hundredth time since he left, Caroline wondered what that answer would be?

She looked down at the pearl ring on her finger. She had given her wedding ring to Ben to give to his bride, telling him it had been his mother's, insisting that his father would want him to have it. She knew he couldn't afford one. But her finger felt naked without it, so she had put the pearl ring in its place. But it only reminded her of the opportunist and the thief who stole it. Suddenly unable to bear it, she slid it off her finger and placed it on the mantle.

'William, tell me what to do,' she murmured. William did not answer.

DREAMS AND ENDEAVORS

All great and honourable actions are accompanied with great difficulties and must be both enterprised and over-come with answerable courages . . . such attempts were not to be made and undertaken without good ground and reason, not rashly or lightly as many have done for curiositie or hope of gain.

From the Journal of William Bradford on the exiled
Puritans in Holland and their decision to
emigrate to New England in 1620

Mid-morning and already the girl was restless. Lucy watched as Princess Elizabeth stared out from the salon windows at the bleak landscape. The grey skies portended ill for another long day of trying to keep her happy. The nurse helped occupy Henry, and Carter – bless his soul – never complained as he went about his daily chores about the boy being underfoot. The long-suffering servant had contrived a miniature feather-duster for the young prince, who wielded it with more industry than result, sometimes teasing the lazy cat that slept beside the hearth until the cat, with Henry chasing after, indignantly walked away to hide behind a cupboard. Elizabeth's occupation was harder won. Since their hurried flight from London, the girl had seemed unsettled, almost as though she had witnessed the dreadful scene from which Lucy had, by sheer good fortune, managed to spare her.

'If Mistress Makin cannot come here, why can you not take me back to her house?' The girl's tone was demanding, as only a royal's can be, but with a pinch of childish whine added for seasoning.

'As I have explained before, Your Grace, it is not safe to travel just now. I thought you were engaged with reading the Hebrew Scriptures.'

'But there are many words I cannot translate. I worry that I might lose what I have already learned if I do not have regular lessons.'

The almost panic in her voice was touching in an odd way. A young girl, with one parent in exile and the other under siege, a child whose world was literally threatened with falling apart, and she was most upset because she could not study with her favorite tutor? Or was she merely anxious without knowing why?

Lucy was no stranger to that kind of nagging anxiety. It first appeared after Wentworth's death. Since John's death, unease had become her closest companion, nudging her like a rapacious lover in the middle of the night, bludgeoning sleep until the day's distractions brought relief. But the fact of the Archbishop's death, even though Lucy had not witnessed his execution, increased her unwelcome companion's constancy. The knowledge that Parliament could be so bold was chilling. Who was outside its reach? Certainly not an unprotected, childless widow.

'I am indeed sorry to see you so distressed,' Lucy said, hugging the child gently. 'Why don't you join Carter and Henry in the kitchen? I think Cook might have some marzipan biscuits.' An ages-old distraction, she thought. But such treats were harder to come by these days.

'May we go to the attic afterward to watch the deer foraging in Richmond Park?'

'Henry has a snotty nose, and it is too cold in the attic today for you as well. Besides, the sky is so overcast you cannot see the deer from that distance.'

The girl looked as if she didn't know whether to cry or protest. Lucy was thinking she couldn't stand either when the idea occurred. 'After you have had your biscuit and Henry has gone down for his nap, you and I will go to my chamber and each write a letter to your mother. Would you like that?'

Elizabeth eyes widened with interest. 'But how shall we send them?'

'Chancellor Hyde has a trusted friend at St James's Palace. He once told me if we needed anything, I could send a message through him. Well, we need something. We need to write a letter to the Queen. The messenger from St James's will deliver it to Oxford, and the next time the chancellor goes to France, he will personally take our letters with him and place them in the Queen's own hand.'

An inspired idea. Henrietta needed to hear from the children, needed to know too about the Archbishop's execution so that she could consider what Parliament's new boldness meant for her and her family. And Lucy needed to make sure her channel to Henrietta was still in good working order.

'You should hurry, before Henry eats all the biscuits. Be sure to ask Cook for milk. It's good for your bones.'

But the girl would not be hurried. 'Shall I write in Latin? Maman's Latin is very good. Though not as good as mine.'

Lucy couldn't help but smile at this girlish pride. 'French, I think,' she said. 'Your mother would like to know her daughter loves her native language. It will give her comfort in your absence. Besides, if you go to visit her in Paris before she returns, you will need the practice.'

The girl visibly brightened, whether at the prospect of pleasing her mother or the promise of exercise for her eager mind, Lucy couldn't surmise.

Lucy's spirit was also refreshed by the idea. It was a little thing, but action, any action, even small ones, helped to push back anxiety. Who knew where this insanity would end?

'You had better hurry,' she said, 'before Henry licks all the marzipan off the biscuits.' Then, to the girl's retreating back, 'Tell Carter I said for him to make time in his schedule to take a message to St James's Palace on the morrow.'

But Elizabeth was scarcely out of sight before Lucy began to question whether it had been prudent to disclose her arrangement with Hyde. What if a delegation from Parliament should show up at her door? They never had, but now that John was gone, it suddenly might occur to some busybody to come nosing around. They would surely question the girl. Not only would learning of Lucy's arrangement with the chancellor put Lucy under suspicion, it could endanger Carter as well.

Hoary-headed worry, her unwelcome companion, had not retreated into the shadows after all, it appeared. Where was the fearless young woman she had once been: The spirit of the girl who had fled the Tower to elope with an aging Scottish courtier; the spirit of the young woman who had stubbornly refused to worship in the Queen's Catholic chapel, risking royal displeasure? But she had been young then and the world ripe with possibility. Pray God she would never have to flee the Tower again. She took a deep breath as a visible shudder passed through her body. It would not be so easy the second time.

Caroline was away from the print shop on the day James returned. Three times she had tried to meet with the officer of the Committee for Three Kingdoms, making a plea for the rights to the second-floor apartment to be returned to her, claiming her late husband had held a legal lease to it and the Covenanters were no longer using it. Twice he had said he would investigate, taking her name, her late husband's name, and telling her to call on the morrow. On the third day, he told her that he was sorry, but inquiries had revealed her husband, Sir William Pendleton of Oxfordshire, had died fighting for the King. Therefore, his lease was forfeit.

'But his son and rightful heir, Arthur Benjamin Pendleton, lost an arm fighting for Parliament. Certainly, that counts for something.'

'Whose regiment?'

When she answered Cromwell's Regiment in Cambridge, he smiled and said he would make inquiries. He wrote down the name and told her to come back on the morrow. The next morning, he told her he was sorry, but the committee would not let her move back into the leased quarters until after the outcome of the war was settled and a special commission was set up to determine which properties should be returned and which sequestered. All he could do was give her leave to maintain the current arrangements.

On her way back to the print shop, she was considering her only option. She had no intention of intruding on the privacy of the newly wedded couple. The hardest part of the winter would be over soon. The attic room would have to do. Without the press there was no longer work for her at the print shop. She would find her lost income somewhere else. Better to make the move before James came back. It would be easier. She would do it today. Or maybe tomorrow morning, she thought, pulling her coat tighter against a sudden gust. The wind was still out of the

North. The attic would be cold as a tomb tonight. Besides, she had retrieved a forgotten jar of pear conserve from the back of her attic cupboard to make fritters for Ben. They were his favorite. Tomorrow she would come earlier and, if the drawing room was deserted, build a fire in the hearth. The warmth would linger in the attic chimney well into the night.

But when she entered the print shop, she heard James's voice, followed by Ben's easy laughter. Her instinct was to turn and run. She could retrieve her personal things later.

'Is that you, Caroline?' Ben called. 'I promised milord you would be here soon. Did you have any luck with the commissioner?'

Too late to leave now. She scarcely glanced at the pair sitting at the table with a pitcher of ale between them. 'Welcome back, my lord,' she said, taking off her cloak and hanging it on a hook by the door. Stepping into the kitchen nook, she put on her apron. 'The lease is in limbo, subject to forfeiture because William died in the King's service,' she said as she began to beat eggs and flour into a bowl. 'But I told him about your service, Ben, and that bought me a little more time. He said the current circumstances were approved until it could all be sorted out after the war.'

'By current circumstances, if you mean that little mousehole,' Ben said, 'you know that will not do, Caroline. There is plenty of room here. Tell her, milord.' Then he must have sensed the tension in the room; his tone lightened as he said, 'James will be off seeking adventure soon. It will be really lonesome here without you.'

As if he was just going away for a little while; as if he was not leaving their lives forever.

'He's all atwitter with his plans. Trying to talk me into coming with him. Said Patience would probably like it fine. If not Roger's "Little Rhody" plantation, then maybe Plymouth Settlement in Boston. Lots of Puritans and independents there.'

She looked up at him then. At them both, her face burning under James's bold, questioning gaze.

'I told him we might join him later,' Ben said lightly. 'After he's charmed all the savages and built us a fine cabin.'

Caroline was grateful for his easy laughter, but she could not look at James as she asked, 'Your trip was successful then?'

'Very. When you came in, I was telling Ben that I have already booked passage on a fine Dutch merchant ship. *Bedrijf* is its name in Dutch. I think that means *Endeavor.* An appropriate name, wouldn't you say?'

'When will you be leaving for good?' she asked, hearing the smallness of her voice.

'Not for a few weeks. I told Jan, the captain, quite a jolly fellow – we became fast friends – that I would let him know for sure in a couple of weeks.'

'Does that mean you are not sure now?' Ben asked.

'Almost sure. Just a few loose ends to clear up.' His gaze at Caroline was so direct, so questioning, that she could not meet it. He talked on. 'It is a very fine ship. Well built. Sturdy enough to weather rough seas. Good heavy cannon for protection. Ample hold for supplies and cargo. Clean bunks for single travelers. And two private cabins for families. Jan makes four crossings a year for the Dutch West India Company to New Amsterdam, bringing back beaver pelts for sale and taking new supplies to the settlements along the Hudson River. I told him I needed a couple of weeks before I would give him surety. I want to see our young man here happily married. Thursday next, right, Ben?'

'A free man for three more days,' Ben said. 'I am glad you are back, so you and Caroline can be our proper witnesses. The only person Patience invited was Mr Milton, but he declined, saying it was on a school day.'

'When do you sail?' she asked, trying to sound as if it were just idle conversation, trying to keep the quiver from her voice.

'The *Endeavor* sets sail on the Ides of March. Ship manifests are due in on the first of March.'

'Do you have to take supplies? How will you know what is needed?' Ben asked.

'Captain Jan set me up with his quartermaster. Gave me a list. Basic stuff: barrels of flour and salt pork, casks of oil, farming tools, seeds for planting, guns, ammunition, some bolts of good English wool. Said he would also advise some crates of chickens and a rooster. A lot would depend on whether I intend to set up my own household or live in a common house with some single freemen.'

Ben sipped his ale and asked, 'Do you? Plan to have your own household?'

With her back turned, Caroline pretended to busy herself.

'I guess that depends on whether I have need of one. Maybe later. If you and Patience come out. Roger promised me, when he was here, that I could stay with them until the next spring if I don't have time to build a cabin before winter. But in either case, the quartermaster suggested I not try to ship furniture. Simple furnishings, tables, chairs, I can buy over there. A few craftsmen are already set up in New Amsterdam and Boston. He said the Narragansett Bay Plantation was more basic than Boston or Plymouth, but ketches and sloops plied the waters all up and down the coast, trading among the settlements. Jan supplies a large trading post in New Amsterdam.'

'So, milord. Are you going to be a farmer, a fisherman, or a trapper? Which is it?' Ben asked.

She was beating the batter too hard. The fritters would be sure to fall apart. Like everything else in her world.

'Won't know until I can get my feet on the ground.'

'What about the small press? The one you started out with. Are you taking that one?'

'Yes, I am taking that one.' He paused, raised his voice. 'You are very quiet, Caroline. Have you nothing to say about my plans?'

She spooned the batter into the hot grease, trying not to let her hand shake. 'I think it all sounds very frightening, James. I will pray for you every day.'

'Umm that smells good,' Ben said, pushing back his chair, coming to look in her skillet. 'There won't be anybody across the ocean who can make fritters like these. Did you know he was coming home today, Caroline? Is that why you made them?'

'I had no idea when or even if he was coming back,' she said. 'No idea at all.'

Her tone was sharper than she meant it to be. Ben noticed. She could tell from his puzzled expression.

'I am going to tell him, Caroline,' James said quietly. 'He is your family. He has a right to know some of what has passed between us.'

'Tell me what?'

'I have asked your stepmother to marry me.'

He said it flatly, bluntly. The words just hung in the air, like overripe fruit, waiting to fall. Caroline dumped the slightly underdone fritters into a platter, so she could escape, and plopped the platter onto the table between them. 'This is not a conversation I wish to have. Not here. Not now,' she said.

'If not now, when, Caroline?' She turned to leave. James caught her by the wrist. 'Please sit down. Let's talk. Don't you think at least you owe me that much?'

He was right. After all that had happened, she did owe him something. But the way he made her feel whenever he was around, a heady stirring of her senses, a rapid beating of her heart, made it hard to think. What could she say? One by one, he untwined his fingers from around her wrist, but she did not walk away.

Ben smiled at her, a warm, sweet smile. 'This is not a total surprise to me, Caroline. At least it would not have been before milord announced that he is leaving us. I thought then I must have misread the signals.'

'Signals, Ben? What signals?' she asked.

'The way you are together. The two of you. Easier, lighter, even when we are just working, than when you and I are alone. When you are with him you remind me of the Caroline I knew as a boy. It is almost as if the world is not tearing itself to pieces.'

She sat down, her senses so raw that the yeasty, greasy smell of the fritters tightened her throat. 'You do not feel that I would be disloyal to your father's memory marrying so soon?'

'Who am I to pass judgment? My own loyalty to my father is certainly questionable. Families are complicated. Sometimes circumstances force us down unexpected paths. You were a good wife to him while he lived. And as to it being too soon? Life happens faster in such times as these. I would be happy to see two people who are very important to me happy together.' Then he turned to ask James, 'But why are you planning to leave and Caroline making plans to stay?'

'She turned me down.'

There it was. He was forcing her to have it out right now. In front of Ben.

She turned to face him directly. 'And what of me, James? What if I do not want to go off with a man of short acquaintance to a wasteland that lies across an ocean?'

'Is it the "wasteland" that frightens you, Caroline? Or is it that you don't trust me?'

'How can I not trust you, James, after all the kindness you have shown to me and Ben? But trust your judgment? Well, that is another matter.' He was the one who looked away first this time. 'There is a recklessness in this man, Ben. Or have you not noticed?'

Ben nodded. 'I have noticed, Caroline. Though what you call reckless some people might call bold. Bold is not always a bad thing. Difficult times call for bold.' Then Ben looked at James as if he was weighing Caroline's words, considering hard. 'You do have somewhat of a reputation. Do you love Caroline truly, milord? The forsaking-all-others kind?'

James furrowed his brow, eyebrows shooting up like crooked blackbird wings. 'Do I seem like the marrying kind to you? Why else would I propose to her, even campaign to overcome her objections, if I did not wish to bind us together forever?'

She was about to complain that she was not some piece of goods to be bargained for when Ben's words startled her.

'Do you love her enough to abandon your longing for this venture, enough to stay here with her?'

'Stop.' She held up her hand. 'That is not a fair question. You do not need to answer that, James.'

He just smiled, that crooked blackbird-wing brow settling into smooth flight, and said, 'I think it is a fair question. I do need to answer it. Yes, Ben, I do love her enough to marry her, even if she decides she cannot leave.' Then he grabbed both her hands, his forthright gaze riveting her own, making it difficult to doubt his sincerity. 'I suppose that is why I did not reserve a berth on the ship. I could not commit to leaving without you. If you agree to marry me and cannot see your way to going with me, I will abandon the venture. Ben is my witness.'

She pulled her hands from his grip, searching for the right words. 'What about all your elaborate plans? You have already sold the press. Even if I agreed and we stayed here as man and wife, how would we live?'

'We could live by my wits and winnings, as we are now. But I don't think you approve of that.' He shrugged. 'If we had to leave London because of pressure or lack of opportunity, we could go to Holland. I could try my hand at trading. Or there is that rock-pile of an estate I abandoned. We could go back there. A few rooms in the house might be habitable. But just barely. An old caretaker lives there now. He raises pigs and pays me quarterly rents.' He paused and ran his long fingers through his hair, sweeping it back in a gesture of frustration. 'A pig farmer's wife? It would not be much of a life for a lady.'

'I was lady to a conscripted knight, a sheep farmer's wife, James. It wasn't such a bad life, was it, Ben?'

'Not a bad life at all,' he smiled. 'I didn't realize how good it was until it was gone.'

'You could just as well be a farmer's wife in Narragansett Bay, and we would be our own masters, make our own living as we choose, paying no rent and only such small taxes as we vote ourselves, no king's palaces or church wards to fund, no religious tyranny . . .' He held up his hand, palm out, in a gesture that said he knew he was pressing too hard, but he couldn't stop. 'Freedom from the oppressor's yoke, Caroline. Isn't that worth a little risk?'

She could see the tension working in the lines on his brow, the tightening of the muscles in his jaw.

'But I will marry you, Caroline Pendleton, and stay here with you because, wherever we live, whatever we do, I will be happier with you than following some freedom dream without you. Does that answer your question, Ben?'

'That answers my question.'

'Do we have your blessing then?'

'You know how much I admire both of you. And I think my father would give his blessing. He was a very practical man. Not much of a risk-taker. In that way you are very different, but he would not like to see Caroline alone. Not that she would be. You would have Patience and me, Caroline, and you would be more than welcome to live with us. All that, to say it is your choice.'

'Well, Caroline, will you be my wife? If we married soon we would still have a little time to consider together our future before some of our options close. Do you trust me enough to know that even though I will make my best case, I will abide by what your heart desires?'

She was weak with exhaustion. 'I can't think about this now.

I realize the time is short. You deserve an answer. I will return tomorrow and give you an answer.'

'Return? Please, Caroline. Whatever your answer, there is no need for you to go back to Gresham Street. Since I have made my intentions known, for propriety's sake, I will take lodgings in the tavern down the street until we are married – or until I go to America alone. Patience and Ben will have the downstairs and you the upstairs. If we decide to marry and stay in London, we'll decide later about our living arrangements.'

The silence in the room pressed on her as they looked at her expectantly. She could not breathe. 'Thank you for that consideration, James. I will bid you both goodnight. Enjoy your fritters. There is some milk hanging in the cistern beside the back door. Best fetch it now so it can thaw.'

Both men stood up as she left the room, their 'goodnights' following her up the stairs.

For a long time, she lay in the dark, her mind a chaotic jumble, listening to the low voices of James and Ben below, not making out their words, but hearing their easy laughter. It was a comforting sound. Yet when she drifted off to troubled sleep, she found no comfort in her dreams, not images of turbulent seas and stormy gales as she might have expected; instead she was haunted by a sea of another kind. Tides of turbulent humanity pressed in upon her. Fear clotted in her throat, threatened to drown her in fury, all howling for the same thing – the bloody head of one frail old man. She woke at dawn, gasping for breath, thinking for one heart-stopping moment that she was being forced to look into the dead eyes of the Archbishop Laud's bloody head.

The sound of Ben, already stirring below as he stoked the banked fire to life, brought her back to reality. But the dream – more memory than dream – had been reality too. She dressed quickly, washed her face in cold water and ran a comb through her hair, braided it into a bun and went downstairs.

'The two of you were up late last night,' she said.

'I hope we didn't disturb you,' Ben said. 'He was telling me all about the ship, about the plans he'd made . . .' He left off brushing some embers back from the hearth to look up at her. 'Tentative plans, all depending on you, of course. And I was feeling a little restless too. It isn't everyday a man takes a wife.'

'Did he say what time he was coming back here?'

'He said he didn't want you to feel pressured. Said he was going to give you a little time. He had some things to tend to. Said he wanted to see about getting an apprenticeship for Ralphie and to check on Little John with Mr Milton. He said to tell you he'd be back well before sunset and for us not to cook. He'd bring a pie and a bottle of wine. And I don't think he meant for me to tell you this, but he was also going to check with the vicar at St Bride's about times. Just in case.'

'Aren't you and Patience being married by the preacher at Norton Folgate?'

'We are. Patience wouldn't stand for anything less. But James thought you would prefer a Church of England service.'

'He sounds quite sure of himself.'

Ben laughed. 'Hardly. I have never seen him so anxious about anything. He really wants this, Caroline.'

'What are your plans for today? Will you be seeing Patience?'

'No, Mr Milton has hired a new girl and Patience is tasked with giving her instructions. She has agreed to keep cooking for him, but the new girl will take on the housekeeping duties. Under Patience's supervision, of course. Then Patience said something that surprised me. She said Mr Milton was expecting his wife to return when it was safe to travel, and could Patience teach her some of his favorite dishes?'

Milton had believed her lie. 'Patience might not be available by then. Could be a long wait. But, for now, you and I have some work to do. We need to make this place more welcoming for your bride. Let's set up William's bed where the press was.'

His grin spread into a big old toothy smile. 'I am tired of sleeping on a mat on the floor. I must keep an appointment at the Stationers' Guild this afternoon, but the morning is young. So, let's do this.'

'We need to air out the linens. Open that chest in the corner. And place that sideboard underneath the window. That other chest has some pewter ware and a pair of candlesticks.'

After they had finished setting up the bed, beating and airing its feather mattress, hanging a pair of damask panels over the window, Caroline surveyed the print shop transformed. It was now an efficient and almost pretty bedchamber.

'Did we save enough in those chests for you to have something? Have you decided what you are going to keep?'

'I have. There is a second set of decent linens and some of the pewter ware. It should all fit into one chest. You and Patience can use the other. Place it at the foot of the bed. With a pretty bolster it can double as a bench. Patience will probably have a few things she will want to bring. What's in that sturdy chest against the back wall?'

'That's my printer tools and some tin-type. I am a journeyman now,' he said with pride. 'Won't need my own press, just my own tools and type. James and I divided them. He's going to take a set with him if he . . . Have you made your decision, Caroline?'

She looked toward the window where dust motes floated in a sunbeam and thought she should get some vinegar and clean that window.

'I guess it depends on which moment you ask, Ben. I do really enjoy his company. He makes me feel protected and cared for: not in the cherishing way your father did, in a more personal way. But he frightens me sometimes too. I can't explain it. I do trust him, I think – but enough to follow him into the unknown? Enough to leave you and the Powells, the only family I have known these twenty-plus years? Maybe forever, not knowing if I will ever see you or see England again. I am just not sure.'

'You can't be sure about everything, Caroline. Sometimes you just need to step out on faith. Do you love him? I mean are you in love with him? You know you don't have to go to America with him. He wants this enough to give that up.'

'I know that's what he said. But if I love him enough to marry him, I should love him enough not to ask that of him.'

The Mermaid Inn only had only one pie left, but it looked fresh enough and there was no time to go anywhere else. James wanted to get back to the print shop while Ben was still away. His 'printer's devil' had been offered a print job by one of the Stationers' Guild masters and was meeting with him this afternoon to learn exactly what the job entailed. He might have to turn it down, he had said with a nervous frown, because to botch his first freelance job would be a very bad beginning. But James had confidence in him and had advised him not to turn it down. He would do just fine on his own.

The timing for Ben's errand was good for James too, since he needed to find Caroline alone. In the bright light of day, he had felt his own self-confidence thinning. What if she turned him down outright? What then? Or what if she offered to marry him per his promise to stay? He had made that bargain on impulse, overcome by her presence and Ben's probing. Had he been rash? But he had only to think of life without her to know he really had no choice and would do whatever it took. A foolish move, telling her about the highway robbery. He'd been close until then – he could feel it. But he had wanted nothing false between them. Not in the beginning. Not ever; unless the keeping of some secret enterprise was for her protection, then maybe. On his way down Cheapside he'd even thought about stopping at one of the gold-smith's shops to buy a wedding ring, but decided that might jinx his chances.

Feeling as jittery as a whore in church, he entered what used to be the main print room. Caroline was standing on a three-legged stool trying to fasten a bit of blue drapery above the shop window. 'Here, let me help,' he said, setting the pie on the kitchen table. Placing his arms around her, he reached up and pushed in the pin, but overcome with the sensation of her body so close to his, he did not let go immediately. He was struggling to control the impulse to bury his face in the hollow of her neck when he felt her shoulders tense.

'Thank you. I believe that will hold. You can let go now.'

'Must I?'

'You must. I expect Ben back any moment.'

He removed his arms, holding only her hand as she stepped down. He stepped back then and suddenly looked around at his improved surroundings. With a low whistle of appreciation, he said, 'What have you done with our print shop?'

'I just finished what you started. You were the one who did away with the print shop and offered the space to Ben and his bride.'

'See how well we complement each other. The room looks wonderful. It just required a woman's touch.' And then he thought about the way that sounded. 'Not any woman's touch. Your touch.'

'Did you bring the pie?'

'The pie? Yes. The pie. Pigeon. I think. It was the only choice and the last one.'

'I will put it on the hob to keep it warm. Too bad the boys are not here to share it.'

'Just as well. This conversation calls for privacy.'

She sat down at the table across from him. 'Is Ben to be included in our private conversation? I mean, you were quick to involve him yesterday.' He noted the edge in her voice. Maybe not a good sign.

'Only because I needed support,' he pleaded. 'I was sure he would approve and thought his approval might influence you.'

'It did. As did your promise.'

The abruptness of her answer startled him. Did that answer imply that she was going to accept him? Was he really going to be a farmer on that desolate pile on the moor with only pigs and sheep for company? A thought that incited panic in his soul. And then came his second thought. She would be there too.

Getting up from the table, she went over to the mantle, swept it with her hands as though scooping up dust, then sat back down across from him, back straight, shoulders square. She inhaled deeply, as if she were giving a rehearsed speech. 'I am honored by your proposal, Lord Whittier. If you have not changed your mind, I will marry you. But first I have two things to give you. I wish to return this to you so that you can give it back to me. It shall be my wedding ring.'

She opened her palm and handed him the pearl ring. He felt hot with shame.

'No, Caroline. No. I can afford to buy you a wedding ring. I even thought about it today, but I wasn't sure—'

'I . . . I want this one,' she said, the catch in her voice belying her rigid posture, but he recognized the steel in her tone – not sharp but firm. He knew he could not counter it, but he had to try. 'For God's sake, Caroline. Every time you look at it you will be reminded of—'

'William? As well I should be. I can honor his memory and remember how blessed I am that two good men have loved me. It does not mean I will love you less or grieve him more.' The old teasing smile returned, 'After all, James, it was this ring that first brought us together.'

'Every time I look at it, I will remember that, and how much I came to regret that deed.'

'Don't you see? It has meaning for both of us. It will be a caution. Not to be guided by foolish impulse, but when we are, to know that sometimes our mistakes and our losses can be redeemed. It will remind us how fleeting and changeable life can be and to embrace the moments we have. Here. Take it. You took it from me by force and gave it back out of conscience. I am giving it freely to you now to give back to me out of love. It is not the same ring.'

With both hands, she reached for his and folded the ring into his palm. He could feel the pulse in her wrist. How could he deny her anything?

'Put it on my finger when we stand at the altar in St Bride's.'

'Ben told you.'

'He did. And I thought it presumptuous of you. But when are you ever not presumptuous, my lord? It seems to serve you well.'

He kissed the hand that handed him the ring. 'You are a complicated and exceptional woman, Caroline Pendleton soon to be Caroline Whittier. You never fail to surprise me.'

He started to pull her toward him, but she held out her hand, halting him. 'Wait. I have one more thing for you,' she said, reaching into her pocket. 'This is my list of demands.' She handed him a folded piece of paper.

He groaned inwardly. The table between them had suddenly become a negotiating table and he was being bested. He was really going to spend his life with this indefatigable woman. Probably on a pig farm. A farmer would need that quality, he supposed.

'Read it. Aloud.'

He looked at her with a question in his eyes but did as he was told. 'Two bolts finely woven linen. One large tub for washing. One dozen bars of soap,' he began haltingly, thinking it a strange list for a trousseau. But what did he know of such things? 'Three woolen blankets. Two lanterns each with a round of wicking. 150 beeswax candles. 200 tallow dips. Two large casks of vinegar?'

'For preventing spread of disease.'

'You must be anticipating plague.' When she made no comment he continued, 'Two iron skillets. Three crock jars. Three jugs. Crockery and plate. One brazier. One small cook stove with a flue if there is room.' He was halfway down the list when he realized what it meant. He could have shouted for the pure pleasure of it, but he restrained himself.

'I have a small cache of silver that I can contribute for the expense,' she said into the pause.

'Does this mean?'

'It means that I am willing to try,' she said. 'On one condition. That we will return to England if the place is not what you expected, or if it is too savage or simply too harsh for a civilized woman to live there. Or too lonely for human habitation – you have not said if there are other women there? Or children? Is there a school? A church?'

Her tone was less assured now. Anxious, worried. He should have told her that first. Such things were important to women. Reassuring words came out in an excited tumble. 'There are already seven families there. The closest doctor is in Boston, but there is one aging midwife who is training Roger's oldest daughter to be her assistant. There is a common meeting room that serves as both church and school and government administration. Not the Church of England, my darling, but not a Puritan church, either. Simple services, I am told – Roger mostly preaches – where all are welcome, but none compelled.'

'No shops or markets, I suppose.'

'A really large trading post just a couple hours' sailing away, I have been assured. All sorts of goods, both local and imported. Sugar from the islands, spices, handmade goods. The colonies – Boston and New Amsterdam in particular – have made remarkable progress in a few short decades. It is not like the stories we heard from Jamestown or even when Winthrop first went out twenty years ago.'

He saw her relax a little. This was a lot for her. Even to agree, she must love him more than he had dared hope.

'But, James, it is so far. You must know, just thinking about the voyage frightens me. Will you promise me fair winds for sailing?' She tried to smile but it quickly faded.

'You know I cannot promise that.' He tried to lighten his tone, to resurrect the smile. 'But I will promise to hold your pretty head while you puke – if I'm not tossing my own over the side.'

It worked. Her smile and quick laughter were two of the things he loved about her. He would do anything not to lose that, even if it meant dirt farming on a god-forsaken English moor. 'Caroline, as God is my witness, I solemnly vow, if you are willing to go with me and give me just one year, that's all I am asking . . . if you are not happy, I will bring you home and we will start over. Ships to and fro about every three months, even in winter.' He held her face between his hands, so she would not fail to see the sincerity in his eyes. 'My darling, my soon-to-be bride, we will come home whenever you say. On the very next ship.'

'Well, then,' she said, 'I suppose you may kiss me, James, to seal this bargain. Quickly, before I change my mind.'

He took her in his arms then and, from the way she responded to his kiss, tentatively at first, and then with real passion, James did not think it likely she was going to change her mind. Whatever happened with his new world plans, this new life was going to mark the beginning of the greatest adventure of his life. It was James who broke the embrace this time. He needed to bank the fire she had started, before it became unstoppable. He wanted to take her right here on the cold stone floor, but this woman was going to be his wife. She would demand, and she deserved, more.

The door opened. Ben came in, calling cheerily, 'I did it. I took the job.' But he pulled up short when he saw the two of them standing there together, daylight scarcely between them.

'Oh. Sorry.' He looked away, then, relieving the awkward moment as he so often did, said, 'I would offer to leave you two alone, and come back later – but I see there is pie.'

'Let go of me, milord, so I can get this hungry lad some pie,' Caroline said. Whether it was the flush in Caroline's cheeks from embarrassment, or something else, James couldn't really say, but he had never seen her look more desirable.

She cut the pie into slices and set them on the table along with three goblets for the wine that was still waiting there.

'Tell us your news first,' James said. 'You have probably already surmised ours.'

'I'll tell you about the job while we eat. I haven't eaten all day. I was too nervous.'

'Me, too,' James said. 'How about you, Caroline, have you eaten anything today?'

'I can't remember,' she said.

'If she were here, Patience would say we should say grace.'

'As soon-to-be-head of our *de facto* family, that would be my honor,' James said, not missing the look of shock that Ben shot Caroline. Her chin quivered with the effort to restrain her smile.

James cleared his throat and intoned. 'Lord, for what we are about to receive, we are truly grateful. Protect us from evil and grant us guidance for all future endeavors. Ever seeking your will and mercy, we beseech blessings on our family and fair winds and smooth seas. Please forgive us of our sins: those we have committed and those we have yet to commit. We ask these things in the Holy Name of Jesus Christ, the Son of God, and our Lord and Savior.'

'Amen and well done,' Ben said. 'Even Patience would approve.'

James winked, 'I didn't go to divinity school for nothing.' He picked up his fork, 'Now let's eat.'

The pigeon pie was savory and tasted uncommonly good. It was an auspicious beginning.

A TIME TO MOURN

Sweetheart, now they will cut off thy father's head and perhaps make thee a king . . . Thou must not be a King so long as thy brothers Charles and James do live. For they will cut off your brothers' heads when they can catch them and cut off thy head too at the last. And therefore, I charge you do not be made a King by them.

Charles I to his youngest son, Henry, Duke of Gloucester, on the eve of his execution

29 January 1649, four years later

The evening before the scheduled execution, Oliver Cromwell escorted the King's youngest children into the King's presence at St James's Palace. Charles had lain awake all during the long night, beset with dread at what he must tell them. Now, the moment was at hand. If only he could have escaped to the Continent to raise an army, but he had been betrayed by those whom he trusted. His loyal Scots, instead of giving him succor, had given him up to Parliament, and others too, whose loyalty had proven false, like Lord Hammond, with whom he'd sought refuge on the Isle of Wight but who had become instead his gaoler at Carisbrooke Castle.

Now Parliament was about to take their revenge and, he had to admit, if truth be told, they had little choice. After three thwarted escape attempts, one for each of the years Parliament had imprisoned him while they tried to form a government, Parliament – or the rump that was left of it after the purge – had come to understand that Charles Stuart would never surrender his kingdom. Not if he had breath.

As eight-year-old Henry and thirteen-year-old Elizabeth entered, Elizabeth clutched her brother's hand and whispered in his ear. The King, from his tall chair in the center of the room, motioned for them to come to him. General Cromwell stood respectfully to one side but not out of earshot.

During his initial imprisonment at Hampton Court in 1647, Charles had been allowed frequent access to them. But after his incarceration at Carisbrooke, that access was curtailed – though he had received letters, smuggled in by Mistress Whorwood, the truest friend Charles had left. Almost all others had been exiled or kept from him, except the remarkably resourceful Jane Whorwood. The plainer his plight became, the more elevated her risk and the stronger her devotion, and if he was to be honest on this evening before he was to meet his maker, he would have to admit, at least to himself, she had brought him more than letters to ease his pain. She gave him physical comfort, mental support, and a higher respect that no one else – not even Henrietta – had given him. Charles had treasured every letter Jane smuggled in: Elizabeth's, written sometimes in perfect Latin; her little brother's in an undisciplined scrawl, often with a crudely sketched picture of a jousting knight with lance and helmet

This youngest son – whom he hardly knew because of the war which separated them – approached tentatively. 'Come closer, children, and greet your father.' *For one last time.* But he did not say that, could scarcely bear to think it. 'I have something to tell you. Something for your ears only.'

Cromwell nodded his understanding and stepped back a couple of paces.

Henry grinned, as if they were to play some secret game.

'Now listen carefully, my darlings,' Charles said, drawing them close. 'I have summoned you today to bid you goodbye. I must go away soon – very soon – and I want you to always remember how much your father loves you.'

Elizabeth questioned him with her eyes. He wondered how much she knew of the goings-on of the kingdom, the fighting, his imprisonment. He had asked that she be shielded from such knowledge, but she was an intelligent child. He had seen her watching, once or twice remarking on the lack of ceremony surrounding him when she visited him at Hampton Court.

'Are you going back to the battlefield, Father? Is there to be more fighting? I thought all that had ended.'

'No. There is to be no more fighting. That will be good, will it not?' He paused, thinking how to proceed, inhaled deeply. 'This time, I am going to a better place, a perfect kingdom where there is never war or grief or pain: a blessed kingdom.'

'May we go with you, Father?' Henry asked, excitement in his voice. 'Please take us with you. You took Charles and James. I am old enough now.'

But Elizabeth's chin quivered. She held her hand to her lips to hide it.

'No, Henry, where I am going you cannot go. Just yet. And your brothers are not going with me this time either. They are already with your mother in France. But all of you will join me later. We will have a wonderful reunion and never be parted again. All of us together in that new kingdom.'

'Maman too?' Elizabeth said in a small voice.

'Oh yes. Maman, too.'

His daughter pinched her mouth and squeezed her eyelids. A tear slid down her cheek. He took her hands in his and kissed them both, straining every nerve in his body not to let her tears draw out his own. He was uncomfortably aware of General Cromwell who, from across the room, cleared his throat and dropped his head. Charles lowered his voice to a whisper.

'But before we meet again in that wonderful kingdom, I need you to do something for me. Chancellor Hyde is working with Parliament leaders to give you and your brother Henry leave to join your mother in France. You will see your little sister for the first time. It will be great fun, Henry, to have a little sister. You can teach her how to play all your favorite games. James and Charles can teach you how to joust like a real knight. You will like Paris, Elizabeth. There are lots of learned scholars there. You will hardly have time to miss me.'

'Why can't you go with us?' she asked, her voice so low he had to strain to hear. His brave little daughter, the brightest of them all. Despite his cryptic language, she knew why.

'When the time comes, Chancellor Hyde will escort you on your grand adventure. But first, this is what you must promise to do for your father.'

The children nodded.

'If you are moved to the royal apartments in the White Tower, you must mind your teachers and behave like the good children that you are. Do not make trouble. Do your lessons. Write down your thoughts – in English, Elizabeth.'

The girl dropped her head and looked at the floor. He gently reached out his hand and tilted up her chin. 'You are a princess of England, not a princess of Rome or France. You are to study the Holy Word and say your prayers – in English.'

He reached inside a satchel on the floor beside him and drew out a heavy leather-bound book, handed it to her. Hesitant, she took it.

'This is for you, Elizabeth. It is my Bible. It is the Bible given me by your grandfather, James Stuart. It was his greatest desire that this book be the official Word in England and Scotland and Ireland. It is yours now. Honor it. Read it and read it to your brother. Every day. And say your prayers every night. Both of you are to attend chapel in the White Tower. There will be an Anglican priest there. Do you have a Book of Common Prayer?'

She shook her head.

'The Anglican priest will be pleased to provide you with one. When you write to your mother and brothers in Paris, you may write in French. Be careful what you write. You must assume your letters will be read by spies.'

He paused, looked firmly at each of them. 'Do you understand?'

'Yes, Father. I am glad we don't have to write in Latin. It is too hard,' Henry said.

'Elizabeth?'

'Yes, Father. I will do as you have said. But may I at least continue my studies of the Greek philosophers? They still allow my tutor. She comes twice a week.'

He sighed. 'I suppose that is permissible. She is a scholar, not a cleric. But don't forget to take your exercise in the garden. You need the sunshine and Henry needs your company. Now, one more thing. This is of the utmost importance. Listen closely. When you are given leave to go to Paris, I want you to take a message to your mother. This is what you must say. Elizabeth, you are to tell your mother that I love her still and that I have always been faithful to her,' he said.

It was no lie. He had always been faithful – in his heart. But Carisbrooke Castle was a lonely, hard place to be imprisoned.

Henrietta would never have to know, and God would forgive him. He had forgiven another King far worse.

'Climb up on my lap, Henry. I have a special instruction for you, also.' He tried to say this cheerfully, struggled to push back the voice in his head reminding him there would be no other chance for his children to sit on his lap. 'My, how you have grown since last you sat in my lap.'

The child straightened his spine to a proud posture.

'Now, your turn, Henry. Are you listening? This is most important of all my instructions. It is something only you can do.'

The young Duke nodded earnestly.

As Charles began his instructions, the child's eyes grew large and round. Elizabeth's sharp intake of breath alerted him, but he warned her with a glance and a shake of his head. When he had finished with the admonition, he repeated, 'Do not be made a king by them.' The little boy straightened himself, took a deep breath, and said resolutely, 'I will be torn in pieces first.'

The spirit with which he said it, this mere child, so earnest and brave, cheered his heart. Smiling, he lifted the child off his lap to stand again beside his sister.

'Now,' he said raising his voice, 'General Cromwell will take you back to the White Tower. You will bide there, until it is time for you to go to Paris to be with your mother. Chancellor Hyde will visit you often to see that you are well provided for. If anyone is unkind to you, tell him. Look out for each other. Remember your promise to me, Henry. I will ask you when we meet again if you were true to it.'

'I will not let them make me King, Father. Not ever.'

'And Elizabeth?'

'I will give your message to Maman, Father.'

He kissed each of them on the cheek and said. 'I have a parting gift. For remembrance of thy father.' He removed two jeweled rings from his finger that he had been allowed to keep, and folded them into a palm of each child's hand, saying, 'Goodbye, my children. I give thee my blessing.'

As Cromwell led them away, Charles turned his back to the wall. He would not let his enemy witness his tears.

*   *   *

The next morning dawned a bitter cold. The King had slept but little. Having passed the emotional hurdle of bidding goodbye to his children, determined not to borrow pain before he had to bear it, he submitted his fate to God and willed his thoughts to a more philosophical bent. What did his death mean for the future of England? Would God wreak yet more havoc on this kingdom for their sin of regicide? The sorry rump of a Parliament had never replaced the leadership of John Pym. If Prince Charles, with Henrietta's help, could raise an army and seize the throne. So many *if's*.

Finally, he saw the gray light seeping through the window and around the door. The last dawn he would ever see. He got up, shivering in his night shirt, pulled back the window curtain to greet it. The fire in his chamber had been unattended since midnight. Charles declined to break his fast but sat beside the dying embers. Bishop William Juxon, an old friend who had once served as the court chaplain, and as Lord High Treasurer, sat with him, prayed with him, read Scripture with him and offered the sacrament. Parliament had appointed a Presbyterian chaplain, but had conceded when Charles asked to be attended by the Bishop of London.

It was a little before ten o'clock in the morning when the Parliament-assigned custodian, Colonel Tomlinson, came to tell him it was time to leave for the processional to Whitehall. 'You will be going on foot, Your Majesty, accompanied by a regiment of the New Model Army, front and rear, to protect the King's dignity and preserve order.'

'Do not worry, Colonel. There will be no rescue party. We are way beyond that. And I agree the King's dignity must be preserved even as they cut off his head.'

Tomlinson had the grace to look embarrassed. But in truth Charles was also worried about the King's dignity – and the King's pain.

'It is a bitter morning. Please tell my servant to bring me an extra shirt to wear beneath my doublet. I would not like my enemies to think I shiver from fear. And instruct him to bring my nightcap. I want the axe to meet no impediment. I hope the blade has been honed and the axe man is a professional.'

Charles tried to dispel the bloody image that had been

placed in his head as a child, the gruesome story of what had happened at the execution of his grandmother, Mary, Queen of Scots; how her head had been hacked off three times, ragged sinews hanging, her mouth still twitching, when the headsman held it up.

'This headsman is an expert, Your Majesty. From France, I think. They could find no Englishman among your subjects who would do it – for any sum. The officers of the Tower have assured us the Committee Blade has been newly honed. It should be swift and . . . painless.'

'Then let us begin,' he said, and walked out into the street to take his place.

As they marched, he couldn't help but observe that General Cromwell's army was impressive, disciplined, marching as one and well turned out, their regiment flags waving in the slight breeze. Charles was grateful for the extra shirt as he walked the short distance to Whitehall, regiments front and back of him, drums beating, flags unfurling. Even in his extremity, he summoned that part of himself that provided intellectual distance and held back fear, much as he had been able to do on the battlefield. He looked right and left at both the loyal and the disloyal, meeting the eyes of his enemies with his head held high and nodding at the occasional tearful face of a faithful friend or loyal subject. He remarked to Colonel Tomlinson, walking beside him, in clear conversational tones of detachment, about the quality of the day, the size of the crowd lining the route.

They were approaching Whitehall when a small disturbance occurred and a tall woman in a hooded cape of forest green rushed forward. Before the startled guards could pull her away, she pulled back her furred hood so that he could see her face and knelt before him.

'Stop. We would speak with this good woman,' he said.

Colonel Tomlinson held up his hand to halt the marchers. The drums stilled. Charles bade the woman stand. 'Mistress Whorwood. Jane.'

He considered her tear-streaked face. She was a comely woman, even in extremity. But not a beautiful one. And yet, she had been able to move him more than any other. In his darkest hours he had been buoyed by her loyalty and exalted by her reckless demonstrations of affection. This one was especially rash, but it would be her last.

'Your love and loyalty to your sovereign has been much appreciated, my dear lady. It was kind of you to wish to bid me farewell.' He said this loudly enough that Colonel Tomlinson and Bishop Juxon behind him could hear clearly. Then, dropping his voice, 'Leave quickly, Jane. Do not linger in this crowd. Go back to Oxford this night. Take with you the memory and love of your King.'

Colonel Tomlinson motioned for one of the soldiers situated at stations along the way. 'See this woman safely away.' Then he signaled for the processional to enter the portal at Whitehall.

As they entered, Charles looked straight ahead, refusing to look at the crudely cut door facing the street through which he would at some near hour meet death. Sooner rather than later was his hope. Waiting would only deplete his strength. The Banqueting House. Henrietta's joy. The King's glory.

Standing beneath Peter Paul Rubens' painted ceiling, he felt himself a small figure. He gazed upward at the magnificent creation of color and light, a riotous celebration of the Stuart Divine Right to rule: James I, his foot on the world, his scepter lifted upwards, his arm supported by the figure of Justice. The infant Charles was there too, presented by figures representing both Scotland and England: Scotland who betrayed him, England who ripped the crown from his head, and would soon slice off the anointed head that bore it. Where now was the triumph of justice and virtue presented in the painting? Where the promised triumph of peace over war? *Beside the still waters, Charles. Death is but a shadow. This world is but a shadow. This broken kingdom is but a shadow.*

Hours later he took, at the urging, a bit of bread and wine to fortify his body so he would not faint. Still they did not come. Some problem with the headsman? Or the sword? Or was this delay just to prolong his suffering? He sipped the wine and nibbled at the bread and a bit of tasteless cheese, then asked to be alone to say his prayers in private. He prayed for Henrietta in France. He should have seen her off at Falmouth Harbor, but it had never occurred to him when he left her so abruptly in Bedford that he would never see his dear heart again. He hoped Elizabeth remembered to give her his message. He prayed for his children, calling each by name, and even the youngest daughter who would never know him. He prayed for the kingdom he was leaving. And finally, he prayed for the courage to die with honor.

Beside the still waters. In the valley of the shadow of death.

This last prayer was answered. An unusual calm descended over him as he prepared to step through the newly cut-out door, fronting onto the street, and onto the black-draped platform prepared for a king's execution. No common scaffolding on Ludgate Hill, this with its black velvet draped platform and lined coffin waiting. A large knot of soldiers stood in front of the scaffolding, a barrier between the spectacle and the large crowd that spilled into the street as far as he could see. He paused and assessed this last earthly convocation he would witness. It was an orderly crowd. Unlike the crowd that witnessed Thomas Wentworth, eight years gone, martyred for his loyalty to his King. Unlike the crowd that witnessed Archbishop William Laud four years gone, martyred for his loyalty to the one true Church of England. No howling mob waited for the King's head. At long last, the burden Charles had carried for nine years would be lifted. That same King, whom these two friends had trusted and who had failed them, would join them. Atonement.

The sonorous pealing of two bells interrupted his thoughts.

'It is time, Your Majesty.'

He stepped through the door.

A hush fell on those assembled. Behind him Bishop Juxon intoned the Lord's prayer. The smell of the new-cut wood assailed his nostrils. Now, treading the raw boards, he bolstered his courage, as before, by voicing aloud to these faithless witnesses, as he had to his children, that he was only exchanging this broken and imperfect kingdom for a perfect kingdom where he would be rewarded for his faithfulness. But at the sight of the black-masked executioner, the block, the waiting coffin, a momentary turbulence troubled the *still waters* of the Psalmist's promise.

'The block is too low. It should be raised.' Charles addressed this to Colonel Hacker – *Please, Christ and all the saints, let not the irony of this man's name be a sign.*

'I am sorry, it cannot be changed. It is already in place.' The man's voice was civil enough, but Charles knew the positioning of the block was an unsubtle attempt at his humiliation.

'My linen cap, please,' he told the servant, 'beneath which to tuck my hair.' He said this matter-of-factly, a King's voice, still giving orders. 'No hindrance between blade and object.' He placed some coins in the executioner's hand. 'Take care that you do not put me to pain, good headsman.' The black-hooded executioner nodded.

As a last chance to cleanse his soul, and as a display of the King's piety, a lesson for the watchers – especially the little congregation in the front rows of those who had condemned him – he knelt to pray for those who had been loyal to him and ask divine forgiveness for his enemies. He prayed for John Pym, pausing to ponder with a sigh how they two would greet each other in Heaven. (In the unlikely event, of course, that Pym was there.) He asked God's guidance for Parliament to realize their grievous error and prayed that the Crown would be restored to Prince Charles, who would heal the land of its bloody wounds.

Crossing himself, he stood up then and, fumbling with the linen cap, tried to tuck his heavy locks beneath it.

'Allow me, Your Highness,' Tomlinson said.

With the image of the Reubens painting still floating before his eyes, he proclaimed as loudly as he could, 'I go from a corruptible to an incorruptible Crown, where no disturbance can be!' Then, after making a joke to the headsman about not harming the blade lest it harm him, he knelt, spread his arms wide, and put his head upon the block.

One clean, quick slice.

In silence, lest his voice be recognized, the headsman lifted the bloody head of their King for the modest crowd of assembled witnesses. The response from the crowd was a stunned silence broken only by a muted 'praise be to God' coming from the chief prosecutors in the front row, who were sufficiently removed so the King's blood would not spatter them. One or two cheers threatened, then faded into the hovering quiet, as one by one the small crowd in the courtyard drifted away with stunned expressions, realization dawning. They had killed an anointed King, God's deputy placed on earth to govern them. Now what? Was it over? Even the prosecutors were restrained in their singular achievement as the body was placed in its velvet-lined coffin and carried away.

The crowd dispersed in a dissipating swarm of murmuring silence.

A few women lingered. One by one, they silently approached the basket that had received a martyr's head. Genuflecting as before an altar, they dipped their handkerchiefs in the King's blood, already thickening into clots, then clutching their relics unobtrusively – lest they be seen by the guards posted at the entrance to the courtyard – they also left. Among them was a tall woman in a forest green hooded cloak.

On the afternoon of the King's execution, Lucy Hay was not among those assembled in the street outside Whitehall. She went instead to St James's Palace to console the condemned man's children. She had visited them often since Parliament had abruptly removed them from Syon House, placing them under the control of Oliver Cromwell's New Model Army. At least St James's Palace was familiar to them. Much to her relief, they had seemed content. Elizabeth had been allowed her tutor and Henry a fencing master – he was always eager to show her his en garde and feint – but she was never left alone with them, a circumstance which troubled her for many reasons.

And today, when they would be most in need of a friend, she was denied entrance.

'The children are indisposed.'

She protested but the chamberlain was adamant. 'Then when will I be allowed access to them?' she asked.

Stone-faced, he replied, 'I cannot say, my lady. Decisions concerning the Stuart children are left to the Committee of Safety.'

The Stuart children. He did not say the King's children.

So, it was finished, Lucy thought. England had no king. Parliament had removed their troublesome sovereign the only way they could, by committing regicide. She should feel some measure of grief, but she could not. Her memory of Thomas Wentworth left no room in her heart for sorrow. It was apt that Charles Stuart should die by arbitrary decree. The circle was complete. She spared a sympathetic thought for his wife who had loved him, though, and wondered if Henrietta knew she was a widow. Surely, he had been allowed to see his children. Even his enemies could not be so cold.

She considered protesting the guard's refusal, appealing to their better angels, even flirting, but she could see it would avail her nothing but her ultimate humiliation. 'I shall speak to the Committee of Safety you may be sure,' she said with a forced smile, and with an air of umbrage walked briskly from the room.

The coachman, huddled in his muffler, looked up in some surprise, then hastened down from his perch to help her into the carriage. Resting her head against the back of the seat and inhaling purposefully to still her racing heart, she stared out the window, not seeing the lowering clouds and the winter-blasted landscape as it passed, seeing only images in her head, her imagination conjuring what she had refused to witness. How did the crowd react? How did Charles conduct himself? Were there any present to protest or speak on his behalf? And what now? These thoughts and more needled her. What did it mean for England? And the most troublesome of all: what did it mean for her? She had not heard from the chancellor since they took the children away, nor had she any news of the Queen. Who would tell the Queen that her enemies had cut off her husband's head? Were her sons with her, or was she alone?

Despite her threat, Lucy did not plan to go into London, to confront the Committee or any other Parliament member. She should not attempt again to see the children, lest her efforts called unwanted attention to her regard for the 'Stuart' children, harming both her and them. Her mind tried to frame an argument. What would she say if some committee called her in for questioning? *What exactly is your concern for the children, Lady Carlisle? Are you part of some conspiracy? Exactly where do your loyalties lie?*

Finding no ready answer, her thoughts turned in another direction. She should not sit at Syon House and wait. Checkpoints at the Lines of Communication would not be closed to her, not yet at least. But they might be soon. Perhaps it was better to go in an unmarked carriage as a yeoman's wife. But where? Northumberland and the ancient Percy family seat at Alnwick? A bleak prospect, to be sure, but she could gain some time to think there in that isolated place. The more she thought about it, the sounder the idea became. If enough Scots in the North were still loyal and should recognize Prince Charles as King, he would surely offer her protection for old times' sake and for her service to his mother and his siblings. There was certainly nobody left in the Rump Parliament to plead her cause. All the moderate voices had been expelled. Best to get out now if she still could.

Large snowflakes had begun to fall, softening the bare branches and muddy fields. How peaceful it looks, she thought. Nature's little white lie, for there was no peace. A kind of helplessness enveloped her, unlike any she had felt since she was a girl held virtual prisoner by her father in the Tower.

She leaned her head out the window and shouted for the driver to make haste. Snowflakes powdered her face. The cold air was bracing, the kiss of a light breeze comforting.

She closed the window and leaned back, listening to another voice in her head. *Dig deep, Lucy. Find some vestige of that girl's spirit. All is not lost. You still have breath and your wits have not waned, if anything only been enhanced by the wisdom of experience; and if no longer a celebrated beauty, you are still a handsome woman – in proper lighting. Tomorrow is not too late. It is a good thing that you were denied access to the children. That was your warning sign, lass, probably the only one you'll get.* James Hay always gave good advice. She would leave early in the morning. In three days she would be close to the Scottish border before anybody knew she was gone – if anybody cared.

4 February 1649

Prince Charles shouted for the footman outside his chamber in Le Louvre to summon his chamberlain. He rolled out of bed reluctantly, pulled on his breeches and belt. The room was cold, his fire unattended. His mother's Paris relations had not been eager in observing the protocols due a Prince of England, not even providing an adequate staff. But that was just as well. They probably were not to be trusted anyway. His loyal chamberlain had come with him when Edward Hyde had successfully pressed the King to send him and his brother into exile in France. The heir and the spare, their lives should be protected for the future of England, Chancellor Hyde had argued, when it became clear that the breach between the King and Parliament was not likely to end in the King's favor.

His father agreed. 'You will be safe there and available to give comfort to your mother, should Providence decree thy father's . . .' But, not wishing to voice this outcome, he had only shrugged. Charles had understood he was being banished because his capture would have been catastrophic for the kingdom, but he had reluctantly quit the field, thinking the action overly cautious and unwelcome. Until Newbury. After that it made more sense, but, still, he was restless here. At nineteen he belonged on the battlefield. At his father's side.

With a sigh of boredom, Charles gazed out the window at the bleak winter scene, last week's snow still patching the black mud along the bank of the Seine and the bare-branched wood beyond. But the sun was shining. His father favored such a day for hunting. Maybe he would be able to join them before the season ended. Yesterday his mother had hurriedly summoned him and his brother, telling them that they were not to worry if they heard some French tales about their father's trial in Parliament. She had heard from one of her spies that the King had escaped, rescued by a party of his loyal Scots, and was on his way to France, where they would rally French troops and put an end to this devil-spawned insurrection . . . Hysterical with relief, she had almost choked on her words.

His back still to the doorway, Charles heard the chamberlain enter. 'Tell my brother to dress for the hunt today. The deer will be easy to spot in the snow. And see if Henry Percy is up for some sport. Bring some bacon with my loaf and some butter and a pot of jam if you can wrangle it out of that stingy cook.'

But there was no response. Only the sound of heavy breathing.

In reflex, Charles's hand went to the small knife attached to his belt and whirled around, but it was only his chamberlain standing there, his face a mask of uncertainty. Gripped tightly in his hand was a . . . news book?

'Speak up man! What ails you? Have they closed our favorite tavern?'

The servant dropped to his knees and, bowing his head, muttered 'Your Majesty.' His hand held out the news book.

Your Majesty? To be thusly addressed could only mean one thing. Charles ripped the quarto from the man's hand. The headline in bold black ink screamed '*Le Parlement Décapite Charles I, Roi d' Angleterre.*' His knees weak, he sank onto the bed, his eyes ravaging the print as he disciplined his mind to register the details.

The weekly *La Gazette* gave eye-witness details, according to which at least after the execution, the English had treated the body of their sovereign with respect . . . sewed the head back onto the body . . . black draped coffin . . . procession escorted by an honor guard of Parliament's cavalry . . . interment in St George's Chapel, Windsor. It also reported that the assemblies along the route were well-behaved and sober, with many crying and kneeling as the King's coffin passed by, including one stunning encounter with a tall blonde woman in forest green.

Charles sat on the bed oblivious to his chamberlain, who was still on his knees. His brain struggled to absorb what he had read and to marshal a response. Such excruciating detail could not reasonably be refuted. It read like an eye-witness account. It could only mean one thing. His father was stone cold dead. Executed by Parliament and . . . he was King now. But a King in exile. He longed to gather a company of horse and invade Westminster to avenge his father's murder. But he dared not go back – at least without an army. Or not without an invitation from Parliament to take up the Crown.

He had never felt so alone in his life. The sentence had been carried out on 30 January. Five days ago. Why had nobody come to tell them? Where was Edward Hyde? And God have mercy, it had befallen to him to tell his mother.

'I am so sorry, Your Majesty. I will pray for his soul.'

Charles looked up then and awkwardly gestured for the chamberlain to stand. 'Summon my mother. I must speak with her. You will probably find her in the chapel at this hour of the morning.'

By the time she arrived, he had composed himself sufficiently to put on his doublet and ring for a footman to build a fire. 'Enter,' he said to a tap on the door.'

'The Queen Mother, Your Majesty,' his servant said as they entered.

She did not look happy. 'You are a bit ahead of yourself,' she said to the man, curtly. Then, 'You are dismissed.' But he just stood there looking uncertain.

Charles nodded, and the chamberlain left, backing out of the door.

'What is wrong with him?'

'Pay him no mind. He means no disrespect. He has had a shock. Please, Mother. Come. Sit here by the fire.'

'No. Just tell me why you have interrupted my morning devotions. What is it now? Your quarters not to your liking? Your meals insufficient? Your service inadequate? I know you would prefer to be in England, but you must temper your expectations. Remember, my son, we are guests here.'

Instead of answering back, he placed his arm around her, his voice scarcely above a whisper. 'Mother, please sit,' he pleaded. But she just straightened her spine. 'Just say whatever it is that spurred you to this urgent summons.'

'I-I bring you the most miserable of news.' He paused for a breath, then without looking at her said, 'It has fallen my sad duty to tell you that your husband and my father has succumbed to the calumny of Parliament. He . . . he was executed at Whitehall five days ago.'

She sat then but did not react as he had expected, and when she spoke her tone was still exasperated.

'Charles, I warned you and James about this. Do not be distressed. It is a lie. I told you—'

'No, Mother. You have been misinformed. It is all here. In this paper. Every excruciating detail. The false news you received from your spy was a scurrilous lie.'

She pushed away the paper he held out to her. 'He wore the livery of St James's Palace. Why would he lie?'

'Delivering bad news is a hard service and not a welcome one. Did you reward him for bringing you good news?'

'*Absolument* . . .' Then understanding dawned in her face. She reached for the paper.

He watched as disbelief, denial and understanding warred in her countenance, contorting her mouth, wrinkling her brow, widening her eyes. When she had finished reading, her face was a frozen mask of pain. He knelt beside her, extended his arms in an embrace. But she did not cry out, nor did she move. The paper fell to the floor, its whisper against the stone flags and the popping of a burnt log breaking in half, the only sounds in the room. Still holding her, he waited for the storm that never came. She might have been a statue except for her trembling hands. He had seen his mother in many moods, but never like this. His legs were cramped from his kneeling position, but still she did not move.

When he could no longer sustain his uncomfortable posture, he stood up. Bending down, he stilled the tremor in her clutched hands beneath his own. 'Mother, may I help you to your chamber? Do you need a physician?'

'No. Leave me. I wish to be alone.'

But he could not leave her. Not like this. 'May I at least send for someone to sit with you? Lord Jermyn?'

'Genevieve,' she whispered. Then, more strongly. 'Assemble Percy and Jermyn and your brother and those of our servants whose loyalty you trust. Show them this,' she said, closing her eyes as she scuffed the offending paper with the toe of her slipper. Charles picked it up and left to fulfill yet another unwanted duty, suspecting it would be the first of many.

Henrietta did not know how long she sat there in her son's empty room. When she next opened her eyes, he was gone. The room was cold, the fire dead.

She thought that she should seek out her sons to comfort them. They had lost their father. She was their mother. They needed her. But she did not move. Her thoughts came quick and fast and disjointed. In killing their King, Parliament had at long last attained their desire. They had finally rid themselves of their despised Catholic Queen, but they would never be rid of her influence. She was the Queen Mother. The son born of her body, sired by their father, was still their rightful King. But their new King was still a boy. He would need guidance, guidance only she could give. They could exile her body but not her influence.

She should cry for her husband, but she had no tears. She should go to her chapel to pray for her husband's soul. But she could not summon the strength.

Ave Maria . . . but the Virgin was silent. Charles was dead. She would never see his face again, feel his touch, hear his voice. At least not in this life. How could she live without him?

He had been the center of her life since she was but a girl. Parliament had robbed her of that. Robbed her children of their father. Still she did not cry.

A hot anger rose inside her, quickening her strength, flowing through her limbs and into her heart. Where was that sycophant Hyde? Why did he not come to her to tell her of the fate of her husband? And what of her youngest children? What would now be their fate?

Only when Genevieve came into the room, knelt beside her and put her arms around her did Henrietta begin to cry. She sobbed in her faithful servant's arms until she had no more tears. Then she straightened her face and the two women went to Henrietta's apartment. It was warm there. Genevieve offered her a posset of honeyed wine, which she accepted gratefully.

'Would you like to lie down, Your Majesty?'

'There will be time for sleeping later, Genevieve. Send a footman to summon the princes and the English exiles to gather outside the chapel within the hour,' she said. 'Tell my sons to wear their blue satin.'

Exactly one hour later, Henrietta gathered with her fellow exiles and loyal servants in the hall outside the chapel. The young princes were elegant in their blue satin but subdued. A hush fell over those assembled as she stood before them. She lifted her chin, cleared her throat and took a deep breath, her voice ringing clear. 'The King is dead.' She reached for the hand of her oldest son and, lifting it high in the air, exclaimed in the strongest voice she could muster, 'Long live the King.'

Charles stood up and those assembled, inspired by the resolve and firmness of the posture and voice of Henrietta Maria, mother of Charles II, echoed, 'Long live the King.' His mother first, his brother next, one by one they knelt before him to swear fealty. Then, led by the Queen's private chaplain, they went into the chapel to pray for the soul of the one who Edward Hyde would later eulogize in his *History of the Rebellion* as 'the worthiest gentleman, the best master, the best friend, the best husband, the best father and the best Christian that the age in which he lived produced.'

HISTORICAL NOTE: INFLUENCES AND OUTCOMES

The historical relevance of England's Civil War, the bloodiest war ever fought on English soil, cannot be overstated. The regicide with which it ended was a watershed event for England and beyond. Not only did it mark the end of absolute rule for the English monarchy, but it birthed the republican ideals and representational government that would provide a foundation stone for the philosophy of governance and constitutional underpinnings of the United States: Freedom of religion, freedom of speech and a free and unfettered press. Within the constraints of my story, I could only deal with portions of the war. The years between 1642 and 1645 – with 1641 prologue and 1649 final chapter – offered the richest vein for mining the emotional and dramatic details wherein I found my story. Within that frame, I have made every effort to remain true to the recorded timelines of events and battles.

The historical characters who captured my imagination in the two volumes of Broken Kingdom were Lucy Percy Hay, Queen Henrietta Maria, and to a lesser extent King Charles I and his chief adversary in Parliament, John Pym. A study in contrast and survival, Lucy's character has been much speculated upon, including by the novelist Alexander Dumas. She is said to be the model for 'Milady de Winter,' the attractive and dangerous spy for Cardinal Richelieu in *The Three Musketeers*. Some historical sources argue that Lucy betrayed her King by warning John Pym of the impending arrest of five leading parliamentarians and that her affair with him was rumored. I found this more than plausible and used it as a plot point. Despite Lucy's duplicity and reputation, I found her to be a sympathetic character in her instinct for survival and her intelligence. She is reputed to have had lovers on both sides of the divide. I also found Queen Henrietta Maria a sympathetic character, even though her determination to deliver

Protestant England to the pope provided the catalyst for the brutal war. Both she and Lucy Hay were strong, determined women in an age when it was not easy to be a woman who could influence policy and affect outcomes – or even her own personal choices.

As the conflict wore on without resolution, Parliament split. Lucy and the Percy family aligned with the moderate faction in pursuit of a peaceful solution. After the King's execution, the Puritan 'Rump Parliament' imprisoned Lucy Hay in the Tower and threatened her with the rack. While in prison – and upon her release – she worked for Charles II's restoration to the throne, acting as an intermediary with the court in exile. It is said she pawned a pearl necklace to support Lord Holland's troops in that cause. She died of apoplexy not long after the Restoration.

The last time Queen Henrietta saw her 'dearest heart' was when he said goodbye to her in Exeter after the birth of their last child. Henrietta's fears regarding Jane Whorwood probably came true – according to historical speculation (based on that young woman's tender ministrations to him while he was imprisoned). After her husband's death, Henrietta wore mourning for the rest of her life and spent some time in a nunnery in France. During Cromwell's Protectorate she worked tirelessly to return the throne to her oldest son, using the same tactics and resources she had used for his father. Until her death, Baron Henry Jermyn remained devoted to her and she to him. Under Charles II, Jermyn became Earl of St Albans. Some historical gossips maintain that he and Henrietta were secretly married and further suggest that the little Princess born in Exeter belonged to him. The Queen Mother returned to England at the Restoration but retired to Paris in 1665. She died in Paris in 1669 and was buried at the abbey church of St Denis.

All the Queen's children joined their mother in France, except Princess Elizabeth, who died at the age of thirteen, two days before Parliament gave the children permission to leave. Young Henry, Duke of Gloucester, became a staunch Protestant and maintained a chilly relationship with his mother throughout her lifetime. The youngest child, baby 'Minette' Henrietta Anne, spent her girlhood in Paris with her mother and grew up Catholic. She was devoted to the Stuart Restoration and, as the Duchess d'Orléans, was a favorite at the court of Louis XIV. After his older brother Charles II died, James became King James II of England (James VII of Scotland) in 1685 to become the last Catholic monarch of England. He was deposed by his Protestant son-in-law William of Orange.

The biography of John Milton, the second greatest poet in the English language, also ignited my imagination. The tension between his literary genius and his unpleasant personality, raw ambition, and destructive self-interest I found intriguing. After the war, Mary Powell came back to John Milton, bringing her dispossessed Royalist family with her. A dutiful Puritan, he took them in. Mary died at the age of twenty-seven while giving birth to their fourth child, a son also named John. He did not thrive and died after a few weeks. Three daughters survived to serve Milton, begrudgingly, into his old age. Under Cromwell, Milton was appointed Secretary of Foreign Tongues and continued to write political tracts, one of which was a defense of the regicide of Charles I. After the Restoration of Charles II, he was briefly imprisoned, but influential literary friends with royal ties gained him a pardon. John Milton's *Areopagitica* is now acknowledged as a seminal document for freedom of speech. After he lost his sight, Milton continued to write poetry and produced the brilliant epic poem *Paradise Lost*.

Other historical figures make cameo appearances, such as Joanna Cartwright, an Englishwoman living in Amsterdam who advocated for the return of the Jews to England. Her meeting with Henrietta is fictional, though it seems logical she would have made such an attempt while the Queen was in The Hague. The English Jews were finally allowed to return under Cromwell. Also, the literary figures with whom Milton – and Lucy Hay – interacted within the narrative are historical characters. The goldsmith, Thomas Simpson, is likewise a name from the period, though the account of Lucy's meeting with him is fictional. The specific kind of enterprise mentioned in the description of his Cheapside vault emerged during the war and became the forerunner for the institution of the Bank of England established at the end of the century (see accounts of the Cheapside Hoard, discovered in 1913, reported by several contemporary sources).

The printer James Whittier and Caroline Pendleton are fictional characters, as are Ben Pendleton and Patience Trapford. They were inspired by accounts of the fractured families and hardships of the war and are emblematic of the burgeoning Fleet Street printing enterprises that still survive today. I did not discover the name of the 'free' printer for Milton's *Doctrine and Discipline of Divorce*, or *The Bloudy Tenent of Persecution* by Roger Williams. James Whittier emerged in my imagination as the kind of risk-taker and free-thinker who would have accepted such a challenge and gone on to embrace the radical freedom experiment in Rhode Island.

HISTORICAL SOURCES

Kishlansky, Mark. *A Monarchy Transformed: Britain 1603–1714.* Penguin Books, 1996.

MacCulloch, Diarmaid. *The Reformation: A History.* Penguin Books, 2003.

Major, Philip. *Writings of Exile in the English Revolution and Restoration.* Ashgate Publishing, 1988.

Purkiss, Diane. *The English Civil War.* Basic Books, 2006.

Spencer, Charles. *Killers of the King: The Men Who Dared to Execute Charles I.* Bloomsbury Press, 2014.

Tombs, Robert. *The English and Their History.* Alfred A. Knopf, 2015.

A general web search for any of the many historical characters and quotes referenced in the novel will produce a variety of sources. For facts, biography, themes and timelines I recommend the site run by the British Civil War Project: http://bcw-project.org.

For more about the history of Henrietta Maria go to: https://history.blog.gov.uk/2014/04/28/henrietta-maria-the-forgotten-queen/

For a summary understanding of Roger Williams and the American connection with the English Civil War, I recommend *Smithsonian Magazine*'s article on Williams: http://www.smithsonianmag.com/history/god-government-and-roger-williams-big-idea-6291280/